THE NEW WESSEX EDITION
OF THE STORIES OF THOMAS HARDY
VOLUME ONE

WESSEX TALES
and
A GROUP OF NOBLE DAMES

THE NEW WESSEX EDITION

Wessex Tales

and

A Group of Noble Dames

THOMAS HARDY

EDITED BY
F. B. Pinion

THE NEW WESSEX EDITION OF THE STORIES OF THOMAS HARDY
VOLUME ONE

Thomas Hardy's text © Macmillan London Ltd

Editorial arrangement, introduction and notes
© Macmillan London Ltd 1977
Typography © Macmillan London Ltd 1977

ISBN: 0 333 19982 0

The New Wessex Edition first published 1977 by
MACMILLAN LONDON LTD
London and Basingstoke
Associated companies in New York Dublin
Melbourne Johannesburg & Delhi

Published in the United States by
ST MARTIN'S PRESS INC.
175 Fifth Avenue, New York

Printed in Great Britain by
WESTERN PRINTING SERVICES LTD
Bristol

Contents

A GROUP OF NOBLE DAMES

The frontispiece is a pencil drawing of Thomas Hardy made in 1919
by William Strang, R.A.

Introduction

THE first two volumes of the New Wessex Edition of Hardy's short stories present his collected tales in their chronological order of publication in book form: *Wessex Tales* with *A Group of Noble Dames*, and *Life's Little Ironies* with *A Changed Man*. No attempt has been made to obtrude critical evaluations, but much that is relevant on the origin and background of the stories will be found at the end of each volume, with bibliographical information and glossaries of Wessex words and place-names.

A third, more miscellaneous volume consists mainly of stories which have never hitherto been collected. Among them are 'Old Mrs Chundle', 'An Indiscretion in the Life of an Heiress', another story intended originally for *A Group of Noble Dames*, and two stories for young people. Plans for others are added, together with *The Famous Tragedy of the Queen of Cornwall*.

As a short-story writer, Hardy undoubtedly reaches a higher stature than any English novelist who preceded him. Like Scott, he believes in telling stories of uncommon events: 'We tale-tellers are all Ancient Mariners, and none of us is warranted in stopping Wedding Guests (in other words, the hurrying public) unless he has something more unusual to relate than the ordinary experience of every average man or woman,' he wrote in 1893. Yet, though an imaginative rather than a realistic writer, he rarely (and never completely) flits into a world of fantasy; his stories are rooted in Wessex. They derive as much from local history, traditions, folklore, and newspapers, as from invention. Truth can be stranger than fiction, and some of the most graphic (and harrowing) details are based on recollections Hardy heard from his parents in his youth.

Since 1895, when he virtually abandoned the writing of prose fiction, many authors have achieved greater sophistication and technical expertise in the short story than Hardy ever aspired to. Yet his virtues as a writer are more enduring. High literary excellence, Longinus wrote, 'is the echo of a great mind'. With Hardy we often feel we are sharing the thoughts, feelings, and vision of a great mind, whether we agree with his philosophical presuppositions or not. He has the creative gift which makes characters and visible scenes live as imaginative realities; he evades sentimentality by combining compassion with critical detachment; he is a master of suspense, the unexpected, and irony of situation; and his range extends from the deeply tragic to the highly humorous and diverting. If he is not one of the greatest short-story writers, his short stories reflect a great writer in many moods.

Satisfying the requirements of magazine editors led to occasional compromises, as Hardy exemplifies at the end of 'The Distracted Preacher'. The short stories vary in length from such a novelette to the very brief, and some of his best are to be found in each of these categories. There is an art in concealing art of which Hardy is master more often than is generally suspected. It is doubtful whether some of his tales, especially the less 'literary', could be told with more life and economy, and a greater air of verisimilitude. Oral methods of narration sometimes contribute effectively towards the latter end, as in 'A Tradition of Eighteen Hundred and Four'; occasionally this fictional device is little more than a parenthetical convention.

Although *Wessex Tales* was the first collection of Hardy's short stories to be published, it contains no suggestion of immaturity. Six of his novels, including *Far from the Madding Crowd* and *The Return of the Native*, had been published before the earliest of its inclusions was written, and the last of them (chronologically) belong to the period of *The Woodlanders* and *Tess of the d'Urbervilles*. The seven stories vary widely not only in length but in character, ranging from the humorous to the tragical, and from the romantic to the more realistic, one being a miniature novel rather than a long short story. Hardy's preface illustrates the reality behind some of their more extraordinary features, and there can be little doubt that Wessex history and tradition add to the fascination of this popular volume.

History and traditions of a very different kind enter most of the stories in *A Group of Noble Dames*. Most of them were written during the interval when the serial publication of *Tess of the d'Urbervilles* was suspended. They form a strange assortment, from the grim to the startling and even amusing. The writer's imagination and lingering legacies of old scandals impart more to their 'palpitating drama', one suspects, than the genealogies of the county families Hardy loved to explore. At crucial points in some of these stories, his presentation and incisive style communicate deep pity for suffering and a condemnation of class pride and cruelty. In this implied or imaginative (as opposed to overt) criticism one can see a link with some of the moving stories which were to appear in *Life's Little Ironies*.

F. B. PINION

WESSEX TALES

Preface to 'Wessex Tales'

AN apology is perhaps needed for the neglect of contrast which is shown by presenting two stories of hangmen and one of a military execution in such a small collection as the following. But as to the former, in the neighbourhood of county-towns hanging matters used to form a large proportion of the local tradition; and though never personally acquainted with any chief operator at such scenes, the writer of these pages had as a boy the privilege of being on speaking terms with a man who applied for the office, and who sank into an incurable melancholy because he failed to get it, some slight mitigation of his grief being to dwell upon striking episodes in the lives of those happier ones who had held it with success and renown. His tale of disappointment used to cause his listener some wonder why his ambition should have taken such an unfortunate form, by limiting itself to a profession of which there could be only one practitioner in England at one time, when it might have aimed at something more commonplace – that would have afforded him more chances – such as the office of a judge, a bishop, or even a member of Parliament – but its nobleness was never questioned. In those days, too, there was still living an old woman who, for the cure of some eating disease, had been taken in her youth to have her 'blood turned' by a convict's corpse, in the manner described in 'The Withered Arm'.

Since writing this story some years ago I have been reminded by an aged friend who knew 'Rhoda Brook' that, in relating her dream, my forgetfulness has weakened the facts out of which the tale grew. In reality it was while lying down on a hot afternoon that the incubus oppressed her and she flung it off, with the results upon the body of the original as described. To my mind the occurrence of such a vision in the daytime is more impressive than if it had happened in a midnight dream. Readers are therefore asked to correct the misrelation, which affords an instance of how our imperfect memories insensibly formalize the fresh originality of living fact – from whose shape they slowly depart, as machine-made castings depart by degrees from the sharp hand-work of the mould.

Among the many devices for concealing smuggled goods in caves and pits of the earth, that of planting an apple-tree in a tray or box which was placed over the mouth of the pit is, I believe, unique, and it is detailed in 'The Distracted Preacher' precisely as described by an old carrier of 'tubs' – a man who was afterwards in my father's employ for over thirty years. I never gathered from his reminiscences what means were adopted for lifting the tree, which, with its roots, earth, and receptacle, must have been of considerable weight. There is no doubt, however, that the thing was done through many years. My informant often spoke, too, of the horribly suffocating sensation produced by the pair of spirit-tubs slung upon the chest and back, after stumbling with the burden of them for several miles inland over a rough country and in darkness. He said that though years of his youth and young manhood were spent in this irregular business, his profits from the same, taken all together, did not average the wages he might have earned in a steady employment, whilst the fatigues and risks were excessive.

I may add that the action of this story is founded on certain smuggling exploits that occurred between 1825 and 1830, and were brought to a close in the latter year by the trial of the chief actors at the Assizes before Baron Bolland for their desperate armed resistance to the Custom-house officers during the landing of a cargo of spirits. This happened only a little time after the doings recorded in the narrative, in which some incidents that came out at the trial are also embodied.

In the culminating affray the character called Owlett was badly wounded, and several of the Preventive-men would have lost their lives through being overpowered by the far more numerous body of smugglers, but for the forbearance and manly conduct of the latter. This served them in good stead at their trial, in which the younger Erskine prosecuted, their defence being entrusted to Erle. Baron Bolland's summing up was strongly in their favour; they were merely ordered to enter into their own recognizances for good behaviour and discharged. (See also as to facts the note at the end of the tale.)

However, the stories are but dreams, and not records. They were first collected and published under their present title, in two volumes, in 1888.

April 1896–May 1912

An experience of the writer in respect of the tale called 'A Tradition of Eighteen Hundred and Four' is curious enough to be mentioned here. The incident of Napoleon's visit to the English coast by night, with a view to discovering a convenient spot for landing his army of invasion, was an invention of the author's on which he had some doubts because of its improbability. This was in 1882, when it was first published. Great was his surprise several years later to be told that it was a real tradition. How far this is true he is unaware.

June 1919   T.H.

The Three Strangers

AMONG the few features of agricultural England which retain an appearance but little modified by the lapse of centuries, may be reckoned the long, grassy and furzy downs, coombs, or ewe-leases, as they are called according to their kind, that fill a large area of certain counties in the south and south-west. If any mark of human occupation is met with hereon, it usually takes the form of the solitary cottage of some shepherd.

Fifty years ago such a lonely cottage stood on such a down, and may possibly be standing there now. In spite of its loneliness, however, the spot, by actual measurement, was not three miles from a county-town. Yet that affected it little. Three miles of irregular upland, during the long inimical seasons, with their sleets, snows, rains, and mists, afford withdrawing space enough to isolate a Timon or a Nebuchadnezzar; much less, in fair weather, to please that less repellent tribe, the poets, philosophers, artists, and others who 'conceive and meditate of pleasant things'.

Some old earthen camp or barrow, some clump of trees, at least some starved fragment of ancient hedge is usually taken advantage of in the erection of these forlorn dwellings. But, in the present case, such a kind of shelter had been disregarded. Higher Crowstairs, as the house was called, stood quite detached and undefended. The only reason for its precise situation seemed to be the crossing of two footpaths at right angles hard by, which may have crossed there and thus for a good five hundred years. Hence the house was exposed to the elements on all sides. But, though the wind up here blew unmistakably when it did blow, and the rain hit hard whenever it fell, the various weathers of the winter season were not quite so formidable on the down as they were imagined to be by dwellers on low ground. The raw rimes were not so pernicious as in the hollows, and the frosts were scarcely so severe. When the shepherd and his family who tenanted the house were pitied for their sufferings from the exposure, they said that upon the whole they were less inconvenienced by 'wuzzes and flames' (hoarses and phlegms) than when they had lived by the stream of a snug neighbouring valley.

The night of March 28, 182–, was precisely one of the nights that were wont to call forth these expressions of commiseration. The level rainstorm smote walls, slopes, and hedges like the clothyard shafts of Senlac and Crecy. Such sheep and outdoor animals as had no shelter stood with their buttocks to the winds; while the tails of little birds trying to roost on some scraggy thorn were blown inside-out like umbrellas. The gable-end of the cottage was stained with wet, and the eavesdroppings flapped against the wall. Yet never was commiseration for the shepherd more misplaced. For that cheerful rustic was entertaining a large party in glorification of the christening of his second girl.

The guests had arrived before the rain began to fall, and they were all now assembled in the chief or living-room of the dwelling. A glance into the apartment at eight o'clock on this eventful evening would have resulted in the opinion that it was as cosy and comfortable a nook as could be wished for in boisterous weather. The calling of its inhabitant was proclaimed by a number of highly-polished sheep-crooks without stems that were hung ornamentally over the fireplace, the curl of each shining crook varying from the antiquated type engraved in the patriarchal pictures of old family Bibles to the most approved fashion of the last local sheep-fair. The room was lighted by half-a-dozen candles, having wicks only a trifle smaller than the grease which enveloped them, in candlesticks that were never used but at high-days, holy-days, and family feasts. The lights were scattered about the room, two of them standing on the chimney-piece. This position of candles was in itself significant. Candles on the chimney-piece always meant a party.

On the hearth, in front of a back-brand to give substance, blazed a fire of thorns, that crackled 'like the laughter of the fool'.

Nineteen persons were gathered here. Of these, five women, wearing gowns of various bright hues, sat in chairs along the wall; girls shy and not shy filled the window-bench; four men, including Charley Jake the hedge-carpenter, Elijah New the parish-clerk, and John Pitcher, a neighbouring dairyman, the shepherd's father-in-law, lolled in the settle; a young man and maid, who were blushing over tentative *pourparlers* on a life-companionship, sat beneath the corner-cupboard; and an elderly engaged man of fifty or upward moved restlessly about from spots where his betrothed was not to the spot where she was. Enjoyment was pretty general, and so much the more prevailed in being unhampered by conventional restrictions. Absolute confidence in each other's good opinion begat perfect ease, while the finishing stroke of manner, amounting to a truly princely serenity, was lent to the majority by the absence of any expression or trait denoting that they wished to get on in the world, enlarge their minds, or do any eclipsing thing whatever – which nowadays so generally nips the bloom and *bonhomie* of all except the two extremes of the social scale.

Shepherd Fennel had married well, his wife being a dairyman's daughter from a vale at a distance, who brought fifty guineas in her pocket – and kept them there, till they should be required for ministering to the needs of a coming family. This frugal woman had been some-what exercised as to the character that should be given to the gathering. A sit-still party had its advantages; but an undisturbed position of ease in chairs and settles was apt to lead on the men to such an unconscionable deal of toping that they would sometimes fairly drink the house dry. A dancing-party was the alternative; but this, while avoiding the foregoing objection on the score of good drink, had a counterbalancing dis-advantage in the matter of good victuals, the ravenous appetites engen-dered by the exercise causing immense havoc in the buttery. Shepherdess Fennel fell back upon the intermediate plan of mingling short dances with short periods of talk and singing, so as to hinder any ungovernable rage in either. But this scheme was entirely confined to her own gentle mind: the shepherd himself was in the mood to exhibit the most reckless phases of hospitality.

The fiddler was a boy of those parts, about twelve years of age, who had a wonderful dexterity in jigs and reels, though his fingers were so small and short as to necessitate a constant shifting for the high notes, from which he scrambled back to the first position with sounds not of unmixed purity of tone. At seven the shrill tweedle-dee of this youngster had begun, accompanied by a booming ground-bass from Elijah New, the parish-clerk, who had thoughtfully brought with him his favourite musical instrument, the serpent. Dancing was instantaneous, Mrs Fennel privately enjoining the players on no account to let the dance exceed the length of a quarter of an hour.

But Elijah and the boy in the excitement of their position quite forgot the injunction. Moreover, Oliver Giles, a man of seventeen, one of the dancers, who was enamoured of his partner, a fair girl of thirty-three rolling years, had recklessly handed a new crown-piece to the musicians,

as a bribe to keep going as long as they had muscle and wind. Mrs
Fennel, seeing the steam begin to generate on the countenances of her
guests, crossed over and touched the fiddler's elbow and put her hand on
the serpent's mouth. But they took no notice, and fearing she might lose
her character of genial hostess if she were to interfere too markedly, she
retired and sat down helpless. And so the dance whizzed on with
cumulative fury, the performers moving in their planet-like courses,
direct and retrograde, from apogee to perigee, till the hand of the well-
kicked clock at the bottom of the room had travelled over the circumference of an hour.

While these cheerful events were in course of enactment within
Fennel's pastoral dwelling an incident having considerable bearing on
the party had occurred in the gloomy night without. Mrs Fennel's
concern about the growing fierceness of the dance corresponded in point
of time with the ascent of a human figure to the solitary hill of Higher
Crowstairs from the direction of the distant town. This personage strode
on through the rain without a pause, following the little-worn path
which, further on in its course, skirted the shepherd's cottage.

It was nearly the time of full moon, and on this account, though the
sky was lined with a uniform sheet of dripping cloud, ordinary objects
out of doors were readily visible. The sad wan light revealed the lonely
pedestrian to be a man of supple frame; his gait suggested that he had
somewhat passed the period of perfect and instinctive agility, though
not so far as to be otherwise than rapid of motion when occasion
required. At a rough guess, he might have been about forty years of age.
He appeared tall, but a recruiting sergeant, or other person accustomed
to the judging of men's heights by the eye, would have discerned that
this was chiefly owing to his gauntness, and that he was not more than
five-feet-eight or nine.

Notwithstanding the regularity of his tread there was caution in it, as
in that of one who mentally feels his way; and despite the fact that it was
not a black coat nor a dark garment of any sort that he wore, there was
something about him which suggested that he naturally belonged to the
black-coated tribes of men. His clothes were of fustian, and his boots
hobnailed, yet in his progress he showed not the mud-accustomed
bearing of hobnailed and fustianed peasantry.

By the time that he had arrived abreast of the shepherd's premises the
rain came down, or rather came along, with yet more determined
violence. The outskirts of the little settlement partially broke the force of

wind and rain, and this induced him to stand still. The most salient of the shepherd's domestic erections was an empty sty at the forward corner of his hedgeless garden, for in these latitudes the principle of masking the homelier features of your establishment by a conventional frontage was unknown. The traveller's eye was attracted to this small building by the pallid shine of the wet slates that covered it. He turned aside, and, finding it empty, stood under the pent-roof for shelter.

While he stood, the boom of the serpent within the adjacent house, and the lesser strains of the fiddler, reached the spot as an accompaniment to the surging hiss of the flying rain on the sod, its louder beating on the cabbage-leaves of the garden, on the straw hackles of eight or ten beehives just discernible by the path, and its dripping from the eaves into a row of buckets and pans that had been placed under the walls of the cottage. For at Higher Crowstairs, as at all such elevated domiciles, the grand difficulty of housekeeping was an insufficiency of water; and a casual rainfall was utilized by turning out, as catchers, every utensil that the house contained. Some queer stories might be told of the contrivances for economy in suds and dish-waters that are absolutely necessitated in upland habitations during the droughts of summer. But at this season there were no such exigencies; a mere acceptance of what the skies bestowed was sufficient for an abundant store.

At last the notes of the serpent ceased and the house was silent. This cessation of activity aroused the solitary pedestrian from the reverie into which he had lapsed, and, emerging from the shed, with an apparently new intention, he walked up the path to the house-door. Arrived here, his first act was to kneel down on a large stone beside the row of vessels, and to drink a copious draught from one of them. Having quenched his thirst he rose and lifted his hand to knock, but paused with his eye upon the panel. Since the dark surface of the wood revealed absolutely nothing, it was evident that he must be mentally looking through the door, as if he wished to measure thereby all the possibilities that a house of this sort might include, and how they might bear upon the question of his entry.

In his indecision he turned and surveyed the scene around. Not a soul was anywhere visible. The garden-path stretched downward from his feet, gleaming like the track of a snail; the roof of the little well (mostly dry), the well-cover, the top rail of the garden-gate, were varnished with the same dull liquid glaze; while, far away in the vale, a faint whiteness of more than usual extent showed that the rivers were high in the meads.

Beyond all this winked a few bleared lamplights through the beating drops – lights that denoted the situation of the county-town from which he had appeared to come. The absence of all notes of life in that direction seemed to clinch his intentions, and he knocked at the door.

Within, a desultory chat had taken the place of movement and musical sound. The hedge-carpenter was suggesting a song to the company, which nobody just then was inclined to undertake, so that the knock afforded a not unwelcome diversion.

'Walk in!' said the shepherd promptly.

The latch clicked upward, and out of the night our pedestrian appeared upon the door-mat. The shepherd arose, snuffed two of the nearest candles, and turned to look at him.

Their light disclosed that the stranger was dark in complexion and not unprepossessing as to feature. His hat, which for a moment he did not remove, hung low over his eyes, without concealing that they were large, open, and determined, moving with a flash rather than a glance round the room. He seemed pleased with his survey, and, baring his shaggy head, said, in a rich deep voice, 'The rain is so heavy, friends, that I ask leave to come in and rest awhile.'

'To be sure, stranger,' said the shepherd. 'And faith, you've been lucky in choosing your time, for we are having a bit of a fling for a glad cause – though, to be sure, a man could hardly wish that glad cause to happen more than once a year.'

'Nor less,' spoke up a woman. 'For 'tis best to get your family over and done with, as soon as you can, so as to be all the earlier out of the fag o't.'

'And what may be this glad cause?' asked the stranger.

'A birth and christening,' said the shepherd.

The stranger hoped his host might not be made unhappy either by too many or too few of such episodes, and being invited by a gesture to a pull at the mug, he readily acquiesced. His manner, which, before entering, had been so dubious, was now altogether that of a careless and candid man.

'Late to be traipsing athwart this coomb – hey?' said the engaged man of fifty.

'Late it is, master, as you say. – I'll take a seat in the chimney-corner, if you have nothing to urge against it, ma'am; for I am a little moist on the side that was next the rain.'

Mrs Shepherd Fennel assented, and made room for the self-invited comer, who, having got completely inside the chimney-corner, stretched out his legs and his arms with the expansiveness of a person quite at home.

'Yes, I am rather cracked in the vamp,' he said freely, seeing that the eyes of the shepherd's wife fell upon his boots, 'and I am not well fitted either. I have had some rough times lately, and have been forced to pick up what I can get in the way of wearing, but I must find a suit better fit for working-days when I reach home.'

'One of hereabouts?' she inquired.

'Not quite that – further up the country.'

'I thought so. And so be I; and by your tongue you come from my neighbourhood.'

'But you would hardly have heard of me,' he said quickly. 'My time would be long before yours, ma'am, you see.'

This testimony to the youthfulness of his hostess had the effect of stopping her cross-examination.

'There is only one thing more wanted to make me happy,' continued the new-comer. 'And that is a little baccy, which I am sorry to say I am out of.'

'I'll fill your pipe,' said the shepherd.

'I must ask you to lend me a pipe likewise.'

'A smoker, and no pipe about 'ee?'

'I have dropped it somewhere on the road.'

The shepherd filled and handed him a new clay pipe, saying, as he did so, 'Hand me your baccy-box – I'll fill that too, now I am about it.'

The man went through the movement of searching his pockets.

'Lost that too?' said his entertainer, with some surprise.

'I am afraid so,' said the man with some confusion. 'Give it to me in a screw of paper.' Lighting his pipe at the candle with a suction that drew the whole flame into the bowl, he resettled himself in the corner and bent his looks upon the faint steam from his damp legs, as if he wished to say no more.

Meanwhile the general body of guests had been taking little notice of this visitor by reason of an absorbing discussion in which they were engaged with the band about a tune for the next dance. The matter being settled, they were about to stand up when an interruption came in the shape of another knock at the door.

At sound of the same the man in the chimney-corner took up the poker and began stirring the brands as if doing it thoroughly were the one aim of his existence; and a second time the shepherd said, 'Walk in!'

In a moment another man stood upon the straw-woven door-mat. He too was a stranger.

This individual was one of a type radically different from the first. There was more of the commonplace in his manner, and a certain jovial cosmopolitanism sat upon his features. He was several years older than the first arrival, his hair being slightly frosted, his eyebrows bristly, and his whiskers cut back from his cheeks. His face was rather full and flabby, and yet it was not altogether a face without power. A few grog-blossoms marked the neighbourhood of his nose. He flung back his long drab greatcoat, revealing that beneath it he wore a suit of cinder-gray shade throughout, large heavy seals, of some metal or other that would take a polish, dangling from his fob as his only personal ornament. Shaking the water-drops from his low-crowned glazed hat, he said, 'I must ask for a few minutes' shelter, comrades, or I shall be wetted to my skin before I get to Casterbridge.'

'Make yourself at home, master,' said the shepherd, perhaps a trifle less heartily than on the first occasion. Not that Fennel had the least tinge of niggardliness in his composition; but the room was far from large, spare chairs were not numerous, and damp companions were not altogether desirable at close quarters for the women and girls in their bright-coloured gowns.

However, the second comer, after taking off his greatcoat, and hanging his hat on a nail in one of the ceiling-beams as if he had been specially invited to put it there, advanced and sat down at the table. This had been pushed so closely into the chimney-corner, to give all available room to the dancers, that its inner edge grazed the elbow of the man who had ensconced himself by the fire; and thus the two strangers were brought into close companionship. They nodded to each other by way of breaking the ice of unacquaintance, and the first stranger handed his neighbour the family mug – a huge vessel of brown ware, having its upper edge worn away like a threshold by the rub of whole generations of thirsty lips that had gone the way of all flesh, and bearing the following inscription burnt upon its rotund side in yellow letters: –

THERE IS NO FUN
UNTILL i CUM

The other man, nothing loth, raised the mug to his lips, and drank on, and on, and on – till a curious blueness overspread the countenance of the shepherd's wife, who had regarded with no little surprise the first stranger's free offer to the second of what did not belong to him to dispense.

'I knew it!' said the toper to the shepherd with much satisfaction. 'When I walked up your garden before coming in, and saw the hives all of a row, I said to myself, "Where there's bees there's honey, and where there's honey there's mead." But mead of such a truly comfortable sort as this I really didn't expect to meet in my older days.' He took yet another pull at the mug, till it assumed an ominous elevation.

'Glad you enjoy it!' said the shepherd warmly.

'It is goodish mead,' assented Mrs Fennel, with an absence of enthusiasm which seemed to say that it was possible to buy praise for one's cellar at too heavy a price. 'It is trouble enough to make – and really I hardly think we shall make any more. For honey sells well, and we ourselves can make shift with a drop o' small mead and metheglin for common use from the comb-washings.'

'O, but you'll never have the heart!' reproachfully cried the stranger in cinder-gray, after taking up the mug a third time and setting it down empty. 'I love mead, when 'tis old like this, as I love to go to church o' Sundays or to relieve the needy any day of the week.'

'Ha, ha, ha!' said the man in the chimney-corner, who, in spite of the taciturnity induced by the pipe of tobacco, could not or would not refrain from this slight testimony to his comrade's humour.

Now the old mead of those days, brewed of the purest first-year or maiden honey, four pounds to the gallon – with its due complement of white of eggs, cinnamon, ginger, cloves, mace, rosemary, yeast, and processes of working, bottling, and cellaring – tasted remarkably strong; but it did not taste so strong as it actually was. Hence, presently, the stranger in cinder-gray at the table, moved by its creeping influence, unbuttoned his waistcoat, threw himself back in his chair, spread his legs, and made his presence felt in various ways.

'Well, well, as I say,' he resumed, 'I am going to Casterbridge, and to Casterbridge I must go. I should have been almost there by this time; but the rain drove me into your dwelling, and I'm not sorry for it.'

'You don't live in Casterbridge?' said the shepherd.

'Not as yet; though I shortly mean to move there.'

'Going to set up in trade, perhaps?'

'No, no,' said the shepherd's wife. 'It is easy to see that the gentleman is rich, and don't want to work at anything.'

The cinder-gray stranger paused, as if to consider whether he would accept that definition of himself. He presently rejected it by answering, 'Rich is not quite the word for me, dame. I do work, and I must work. And even if I only get to Casterbridge by midnight I must begin work there at eight to-morrow morning. Yes, het or wet, blow or snow, famine or sword, my day's work to-morrow must be done.'

'Poor man! Then, in spite o' seeming, you be worse off than we?' replied the shepherd's wife.

' 'Tis the nature of my trade, men and maidens. 'Tis the nature of my trade more than my poverty. . . . But really and truly I must up and off, or I shan't get a lodging in the town.' However, the speaker did not move, and directly added, 'There's time for one more draught of friendship before I go; and I'd perform it at once if the mug were not dry.'

'Here's a mug o' small,' said Mrs Fennel. 'Small, we call it, though to be sure 'tis only the first wash o' the combs.'

'No,' said the stranger disdainfully. 'I won't spoil your first kindness by partaking o' your second.'

'Certainly not,' broke in Fennel. 'We don't increase and multiply every day, and I'll fill the mug again.' He went away to the dark place under the stairs where the barrel stood. The shepherdess followed him.

'Why should you do this?' she said reproachfully, as soon as they were alone. 'He's emptied it once, though it held enough for ten people; and now he's not contented wi' the small, but must needs call for more o' the strong! And a stranger unbeknown to any of us. For my part, I don't like the look o' the man at all.'

'But he's in the house, my honey; and 'tis a wet night, and a christening. Daze it, what's a cup of mead more or less? There'll be plenty more next bee-burning.'

'Very well – this time, then,' she answered, looking wistfully at the barrel. 'But what is the man's calling, and where is he one of, that he should come in and join us like this?'

'I don't know. I'll ask him again.'

The catastrophe of having the mug drained dry at one pull by the stranger in cinder-gray was effectually guarded against this time by Mrs Fennel. She poured out his allowance in a small cup, keeping the large one at a discreet distance from him. When he had tossed off his portion the shepherd renewed his inquiry about the stranger's occupation.

The latter did not immediately reply, and the man in the chimney-corner, with sudden demonstrativeness, said, 'Anybody may know my trade – I'm a wheelwright.'

'A very good trade for these parts,' said the shepherd.

'And anybody may know mine – if they've the sense to find it out,' said the stranger in cinder-gray.

'You may generally tell what a man is by his claws,' observed the hedge-carpenter, looking at his own hands. 'My fingers be as full of thorns as an old pin-cushion is of pins.'

The hands of the man in the chimney-corner instinctively sought the shade, and he gazed into the fire as he resumed his pipe. The man at the table took up the hedge-carpenter's remark, and added smartly, 'True; but the oddity of my trade is that, instead of setting a mark upon me, it sets a mark upon my customers.'

No observation being offered by anybody in elucidation of this enigma the shepherd's wife once more called for a song. The same obstacles presented themselves as at the former time – one had no voice, another had forgotten the first verse. The stranger at the table, whose soul had now risen to a good working temperature, relieved the difficulty by exclaiming that, to start the company, he would sing himself. Thrusting one thumb into the arm-hole of his waistcoat, he waved the other hand in the air, and, with an extemporizing gaze at the shining sheep-crooks above the mantelpiece, began: –

> 'O my trade it is the rarest one,
> Simple shepherds all –
> My trade is a sight to see;
> For my customers I tie, and take them up on high,
> And waft 'em to a far countree!'

The room was silent when he had finished the verse – with one exception, that of the man in the chimney-corner, who, at the singer's word, 'Chorus!' joined him in a deep bass voice of musical relish –

> 'And waft 'em to a far countree!'

Oliver Giles, John Pitcher the dairyman, the parish-clerk, the engaged man of fifty, the row of young women against the wall, seemed lost in thought not of the gayest kind. The shepherd looked meditatively on the ground, the shepherdess gazed keenly at the singer, and with some suspicion; she was doubting whether this stranger were merely singing an old song from recollection, or was composing one there and then for the occasion. All were as perplexed at the obscure revelation as the guests at Belshazzar's Feast, except the man in the chimney-corner, who quietly said, 'Second verse, stranger,' and smoked on.

The singer thoroughly moistened himself from his lips inwards, and
went on with the next stanza as requested: –

> 'My tools are but common ones,
> Simple shepherds all –
> My tools are no sight to see:
> A little hempen string, and a post whereon to swing,
> Are implements enough for me!'

Shepherd Fennel glanced round. There was no longer any doubt that
the stranger was answering his question rhythmically. The guests one
and all started back with suppressed exclamations. The young woman
engaged to the man of fifty fainted half-way, and would have proceeded,
but finding him wanting in alacrity for catching her she sat down
trembling.

'O, he's the ——!' whispered the people in the background, mentioning the name of an ominous public officer. 'He's come to do it! 'Tis to be
at Casterbridge jail to-morrow – the man for sheep-stealing – the poor
clockmaker we heard of, who used to live away at Shottsford and had
no work to do – Timothy Summers, whose family were a-starving, and
so he went out of Shottsford by the high-road, and took a sheep in open
daylight, defying the farmer and the farmer's wife and the farmer's lad,
and every man jack among 'em. He' (and they nodded towards the
stranger of the deadly trade) 'is come from up the country to do it
because there's not enough to do in his own county-town, and he's got
the place here now our own county man's dead; he's going to live in the
same cottage under the prison wall.'

The stranger in cinder-gray took no notice of this whispered string of
observations, but again wetted his lips. Seeing that his friend in the
chimney-corner was the only one who reciprocated his joviality in any
way, he held out his cup towards that appreciative comrade, who also
held out his own. They clinked together, the eyes of the rest of the
room hanging upon the singer's actions. He parted his lips for the third
verse; but at that moment another knock was audible upon the door.
This time the knock was faint and hesitating.

The company seemed scared; the shepherd looked with consternation
towards the entrance, and it was with some effort that he resisted his
alarmed wife's deprecatory glance, and uttered for the third time the
welcoming words, 'Walk in!'

The door was gently opened, and another man stood upon the mat.
He, like those who had preceded him, was a stranger. This time it was a

short, small personage, of fair complexion, and dressed in a decent suit
of dark clothes.

'Can you tell me the way to—?' he began: when, gazing round the
room to observe the nature of the company amongst whom he had fallen,
his eyes lighted on the stranger in cinder-gray. It was just at the instant
when the latter, who had thrown his mind into his song with such a will
that he scarcely heeded the interruption, silenced all whispers and
inquiries by bursting into his third verse: –

> 'To-morrow is my working day,
>   Simple shepherds all –
>   To-morrow is a working day for me:
> For the farmer's sheep is slain, and the lad who did it ta'en,
>   And on his soul may God ha' merc-y!'

The stranger in the chimney-corner, waving cups with the singer so
heartily that his mead splashed over on the hearth, repeated in his bass
voice as before: –

> 'And on his soul may God ha' merc-y!'

All this time the third stranger had been standing in the doorway.
Finding now that he did not come forward or go on speaking, the guests
particularly regarded him. They noticed to their surprise that he stood
before them the picture of abject terror – his knees trembling, his hand
shaking so violently that the door-latch by which he supported himself
rattled audibly: his white lips were parted, and his eyes fixed on the
merry officer of justice in the middle of the room. A moment more and
he had turned, closed the door, and fled.

'What a man can it be?' said the shepherd.

The rest, between the awfulness of their late discovery and the odd
conduct of this third visitor, looked as if they knew not what to think,
and said nothing. Instinctively they withdrew further and further from
the grim gentleman in their midst, whom some of them seemed to take
for the Prince of Darkness himself, till they formed a remote circle, an
empty space of floor being left between them and him –

> '. . . circulus, cujus centrum diabolus'.

The room was so silent – though there were more than twenty people in
it – that nothing could be heard but the patter of the rain against the
window-shutters, accompanied by the occasional hiss of a stray drop

that fell down the chimney into the fire, and the steady puffing of the man in the corner, who had now resumed his pipe of long clay.

The stillness was unexpectedly broken. The distant sound of a gun reverberated through the air – apparently from the direction of the county-town.

'Be jiggered!' cried the stranger who had sung the song, jumping up.

'What does that mean?' asked several.

'A prisoner escaped from the jail – that's what it means.'

All listened. The sound was repeated, and none of them spoke but the man in the chimney-corner, who said quietly, 'I've often been told that in this county they fire a gun at such times; but I never heard it till now.'

'I wonder if it is *my* man?' murmured the personage in cinder-gray.

'Surely it is!' said the shepherd involuntarily. 'And surely we've zeed him! That little man who looked in at the door by now, and quivered like a leaf when he zeed ye and heard your song!'

'His teeth chattered, and the breath went out of his body,' said the dairyman.

'And his heart seemed to sink within him like a stone,' said Oliver Giles.

'And he bolted as if he'd been shot at,' said the hedge-carpenter.

'True – his teeth chattered, and his heart seemed to sink; and he bolted as if he'd been shot at,' slowly summed up the man in the chimney-corner.

'I didn't notice it,' remarked the hangman.

'We were all a-wondering what made him run off in such a fright,' faltered one of the women against the wall, 'and now 'tis explained!'

The firing of the alarm-gun went on at intervals, low and sullenly, and their suspicions became a certainty. The sinister gentleman in cinder-gray roused himself. 'Is there a constable here?' he asked, in thick tones. 'If so, let him step forward.'

The engaged man of fifty stepped quavering out from the wall, his betrothed beginning to sob on the back of the chair.

'You are a sworn constable?'

'I be, sir.'

'Then pursue the criminal at once, with assistance, and bring him back here. He can't have gone far.'

'I will, sir, I will – when I've got my staff. I'll go home and get it, and come sharp here, and start in a body.'

'Staff! – never mind your staff; the man'll be gone!'

'But I can't do nothing without my staff – can I, William, and John, and Charles Jake? No; for there's the king's royal crown a painted on en in yaller and gold, and the lion and the unicorn, so as when I raise en up and hit my prisoner, 'tis made a lawful blow thereby. I wouldn't 'tempt to take up a man without my staff – no, not I. If I hadn't the law to gie me courage, why, instead o' my taking up him he might take up me!'

'Now, I'm a king's man myself, and can give you authority enough for this,' said the formidable officer in gray. 'Now then, all of ye, be ready. Have ye any lanterns?'

'Yes – have ye any lanterns? – I demand it!' said the constable.

'And the rest of you able-bodied—'

'Able-bodied men – yes – the rest of ye!' said the constable.

'Have you some good stout staves and pitchforks—'

'Staves and pitchforks – in the name o' the law! And take 'em in yer hands and go in quest, and do as we in authority tell ye!'

Thus aroused, the men prepared to give chase. The evidence was, indeed, though circumstantial, so convincing, that but little argument was needed to show the shepherd's guests that after what they had seen it would look very much like connivance if they did not instantly pursue the unhappy third stranger, who could not as yet have gone more than a few hundred yards over such uneven country.

A shepherd is always well provided with lanterns; and, lighting these hastily, and with hurdle-staves in their hands, they poured out of the door, taking a direction along the crest of the hill, away from the town, the rain having fortunately a little abated.

Disturbed by the noise, or possibly by unpleasant dreams of her baptism, the child who had been christened began to cry heart-brokenly in the room overhead. These notes of grief came down through the chinks of the floor to the ears of the women below, who jumped up one by one, and seemed glad of the excuse to ascend and comfort the baby, for the incidents of the last half-hour greatly oppressed them. Thus in the space of two or three minutes the room on the ground-floor was deserted quite.

But it was not for long. Hardly had the sound of footsteps died away when a man returned round the corner of the house from the direction the pursuers had taken. Peeping in at the door, and seeing nobody there, he entered leisurely. It was the stranger of the chimney-corner, who had gone out with the rest. The motive of his return was shown by his helping himself to a cut piece of skimmer-cake that lay on a ledge beside where he had sat, and which he had apparently forgotten to take with him. He also poured out half a cup more mead from the quantity that remained, ravenously eating and drinking these as he stood. He had not finished when another figure came in just as quietly – his friend in cinder-gray.

'O – you here?' said the latter, smiling. 'I thought you had gone to help in the capture.' And this speaker also revealed the object of his return by looking solicitously round for the fascinating mug of old mead.

'And I thought you had gone,' said the other, continuing his skimmer-cake with some effort.

'Well, on second thoughts, I felt there were enough without me,' said the first confidentially, 'and such a night as it is, too. Besides, 'tis the business o' the Government to take care of its criminals – not mine.'

'True; so it is. And I felt as you did, that there were enough without me.'

'I don't want to break my limbs running over the humps and hollows of this wild country.'

'Nor I neither, between you and me.'

'These shepherd-people are used to it – simple-minded souls, you know, stirred up to anything in a moment. They'll have him ready for me before the morning, and no trouble to me at all.'

'They'll have him, and we shall have saved ourselves all labour in the matter.'

'True, true. Well, my way is to Casterbridge; and 'tis as much as my legs will do to take me that far. Going the same way?'

'No, I am sorry to say! I have to get home over there' (he nodded indefinitely to the right), 'and I feel as you do, that it is quite enough for my legs to do before bedtime.'

The other had by this time finished the mead in the mug, after which, shaking hands heartily at the door, and wishing each other well, they went their several ways.

In the meantime the company of pursuers had reached the end of the hog's-back elevation which dominated this part of the down. They had decided on no particular plan of action; and, finding that the man of the baleful trade was no longer in their company, they seemed quite unable to form any such plan now. They descended in all directions down the hill, and straightway several of the party fell into the snare set by Nature for all misguided midnight ramblers over this part of the cretaceous formation. The 'lanchets', or flint slopes, which belted the escarpment at intervals of a dozen yards, took the less cautious ones unawares, and losing their footing on the rubbly steep they slid sharply downwards, the lanterns rolling from their hands to the bottom, and there lying on their sides till the horn was scorched through.

When they had again gathered themselves together the shepherd, as the man who knew the country best, took the lead, and guided them round these treacherous inclines. The lanterns, which seemed rather to dazzle their eyes and warn the fugitive than to assist them in the exploration, were extinguished, due silence was observed; and in this more rational order they plunged into the vale. It was a grassy, briery, moist defile, affording some shelter to any person who had sought it; but the party perambulated it in vain, and ascended on the other side. Here they wandered apart, and after an interval closed together again to report progress. At the second time of closing in they found themselves near a lonely ash, the single tree on this part of the coomb, probably sown there by a passing bird some fifty years before. And here, standing a little to one side of the trunk, as motionless as the trunk itself, appeared the man they were in quest of, his outline being well defined against the sky beyond. The band noiselessly drew up and faced him.

'Your money or your life!' said the constable sternly to the still figure.

'No, no,' whispered John Pitcher. ' 'Tisn't our side ought to say that. That's the doctrine of vagabonds like him, and we be on the side of the law.'

'Well, well,' replied the constable impatiently; 'I must say something, mustn't I? and if you had all the weight o' this undertaking upon your mind, perhaps you'd say the wrong thing too! – Prisoner at the bar, surrender, in the name of the Father – the Crown, I mane!'

The man under the tree seemed now to notice them for the first time, and, giving them no opportunity whatever for exhibiting their courage, he strolled slowly towards them. He was, indeed, the little man, the third stranger; but his trepidation had in a great measure gone.

'Well, travellers,' he said, 'did I hear ye speak to me?'

'You did: you've got to come and be our prisoner at once!' said the constable. 'We arrest 'ee on the charge of not biding in Casterbridge jail in a decent proper manner to be hung to-morrow morning. Neighbours, do your duty, and seize the culpet!'

On hearing the charge the man seemed enlightened, and, saying not another word, resigned himself with preternatural civility to the search-party, who, with their staves in their hands, surrounded him on all sides, and marched him back towards the shepherd's cottage.

It was eleven o'clock by the time they arrived. The light shining from the open door, a sound of men's voices within, proclaimed to them as they approached the house that some new events had arisen in their absence. On entering they discovered the shepherd's living-room to be invaded by two officers from Casterbridge jail, and a well-known magistrate who lived at the nearest country-seat, intelligence of the escape having become generally circulated.

'Gentlemen,' said the constable, 'I have brought back your man – not without risk and danger; but every one must do his duty! He is inside this circle of able-bodied persons, who have lent me useful aid, considering their ignorance of Crown work. Men, bring forward your prisoner!' And the third stranger was led to the light.

'Who is this?' said one of the officials.

'The man,' said the constable.

'Certainly not,' said the turnkey; and the first corroborated his statement.

'But how can it be otherwise?' asked the constable. 'Or why was he so terrified at sight o' the singing instrument of the law who sat there?' Here he related the strange behaviour of the third stranger on entering the house during the hangman's song.

'Can't understand it,' said the officer coolly. 'All I know is that it is not the condemned man. He's quite a different character from this one; a gauntish fellow, with dark hair and eyes, rather good-looking, and with a musical bass voice that if you heard it once you'd never mistake as long as you lived.'

'Why, souls – 'twas the man in the chimney-corner!'

'Hey – what?' said the magistrate, coming forward after inquiring particulars from the shepherd in the background. 'Haven't you got the man after all?'

'Well, sir,' said the constable, 'he's the man we were in search of, that's true; and yet he's not the man we were in search of. For the man we were in search of was not the man we wanted, sir, if you understand my every-day way; for 'twas the man in the chimney-corner!'

'A pretty kettle of fish altogether!' said the magistrate. 'You had better start for the other man at once.'

The prisoner now spoke for the first time. The mention of the man in the chimney-corner seemed to have moved him as nothing else could do. 'Sir,' he said, stepping forward to the magistrate, 'take no more trouble about me. The time is come when I may as well speak. I have done nothing; my crime is that the condemned man is my brother. Early this afternoon I left home at Shottsford to tramp it all the way to Caster-bridge jail to bid him farewell. I was benighted, and called here to rest and ask the way. When I opened the door I saw before me the very man, my brother, that I thought to see in the condemned cell at Casterbridge. He was in this chimney-corner; and jammed close to him, so that he could not have got out if he had tried, was the executioner who'd come to take his life, singing a song about it and not knowing that it was his victim who was close by, joining in to save appearances. My brother threw a glance of agony at me, and I knew he meant, 'Don't reveal what you see; my life depends on it.' I was so terror-struck that I could hardly stand, and, not knowing what I did, I turned and hurried away.'

The narrator's manner and tone had the stamp of truth, and his story made a great impression on all around.

'And do you know where your brother is at the present time?' asked the magistrate.

'I do not. I have never seen him since I closed this door.'

'I can testify to that, for we've been between ye ever since,' said the constable.

'Where does he think to fly to? – what is his occupation?'

'He's a watch-and-clock-maker, sir.'

' 'A said 'a was a wheelwright – a wicked rogue,' said the constable.

'The wheels of clocks and watches he meant, no doubt,' said Shepherd Fennel. 'I thought his hands were palish for's trade.'

'Well, it appears to me that nothing can be gained by retaining this poor man in custody,' said the magistrate; 'your business lies with the other, unquestionably.'

And so the little man was released off-hand; but he looked nothing the less sad on that account, it being beyond the power of magistrate or constable to raze out the written troubles in his brain, for they concerned another whom he regarded with more solicitude than himself. When this was done, and the man had gone his way, the night was found to be so far advanced that it was deemed useless to renew the search before the next morning.

Next day, accordingly, the quest for the clever sheep-stealer became general and keen, to all appearance at least. But the intended punishment was cruelly disproportioned to the transgression, and the sympathy of a great many country-folk in that district was strongly on the side of the fugitive. Moreover, his marvellous coolness and daring in hob-and-nobbing with the hangman, under the unprecedented circumstances of the shepherd's party, won their admiration. So that it may be questioned if all those who ostensibly made themselves so busy in exploring woods and fields and lanes were quite so thorough when it came to the private examination of their own lofts and outhouses. Stories were afloat of a mysterious figure being occasionally seen in some old overgrown trackway or other, remote from turnpike roads; but when a search was instituted in any of these suspected quarters nobody was found. Thus the days and weeks passed without tidings.

In brief, the bass-voiced man of the chimney-corner was never recaptured. Some said that he went across the sea, others that he did not, but buried himself in the depths of a populous city. At any rate, the gentleman in cinder-gray never did his morning's work at Casterbridge, nor met anywhere at all, for business purposes, the genial comrade with whom he had passed an hour of relaxation in the lonely house on the slope of the coomb.

The grass has long been green on the graves of Shepherd Fennel and his frugal wife; the guests who made up the christening party have mainly followed their entertainers to the tomb; the baby in whose honour they all had met is a matron in the sere and yellow leaf. But the arrival of the three strangers at the shepherd's that night, and the details connected therewith, is a story as well known as ever in the country about Higher Crowstairs.

March 1883

A Tradition of Eighteen Hundred and Four

THE widely discussed possibility of an invasion of England through a Channel tunnel has more than once recalled old Solomon Selby's story to my mind.

The occasion on which I numbered myself among his audience was one evening when he was sitting in the yawning chimney-corner of the inn-kitchen, with some others who had gathered there, and I entered for shelter from the rain. Withdrawing the stem of his pipe from the dental notch in which it habitually rested, he leaned back in the recess behind him and smiled into the fire. The smile was neither mirthful nor sad, not precisely humorous nor altogether thoughtful. We who knew him recognized it in a moment: it was his narrative smile. Breaking off our few desultory remarks we drew up closer, and he thus began: –

'My father, as you mid know, was a shepherd all his life, and lived out by the Cove four miles yonder, where I was born and lived likewise, till I moved here shortly afore I was married. The cottage that first knew me stood on the top of the down, near the sea; there was no house within a mile and a half of it; it was built o' purpose for the farm-shepherd, and had no other use. They tell me that it is now pulled down, but that you can see where it stood by the mounds of earth and a few broken bricks that are still lying about. It was a bleak and dreary place in winter-time, but in summer it was well enough, though the garden never came to much, because we could not get up a good shelter for the vegetables and currant bushes; and where there is much wind they don't thrive.

'Of all the years of my growing up the ones that bide clearest in my mind were eighteen hundred and three, four, and five. This was for two reasons: I had just then grown to an age when a child's eyes and ears take in and note down everything about him, and there was more at that date to bear in mind than there ever has been since with me. It was, as I

need hardly tell ye, the time after the first peace, when Bonaparte was
scheming his descent upon England. He had crossed the great Alp
mountains, fought in Egypt, drubbed the Turks, the Austrians, and the
Proossians, and now thought he'd have a slap at us. On the other side of
the Channel, scarce out of sight and hail of a man standing on our
English shore, the French army of a hundred and sixty thousand men
and fifteen thousand horses had been brought together from all parts,
and were drilling every day. Bonaparte had been three years a-making
his preparations; and to ferry these soldiers and cannon and horses
across he had contrived a couple of thousand flat-bottomed boats.
These boats were small things, but wonderfully built. A good few of
'em were so made as to have a little stable on board each for the two
horses that were to haul the cannon carried at the stern. To get in order
all these, and other things required, he had assembled there five or six
thousand fellows that worked at trades – carpenters, blacksmiths,
wheelwrights, saddlers, and what not. O 'twas a curious time!

'Every morning Neighbour Boney would muster his multitude of
soldiers on the beach, draw 'em up in line, practise 'em in the manœuvre
of embarking, horses and all, till they could do it without a single hitch.
My father drove a flock of ewes up into Sussex that year, and as he went
along the drover's track over the high downs thereabout he could see
this drilling actually going on – the accoutrements of the rank and file
glittering in the sun like silver. It was thought and always said by my
uncle Job, sergeant of foot (who used to know all about these matters),
that Bonaparte meant to cross with oars on a calm night. The grand
query with us, was, Where would my gentleman land? Many of the
common people thought it would be at Dover; others, who knew how
unlikely it was that any skilful general would make a business of landing
just where he was expected, said he'd go either east into the River
Thames, or west'ard to some convenient place, most likely one of the
little bays inside the Isle of Portland, between the Beal and St Alban's
Head – and for choice the three-quarter-round Cove screened from
every mortal eye, that seemed made o' purpose, out by where we lived,
and which I've climmed up with two tubs of brandy across my shoulders
on scores o' dark nights in my younger days. Some had heard that a part
o' the French fleet would sail right round Scotland, and come up the
Channel to a suitable haven. However, there was much doubt upon the
matter; and no wonder, for after-years proved that Bonaparte himself
could hardly make up his mind upon that great and very particular

point, where to land. His uncertainty came about in this wise, that he could get no news as to where and how our troops lay in waiting, and that his knowledge of possible places where flat-bottomed boats might be quietly run ashore, and the men they brought marshalled in order, was dim to the last degree. Being flat-bottomed, they didn't require a harbour for unshipping their cargo of men, but a good shelving beach away from sight, and with a fair open road toward London. How the question posed that great Corsican tyrant (as we used to call him), what pains he took to settle it, and, above all, what a risk he ran on one particular night in trying to do so, were known only to one man here and there; and certainly to no maker of newspapers or printer of books, or my account o't would not have had so many heads shaken over it as it has by gentry who only believe what they see in printed lines.

'The flocks my father had charge of fed all about the downs near our house, overlooking the sea and shore each way for miles. In winter and early spring father was up a deal at nights, watching and tending the lambing. Often he'd go to bed early, and turn out at twelve or one; and on the other hand, he'd sometimes stay up till twelve or one, and then turn in to bed. As soon as I was old enough I used to help him, mostly in the way of keeping an eye upon the ewes while he was gone home to rest. This is what I was doing in a particular month in either the year four or five – I can't certainly fix which, but it was long before I was took away from the sheepkeeping to be bound prentice to a trade. Every night at that time I was at the fold, about half a mile, or it may be a little more, from our cottage, and no living thing at all with me but the ewes and young lambs. Afeared? No; I was never afeared of being alone at these times; for I had been reared in such an out-step place that the lack o' human beings at night made me less fearful than the sight of 'em. Directly I saw a man's shape after dark in a lonely place I was frightened out of my senses.

'One day in that month we were surprised by a visit from my uncle Job, the sergeant in the Sixty-first foot, then in camp on the downs above King George's watering-place, several miles to the west yonder. Uncle Job dropped in about dusk, and went up with my father to the fold for an hour or two. Then he came home, had a drop to drink from the tub of sperrits that the smugglers kept us in for housing their liquor when they'd made a run, and for burning 'em off when there was danger. After that he stretched himself out on the settle to sleep. I went to bed: at one o'clock father came home, and waking me to go and take his place, according to custom, went to bed himself. On my way out of the house I passed Uncle Job on the settle. He opened his eyes, and upon my telling him where I was going he said it was a shame that such a youngster as I should go up there all alone; and when he had fastened up his stock and waist-belt he set off along with me, taking a drop from the sperrit-tub in a little flat bottle that stood in the corner-cupboard.

'By and by we drew up to the fold, saw that all was right, and then, to keep ourselves warm, curled up in a heap of straw that lay inside the thatched hurdles we had set up to break the stroke of the wind when there was any. To-night, however, there was none. It was one of those very still nights when, if you stand on the high hills anywhere within two or three miles of the sea, you can hear the rise and fall of the tide along the shore, coming and going every few moments like a sort of great snore of the sleeping world. Over the lower ground there was a bit of a mist, but on the hill where we lay the air was clear, and the moon, then in her last quarter, flung a fairly good light on the grass and scattered straw.

'While we lay there Uncle Job amused me by telling me strange stories of the wars he had served in and the wownds he had got. He had already fought the French in the Low Countries, and hoped to fight 'em again. His stories lasted so long that at last I was hardly sure that I was not a soldier myself, and had seen such service as he told of. The wonders of his tales quite bewildered my mind, till I fell asleep and dreamed of battle, smoke, and flying soldiers, all of a kind with the doings he had been bringing up to me.

'How long my nap lasted I am not prepared to say. But some faint sounds over and above the rustle of the ewes in the straw, the bleat of the lambs, and the tinkle of the sheep-bell brought me to my waking senses. Uncle Job was still beside me; but he too had fallen asleep. I looked out from the straw, and saw what it was that had aroused me. Two men, in boat-cloaks, cocked hats, and swords, stood by the hurdles about twenty yards off.

'I turned my ear thitherward to catch what they were saying, but though I heard every word o't, not one did I understand. They spoke in a tongue that was not ours – in French, as I afterward found. But if I could not gain the meaning of a word, I was shrewd boy enough to find out a deal of the talkers' business. By the light o' the moon I could see that one of 'em carried a roll of paper in his hand, while every moment he spoke quick to his comrade, and pointed right and left with the other hand to spots along the shore. There was no doubt that he was explaining to the second gentleman the shapes and features of the coast. What happened soon after made this still clearer to me.

'All this time I had not waked Uncle Job, but now I began to be afeared that they might light upon us, because uncle breathed so heavily through's nose. I put my mouth to his ear and whispered, "Uncle Job."

' "What is it, my boy?" he said, just as if he hadn't been asleep at all.

' "Hush!" says I. "Two French generals—"

' "French?" says he.

' "Yes," says I. "Come to see where to land their army!"

'I pointed 'em out; but I could say no more, for the pair were coming at that moment much nearer to where we lay. As soon as they got as near as eight or ten yards, the officer with a roll in his hand stooped down to a slanting hurdle, unfastened his roll upon it, and spread it out. Then suddenly he sprung a dark lantern open on the paper, and showed it to be a map.

' "What be they looking at?" I whispered to Uncle Job.

' "A chart of the Channel," says the sergeant (knowing about such things).

'The other French officer now stooped likewise, and over the map they had a long consultation, as they pointed here and there on the paper, and then hither and thither at places along the shore beneath us. I noticed that the manner of one officer was very respectful toward the other, who seemed much his superior, the second in rank calling him by a sort of title that I did not know the sense of. The head one, on the other hand, was quite familiar with his friend, and more than once clapped him on the shoulder.

'Uncle Job had watched as well as I, but though the map had been in the lantern-light, their faces had always been in shade. But when they rose from stooping over the chart the light flashed upward, and fell smart upon one of 'em's features. No sooner had this happened than Uncle Job gasped, and sank down as if he'd been in a fit.

' "What is it – what is it, Uncle Job?" said I.

' "O good God!" says he, under the straw.

' "What?" says I.

' "Boney!" he groaned out.

' "Who?" says I.

' "Bonaparty," he said. "The Corsican ogre. O that I had got but my new-flinted firelock, that there man should die! But I haven't got my new-flinted firelock, and that there man must live. So lie low, as you value your life!"

'I did lie low, as you mid suppose. But I couldn't help peeping. And then I too, lad as I was, knew that it was the face of Bonaparte. Not know Boney? I should think I did know Boney. I should have known him by half the light o' that lantern. If I had seen a picture of his features once, I had seen it a hundred times. There was his bullet head, his short neck, his round yaller cheeks and chin, his gloomy face, and his great glowing eyes. He took off his hat to blow himself a bit, and there was the forelock in the middle of his forehead, as in all the draughts of him. In moving, his cloak fell a little open, and I could see for a moment his white-fronted jacket and one of the epaulettes.

'But none of this lasted long. In a minute he and his general had rolled up the map, shut the lantern, and turned to go down toward the shore.

'Then Uncle Job came to himself a bit. "Slipped across in the night-time to see how to put his men ashore," he said. "The like o' that man's coolness eyes will never again see! Nephew, I must act in this, and immediate, or England's lost!"

'When they were over the brow, we crope out, and went some little way to look after them. Half-way down they were joined by two others, and six or seven minutes brought them to the shore. Then, from behind a rock, a boat came out into the weak moonlight of the Cove, and they jumped in; it put off instantly, and vanished in a few minutes between the two rocks that stand at the mouth of the Cove as we all know. We climmed back to where we had been before, and I could see, a short way out, a larger vessel, though still not very large. The little boat drew up alongside, was made fast at the stern as I suppose, for the largest sailed away, and we saw no more.

'My uncle Job told his officers as soon as he got back to camp; but what they thought of it I never heard – neither did he. Boney's army never came, and a good job for me; for the Cove below my father's house was where he meant to land, as this secret visit showed. We coast-folk should have been cut down one and all, and I should not have sat here to tell this tale.'

We who listened to old Selby that night have been familiar with his simple grave-stone for these ten years past. Thanks to the incredulity of the age his tale has been seldom repeated. But if anything short of the direct testimony of his own eyes could persuade an auditor that Bonaparte had examined these shores for himself with a view to a practicable landing-place, it would have been Solomon Selby's manner of narrating the adventure which befell him on the down.

Christmas, 1882

The Melancholy Hussar of the German Legion

I

HERE stretch the downs, high and breezy and green, absolutely un-changed since those eventful days. A plough has never disturbed the turf, and the sod that was uppermost then is uppermost now. Here stood the camp; here are distinct traces of the banks thrown up for the horses of the cavalry, and spots where the midden-heaps lay are still to be observed. At night, when I walk across the lonely place, it is impossible to avoid hearing, amid the scourings of the wind over the grass-bents and thistles, the old trumpet and bugle calls, the rattle of the halters; to help seeing rows of spectral tents and the *impedimenta* of the soldiery. From within the canvases come guttural syllables of foreign tongues, and broken songs of the fatherland; for they were mainly regiments of the King's German Legion that slept round the tent-poles hereabout at that time.

It was nearly ninety years ago. The British uniform of the period, with its immense epaulettes, queer cocked-hat, breeches, gaiters, ponderous cartridge-box, buckled shoes, and what not, would look strange and barbarous now. Ideas have changed; invention has followed invention. Soldiers were monumental objects then. A divinity still hedged kings here and there; and war was considered a glorious thing.

Secluded old manor-houses and hamlets lie in the ravines and hollows among these hills, where a stranger had hardly ever been seen till the King chose to take the baths yearly at the sea-side watering-place a few miles to the south; as a consequence of which battalions descended in a cloud upon the open country around. Is it necessary to add that the echoes of many characteristic tales, dating from that picturesque time, still linger about here in more or less fragmentary form, to be caught by the attentive ear? Some of them I have repeated; most of them I have forgotten; one I have never repeated, and assuredly can never forget.

Phyllis told me the story with her own lips. She was then an old lady of seventy-five, and her auditor a lad of fifteen. She enjoined silence as to her share in the incident, till she should be 'dead, buried, and forgotten'. Her life was prolonged twelve years after the day of her narration, and she has now been dead nearly twenty. The oblivion which in her modesty and humility she courted for herself has only partially fallen on her, with the unfortunate result of inflicting an injustice upon her memory; since such fragments of her story as got abroad at the time, and have been kept alive ever since, are precisely those which are most unfavourable to her character.

It all began with the arrival of the York Hussars, one of the foreign regiments above alluded to. Before that day scarcely a soul had been seen near her father's house for weeks. When a noise like the brushing skirt of a visitor was heard on the doorstep, it proved to be a scudding leaf; when a carriage seemed to be nearing the door, it was her father grinding his sickle on the stone in the garden for his favourite relaxation of trimming the box-tree borders to the plots. A sound like luggage thrown down from the coach was a gun far away at sea; and what looked like a tall man by the gate at dusk was a yew bush cut into a quaint and attenuated shape. There is no such solitude in country places now as there was in those old days.

Yet all the while King George and his Court were at his favourite seaside resort, not more than five miles off.

The daughter's seclusion was great, but beyond the seclusion of the girl lay the seclusion of the father. If her social condition was twilight, his was darkness. Yet he enjoyed his darkness, while her twilight oppressed her. Dr Grove had been a professional man whose taste for lonely meditation over metaphysical questions had diminished his practice till it no longer paid him to keep it going; after which he had relinquished it and hired at a nominal rent the small, dilapidated, half farm, half manor-house of this obscure inland nook, to make a sufficiency of an income which in a town would have been inadequate for their maintenance. He stayed in his garden the greater part of the day, growing more and more irritable with the lapse of time, and the increasing perception that he had wasted his life in the pursuit of illusions. He saw his friends less and less frequently. Phyllis became so shy that if she met a stranger anywhere in her short rambles she felt ashamed at his gaze, walked awkwardly, and blushed to her shoulders.

Yet Phyllis was discovered even here by an admirer, and her hand most unexpectedly asked in marriage.

The King, as aforesaid, was at the neighbouring town, where he had taken up his abode at Gloucester Lodge; and his presence in the town naturally brought many county people thither. Among these idlers – many of whom professed to have connections and interests with the Court – was one Humphrey Gould, a bachelor; a personage neither young nor old; neither good-looking nor positively plain. Too steady-going to be 'a buck' (as fast and unmarried men were then called), he was an approximately fashionable man of a mild type. This bachelor of thirty found his way to the village on the down: beheld Phyllis; made her father's acquaintance in order to make hers; and by some means or other she sufficiently inflamed his heart to lead him in that direction almost daily; till he became engaged to marry her.

As he was of an old local family, some of whose members were held in respect in the county, Phyllis, in bringing him to her feet, had accomplished what was considered a brilliant move for one in her constrained position. How she had done it was not quite known to Phyllis herself. In those days unequal marriages were regarded rather as a violation of the laws of nature than as a mere infringement of convention, the more modern view, and hence when Phyllis, of the watering-place *bourgeoisie*, was chosen by such a gentlemanly fellow, it was as if she were going to be taken to heaven, though perhaps the uninformed would have seen no great difference in the respective positions of the pair, the said Gould being as poor as a crow.

This pecuniary condition was his excuse – probably a true one – for postponing their union, and as the winter drew nearer, and the King departed for the season, Mr Humphrey Gould set out for Bath, promising to return to Phyllis in a few weeks. The winter arrived, the date of his promise passed, yet Gould postponed his coming, on the ground that he could not very easily leave his father in the city of their sojourn, the elder having no other relative near him. Phyllis, though lonely in the extreme, was content. The man who had asked her in marriage was a desirable husband for her in many ways; her father highly approved of his suit; but this neglect of her was awkward, if not painful, for Phyllis. Love him in the true sense of the word she assured me she never did, but she had a genuine regard for him; admired a certain methodical and dogged way in which he sometimes took his pleasure; valued his knowledge of what the Court was doing, had done, or was about to do; and she was not without a feeling of pride that he had chosen her when he might have exercised a more ambitious choice.

But he did not come; and the spring developed. His letters were regular though formal; and it is not to be wondered that the uncertainty of her position, linked with the fact that there was not much passion in her thoughts of Humphrey, bred an indescribable dreariness in the heart of Phyllis Grove. The spring was soon summer, and the summer brought the King; but still no Humphrey Gould. All this while the engagement by letter was maintained intact.

At this point of time a golden radiance flashed in upon the lives of people here, and charged all youthful thought with emotional interest. This radiance was the aforesaid York Hussars.

II

The present generation has probably but a very dim notion of the celebrated York Hussars of ninety years ago. They were one of the regiments of the King's German Legion, and (though they somewhat degenerated later on) their brilliant uniform, their splendid horses, and above all, their foreign air and mustachios (rare appendages then), drew crowds of admirers of both sexes wherever they went. These with other regiments had come to encamp on the downs and pastures, because of the presence of the King in the neighbouring town.

The spot was high and airy, and the view extensive, commanding Portland – the Isle of Slingers – in front, and reaching to St Aldhelm's Head eastward, and almost to the Start on the west.

Phyllis, though not precisely a girl of the village, was as interested as any of them in this military investment. Her father's home stood somewhat apart, and on the highest point of ground to which the lane ascended, so that it was almost level with the top of the church tower in the lower part of the parish. Immediately from the outside of the garden-wall the grass spread away to a great distance, and it was crossed by a path which came close to the wall. Ever since her childhood it had been Phyllis's pleasure to clamber up this fence and sit on the top – a feat not so difficult as it may seem, the walls in this district being built of rubble, without mortar, so that there were plenty of crevices for small toes.

She was sitting up here one day, listlessly surveying the pasture without, when her attention was arrested by a solitary figure walking along the path. It was one of the renowned German Hussars, and he moved onward with his eyes on the ground, and with the manner of one who

wished to escape company. His head would probably have been bent
like his eyes but for his stiff neck-gear. On nearer view she perceived
that his face was marked with deep sadness. Without observing her, he
advanced by the footpath till it brought him almost immediately under
the wall.

Phyllis was much surprised to see a fine, tall soldier in such a mood as
this. Her theory of the military, and of the York Hussars in particular
(derived entirely from hearsay, for she had never talked to a soldier in
her life), was that their hearts were as gay as their accoutrements.

At this moment the Hussar lifted his eyes and noticed her on her
perch, the white muslin neckerchief which covered her shoulders and
neck where left bare by her low gown, and her white raiment in
general, showing conspicuously in the bright sunlight of this summer
day. He blushed a little at the suddenness of the encounter, and without
halting a moment from his pace passed on.

All that day the foreigner's face haunted Phyllis; its aspect was so
striking, so handsome, and his eyes were so blue, and sad, and abstracted.
It was perhaps only natural that on some following day at the same hour
she should look over that wall again, and wait till he had passed a second
time. On this occasion he was reading a letter, and at the sight of her his
manner was that of one who had half expected or hoped to discover her.
He almost stopped, smiled, and made a courteous salute. The end of the
meeting was that they exchanged a few words. She asked him what he
was reading, and he readily informed her that he was re-perusing letters
from his mother in Germany; he did not get them often, he said, and
was forced to read the old ones a great many times. This was all that
passed at the present interview, but others of the same kind followed.

Phyllis used to say that his English, though not good, was quite
intelligible to her, so that their acquaintance was never hindered by
difficulties of speech. Whenever the subject became too delicate, subtle,
or tender, for such words of English as were at his command, the eyes no
doubt helped out the tongue, and – though this was later on – the lips
helped out the eyes. In short, this acquaintance, unguardedly made, and
rash enough on her part, developed and ripened. Like Desdemona, she
pitied him, and learnt his history.

His name was Matthäus Tina, and Saarbrück his native town, where
his mother was still living. His age was twenty-two, and he had already
risen to the grade of corporal, though he had not long been in the army.
Phyllis used to assert that no such refined or well-educated young man

could have been found in the ranks of the purely English regiments, some of these foreign soldiers having rather the graceful manner and presence of our native officers than of our rank and file.

She by degrees learnt from her foreign friend a circumstance about himself and his comrades which Phyllis would least have expected of the York Hussars. So far from being as gay as its uniform, the regiment was pervaded by a dreadful melancholy, a chronic home-sickness, which depressed many of the men to such an extent that they could hardly attend to their drill. The worst sufferers were the younger soldiers who had not been over here long. They hated England and English life; they took no interest whatever in King George and his island kingdom, and they only wished to be out of it and never to see it any more. Their bodies were here, but their hearts and minds were always far away in their dear fatherland, of which – brave men and stoical as they were in many ways – they would speak with tears in their eyes. One of the worst of the sufferers from this home-woe, as he called it in his own tongue, was Matthäus Tina, whose dreamy musing nature felt the gloom of exile still more intensely from the fact that he had left a lonely mother at home with nobody to cheer her.

Though Phyllis, touched by all this, and interested in his history, did not disdain her soldier's acquaintance, she declined (according to her own account, at least) to permit the young man to overstep the line of mere friendship for a long while – as long, indeed, as she considered herself likely to become the possession of another; though it is probable that she had lost her heart to Matthäus before she was herself aware. The stone wall of necessity made anything like intimacy difficult; and he had never ventured to come, or to ask to come, inside the garden, so that all their conversation had been overtly conducted across this boundary.

III

But news reached the village from a friend of Phyllis's father concerning Mr Humphrey Gould, her remarkably cool and patient betrothed. This gentleman had been heard to say in Bath that he considered his overtures to Miss Phyllis Grove to have reached only the stage of a half-understanding; and in view of his enforced absence on his father's account, who was too great an invalid now to attend to his affairs, he thought it best that there should be no definite promise as yet on either side. He was not sure, indeed, that he might not cast his eyes elsewhere.

This account – though only a piece of hearsay, and as such entitled to no absolute credit – tallied so well with the infrequency of his letters and their lack of warmth, that Phyllis did not doubt its truth for one moment; and from that hour she felt herself free to bestow her heart as she should choose. Not so her father; he declared the whole story to be a fabrication. He had known Mr Gould's family from his boyhood; and if there was one proverb which expressed the matrimonial aspect of that family well, it was 'Love me little, love me long.' Humphrey was an honourable man, who would not think of treating his engagement so lightly. 'Do you wait in patience,' he said; 'all will be right enough in time.'

From these words Phyllis at first imagined that her father was in correspondence with Mr Gould; and her heart sank within her; for in spite of her original intentions she had been relieved to hear that her engagement had come to nothing. But she presently learnt that her father had heard no more of Humphrey Gould than she herself had done; while he would not write and address her affianced directly on the subject, lest it should be deemed an imputation on that bachelor's honour.

'You want an excuse for encouraging one or other of those foreign fellows to flatter you with his unmeaning attentions,' her father exclaimed, his mood having of late been a very unkind one towards her. 'I see more than I say. Don't you ever set foot outside that garden-fence without my permission. If you want to see the camp I'll take you myself some Sunday afternoon.'

Phyllis had not the smallest intention of disobeying him in her actions, but she assumed herself to be independent with respect to her feelings. She no longer checked her fancy for the Hussar, though she was far from regarding him as her lover in the serious sense in which an Englishman might have been regarded as such. The young foreign soldier was almost an ideal being to her, with none of the appurtenances of an ordinary house-dweller; one who had descended she knew not whence, and would disappear she knew not whither; the subject of a fascinating dream – no more.

They met continually now – mostly at dusk – during the brief interval between the going down of the sun and the minute at which the last trumpet-call summoned him to his tent. Perhaps her manner had become less restrained latterly; at any rate that of the Hussar was so; he had grown more tender every day, and at parting after these hurried interviews she reached down her hand from the top of the wall that he might press it. One evening he held it such a while that she exclaimed, 'The wall is white, and somebody in the field may see your shape against it!'

He lingered so long that night that it was with the greatest difficulty that he could run across the intervening stretch of ground and enter the camp in time. On the next occasion of his awaiting her she did not appear in her usual place at the usual hour. His disappointment was unspeakably keen; he remained staring blankly at the spot, like a man in a trance. The trumpets and tattoo sounded, and still he did not go.

She had been delayed purely by an accident. When she arrived she was anxious because of the lateness of the hour, having heard as well as he the sounds denoting the closing of the camp. She implored him to leave immediately.

'No,' he said gloomily. 'I shall not go in yet – the moment you come – I have thought of your coming all day.'

'But you may be disgraced at being after time?'

'I don't mind that. I should have disappeared from the world some time ago if it had not been for two persons – my beloved, here, and my mother in Saarbrück. I hate the army. I care more for a minute of your company than for all the promotion in the world.'

Thus he stayed and talked to her, and told her interesting details of his native place, and incidents of his childhood, till she was in a simmer of distress at his recklessness in remaining. It was only because she insisted on bidding him good-night, and leaving the wall, that he returned to his quarters.

The next time that she saw him he was without the stripes that had adorned his sleeve. He had been broken to the level of private for his lateness that night; and as Phyllis considered herself to be the cause of his disgrace her sorrow was great. But the position was now reversed; it was his turn to cheer her.

'Don't grieve, meine Liebliche!' he said. 'I have got a remedy for whatever comes. First, even supposing I regain my stripes, would your father allow you to marry a non-commissioned officer in the York Hussars?'

She flushed. This practical step had not been in her mind in relation to such an unrealistic person as he was; and a moment's reflection was enough for it. 'My father would not – certainly would not,' she answered unflinchingly. 'It cannot be thought of! My dear friend, please do forget me: I fear I am ruining you and your prospects!'

'Not at all!' said he. 'You are giving this country of yours just sufficient interest to me to make me care to keep alive in it. If my dear land were here also, and my old parent, with you, I could be happy as I am, and would do my best as a soldier. But it is not so. And now listen. This is my plan. That you go with me to my own country, and be my wife there, and live there with my mother and me. I am not a Hanoverian, as you know, though I entered the army as such; my country is by the Saar, and is at peace with France, and if I were once in it I should be free.'

'But how get there?' she asked. Phyllis had been rather amazed than shocked at his proposition. Her position in her father's house was growing irksome and painful in the extreme; his parental affection seemed to be quite dried up. She was not a native of the village, like all the joyous girls around her; and in some way Matthäus Tina had infected her with his own passionate longing for his country, and mother, and home.

'But how?' she repeated, finding that he did not answer. 'Will you buy your discharge?'

'Ah, no,' he said. 'That's impossible in these times. No; I came here against my will; why should I not escape? Now is the time, as we shall soon be striking camp, and I might see you no more. This is my scheme. I will ask you to meet me on the highway two miles off, on some calm night next week that may be appointed. There will be nothing unbecoming in it, or to cause you shame; you will not fly alone with me, for I will bring with me my devoted young friend, Christoph, an Alsatian, who has lately joined the regiment, and who has agreed to assist in this enterprise. We shall have come from yonder harbour, where we shall have examined the boats, and found one suited to our purpose. Christoph has already a chart of the Channel, and we will then go to the harbour, and at midnight cut the boat from her moorings, and row away round the point out of sight; and by the next morning we are on the coast of France, near Cherbourg. The rest is easy, for I have saved money for the land journey, and can get a change of clothes. I will write to my mother, who will meet us on the way.'

He added details in reply to her inquiries, which left no doubt in Phyllis's mind of the feasibility of the undertaking. But its magnitude

almost appalled her; and it is questionable if she would ever have gone
further in the wild adventure if, on entering the house that night, her
father had not accosted her in the most significant terms.

'How about the York Hussars?' he said.

'They are still at the camp; but they are soon going away, I believe.'

'It is useless for you to attempt to cloak your actions in that way. You
have been meeting one of those fellows; you have been seen walking
with him – foreign barbarians, not much better than the French themselves! I have made up my mind – don't speak a word till I have
done, please! – I have made up my mind that you shall stay here no
longer while they are on the spot. You shall go to your aunt's.'

It was useless for her to protest that she had never taken a walk with
any soldier or man under the sun except himself. Her protestations were
feeble, too, for though he was not literally correct in his assertion, he
was virtually only half in error.

The house of her father's sister was a prison to Phyllis. She had quite
recently undergone experience of its gloom; and when her father went
on to direct her to pack what would be necessary for her to take, her
heart died within her. In after-years she never attempted to excuse her
conduct during this week of agitation; but the result of her self-
communing was that she decided to join in the scheme of her lover and
his friend, and fly to the country which he had coloured with such
lovely hues in her imagination. She always said that the one feature in
his proposal which overcame her hesitation was the obvious purity and
straightforwardness of his intentions. He showed himself to be so
virtuous and kind; he treated her with a respect to which she had never
before been accustomed; and she was braced to the obvious risks of
the voyage by her confidence in him.

IV

It was on a soft, dark evening of the following week that they engaged in
the adventure. Tina was to meet her at a point in the highway at which
the lane to the village branched off. Christoph was to go ahead of them
to the harbour where the boat lay, row it round the Nothe – or Look-out
as it was called in those days – and pick them up on the other side of the
promontory, which they were to reach by crossing the harbour-bridge
on foot, and climbing over the Look-out hill.

As soon as her father had ascended to his room she left the house, and, bundle in hand, proceeded at a trot along the lane. At such an hour not a soul was afoot anywhere in the village, and she reached the junction of the lane with the highway unobserved. Here she took up her position in the obscurity formed by the angle of a fence, whence she could discern every one who approached along the turnpike-road, without being herself seen.

She had not remained thus waiting for her lover longer than a minute – though from the tension of her nerves the lapse of even that short time was trying – when, instead of the expected footsteps, the stage-coach could be heard descending the hill. She knew that Tina would not show himself till the road was clear, and waited impatiently for the coach to pass. Nearing the corner where she was it slackened speed, and, instead of going by as usual, drew up within a few yards of her. A passenger alighted, and she heard his voice. It was Humphrey Gould's.

He had brought a friend with him, and luggage. The luggage was deposited on the grass, and the coach went on its route to the royal watering-place.

'I wonder where that young man is with the horse and trap?' said her former admirer to his companion. 'I hope we shan't have to wait here long. I told him half-past nine o'clock precisely.'

'Have you got her present safe?'

'Phyllis's? O, yes. It is in this trunk. I hope it will please her.'

'Of course it will. What woman would not be pleased with such a handsome peace-offering?'

'Well – she deserves it. I've treated her rather badly. But she has been in my mind these last two days much more than I should care to confess to everybody. Ah, well; I'll say no more about that. It cannot be that she is so bad as they make out. I am quite sure that a girl of her good wit would know better than to get entangled with any of those Hanoverian soldiers. I won't believe it of her, and there's an end on't.'

More words in the same strain were casually dropped as the two men waited; words which revealed to her, as by a sudden illumination, the enormity of her conduct. The conversation was at length cut off by the arrival of the man with the vehicle. The luggage was placed in it, and they mounted, and were driven on in the direction from which she had just come.

Phyllis was so conscience-stricken that she was at first inclined to follow them; but a moment's reflection led her to feel that it would only be bare justice to Matthäus to wait till he arrived, and explain candidly that she had changed her mind – difficult as the struggle would be when she stood face to face with him. She bitterly reproached herself for having believed reports which represented Humphrey Gould as false to his engagement, when, from what she now heard from his own lips, she gathered that he had been living full of trust in her. But she knew well enough who had won her love. Without him her life seemed a dreary prospect, yet the more she looked at his proposal the more she feared to accept it – so wild as it was, so vague, so venturesome. She had promised Humphrey Gould, and it was only his assumed faithlessness which had led her to treat that promise as nought. His solicitude in bringing her these gifts touched her; her promise must be kept, and esteem must take the place of love. She would preserve her self-respect. She would stay at home, and marry him, and suffer.

Phyllis had thus braced herself to an exceptional fortitude when, a few minutes later, the outline of Matthäus Tina appeared behind a field-gate, over which he lightly leapt as she stepped forward. There was no evading it, he pressed her to his breast.

'It is the first and last time!' she wildly thought as she stood encircled by his arms.

How Phyllis got through the terrible ordeal of that night she could never clearly recollect. She always attributed her success in carrying out her resolve to her lover's honour, for as soon as she declared to him in feeble words that she had changed her mind, and felt that she could not, dared not, fly with him, he forbore to urge her, grieved as he was at her decision. Unscrupulous pressure on his part, seeing how romantically she had become attached to him, would no doubt have turned the balance in his favour. But he did nothing to tempt her unduly or un-fairly.

On her side, fearing for his safety, she begged him to remain. This, he declared, could not be. 'I cannot break faith with my friend,' said he. Had he stood alone he would have abandoned his plan. But Christoph, with the boat and compass and chart, was waiting on the shore; the tide would soon turn; his mother had been warned of his coming; go he must.

Many precious minutes were lost while he tarried, unable to tear himself away. Phyllis held to her resolve, though it cost her many a bitter pang. At last they parted, and he went down the hill. Before his footsteps had quite died away she felt a desire to behold at least his out-line once more, and running noiselessly after him regained view of his diminishing figure. For one moment she was sufficiently excited to be on the point of rushing forward and linking her fate with his. But she could not. The courage which at the critical instant failed Cleopatra of Egypt could scarcely be expected of Phyllis Grove.

A dark shape, similar to his own, joined him in the highway. It was Christoph, his friend. She could see no more; they had hastened on in the direction of the town and harbour, four miles ahead. With a feeling akin to despair she turned and slowly pursued her way homeward.

Tattoo sounded in the camp; but there was no camp for her now. It was as dead as the camp of the Assyrians after the passage of the Destroying Angel.

She noiselessly entered the house, seeing nobody, and went to bed. Grief, which kept her awake at first, ultimately wrapped her in a heavy sleep. The next morning her father met her at the foot of the stairs.

'Mr Gould is come!' he said triumphantly.

Humphrey was staying at the inn, and had already called to inquire for her. He had brought her a present of a very handsome looking-glass in a frame of *repoussé* silverwork, which her father held in his hand. He had promised to call again in the course of an hour, to ask Phyllis to walk with him.

Pretty mirrors were rarer in country-houses at that day than they are now, and the one before her won Phyllis's admiration. She looked into it, saw how heavy her eyes were, and endeavoured to brighten them. She was in that wretched state of mind which leads a woman to move mechanically onward in what she conceives to be her allotted path. Mr Humphrey had, in his undemonstrative way, been adhering all along to the old understanding; it was for her to do the same, and to say not a word of her own lapse. She put on her bonnet and tippet, and when he arrived at the hour named she was at the door awaiting him.

V

Phyllis thanked him for his beautiful gift; but the talking was soon entirely on Humphrey's side as they walked along. He told her of the latest movements of the world of fashion – a subject which she willingly discussed to the exclusion of anything more personal – and his measured language helped to still her disquieted heart and brain. Had not her own sadness been what it was she must have observed his embarrassment. At last he abruptly changed the subject.

'I am glad you are pleased with my little present,' he said. 'The truth is that I brought it to propitiate 'ee, and to get you to help me out of a mighty difficulty.'

It was inconceivable to Phyllis that this independent bachelor – whom she admired in some respects – could have a difficulty.

'Phyllis – I'll tell you my secret at once; for I have a monstrous secret to confide before I can ask your counsel. The case is, then, that I am married: yes, I have privately married a dear young belle; and if you knew her, and I hope you will, you would say everything in her praise. But she is not quite the one that my father would have chose for me – you know the paternal idea as well as I – and I have kept it secret. There will be a terrible noise, no doubt; but I think that with your help I may get over it. If you would only do me this good turn – when I have told my father, I mean – say that you never could have married me, you know, or something of that sort – 'pon my life it will help to smooth the way vastly. I am so anxious to win him round to my point of view, and not to cause any estrangement.'

What Phyllis replied she scarcely knew, or how she counselled him as to his unexpected situation. Yet the relief that his announcement brought her was perceptible. To have confided her trouble in return was what her aching heart longed to do; and had Humphrey been a woman she would instantly have poured out her tale. But to him she feared to confess; and there was a real reason for silence, till a sufficient time had elapsed to allow her lover and his comrade to get out of harm's way.

As soon as she reached home again she sought a solitary place, and spent the time in half regretting that she had not gone away, and in dreaming over the meetings with Matthäus Tina from their beginning to their end. In his own country, amongst his own countrywomen, he would possibly soon forget her, even to her very name.

Her listlessness was such that she did not go out of the house for several days. There came a morning which broke in fog and mist, behind which the dawn could be discerned in greenish grey; and the outlines of the tents, and the rows of horses at the ropes. The smoke from the canteen fires drooped heavily.

The spot at the bottom of the garden where she had been accustomed to climb the wall to meet Matthäus was the only inch of English ground in which she took any interest; and in spite of the disagreeable haze prevailing she walked out there till she reached the well-known corner. Every blade of grass was weighted with little liquid globes, and slugs and snails had crept out upon the plots. She could hear the usual faint noises from the camp, and in the other direction the trot of farmers on the road to the town, for it was market-day. She observed that her frequent visits to this corner had quite trodden down the grass in the angle of the wall, and left marks of garden soil on the stepping-stones by which she had mounted to look over the top. Seldom having gone there till dusk, she had not considered that her traces might be visible by day. Perhaps it was these which had revealed her trysts to her father.

While she paused in melancholy regard, she fancied that the customary sounds from the tents were changing their character. Indifferent as Phyllis was to camp doings now, she mounted by the steps to the old place. What she beheld at first awed and perplexed her; then she stood rigid, her fingers hooked to the wall, her eyes staring out of her head, and her face as if hardened to stone.

On the open green stretching before her all the regiments in the camp were drawn up in line, in the mid-front of which two empty coffins lay on the ground. The unwonted sounds which she had noticed came from an advancing procession. It consisted of the band of the York Hussars playing a dead march; next two soldiers of that regiment in a mourning coach, guarded on each side, and accompanied by two priests. Behind came a crowd of rustics who had been attracted by the event. The melancholy procession marched along the front of the line, returned to the centre, and halted beside the coffins, where the two condemned men were blindfolded, and each placed kneeling on his coffin; a few minutes' pause was now given while they prayed.

A firing-party of twenty-four men stood ready with levelled carbines. The commanding officer, who had his sword drawn, waved it through some cuts of the sword-exercise till he reached the downward stroke, whereat the firing-party discharged their volley. The two victims fell, one upon his face across his coffin, the other backwards.

As the volley resounded there arose a shriek from the wall of Dr Grove's garden, and some one fell down inside; but nobody among the spectators without noticed it at the time. The two executed Hussars were Matthäus Tina and his friend Christoph. The soldiers on guard placed the bodies in the coffins almost instantly; but the colonel of the regiment, an Englishman, rode up and exclaimed in a stern voice: 'Turn them out – as an example to the men!'

The coffins were lifted endwise, and the dead Germans flung out upon their faces on the grass. Then all the regiments wheeled in sections, and marched past the spot in slow time. When the survey was over the corpses were again coffined, and borne away.

Meanwhile Dr Grove, attracted by the noise of the volley, had rushed out into his garden, where he saw his wretched daughter lying motionless against the wall. She was taken indoors, but it was long before she recovered consciousness; and for weeks they despaired of her reason.

It transpired that the luckless deserters from the York Hussars had cut the boat from her moorings in the adjacent harbour, according to their plan, and, with two other comrades who were smarting under ill-treatment from their colonel, had sailed in safety across the Channel. But mistaking their bearings they steered into Jersey, thinking that island the French coast. Here they were perceived to be deserters, and delivered up to the authorities. Matthäus and Christoph interceded for the other two at the court-martial, saying that it was entirely by the former's representations that these were induced to go. Their sentence was accordingly commuted to flogging, the death punishment being reserved for their leaders.

The visitor to the well-known old Georgian watering-place, who may care to ramble to the neighbouring village under the hills, and examine the register of burials, will there find two entries in these words: –

'Matth: Tina (Corpl) in His Majesty's Regmt of York Hussars, and Shot for Desertion, was Buried June 30th, 1801, aged 22 years. Born in the town of Sarrbruk, Germany.
'Christoph Bless, belonging to His Majesty's Regmt of York Hussars, who was Shot for Desertion, was Buried June 30th, 1801, aged 22 years. Born at Lothaargen, Alsatia.'

Their graves were dug at the back of the little church, near the wall. There is no memorial to mark the spot, but Phyllis pointed it out to me. While she lived she used to keep their mounds neat; but now they are overgrown with nettles, and sunk nearly flat. The older villagers, however, who know of the episode from their parents, still recollect the place where the soldiers lie. Phyllis lies near.

October 1889

The Withered Arm

I. A LORN MILKMAID

IT was an eighty-cow dairy, and the troop of milkers, regular and
supernumerary, were all at work; for, though the time of year was as yet
but early April, the feed lay entirely in water-meadows, and the cows
were 'in full pail'. The hour was about six in the evening, and three-
fourths of the large, red, rectangular animals having been finished off,
there was opportunity for a little conversation.

'He do bring home his bride to-morrow, I hear. They've come as far
as Anglebury to-day.'

The voice seemed to proceed from the belly of the cow called Cherry,
but the speaker was a milking-woman, whose face was buried in the
flank of that motionless beast.

'Hav' anybody seen her?' said another.

There was a negative response from the first. 'Though they say she's a
rosy-cheeked, tisty-tosty little body enough,' she added; and as the
milkmaid spoke she turned her face so that she could glance past her
cow's tail to the other side of the barton, where a thin, fading woman of
thirty milked somewhat apart from the rest.

'Years younger than he, they say,' continued the second, with also a
glance of reflectiveness in the same direction.

'How old do you call him, then?'

'Thirty or so.'

'More like forty,' broke in an old milkman near, in a long white
pinafore or 'wropper', and with the brim of his hat tied down, so that he
looked like a woman. ' 'A was born before our Great Weir was builded,
and I hadn't man's wages when I laved water there.'

The discussion waxed so warm that the purr of the milk-streams
became jerky, till a voice from another cow's belly cried with authority,
'Now then, what the Turk do it matter to us about Farmer Lodge's age,

or Farmer Lodge's new mis'ess? I shall have to pay him nine pound a year for the rent of every one of these milchers, whatever his age or hers. Get on with your work, or 'twill be dark afore we have done. The evening is pinking in a'ready.' This speaker was the dairyman himself, by whom the milkmaids and men were employed.

Nothing more was said publicly about Farmer Lodge's wedding, but the first woman murmured under her cow to her next neighbour, ' 'Tis hard for *she*,' signifying the thin worn milkmaid aforesaid.

'O no,' said the second. 'He ha'n't spoke to Rhoda Brook for years.'

When the milking was done they washed their pails and hung them on a many-forked stand made as usual of the peeled limb of an oak-tree, set upright in the earth, and resembling a colossal antlered horn. The majority then dispersed in various directions homeward. The thin woman who had not spoken was joined by a boy of twelve or thereabout, and the twain went away up the field also.

Their course lay apart from that of the others, to a lonely spot high above the water-meads, and not far from the border of Egdon Heath, whose dark countenance was visible in the distance as they drew nigh to their home.

'They've just been saying down in barton that your father brings his young wife home from Anglebury to-morrow,' the woman observed. 'I shall want to send you for a few things to market, and you'll be pretty sure to meet 'em.'

'Yes, mother,' said the boy. 'Is father married then?'

'Yes.... You can give her a look, and tell me what she's like, if you do see her.'

'Yes, mother.'

'If she's dark or fair, and if she's tall – as tall as I. And if she seems like a woman who has ever worked for a living, or one that has been always well off, and has never done anything, and shows marks of the lady on her, as I expect she do.'

'Yes.'

They crept up the hill in the twilight and entered the cottage. It was built of mud-walls, the surface of which had been washed by many rains into channels and depressions that left none of the original flat face visible; while here and there in the thatch above a rafter showed like a bone protruding through the skin.

She was kneeling down in the chimney-corner, before two pieces of turf laid together with the heather inwards, blowing at the red-hot ashes with her breath till the turves flamed. The radiance lit her pale cheek, and made her dark eyes, that had once been handsome, seem handsome anew. 'Yes,' she resumed, 'see if she is dark or fair, and if you can, notice if her hands be white; if not, see if they look as though she had ever done housework, or are milker's hands like mine.'

The boy again promised, inattentively this time, his mother not observing that he was cutting a notch with his pocket-knife in the beech-backed chair.

II. THE YOUNG WIFE

The road from Anglebury to Holmstoke is in general level; but there is one place where a sharp ascent breaks its monotony. Farmers homeward-bound from the former market-town, who trot all the rest of the way, walk their horses up this short incline.

The next evening while the sun was yet bright a handsome new gig, with a lemon-coloured body and red wheels, was spinning west-ward along the level highway at the heels of a powerful mare. The driver was a yeoman in the prime of life, cleanly shaven like an actor, his face being toned to that bluish-vermilion hue which so often graces a thriving farmer's features when returning home after successful dealings in the town. Beside him sat a woman, many years his junior – almost, indeed, a girl. Her face too was fresh in colour, but it was of a totally different quality – soft and evanescent, like the light under a heap of rose-petals.

Few people travelled this way, for it was not a main road, and the long white riband of gravel that stretched before them was empty, save of one small scarce-moving speck, which presently resolved itself into the figure of a boy, who was creeping on at a snail's pace, and continually looking behind him – the heavy bundle he carried being some excuse for, if not the reason of, his dilatoriness. When the bouncing gig-party slowed at the bottom of the incline above mentioned, the pedestrian was only a few yards in front. Supporting the large bundle by putting one hand on his hip, he turned and looked straight at the farmer's wife as though he would read her through and through, pacing along abreast of the horse.

The low sun was full in her face, rendering every feature, shade, and contour distinct, from the curve of her little nostril to the colour of her eyes. The farmer, though he seemed annoyed at the boy's persistent presence, did not order him to get out of the way; and thus the lad preceded them, his hard gaze never leaving her, till they reached the top of the ascent, when the farmer trotted on with relief in his lineaments – having taken no outward notice of the boy whatever.

'How that poor lad stared at me!' said the young wife.

'Yes, dear; I saw that he did.'

'He is one of the village, I suppose?'

'One of the neighbourhood. I think he lives with his mother a mile or two off.'

'He knows who we are, no doubt?'

'O yes. You must expect to be stared at just at first, my pretty Gertrude.'

'I do, – though I think the poor boy may have looked at us in the hope we might relieve him of his heavy load, rather than from curiosity.'

'O no,' said her husband off-handedly. 'These country lads will carry a hundredweight once they get it on their backs; besides, his pack had more size than weight in it. Now, then, another mile and I shall be able to show you our house in the distance – if it is not too dark before we get there.' The wheels spun round, and particles flew from their periphery as before, till a white house of ample dimensions revealed itself, with farm-buildings and ricks at the back.

Meanwhile the boy had quickened his pace, and turning up a by-lane some mile and half short of the white farmstead, ascended towards the leaner pastures, and so on to the cottage of his mother.

She had reached home after her day's milking at the outlying dairy, and was washing cabbage at the doorway in the declining light. 'Hold up the net a moment,' she said, without preface, as the boy came up.

He flung down his bundle, held the edge of the cabbage-net, and as she filled its meshes with the dripping leaves she went on, 'Well, did you see her?'

'Yes; quite plain.'

'Is she ladylike?'

'Yes; and more. A lady complete.'

'Is she young?'

'Well, she's growed up, and her ways be quite a woman's.'

'Of course. What colour is her hair and face?'

'Her hair is lightish, and her face as comely as a live doll's.'

'Her eyes, then, are not dark like mine?'

'No – of a bluish turn, and her mouth is very nice and red; and when she smiles, her teeth show white.'

'Is she tall?' said the woman sharply.

'I couldn't see. She was sitting down.'

'Then do you go to Holmstoke church to-morrow morning: she's sure to be there. Go early and notice her walking in, and come home and tell me if she's taller than I.'

'Very well, mother. But why don't you go and see for yourself?'

'*I* go to see her! I wouldn't look up at her if she were to pass my window this instant. She was with Mr Lodge, of course. What did he say or do?'

'Just the same as usual.'

'Took no notice of you?'

'None.'

Next day the mother put a clean shirt on the boy, and started him off for Holmstoke church. He reached the ancient little pile when the door was just being opened and he was the first to enter. Taking his seat by the font, he watched all the parishioners file in. The well-to-do Farmer Lodge came nearly last, and his young wife, who accompanied him, walked up the aisle with the shyness natural to a modest woman who had appeared thus for the first time. As all other eyes were fixed upon her, the youth's stare was not noticed now.

When he reached home his mother said, 'Well?' before he had entered the room.

'She is not tall. She is rather short,' he replied.

'Ah!' said his mother, with satisfaction.

'But she's very pretty – very. In fact, she's lovely.' The youthful freshness of the yeoman's wife had evidently made an impression even on the somewhat hard nature of the boy.

'That's all I want to hear,' said his mother quickly. 'Now, spread the tablecloth. The hare you wired is very tender; but mind that nobody catches you. – You've never told me what sort of hands she had.'

'I have never seen 'em. She never took off her gloves.'

'What did she wear this morning?'

'A white bonnet and a silver-coloured gownd. It whewed and whistled so loud when it rubbed against the pews that the lady coloured up more than ever for very shame at the noise, and pulled it in to keep it from touching; but when she pushed into her seat, it whewed more than ever. Mr Lodge, he seemed pleased, and his waistcoat stuck out, and his great golden seals hung like a lord's; but she seemed to wish her noisy gownd anywhere but on her.'

'Not she! However, that will do now.'

These descriptions of the newly-married couple were continued from time to time by the boy at his mother's request, after any chance encounter he had had with them. But Rhoda Brook, though she might easily have seen young Mrs Lodge for herself by walking a couple of miles, would never attempt an excursion towards the quarter where the farmhouse lay. Neither did she, at the daily milking in the dairyman's yard on Lodge's outlying second farm, ever speak on the subject of the recent marriage. The dairyman, who rented the cows of Lodge, and knew perfectly the tall milkmaid's history, with manly kindliness always kept the gossip in the cow-barton from annoying Rhoda. But the atmosphere thereabout was full of the subject during the first days of Mrs Lodge's arrival, and from her boy's description and the casual words of the other milkers, Rhoda Brook could raise a mental image of the unconscious Mrs Lodge that was realistic as a photograph.

III. A VISION

One night, two or three weeks after the bridal return, when the boy was gone to bed, Rhoda sat a long time over the turf ashes that she had raked out in front of her to extinguish them. She contemplated so intently the new wife, as presented to her in her mind's eye over the embers, that she forgot the lapse of time. At last, wearied with her day's work, she too retired.

But the figure which had occupied her so much during this and the previous days was not to be banished at night. For the first time Gertrude Lodge visited the supplanted woman in her dreams. Rhoda Brook dreamed – since her assertion that she really saw, before falling asleep, was not to be believed – that the young wife, in the pale silk dress and white bonnet, but with features shockingly distorted, and wrinkled as by age, was sitting upon her chest as she lay. The pressure of Mrs Lodge's person grew heavier; the blue eyes peered cruelly into her face, and then the figure thrust forward its left hand mockingly, so as to make the wedding-ring it wore glitter in Rhoda's eyes. Maddened mentally, and nearly suffocated by pressure, the sleeper struggled; the incubus, still regarding her, withdrew to the foot of the bed, only, however, to come forward by degrees, resume her seat, and flash her left hand as before.

Gasping for breath, Rhoda, in a last desperate effort, swung out her right hand, seized the confronting spectre by its obtrusive left arm, and whirled it backward to the floor, starting up herself as she did so with a low cry.

'O, merciful heaven!' she cried, sitting on the edge of the bed in a cold sweat; 'that was not a dream – she was here!'

She could feel her antagonist's arm within her grasp even now – the very flesh and bone of it, as it seemed. She looked on the floor whither she had whirled the spectre, but there was nothing to be seen.

Rhoda Brook slept no more that night, and when she went milking at the next dawn they noticed how pale and haggard she looked. The milk that she drew quivered into the pail: her hand had not calmed even yet, and still retained the feel of the arm. She came home to breakfast as wearily as if it had been supper-time.

'What was that noise in your chimmer, mother, last night?' said her son. 'You fell off the bed, surely?'

'Did you hear anything fall? At what time?'

'Just when the clock struck two.'

She could not explain, and when the meal was done went silently about her household work, the boy assisting her, for he hated going afield on the farms, and she indulged his reluctance. Between eleven and twelve the garden-gate clicked, and she lifted her eyes to the window. At the bottom of the garden, within the gate, stood the woman of her vision. Rhoda seemed transfixed.

'Ah, she said she would come!' exclaimed the boy, also observing her.

'Said so – when? How does she know us?'

'I have seen and spoken to her. I talked to her yesterday.'

'I told you,' said the mother, flushing indignantly, 'never to speak to anybody in that house, or go near the place.'

'I did not speak to her till she spoke to me. And I did not go near the place. I met her in the road.'

'What did you tell her?'

'Nothing. She said, "Are you the poor boy who had to bring the heavy load from market?" And she looked at my boots, and said they would not keep my feet dry if it came on wet, because they were so cracked. I told her I lived with my mother, and we had enough to do to keep ourselves, and that's how it was; and she said then, "I'll come and

bring you some better boots, and see your mother." She gives away
things to other folks in the meads besides us.'

Mrs Lodge was by this time close to the door – not in her silk, as
Rhoda had dreamt of in the bed-chamber, but in a morning hat, and
gown of common light material, which became her better than silk. On
her arm she carried a basket.

The impression remaining from the night's experience was still
strong. Brook had almost expected to see the wrinkles, the scorn, and
the cruelty on her visitor's face. She would have escaped an interview
had escape been possible. There was, however, no backdoor to the
cottage, and in an instant the boy had lifted the latch to Mrs Lodge's
gentle knock.

'I see I have come to the right house,' said she, glancing at the lad, and
smiling. 'But I was not sure till you opened the door.'

The figure and action were those of the phantom; but her voice was
so indescribably sweet, her glance so winning, her smile so tender, so
unlike that of Rhoda's midnight visitant, that the latter could hardly
believe the evidence of her senses. She was truly glad that she had not
hidden away in sheer aversion, as she had been inclined to do. In her
basket Mrs Lodge brought the pair of boots that she had promised to
the boy, and other useful articles.

At these proofs of a kindly feeling towards her and hers Rhoda's heart
reproached her bitterly. This innocent young thing should have her
blessing and not her curse. When she left them a light seemed gone from
the dwelling. Two days later she came again to know if the boots fitted,
and less than a fortnight after that paid Rhoda another call. On this
occasion the boy was absent.

'I walk a good deal,' said Mrs Lodge, 'and your house is the nearest
outside our own parish. I hope you are well. You don't look quite
well.'

Rhoda said she was well enough, and, indeed, though the paler of the
two, there was more of the strength that endures in her well-defined
features and large frame than in the soft-cheeked young woman before
her. The conversation became quite confidential as regarded their
powers and weaknesses; and when Mrs Lodge was leaving, Rhoda said,
'I hope you will find this air agree with you, ma'am, and not suffer from
the damp of the water-meads.'

The younger one replied that there was not much doubt of it, her
general health being usually good. 'Though, now you remind me,' she

added, 'I have one little ailment which puzzles me. It is nothing serious, but I cannot make it out.'

She uncovered her left hand and arm, and their outline confronted Rhoda's gaze as the exact original of the limb she had beheld and seized in her dream. Upon the pink round surface of the arm were faint marks of an unhealthy colour, as if produced by a rough grasp. Rhoda's eyes became riveted on the discolorations; she fancied that she discerned in them the shape of her own four fingers.

'How did it happen?' she said mechanically.

'I cannot tell,' replied Mrs Lodge, shaking her head. 'One night when I was sound asleep, dreaming I was away in some strange place, a pain suddenly shot into my arm there, and was so keen as to awaken me. I must have struck it in the daytime, I suppose, though I don't remember doing so.' She added, laughing, 'I tell my dear husband that it looks just as if he had flown into a rage and struck me there. O, I daresay it will soon disappear.'

'Ha, ha! Yes. . . . On what night did it come?'

Mrs Lodge considered, and said it would be a fortnight ago on the morrow. 'When I awoke I could not remember where I was,' she added, 'till the clock striking two reminded me.'

She had named the night and the hour of Rhoda's spectral encounter, and Brook felt like a guilty thing. The artless disclosure startled her; she did not reason on the freaks of coincidence, and all the scenery of that ghastly night returned with double vividness to her mind.

'O, can it be,' she said to herself, when her visitor had departed, 'that I exercise a malignant power over people against my own will?' She knew that she had been slily called a witch since her fall; but never having understood why that particular stigma had been attached to her, it had passed disregarded. Could this be the explanation, and had such things as this ever happened before?

IV. A SUGGESTION

The summer drew on, and Rhoda Brook almost dreaded to meet Mrs Lodge again, notwithstanding that her feeling for the young wife amounted wellnigh to affection. Something in her own individuality seemed to convict Rhoda of crime. Yet a fatality sometimes would direct the steps of the latter to the outskirts of Holmstoke whenever she left her

house for any other purpose than her daily work, and hence it happened
that their next encounter was out of doors. Rhoda could not avoid the
subject which had so mystified her, and after the first few words she
stammered, 'I hope your – arm is well again, ma'am?' She had perceived with consternation that Gertrude Lodge carried her left arm
stiffly.

'No; it is not quite well. Indeed, it is no better at all; it is rather
worse. It pains me dreadfully sometimes.'

'Perhaps you had better go to a doctor, ma'am.'

She replied that she had already seen a doctor. Her husband had
insisted upon her going to one. But the surgeon had not seemed to
understand the afflicted limb at all; he had told her to bathe it in hot
water, and she had bathed it, but the treatment had done no good.

'Will you let me see it?' said the milkwoman.

Mrs Lodge pushed up her sleeve and disclosed the place, which was a
few inches above the wrist. As soon as Rhoda Brook saw it, she could
hardly preserve her composure. There was nothing of the nature of a
wound, but the arm at that point had a shrivelled look, and the outline
of the four fingers appeared more distinct than at the former time. Moreover, she fancied that they were imprinted in precisely the relative
position of her clutch upon the arm in the trance: the first finger towards
Gertrude's wrist, and the fourth towards her elbow.

What the impress resembled seemed to have struck Gertrude herself
since their last meeting. 'It looks almost like finger-marks,' she said;
adding with a faint laugh, 'My husband says it is as if some witch, or the
devil himself, had taken hold of me there, and blasted the flesh.'

Rhoda shivered. 'That's fancy,' she said hurriedly. 'I wouldn't mind
it, if I were you.'

'I shouldn't so much mind it,' said the younger, with hesitation, 'if –
if I hadn't a notion that it makes my husband – dislike me – no, love
me less. Men think so much of personal appearance.'

'Some do – he for one.'

'Yes; and he was very proud of mine, at first.'

'Keep your arm covered from his sight.'

'Ah – he knows the disfigurement is there!' She tried to hide the tears
that filled her eyes.

'Well, ma'am, I earnestly hope it will go away soon.'

And so the milkwoman's mind was chained anew to the subject by a
horrid sort of spell as she returned home. The sense of having been

guilty of an act of malignity increased, affect as she might to ridicule her superstition. In her secret heart Rhoda did not altogether object to a slight diminution of her successor's beauty, by whatever means it had come about; but she did not wish to inflict upon her physical pain. For though this pretty young woman had rendered impossible any reparation which Lodge might have made Rhoda for his past conduct, everything like resentment at the unconscious usurpation had quite passed away from the elder's mind.

If the sweet and kindly Gertrude Lodge only knew of the dream-scene in the bed-chamber, what would she think? Not to inform her of it seemed treachery in the presence of her friendliness; but tell she could not of her own accord – neither could she devise a remedy.

She mused upon the matter the greater part of the night, and the next day, after the morning milking, set out to obtain another glimpse of Gertrude Lodge if she could, being held to her by a gruesome fascination. By watching the house from a distance the milkmaid was presently able to discern the farmer's wife in a ride she was taking alone – probably to join her husband in some distant field. Mrs Lodge perceived her, and cantered in her direction.

'Good morning, Rhoda!' Gertrude said, when she had come up. 'I was going to call.'

Rhoda noticed that Mrs Lodge held the reins with some difficulty.

'I hope – the bad arm,' said Rhoda.

'They tell me there is possibly one way by which I might be able to find out the cause, and so perhaps the cure, of it,' replied the other anxiously. 'It is by going to some clever man over in Egdon Heath. They did not know if he was still alive – and I cannot remember his name at this moment; but they said that you knew more of his movements than anybody else hereabout, and could tell me if he were still to be consulted. Dear me – what was his name? But you know.'

'Not Conjuror Trendle?' said her thin companion, turning pale.

'Trendle – yes. Is he alive?'

'I believe so,' said Rhoda, with reluctance.

'Why do you call him conjuror?'

'Well – they say – they used to say he was a – he had powers other folks have not.'

'O, how could my people be so superstitious as to recommend a man of that sort! I thought they meant some medical man. I shall think no more of him.'

Rhoda looked relieved, and Mrs Lodge rode on. The milkwoman had inwardly seen, from the moment she heard of her having been mentioned as a reference for this man, that there must exist a sarcastic feeling among the workfolk that a sorceress would know the whereabouts of the exorcist. They suspected her, then. A short time ago this would have given no concern to a woman of her common sense. But she had a haunting reason to be superstitious now; and she had been seized with sudden dread that this Conjuror Trendle might name her as the malignant influence which was blasting the fair person of Gertrude and so lead her friend to hate her for ever, and to treat her as some fiend in human shape.

But all was not over. Two days after, a shadow intruded into the window-pattern thrown on Rhoda Brook's floor by the afternoon sun. The woman opened the door at once, almost breathlessly.

'Are you alone?' said Gertrude. She seemed to be no less harassed and anxious than Brook herself.

'Yes,' said Rhoda.

'The place on my arm seems worse, and troubles me!' the young farmer's wife went on. 'It is so mysterious! I do hope it will not be an incurable wound. I have again been thinking of what they said about Conjuror Trendle. I don't really believe in such men, but I should not mind just visiting him, from curiosity – though on no account must my husband know. Is it far to where he lives?'

'Yes – five miles,' said Rhoda backwardly. 'In the heart of Egdon.'

'Well, I should have to walk. Could not you go with me to show me the way – say to-morrow afternoon?'

'O, not I – that is,' the milkwoman murmured, with a start of dismay. Again the dread seized her that something to do with her fierce act in the dream might be revealed, and her character in the eyes of the most useful friend she had ever had be ruined irretrievably.

Mrs Lodge urged, and Rhoda finally assented, though with much misgiving. Sad as the journey would be to her, she could not conscientiously stand in the way of a possible remedy for her patron's strange affliction. It was agreed that, to escape suspicion of their mystic intent, they should meet at the edge of the heath at the corner of a plantation which was visible from the spot where they now stood.

V. CONJUROR TRENDLE

By the next afternoon Rhoda would have done anything to escape this
inquiry. But she had promised to go. Moreover, there was a horrid
fascination at times in becoming instrumental in throwing such possible
light on her own character as would reveal her to be something greater
in the occult world than she had ever herself suspected.

She started just before the time of day mentioned between them, and
half-an-hour's brisk walking brought her to the south-eastern extension
of the Egdon tract of country, where the fir plantation was. A slight
figure, cloaked and veiled, was already there. Rhoda recognized, almost
with a shudder, that Mrs Lodge bore her left arm in a sling.

They hardly spoke to each other, and immediately set out on their
climb into the interior of this solemn country, which stood high above
the rich alluvial soil they had left half-an-hour before. It was a long
walk; thick clouds made the atmosphere dark, though it was as yet only
early afternoon; and the wind howled dismally over the slopes of the
heath – not improbably the same heath which had witnessed the agony
of the Wessex King Ina, presented to after-ages as Lear. Gertrude
Lodge talked most, Rhoda replying with monosyllabic preoccupation.
She had a strange dislike to walking on the side of her companion
where hung the afflicted arm, moving round to the other when in-
advertently near it. Much heather had been brushed by their feet when
they descended upon a cart-track, beside which stood the house of the
man they sought.

He did not profess his remedial practices openly, or care anything
about their continuance, his direct interests being those of a dealer in
furze, turf, 'sharp sand', and other local products. Indeed, he affected
not to believe largely in his own powers, and when warts that had been
shown him for cure miraculously disappeared – which it must be
owned they infallibly did – he would say lightly, 'O, I only drink a glass
of grog upon 'em at your expense – perhaps it's all chance,' and immediately turn the subject.

He was at home when they arrived, having in fact seen them descending into his valley. He was a grey-bearded man, with a reddish face,
and he looked singularly at Rhoda the first moment he beheld her. Mrs
Lodge told him her errand; and then with words of self-disparagement
he examined her arm.

'Medicine can't cure it,' he said promptly. ' 'Tis the work of an enemy.'

Rhoda shrank into herself, and drew back.

'An enemy? What enemy?' asked Mrs Lodge.

He shook his head. 'That's best known to yourself,' he said. 'If you like, I can show the person to you, though I shall not myself know who it is. I can do no more; and don't wish to do that.'

She pressed him; on which he told Rhoda to wait outside where she stood, and took Mrs Lodge into the room. It opened immediately from the door; and, as the latter remained ajar, Rhoda Brook could see the proceedings without taking part in them. He brought a tumbler from the dresser, nearly filled it with water, and fetching an egg, prepared it in some private way; after which he broke it on the edge of the glass, so that the white went in and the yolk remained. As it was getting gloomy, he took the glass and its contents to the window, and told Gertrude to watch the mixture closely. They leant over the table together, and the milkwoman could see the opaline hue of the egg-fluid changing form as it sank in the water, but she was not near enough to define the shape that it assumed.

'Do you catch the likeness of any face or figure as you look?' demanded the conjuror of the young woman.

She murmured a reply, in tones so low as to be inaudible to Rhoda, and continued to gaze intently into the glass. Rhoda turned, and walked a few steps away.

When Mrs Lodge came out, and her face was met by the light, it appeared exceedingly pale – as pale as Rhoda's – against the sad dun shades of the upland's garniture. Trendle shut the door behind her, and they at once started homeward together. But Rhoda perceived that her companion had quite changed.

'Did he charge much?' she asked tentatively.

'O no – nothing. He would not take a farthing,' said Gertrude.

'And what did you see?' inquired Rhoda.

'Nothing I – care to speak of.' The constraint in her manner was remarkable; her face was so rigid as to wear an oldened aspect, faintly suggestive of the face in Rhoda's bed-chamber.

'Was it you who first proposed coming here?' Mrs Lodge suddenly inquired, after a long pause. 'How very odd, if you did!'

'No. But I am not sorry we have come, all things considered,' she replied. For the first time a sense of triumph possessed her, and she did

not altogether deplore that the young thing at her side should learn that
their lives had been antagonized by other influences than their own.

The subject was no more alluded to during the long and dreary walk
home. But in some way or other a story was whispered about the many-
dairied lowland that winter that Mrs Lodge's gradual loss of the use of
her left arm was owing to her being 'overlooked' by Rhoda Brook. The
latter kept her own counsel about the incubus, but her face grew sadder
and thinner; and in the spring she and her boy disappeared from the
neighbourhood of Holmstoke.

VI. A SECOND ATTEMPT

Half a dozen years passed away, and Mr and Mrs Lodge's married
experience sank into prosiness, and worse. The farmer was usually
gloomy and silent; the woman whom he had wooed for her grace and
beauty was contorted and disfigured in the left limb; moreover, she had
brought him no child, which rendered it likely that he would be the last
of a family who had occupied that valley for some two hundred years.
He thought of Rhoda Brook and her son; and feared this might be a
judgment from heaven upon him.

The once blithe-hearted and enlightened Gertrude was changing into
an irritable, superstitious woman, whose whole time was given to
experimenting upon her ailment with every quack remedy she came
across. She was honestly attached to her husband, and was ever secretly
hoping against hope to win back his heart again by regaining some at
least of her personal beauty. Hence it arose that her closet was lined with
bottles, packets, and ointment-pots of every description – nay, bunches
of mystic herbs, charms, and books of necromancy, which in her
schoolgirl time she would have ridiculed as folly.

'Damned if you won't poison yourself with these apothecary messes
and witch mixtures some time or other,' said her husband, when his eye
chanced to fall upon the multitudinous array.

She did not reply, but turned her sad, soft glance upon him in such
heart-swollen reproach that he looked sorry for his words, and added, 'I
only meant it for your good, you know, Gertrude.'

'I'll clear out the whole lot, and destroy them,' said she huskily, 'and
try such remedies no more!'

'You want somebody to cheer you,' he observed. 'I once thought of adopting a boy; but he is too old now. And he is gone away I don't know where.'

She guessed to whom he alluded; for Rhoda Brook's story had in the course of years become known to her; though not a word had ever passed between her husband and herself on the subject. Neither had she ever spoken to him of her visit to Conjuror Trendle, and of what was revealed to her, or she thought was revealed to her, by that solitary heathman.

She was now five-and-twenty; but she seemed older. 'Six years of marriage, and only a few months of love,' she sometimes whispered to herself. And then she thought of the apparent cause, and said, with a tragic glance at her withering limb, 'If I could only again be as I was when he first saw me!'

She obediently destroyed her nostrums and charms; but there remained a hankering wish to try something else – some other sort of cure altogether. She had never revisited Trendle since she had been conducted to the house of the solitary by Rhoda against her will; but it now suddenly occurred to Gertrude that she would, in a last desperate effort at deliverance from this seeming curse, again seek out the man, if he yet lived. He was entitled to a certain credence, for the indistinct form he had raised in the glass had undoubtedly resembled the only woman in the world who – as she now knew, though not then – could have a reason for bearing her ill-will. The visit should be paid.

This time she went alone, though she nearly got lost on the heath, and roamed a considerable distance out of her way. Trendle's house was reached at last, however; he was not indoors, and instead of waiting at the cottage, she went to where his bent figure was pointed out to her at work a long way off. Trendle remembered her, and laying down the handful of furze-roots which he was gathering and throwing into a heap, he offered to accompany her in her homeward direction, as the distance was considerable and the days were short. So they walked together, his head bowed nearly to the earth, and his form of a colour with it.

'You can send away warts and other excrescences, I know,' she said; 'why can't you send away this?' And the arm was uncovered.

'You think too much of my powers!' said Trendle; 'and I am old and weak now, too. No, no; it is too much for me to attempt in my own person. What have ye tried?'

She named to him some of the hundred medicaments and counter-spells which she had adopted from time to time. He shook his head.

'Some were good enough,' he said approvingly; 'but not many of them for such as this. This is of the nature of a blight, not of the nature of a wound, and if you ever do throw it off, it will be all at once.'

'If I only could!'

'There is only one chance of doing it known to me. It has never failed in kindred afflictions – that I can declare. But it is hard to carry out, and especially for a woman.'

'Tell me!' said she.

'You must touch with the limb the neck of a man who's been hanged.'

She started a little at the image he had raised.

'Before he's cold – just after he's cut down,' continued the conjuror impassively.

'How can that do good?'

'It will turn the blood and change the constitution. But, as I say, to do it is hard. You must go to the jail when there's a hanging, and wait for him when he's brought off the gallows. Lots have done it, though perhaps not such pretty women as you. I used to send dozens for skin complaints. But that was in former times. The last I sent was in '13 – near twelve years ago.'

He had no more to tell her, and, when he had put her into a straight track homeward, turned and left her, refusing all money as at first.

VII. A RIDE

The communication sank deep into Gertrude's mind. Her nature was rather a timid one; and probably of all remedies that the white wizard could have suggested there was not one which would have filled her with so much aversion as this, not to speak of the immense obstacles in the way of its adoption.

Casterbridge, the county-town, was a dozen or fifteen miles off; and though in those days, when men were executed for horse-stealing, arson, and burglary, an assize seldom passed without a hanging, it was not likely that she could get access to the body of the criminal unaided. And the fear of her husband's anger made her reluctant to breathe a word of Trendle's suggestion to him or to anybody about him.

She did nothing for months, and patiently bore her disfigurement as before. But her woman's nature, craving for renewed love, through the medium of renewed beauty (she was but twenty-five), was ever stimulating her to try what, at any rate, could hardly do her any harm. 'What came by a spell will go by a spell surely,' she would say. Whenever her imagination pictured the act she shrank in terror from the possibility of it; then the words of the conjuror, 'It will turn your blood,' were seen to be capable of a scientific no less than a ghastly interpretation; the mastering desire returned, and urged her on again.

There was at this time but one county paper, and that her husband only occasionally borrowed. But old-fashioned days had old-fashioned means, and news was extensively conveyed by word of mouth from market to market, or from fair to fair, so that, whenever such an event as an execution was about to take place, few within a radius of twenty miles were ignorant of the coming sight; and, so far as Holmstoke was concerned, some enthusiasts had been known to walk all the way to Casterbridge and back in one day, solely to witness the spectacle. The next assizes were in March; and when Gertrude Lodge heard that they had been held, she inquired stealthily at the inn as to the result, as soon as she could find opportunity.

She was, however, too late. The time at which the sentences were to be carried out had arrived, and to make the journey and obtain admission at such short notice required at least her husband's assistance. She dared not tell him, for she had found by delicate experiment that these smouldering village beliefs made him furious if mentioned, partly because he half entertained them himself. It was therefore necessary to wait for another opportunity.

Her determination received a fillip from learning that two epileptic children had attended from this very village of Holmstoke many years before with beneficial results, though the experiment had been strongly condemned by the neighbouring clergy. April, May, June passed; and it is no overstatement to say that by the end of the last-named month Gertrude wellnigh longed for the death of a fellow-creature. Instead of her formal prayers each night, her unconscious prayer was, 'O Lord, hang some guilty or innocent person soon!'

This time she made earlier inquiries, and was altogether more systematic in her proceedings. Moreover, the season was summer, between the haymaking and the harvest, and in the leisure thus afforded him her husband had been holiday-taking away from home.

The assizes were in July, and she went to the inn as before. There was to be one execution – only one – for arson.

Her greatest problem was not how to get to Casterbridge, but what means she should adopt for obtaining admission to the jail. Though access for such purposes had formerly never been denied, the custom had fallen into desuetude; and in contemplating her possible difficulties, she was again almost driven to fall back upon her husband. But, on sounding him about the assizes, he was so uncommunicative, so more than usually cold, that she did not proceed, and decided that whatever she did she would do alone.

Fortune, obdurate hitherto, showed her unexpected favour. On the Thursday before the Saturday fixed for the execution, Lodge remarked to her that he was going away from home for another day or two on business at a fair, and that he was sorry he could not take her with him.

She exhibited on this occasion so much readiness to stay at home that he looked at her in surprise. Time had been when she would have shown deep disappointment at the loss of such a jaunt. However, he lapsed into his usual taciturnity, and on the day named left Holmstoke.

It was now her turn. She at first had thought of driving, but on reflection held that driving would not do, since it would necessitate her keeping to the turnpike-road, and so increase by tenfold the risk of her ghastly errand being found out. She decided to ride, and avoid the beaten track, notwithstanding that in her husband's stables there was no animal just at present which by any stretch of imagination could be considered a lady's mount, in spite of his promise before marriage to always keep a mare for her. He had, however, many cart-horses, fine ones of their kind; and among the rest was a serviceable creature, an equine Amazon, with a back as broad as a sofa, on which Gertrude had occasionally taken an airing when unwell. This horse she chose.

On Friday afternoon one of the men brought it round. She was dressed, and before going down looked at her shrivelled arm. 'Ah!' she said to it, 'if it had not been for you this terrible ordeal would have been saved me!'

When strapping up the bundle in which she carried a few articles of clothing, she took occasion to say to the servant, 'I take these in case I should not get back to-night from the person I am going to visit. Don't be alarmed if I am not in by ten, and close up the house as usual. I shall be at home to-morrow for certain.' She meant then to tell her husband privately; the deed accomplished was not like the deed projected. He would almost certainly forgive her.

And then the pretty palpitating Gertrude Lodge went from her husband's homestead; but though her goal was Casterbridge she did not take the direct route thither through Stickleford. Her cunning course at first was in precisely the opposite direction. As soon as she was out of sight, however, she turned to the left, by a road which led into Egdon, and on entering the heath wheeled round, and set out in the true course, due westerly. A more private way down the county could not be imagined; and as to direction, she had merely to keep her horse's head to a point a little to the right of the sun. She knew that she would light upon a furze-cutter or cottager of some sort from time to time, from whom she might correct her bearing.

Though the date was comparatively recent, Egdon was much less fragmentary in character than now. The attempts – successful and otherwise – at cultivation on the lower slopes, which intrude and break up the original heath into small detached heaths, had not been carried far; Enclosure Acts had not taken effect, and the banks and fences which now exclude the cattle of those villagers who formerly enjoyed rights of commonage thereon, and the carts of those who had turbary privileges which kept them in firing all the year round, were not erected. Gertrude, therefore, rode along with no other obstacles than the prickly furze-bushes, the mats of heather, the white water-courses, and the natural steeps and declivities of the ground.

Her horse was sure, if heavy-footed and slow, and though a draught animal, was easy-paced; had it been otherwise, she was not a woman who could have ventured to ride over such a bit of country with a half-dead arm. It was therefore nearly eight o'clock when she drew rein to breathe her bearer on the last outlying high point of heath-land towards Casterbridge, previous to leaving Egdon for the cultivated valleys.

She halted before a pool called Rushy-pond, flanked by the ends of two hedges; a railing ran through the centre of the pond, dividing it in half. Over the railing she saw the low green country; over the green trees the roofs of the town; over the roofs a white flat façade, denoting the entrance to the county jail. On the roof of this front specks were moving about; they seemed to be workmen erecting something. Her flesh crept. She descended slowly, and was soon amid corn-fields and pastures. In another half-hour, when it was almost dusk, Gertrude reached the White Hart, the first inn of the town on that side.

Little surprise was excited by her arrival; farmers' wives rode on horseback then more than they do now; though, for that matter, Mrs Lodge was not imagined to be a wife at all; the innkeeper supposed her some harum-skarum young woman who had come to attend 'hang-fair' next day. Neither her husband nor herself ever dealt in Casterbridge market, so that she was unknown. While dismounting she beheld a crowd of boys standing at the door of a harness-maker's shop just above the inn, looking inside it with deep interest.

'What is going on there?' she asked of the ostler.

'Making the rope for to-morrow.'

She throbbed responsively, and contracted her arm.

' 'Tis sold by the inch afterwards,' the man continued. 'I could get you a bit, miss, for nothing, if you'd like?'

She hastily repudiated any such wish, all the more from a curious creeping feeling that the condemned wretch's destiny was becoming interwoven with her own; and having engaged a room for the night, sat down to think.

Up to this time she had formed but the vaguest notions about her means of obtaining access to the prison. The words of the cunning-man returned to her mind. He had implied that she should use her beauty, impaired though it was, as a pass-key. In her inexperience she knew little about jail functionaries; she had heard of a high-sheriff and an under-sheriff, but dimly only. She knew, however, that there must be a hangman, and to the hangman she determined to apply.

VIII. A WATER-SIDE HERMIT

At this date, and for several years after, there was a hangman to almost every jail. Gertrude found, on inquiry, that the Casterbridge official dwelt in a lonely cottage by a deep slow river flowing under the cliff on which the prison buildings were situate – the stream being the self-same one, though she did not know it, which watered the Stickleford and Holmstoke meads lower down in its course.

Having changed her dress, and before she had eaten or drunk – for she could not take her ease till she had ascertained some particulars – Gertrude pursued her way by a path along the water-side to the cottage indicated. Passing thus the outskirts of the jail, she discerned on the level roof over the gateway three rectangular lines against the sky, where the specks had been moving in her distant view; she recognized what the erection was, and passed quickly on. Another hundred yards brought her to the executioner's house, which a boy pointed out. It stood close to the same stream, and was hard by a weir, the waters of which emitted a steady roar.

While she stood hesitating the door opened, and an old man came forth, shading a candle with one hand. Locking the door on the outside, he turned to a flight of wooden steps fixed against the end of the cottage, and began to ascend them, this being evidently the staircase to his bedroom. Gertrude hastened forward, but by the time she reached the foot of the ladder he was at the top. She called to him loudly enough to be heard above the roar of the weir; he looked down and said, 'What d'ye want here?'

'To speak to you a minute.'

The candlelight, such as it was, fell upon her imploring, pale, upturned face, and Davies (as the hangman was called) backed down the ladder. 'I was just going to bed,' he said. ' "Early to bed and early to rise", but I don't mind stopping a minute for such a one as you. Come into house.' He reopened the door, and preceded her to the room within.

The implements of his daily work, which was that of a jobbing gardener, stood in a corner, and seeing probably that she looked rural, he said, 'If you want me to undertake country work I can't come, for I never leave Casterbridge for gentle nor simple – not I. My real calling is officer of justice,' he added formally.

'Yes, yes! That's it. To-morrow!'

'Ah! I thought so. Well, what's the matter about that? 'Tis no use to come here about the knot – folks do come continually, but I tell 'em one knot is as merciful as another if ye keep it under the ear. Is the unfortunate man a relation; or, I should say, perhaps' (looking at her dress) 'a person who's been in your employ?'

'No. What time is the execution?'

'The same as usual – twelve o'clock, or as soon after as the London mail-coach gets in. We always wait for that, in case of a reprieve.'

'O – a reprieve – I hope not!' she said involuntarily.

'Well, – hee, hee! – as a matter of business, so do I! But still, if ever a young fellow deserved to be let off, this one does; only just turned eighteen, and only present by chance when the rick was fired. How-somever, there's not much risk of it, as they are obliged to make an example of him, there having been so much destruction of property that way lately.'

'I mean,' she explained, 'that I want to touch him for a charm, a cure of an affliction, by the advice of a man who has proved the virtue of the remedy.'

'O yes, miss! Now I understand. I've had such people come in past years. But it didn't strike me that you looked of a sort to require blood-turning. What's the complaint? The wrong kind for this, I'll be bound.'

'My arm.' She reluctantly showed the withered skin.

'Ah! – 'tis all a-scram!' said the hangman, examining it.

'Yes,' said she.

'Well,' he continued, with interest, 'that *is* the class o' subject, I'm bound to admit! I like the look of the wownd; it is truly as suitable for the cure as any I ever saw. 'Twas a knowing-man that sent 'ee, whoever he was.'

'You can contrive for me all that's necessary?' she said breathlessly.

'You should really have gone to the governor of the jail, and your doctor with 'ee, and given your name and address – that's how it used to be done, if I recollect. Still, perhaps, I can manage it for a trifling fee.'

'O, thank you! I would rather do it this way, as I should like it kept private.'

'Lover not to know, eh?'

'No – husband.'

'Aha! Very well. I'll get 'ee a touch of the corpse.'

'Where is it now?' she said, shuddering.

'It? – *he*, you mean; he's living yet. Just inside that little small winder up there in the glum.' He signified the jail on the cliff above.

She thought of her husband and her friends. 'Yes, of course,' she said; 'and how am I to proceed?'

He took her to the door. 'Now, do you be waiting at the little wicket in the wall, that you'll find up there in the lane, not later than one o'clock. I will open it from the inside, as I shan't come home to dinner till he's cut down. Good-night. Be punctual; and if you don't want anybody to know 'ee, wear a veil. Ah – once I had such a daughter as you!'

She went away, and climbed the path above, to assure herself that she would be able to find the wicket next day. Its outline was soon visible to her – a narrow opening in the outer wall of the prison precincts. The steep was so great that, having reached the wicket, she stopped a moment to breathe; and, looking back upon the water-side cot, saw the hangman again ascending his outdoor staircase. He entered the loft or chamber to which it led, and in a few minutes extinguished his light.

The town clock struck ten, and she returned to the White Hart as she had come.

IX. A RENCOUNTER

It was one o'clock on Saturday. Gertrude Lodge, having been admitted to the jail as above described, was sitting in a waiting-room within the second gate, which stood under a classic archway of ashlar, then comparatively modern, and bearing the inscription, 'COVNTY JAIL: 1793'. This had been the façade she saw from the heath the day before. Near at hand was a passage to the roof on which the gallows stood.

The town was thronged, and the market suspended; but Gertrude had seen scarcely a soul. Having kept her room till the hour of the appointment, she had proceeded to the spot by a way which avoided the open space below the cliff where the spectators had gathered; but she could, even now, hear the multitudinous babble of their voices, out of which rose at intervals the hoarse croak of a single voice uttering the words, 'Last dying speech and confession!' There had been no reprieve, and the execution was over; but the crowd still waited to see the body taken down.

Soon the persistent woman heard a trampling overhead, then a hand beckoned to her, and, following directions, she went out and crossed the inner paved court beyond the gatehouse, her knees trembling so that she could scarcely walk. One of her arms was out of its sleeve, and only covered by her shawl.

On the spot at which she had now arrived were two trestles, and before she could think of their purpose she heard heavy feet descending stairs somewhere at her back. Turn her head she would not, or could not, and, rigid in this position, she was conscious of a rough coffin passing her shoulder, borne by four men. It was open, and in it lay the body of a young man, wearing the smockfrock of a rustic, and fustian breeches. The corpse had been thrown into the coffin so hastily that the skirt of the smockfrock was hanging over. The burden was temporarily deposited on the trestles.

By this time the young woman's state was such that a gray mist seemed to float before her eyes, on account of which, and the veil she

wore, she could scarcely discern anything: it was as though she had
nearly died, but was held up by a sort of galvanism.

'Now!' said a voice close at hand, and she was just conscious that the
word had been addressed to her.

By a last strenuous effort she advanced, at the same time hearing
persons approaching behind her. She bared her poor curst arm; and
Davies, uncovering the face of the corpse, took Gertrude's hand, and
held it so that her arm lay across the dead man's neck, upon a line the
colour of an unripe blackberry, which surrounded it.

Gertrude shrieked: 'the turn o' the blood', predicted by the conjuror,
had taken place. But at that moment a second shriek rent the air of the
enclosure: it was not Gertrude's, and its effect upon her was to make her
start round.

Immediately behind her stood Rhoda Brook, her face drawn, and her
eyes red with weeping. Behind Rhoda stood Gertrude's own husband;
his countenance lined, his eyes dim, but without a tear.

'D—n you! what are you doing here?' he said hoarsely.

'Hussy – to come between us and our child now!' cried Rhoda. 'This
is the meaning of what Satan showed me in the vision! You are like her
at last!' And clutching the bare arm of the younger woman, she pulled
her unresistingly back against the wall. Immediately Brook had loosened
her hold the fragile young Gertrude slid down against the feet of her
husband. When he lifted her up she was unconscious.

The mere sight of the twain had been enough to suggest to her that
the dead young man was Rhoda's son. At that time the relatives of an
executed convict had the privilege of claiming the body for burial, if
they chose to do so; and it was for this purpose that Lodge was awaiting
the inquest with Rhoda. He had been summoned by her as soon as the
young man was taken in the crime, and at different times since; and he
had attended in court during the trial. This was the 'holiday' he had
been indulging in of late. The two wretched parents had wished to
avoid exposure; and hence had come themselves for the body, a
waggon and sheet for its conveyance and covering being in waiting
outside.

Gertrude's case was so serious that it was deemed advisable to call to
her the surgeon who was at hand. She was taken out of the jail into the
town; but she never reached home alive. Her delicate vitality, sapped
perhaps by the paralyzed arm, collapsed under the double shock that
followed the severe strain, physical and mental, to which she had

subjected herself during the previous twenty-four hours. Her blood had
been 'turned' indeed – too far. Her death took place in the town three
days after.

Her husband was never seen in Casterbridge again; once only in the
old market-place at Anglebury, which he had so much frequented, and
very seldom in public anywhere. Burdened at first with moodiness and
remorse, he eventually changed for the better, and appeared as a
chastened and thoughtful man. Soon after attending the funeral of his
poor young wife he took steps towards giving up the farms in Holmstoke
and the adjoining parish, and, having sold every head of his stock, he
went away to Port-Bredy, at the other end of the county, living there in
solitary lodgings till his death two years later of a painless decline. It
was then found that he had bequeathed the whole of his not inconsider-
able property to a reformatory for boys, subject to the payment of a
small annuity to Rhoda Brook, if she could be found to claim it.

For some time she could not be found; but eventually she reappeared
in her old parish, – absolutely refusing, however, to have anything to do
with the provision made for her. Her monotonous milking at the dairy
was resumed, and followed for many long years, till her form became
bent, and her once abundant dark hair white and worn away at the
forehead – perhaps by long pressure against the cows. Here, sometimes,
those who knew her experiences would stand and observe her, and
wonder what sombre thoughts were beating inside that impassive,
wrinkled brow, to the rhythm of the alternating milk-streams.

'Blackwood's Magazine',
January 1888

Fellow-Townsmen

I

THE shepherd on the east hill could shout out lambing intelligence to the shepherd on the west hill, over the intervening town chimneys, without great inconvenience to his voice, so nearly did the steep pastures encroach upon the burghers' backyards. And at night it was possible to stand in the very midst of the town and hear from their native paddocks on the lower levels of greensward the mild lowing of the farmer's heifers, and the profound, warm blowings of breath in which those creatures indulge. But the community which had jammed itself in the valley thus flanked formed a veritable town, with a real mayor and corporation, and a staple manufacture.

During a certain damp evening five-and-thirty years ago, before the twilight was far advanced, a pedestrian of professional appearance, carrying a small bag in his hand and an elevated umbrella, was descending one of these hills by the turnpike road when he was overtaken by a phaeton.

'Hullo, Downe – is that you?' said the driver of the vehicle, a young man of pale and refined appearance. 'Jump up here with me, and ride down to your door.'

The other turned a plump, cheery, rather self-indulgent face over his shoulder towards the hailer.

'O, good evening, Mr Barnet – thanks,' he said, and mounted beside his acquaintance.

They were fellow-burgesses of the town which lay beneath them, but though old and very good friends they were differently circumstanced. Barnet was a richer man than the struggling young lawyer Downe, a fact which was to some extent perceptible in Downe's manner towards his companion, though nothing of it ever showed in Barnet's manner towards the solicitor. Barnet's position in the town was none of his own

making; his father had been a very successful flax-merchant in the same
place, where the trade was still carried on as briskly as the small capacities
of its quarters would allow. Having acquired a fair fortune, old Mr
Barnet had retired from business, bringing up his son as a gentleman-
burgher, and, it must be added, as a well-educated, liberal-minded
young man.

'How is Mrs Barnet ?' asked Downe.

'Mrs Barnet was very well when I left home,' the other answered
constrainedly, exchanging his meditative regard of the horse for one of
self-consciousness.

Mr Downe seemed to regret his inquiry, and immediately took up
another thread of conversation. He congratulated his friend on his
election as a councilman; he thought he had not seen him since that
event took place; Mrs Downe had meant to call and congratulate Mrs
Barnet, but he feared that she had failed to do so as yet.

Barnet seemed hampered in his replies. 'We should have been glad to
see you. I – my wife would welcome Mrs Downe at any time, as you
know. . . . Yes, I am a member of the corporation – rather an inexperienced member, some of them say. It is quite true; and I should have
declined the honour as premature – having other things on my hands
just now, too – if it had not been pressed upon me so very heartily.'

'There is one thing you have on your hands which I can never quite
see the necessity for,' said Downe, with good-humoured freedom.
'What the deuce do you want to build that new mansion for, when you
have already got such an excellent house as the one you live in ?'

Barnet's face acquired a warmer shade of colour; but as the question
had been idly asked by the solicitor while regarding the surrounding
flocks and fields, he answered after a moment with no apparent embarrassment –

'Well, we wanted to get out of the town, you know; the house I am
living in is rather old and inconvenient.'

Mr Downe declared that he had chosen a pretty site for the new
building. They would be able to see for miles and miles from the
windows. Was he going to give it a name ? He supposed so.

Barnet thought not. There was no other house near that was likely to
be mistaken for it. And he did not care for a name.

'But I think it has a name!' Downe observed: 'I went past – when was
it ? – this morning; and I saw something, – "Château Ringdale", I
think it was, stuck up on a board!'

'It was an idea she – we had for a short time,' said Barnet hastily.
'But we have decided finally to do without a name – at any rate such a
name as that. It must have been a week ago that you saw it. It was
taken down last Saturday. . . . Upon that matter I am firm!' he added
grimly.

Downe murmured in an unconvinced tone that he thought he had
seen it yesterday.

Talking thus they drove into the town. The street was unusually
still for the hour of seven in the evening; an increasing drizzle from the
sea had prevailed since the afternoon, and now formed a gauze across
the yellow lamps, and trickled with a gentle rattle down the heavy roofs
of stone tile, that bent the house-ridges hollow-backed with its weight,
and in some instances caused the walls to bulge outwards in the upper
story. Their route took them past the little town-hall, the Black-Bull
Hotel, and onward to the junction of a small street on the right, consisting of a row of those two-and-two windowed brick residences of no
particular age, which are exactly alike wherever found, except in the
people they contain.

'Wait – I'll drive you up to your door,' said Barnet, when Downe
prepared to alight at the corner. He thereupon turned into the narrow
street, when the faces of three little girls could be discerned close to the
panes of a lighted window a few yards ahead, surmounted by that of a
young matron, the gaze of all four being directed eagerly up the empty
street. 'You are a fortunate fellow, Downe,' Barnet continued, as mother
and children disappeared from the window to run to the door. 'You
must be happy if any man is. I would give a hundred such houses as my
new one to have a home like yours.'

'Well – yes, we get along pretty comfortably,' replied Downe com-
placently.

'That house, Downe, is none of my ordering,' Barnet broke out,
revealing a bitterness hitherto suppressed, and checking the horse a
moment to finish his speech before delivering up his passenger. 'The
house I have already is good enough for me, as you supposed. It is my
own freehold; it was built by my grandfather, and is stout enough for a
castle. My father was born there, lived there, and died there. I was born
there, and have always lived there; yet I must needs build a new one.'

'Why do you?' said Downe.

'Why do I? To preserve peace in the household. I do anything for
that; but I don't succeed. I was firm in resisting "Château Ringdale",

however; not that I would not have put up with the absurdity of the name, but it was too much to have your house christened after Lord Ringdale, because your wife once had a fancy for him. If you only knew everything, you would think all attempt at reconciliation hopeless. In your happy home you have had no such experiences; and God forbid that you ever should. See, here they are all ready to receive you!'

'Of course! And so will your wife be waiting to receive you,' said Downe. 'Take my word for it she will! And with a dinner prepared for you far better than mine.'

'I hope so,' Barnet replied dubiously.

He moved on to Downe's door, which the solicitor's family had already opened. Downe descended, but being encumbered with his bag and umbrella, his foot slipped, and he fell upon his knees in the gutter.

'O, my dear Charles!' said his wife, running down the steps; and, quite ignoring the presence of Barnet, she seized hold of her husband, pulled him to his feet, and kissed him, exclaiming, 'I hope you are not hurt, darling!' The children crowded round, chiming in piteously, 'Poor papa!'

'He's all right,' said Barnet, perceiving that Downe was only a little muddy, and looking more at the wife than at the husband. Almost at any other time – certainly during his fastidious bachelor years – he would have thought her a too demonstrative woman; but those recent circumstances of his own life to which he had just alluded made Mrs Downe's solicitude so affecting that his eye grew damp as he witnessed it. Bidding the lawyer and his family good-night he left them, and drove slowly into the main street towards his own house.

The heart of Barnet was sufficiently impressionable to be influenced by Downe's parting prophecy that he might not be so unwelcome home as he imagined: the dreary night might, at least on this one occasion, make Downe's forecast true. Hence it was in a suspense that he could hardly have believed possible that he halted at his door. On entering his wife was nowhere to be seen, and he inquired for her. The servant informed him that her mistress had the dressmaker with her, and would be engaged for some time.

'Dressmaker at this time of day!'

'She dined early, sir, and hopes you will excuse her joining you this evening.'

'But she knew I was coming to-night?'

'O yes, sir.'

'Go up and tell her I am come.'

The servant did so; but the mistress of the house merely transmitted her former words.

Barnet said nothing more, and presently sat down to his lonely meal, which was eaten abstractedly, the domestic scene he had lately witnessed still impressing him by its contrast with the situation here. His mind fell back into past years upon a certain pleasing and gentle being whose face would loom out of their shades at such times as these. Barnet turned in his chair, and looked with unfocused eyes in a direction southward from where he sat, as if he saw not the room but a long way beyond. 'I wonder if she lives there still!' he said.

II

He rose with a sudden rebelliousness, put on his hat and coat, and went out of the house, pursuing his way along the glistening pavement while eight o'clock was striking from St Mary's tower, and the apprentices and shopmen were slamming up the shutters from end to end of the town. In two minutes only those shops which could boast of no attendant save the master or the mistress remained with open eyes. These were ever somewhat less prompt to exclude customers than the others: for their owners' ears the closing hour had scarcely the cheerfulness that it possessed for the hired servants of the rest. Yet the night being dreary the delay was not for long, and their windows, too, blinked together one by one.

During this time Barnet had proceeded with decided step in a direction at right angles to the broad main thoroughfare of the town, by a long street leading due southward. Here, though his family had no more to do with the flax manufacture, his own name occasionally greeted him on gates and warehouses, being used allusively by small rising tradesmen as a recommendation, in such words as 'Smith, from Barnet & Co.' – 'Robinson, late manager at Barnet's'. The sight led him to reflect upon his father's busy life, and he questioned if it had not been far happier than his own.

The houses along the road became fewer, and presently open ground appeared between them on either side, the track on the right hand rising to a higher level till it merged in a knoll. On the summit a row of builders' scaffold-poles probed the indistinct sky like spears, and at their bases could be discerned the lower courses of a building lately begun. Barnet slackened his pace and stood for a few moments without leaving the centre of the road, apparently not much interested in the sight, till suddenly his eye was caught by a post in the fore part of the ground bearing a white board at the top. He went to the rails, vaulted over, and walked in far enough to discern painted upon the board 'Château Ringdale'.

A dismal irony seemed to lie in the words, and its effect was to irritate him. Downe, then, had spoken truly. He stuck his umbrella into the sod, and seized the post with both hands, as if intending to loosen and throw it down. Then, like one bewildered by an opposition which would exist none the less though its manifestations were removed, he allowed his arms to sink to his side.

'Let it be,' he said to himself. 'I have declared there shall be peace – if possible.'

Taking up his umbrella, he quietly left the enclosure, and went on his way, still keeping his back to the town. He had advanced with more decision since passing the new building, and soon a hoarse murmur rose upon the gloom; it was the sound of the sea. The road led to the harbour, at a distance of a mile from the town, from which the trade of the district was fed. After seeing the obnoxious name-board Barnet had forgotten to open his umbrella, and the rain tapped smartly on his hat, and occasionally stroked his face as he went on.

Though the lamps were still continued at the roadside they stood at wider intervals than before, and the pavement had given place to rough gravel. Every time he came to a lamp an increasing shine made itself visible upon his shoulders, till at last they quite glistened with wet. The murmur from the shore grew stronger, but it was still some distance off when he paused before one of the smallest of the detached houses by the wayside, standing in its own garden, the latter being divided from the road by a row of wooden palings. Scrutinizing the spot to ensure that he was not mistaken, he opened the gate and gently knocked at the cottage door.

When he had patiently waited minutes enough to lead any man in ordinary cases to knock again, the door was heard to open, though it was impossible to see by whose hand, there being no light in the passage. Barnet said at random, 'Does Miss Savile live here?'

A youthful voice assured him that she did live there, and by a sudden afterthought asked him to come in. It would soon get a light, it said: but the night being wet, mother had not thought it worth while to trim the passage lamp.

'Don't trouble yourself to get a light for me,' said Barnet hastily; 'it is not necessary at all. Which is Miss Savile's sitting-room?'

The young person, whose white pinafore could just be discerned, signified a door in the side of the passage, and Barnet went forward at the same moment, so that no light should fall upon his face. On entering the room he closed the door behind him, pausing till he heard the retreating footsteps of the child.

He found himself in an apartment which was simply and neatly, though not poorly furnished; everything, from the miniature chiffonnier to the shining little daguerreotype which formed the central ornament of the mantelpiece, being in scrupulous order. The picture was enclosed by a frame of embroidered card-board – evidently the work of feminine hands – and it was the portrait of a thin-faced, elderly lieutenant in the navy. From behind the lamp on the table a female form now rose into view, that of a young girl, and a resemblance between her and the portrait was early discoverable. She had been so absorbed in some occupation on the other side of the lamp as to have barely found time to realize her visitor's presence.

They both remained standing for a few seconds without speaking. The face that confronted Barnet had a beautiful outline; the Raffaelesque oval of its contour was remarkable for an English countenance, and that countenance housed in a remote country-road to an unheard-of harbour. But her features did not do justice to this splendid beginning: Nature had recollected that she was not in Italy; and the young lady's lineaments, though not so inconsistent as to make her plain, would have been accepted rather as pleasing than as correct. The preoccupied expression which, like images on the retina, remained with her for a moment after the state that caused it had ceased, now changed into a reserved, half-proud, and slightly indignant look, in which the blood diffused itself quickly across her cheek, and additional brightness broke the shade of her rather heavy eyes.

'I know I have no business here,' he said, answering the look. 'But I had a great wish to see you, and inquire how you were. You can give your hand to me, seeing how often I have held it in past days?'

'I would rather forget than remember all that, Mr Barnet,' she answered, as she coldly complied with the request. 'When I think of the circumstances of our last meeting, I can hardly consider it kind of you to allude to such a thing as our past – or, indeed, to come here at all.'

'There was no harm in it surely? I don't trouble you often, Lucy.'

'I have not had the honour of a visit from you for a very long time, certainly, and I did not expect it now,' she said, with the same stiffness in her air. 'I hope Mrs Barnet is very well?'

'Yes, yes!' he impatiently returned. 'At least, I suppose so – though I only speak from inference!'

'But she is your wife, sir,' said the young girl tremulously.

The unwonted tones of a man's voice in that feminine chamber had startled a canary that was roosting in its cage by the window; the bird awoke hastily, and fluttered against the bars. She went and stilled it by laying her face against the cage and murmuring a coaxing sound. It might partly have been done to still herself.

'I didn't come to talk of Mrs Barnet,' he pursued; 'I came to talk of you, of yourself alone; to inquire how you are getting on since your great loss.' And he turned towards the portrait of her father.

'I am getting on fairly well, thank you.'

The force of her utterance was scarcely borne out by her look; but Barnet courteously reproached himself for not having guessed a thing so natural; and to dissipate all embarrassment added, as he bent over the table, 'What were you doing when I came? – painting flowers, and by candlelight?'

'O no,' she said, 'not painting them – only sketching the outlines. I do that at night to save time – I have to get three dozen done by the end of the month.'

Barnet looked as if he regretted it deeply. 'You will wear your poor eyes out,' he said, with more sentiment than he had hitherto shown. 'You ought not to do it. There was a time when I should have said you must not. Well – I almost wish I had never seen light with my own eyes when I think of that!'

'Is this a time or place for recalling such matters?' she asked, with dignity. 'You used to have a gentlemanly respect for me, and for your-self. Don't speak any more as you have spoken, and don't come again. I cannot think that this visit is serious, or was closely considered by you.'

'Considered: well, I came to see you as an old and good friend – not to mince matters, to visit a woman I loved. Don't be angry! I could not help doing it, so many things brought you into my mind. . . . This evening I fell in with an acquaintance, and when I saw how happy he was with his wife and family welcoming him home, though with only one-tenth of my income and chances, and thought what might have been in my case, it fairly broke down my discretion, and off I came here. Now I am here I feel that I am wrong to some extent. But the feeling that I should like to see you, and talk of those we used to know in common, was very strong.'

'Before that can be the case a little more time must pass,' said Miss Savile quietly; 'a time long enough for me to regard with some calmness what at present I remember far too impatiently – though it may be you almost forget it. Indeed you must have forgotten it long before you acted as you did.' Her voice grew stronger and more vivacious as she added: 'But I am doing my best to forget it too, and I know I shall succeed from the progress I have made already!'

She had remained standing till now, when she turned and sat down, facing half away from him.

Barnet watched her moodily. 'Yes, it is only what I deserve,' he said. 'Ambition pricked me on – no, it was not ambition, it was wrongheadedness! Had I but reflected. . . .' He broke out vehemently: 'But always remember this, Lucy: if you had written to me only one little line after that misunderstanding, I declare I should have come back to you. That ruined me!' He slowly walked as far as the little room would allow him to go, and remained with his eyes on the skirting.

'But, Mr Barnet, how could I write to you? There was no opening for my doing so.'

'Then there ought to have been,' said Barnet, turning. 'That was my fault!'

'Well, I don't know anything about that; but as there had been nothing said by me which required any explanation by letter, I did not send one. Everything was so indefinite, and feeling your position to be so much wealthier than mine, I fancied I might have mistaken your meaning. And when I heard of the other lady – a woman of whose family even you might be proud – I thought how foolish I had been, and said nothing.'

'Then I suppose it was destiny – accident – I don't know what, that separated us, dear Lucy. Anyhow, you were the woman I ought to have made my wife – and I let you slip, like the foolish man that I was!'

'O, Mr Barnet,' she said, almost in tears, 'don't revive the subject to me; I am the wrong one to console you – think, sir, – you should not be here – it would be so bad for me if it were known!'

'It would – it would, indeed,' he said hastily. 'I am not right in doing this, and I won't do it again.'

'It is a very common folly of human nature, you know, to think the course you did *not* adopt must have been the best,' she continued, with gentle solicitude, as she followed him to the door of the room. 'And you don't know that I should have accepted you, even if you had asked me to be your wife.' At this his eye met hers, and she dropped her gaze. She knew that her voice belied her. There was a silence till she looked up to add, in a voice of soothing playfulness, 'My family was so much poorer than yours, even before I lost my dear father, that – perhaps your companions would have made it unpleasant for us on account of my deficiencies.'

'Your disposition would soon have won them round,' said Barnet.

She archly expostulated: 'Now, never mind my disposition; try to make it up with your wife! Those are my commands to you. And now you are to leave me at once.'

'I will. I must make the best of it all, I suppose,' he replied, more cheerfully than he had as yet spoken. 'But I shall never again meet with such a dear girl as you!' And he suddenly opened the door and left her alone. When his glance again fell on the lamps that were sparsely ranged along the dreary level road, his eyes were in a state which showed straw-like motes of light radiating from each flame into the surrounding air.

On the other side of the way Barnet observed a man under an umbrella, walking parallel with himself. Presently this man left the footway, and gradually converged on Barnet's course. The latter then saw that it was Charlson, a surgeon of the town, who owed him money. Charlson was a man not without ability; yet he did not prosper. Sundry circumstances stood in his way as a medical practitioner: he was needy; he was not a coddle; he gossiped with men instead of with women; he had married a stranger instead of one of the town young ladies; and he was given to conversational buffoonery. Moreover, his look was quite erroneous. Those only proper features in the family doctor, the quiet eye, and the thin straight passionless lips which never curl in public either for laughter or for scorn, were not his; he had a full-curved mouth, and a bold black eye that made timid people nervous. His companions were what in old times would have been called boon companions – an expression which, though of irreproachable root, suggests fraternization carried to the point of unscrupulousness. All this was against him in the little town of his adoption.

Charlson had been in difficulties, and to oblige him Barnet had put
his name to a bill; and, as he had expected, was called upon to meet it
when it fell due. It had been only a matter of fifty pounds, which Barnet
could well afford to lose, and he bore no ill-will to the thriftless surgeon
on account of it. But Charlson had a little too much brazen indifferentism
in his composition to be altogether a desirable acquaintance.

'I hope to be able to make that little bill-business right with you in
the course of three weeks, Mr Barnet,' said Charlson with hail-fellow
friendliness.

Barnet replied good-naturedly that there was no hurry.

This particular three weeks had moved on in advance of Charlson's
present with the precision of a shadow for some considerable time.

'I've had a dream,' Charlson continued. Barnet knew from his tone
that the surgeon was going to begin his characteristic nonsense, and did
not encourage him. 'I've had a dream,' repeated Charlson, who required
no encouragement. 'I dreamed that a gentleman, who has been very
kind to me, married a haughty lady in haste, before he had quite forgotten a nice little girl he knew before, and that one wet evening, like the
present, as I was walking up the harbour-road, I saw him come out of
that dear little girl's present abode.'

Barnet glanced towards the speaker. The rays from a neighbouring
lamp struck through the drizzle under Charlson's umbrella, so as just
to illumine his face against the shade behind, and show that his eye was
turned up under the outer corner of its lid, whence it leered with
impish jocoseness as he thrust his tongue into his cheek.

'Come,' said Barnet gravely, 'we'll have no more of that.'

'No, no – of course not,' Charlson hastily answered, seeing that his
humour had carried him too far, as it had done many times before. He
was profuse in his apologies, but Barnet did not reply. Of one thing he
was certain – that scandal was a plant of quick root, and that he was
bound to obey Lucy's injunction for Lucy's own sake.

III

He did so, to the letter; and though, as the crocus followed the snow-
drop and the daffodil the crocus in Lucy's garden, the harbour-road
was a not unpleasant place to walk in, Barnet's feet never trod its stones,
much less approached her door. He avoided a saunter that way as he

would have avoided a dangerous dram, and took his airings a long distance
northward, among severely square and brown ploughed fields, where no
other townsman came. Sometimes he went round by the lower lanes of
the borough, where the rope-walks stretched in which his family
formerly had share, and looked at the rope-makers walking backwards,
overhung by apple-trees and bushes, and intruded on by cows and
calves, as if trade had established itself there at considerable inconvenience to Nature.

One morning, when the sun was so warm as to raise a steam from the
south-eastern slopes of those flanking hills that looked so lovely above
the old roofs, but made every low-chimneyed house in the town as
smoky as Tophet, Barnet glanced from the windows of the town-council
room for lack of interest in what was proceeding within. Several
members of the corporation were present, but there was not much
business doing, and in a few minutes Downe came leisurely across to
him, saying that he seldom saw Barnet now.

Barnet owned that he was not often present.

Downe looked at the crimson curtain which hung down beside the
panes, reflecting its hot hues into their faces, and then out of the
window. At that moment there passed along the street a tall commanding lady, in whom the solicitor recognized Barnet's wife. Barnet had
done the same thing, and turned away.

'It will be all right some day,' said Downe, with cheering sympathy.

'You have heard, then, of her last outbreak?'

Downe depressed his cheerfulness to its very reverse in a moment.
'No, I have not heard of anything serious,' he said, with as long a face as
one naturally round could be turned into at short notice. 'I only hear
vague reports of such things.'

'You may think it will be all right,' said Barnet drily. 'But I have a
different opinion. . . . No, Downe, we must look the thing in the face.
Not poppy nor mandragora – however, how are your wife and children?'

Downe said that they were all well, thanks; they were out that
morning somewhere; he was just looking to see if they were walking that
way. Ah, there they were, just coming down the street; and Downe
pointed to the figures of two children with a nursemaid, and a lady
walking behind them.

'You will come out and speak to her?' he asked.

'Not this morning. The fact is I don't care to speak to anybody just
now.'

'You are too sensitive, Mr Barnet. At school I remember you used to
get as red as a rose if anybody uttered a word that hurt your feelings.'

Barnet mused. 'Yes,' he admitted, 'there is a grain of truth in that. It
is because of that I often try to make peace at home. Life would be
tolerable then at any rate, even if not particularly bright.'

'I have thought more than once of proposing a little plan to you,' said
Downe with some hesitation. 'I don't know whether it will meet your
views, but take it or leave it, as you choose. In fact, it was my wife who
suggested it: that she would be very glad to call on Mrs Barnet and get
into her confidence. She seems to think that Mrs Barnet is rather alone
in the town, and without advisers. Her impression is that your wife will
listen to reason. Emily has a wonderful way of winning the hearts of
people of her own sex.'

'And of the other sex too, I think. She is a charming woman, and you
were a lucky fellow to find her.'

'Well, perhaps I was,' simpered Downe, trying to wear an aspect of
being the last man in the world to feel pride. 'However, she will be
likely to find out what ruffles Mrs Barnet. Perhaps it is some misunderstanding, you know – something that she is too proud to ask you to
explain, or some little thing in your conduct that irritates her because
she does not fully comprehend you. The truth is, Emily would have
been more ready to make advances if she had been quite sure of her
fitness for Mrs Barnet's society, who has of course been accustomed to
London people of good position, which made Emily fearful of intruding.'

Barnet expressed his warmest thanks for the well-intentioned
proposition. There was reason in Mrs Downe's fear – that he owned.
'But do let her call,' he said. 'There is no woman in England I would so
soon trust on such an errand. I am afraid there will not be any brilliant
result; still, I shall take it as the kindest and nicest thing if she will try
it, and not be frightened at a repulse.'

When Barnet and Downe had parted, the former went to the Town
Savings-Bank, of which he was a trustee, and endeavoured to forget his
troubles in the contemplation of low sums of money, and figures in a
network of red and blue lines. He sat and watched the working-people
making their deposits, to which at intervals he signed his name. Before
he left in the afternoon Downe put his head inside the door.

'Emily has seen Mrs Barnet,' he said in a low voice. 'She has got Mrs

Barnet's promise to take her for a drive down to the shore to-morrow, if it is fine. Good afternoon!'

Barnet shook Downe by the hand without speaking, and Downe went away.

IV

The next day was as fine as the arrangement could possibly require. As the sun passed the meridian and declined westward, the tall shadows from the scaffold-poles of Barnet's rising residence streaked the ground as far as to the middle of the highway. Barnet himself was there inspecting the progress of the works for the first time during several weeks. A building in an old-fashioned town five-and-thirty years ago did not, as in the modern fashion, rise from the sod like a booth at a fair. The foundations and lower courses were put in and allowed to settle for many weeks before the superstructure was built up, and a whole summer of drying was hardly sufficient to do justice to the important issues involved. Barnet stood within a window-niche which had as yet received no frame, and thence looked down a slope into the road. The wheels of a chaise were heard, and then his handsome Xantippe, in the company of Mrs Downe, drove past on their way to the shore. They were driving slowly; there was a pleasing light in Mrs Downe's face, which seemed faintly to reflect itself upon the countenance of her companion – that *politesse du cœur* which was so natural to her having possibly begun already to work results. But whatever the situation, Barnet resolved not to interfere, or do anything to hazard the promise of the day. He might well afford to trust the issue to another when he could never direct it but to ill himself. His wife's clenched rein-hand in its lemon-coloured glove, her stiff erect figure, clad in velvet and lace, and her boldly-outlined face, passed on, exhibiting their owner as one fixed for ever above the level of her companion – socially by her early breeding, and materially by her higher cushion.

Barnet decided to allow them a proper time to themselves, and then stroll down to the shore and drive them home. After lingering on at the house for another hour he started with this intention. A few hundred yards below 'Château Ringdale' stood the cottage in which the late lieutenant's daughter had her lodging. Barnet had not been so far that way for a long time, and as he approached the forbidden ground a

curious warmth passed into him, which led him to perceive that, unless
he were careful, he might have to fight the battle with himself about
Lucy over again. A tenth of his present excuse would, however, have
justified him in travelling by that road to-day.

He came opposite the dwelling, and turned his eyes for a momentary
glance into the little garden that stretched from the palings to the door.
Lucy was in the enclosure; she was walking and stooping to gather some
flowers, possibly for the purpose of painting them, for she moved about
quickly, as if anxious to save time. She did not see him; he might have
passed unnoticed; but a sensation which was not in strict unison with
his previous sentiments that day led him to pause in his walk and watch
her. She went nimbly round and round the beds of anemones, tulips,
jonquils, polyanthuses, and other old-fashioned flowers, looking a very
charming figure in her half-mourning bonnet, and with an incomplete
nosegay in her left hand. Raising herself to pull down a lilac blossom she
observed him.

'Mr Barnet!' she said, innocently smiling. 'Why, I have been thinking
of you many times since Mrs Barnet went by in the pony-carriage, and
now here you are!'

'Yes, Lucy,' he said.

Then she seemed to recall particulars of their last meeting, and he
believed that she flushed, though it might have been only the fancy of
his own supersensitiveness.

'I am going to the harbour,' he added.

'Are you?' Lucy remarked simply. 'A great many people begin to go
there now the summer is drawing on.'

Her face had come more into his view as she spoke, and he noticed
how much thinner and paler it was than when he had seen it last. 'Lucy,
how weary you look! tell me, can I help you?' he was going to cry out. –
'If I do,' he thought, 'it will be the ruin of us both!' He merely said that
the afternoon was fine, and went on his way.

As he went a sudden blast of air came over the hill as if in contradic-
tion to his words, and spoilt the previous quiet of the scene. The wind
had already shifted violently, and now smelt of the sea.

The harbour-road soon began to justify its name. A gap appeared in
the rampart of hills which shut out the sea, and on the left of the opening
rose a vertical cliff, coloured a burning orange by the sunlight, the
companion cliff on the right being livid in shade. Between these cliffs,
like the Libyan bay which sheltered the shipwrecked Trojans, was a

little haven, seemingly a beginning made by Nature herself of a perfect harbour, which appealed to the passer-by as only requiring a little human industry to finish it and make it famous, the ground on each side as far back as the daisied slopes that bounded the interior valley being a mere layer of blown sand. But the Port-Bredy burgesses a mile inland had, in the course of ten centuries, responded many times to that mute appeal, with the result that the tides had invariably choked up their works with sand and shingle as soon as completed. There were but few houses here: a rough pier, a few boats, some stores, an inn, a residence or two, a ketch unloading in the harbour, were the chief features of the settlement. On the open ground by the shore stood his wife's pony-carriage, empty, the boy in attendance holding the horse.

When Barnet drew nearer, he saw an indigo-coloured spot moving swiftly along beneath the radiant base of the eastern cliff, which proved to be a man in a jersey, running with all his might. He held up his hand to Barnet, as it seemed, and they approached each other. The man was local, but a stranger to him.

'What is it, my man?' said Barnet.

'A terrible calamity!' the boatman hastily explained. Two ladies had been capsized in a boat – they were Mrs Downe and Mrs Barnet of the old town; they had driven down there that afternoon – they had alighted, and it was so fine, that, after walking about a little while, they had been tempted to go out for a short sail round the cliff. Just as they were putting in to the shore, the wind shifted with a sudden gust, the boat listed over, and it was thought they were both drowned. How it could have happened was beyond his mind to fathom, for John Green knew how to sail a boat as well as any man there.

'Which is the way to the place?' said Barnet.

It was just round the cliff.

'Run to the carriage and tell the boy to bring it to the place as soon as you can. Then go to the Harbour Inn and tell them to ride to town for a doctor. Have they been got out of the water?'

'One lady has.'

'Which?'

'Mrs Barnet. Mrs Downe, it is feared, has fleeted out to sea.'

Barnet ran on to that part of the shore which the cliff had hitherto obscured from his view, and there discerned, a long way ahead, a group of fishermen standing. As soon as he came up one or two recognized him, and, not liking to meet his eye, turned aside with misgiving. He went amidst them and saw a small sailing-boat lying draggled at the water's edge; and, on the sloping shingle beside it, a soaked and sandy woman's form in the velvet dress and yellow gloves of his wife.

V

All had been done that could be done. Mrs Barnet was in her own house under medical hands, but the result was still uncertain. Barnet had acted as if devotion to his wife were the dominant passion of his existence. There had been much to decide – whether to attempt restoration of the apparently lifeless body as it lay on the shore – whether to carry her to the Harbour Inn – whether to drive with her at once to his own house. The first course, with no skilled help or appliances near at hand, had seemed hopeless. The second course would have occupied nearly as much time as a drive to the town, owing to the intervening ridges of shingle, and the necessity of crossing the harbour by boat to get to the house, added to which much time must have elapsed before a doctor could have arrived down there. By bringing her home in the carriage some precious moments had slipped by; but she had been laid in her own bed in seven minutes, a doctor called to her side, and every possible restorative brought to bear upon her.

At what a tearing pace he had driven up that road, through the yellow evening sunlight, the shadows flapping irksomely into his eyes as each wayside object rushed past between him and the west! Tired workmen with their baskets at their backs had turned on their homeward journey to wonder at his speed. Half-way between the shore and Port-Bredy town he had met Charlson, who had been the first surgeon to hear of the accident. He was accompanied by his assistant in a gig. Barnet had sent on the latter to the coast in case that Downe's poor wife should by that time have been reclaimed from the waves, and had brought Charlson back with him to the house.

Barnet's presence was not needed here, and he felt it to be his next duty to set off at once and find Downe, that no other than himself might break the news to him.

He was quite sure that no chance had been lost for Mrs Downe by his leaving the shore. By the time that Mrs Barnet had been laid in the carriage a much larger group had assembled to lend assistance in finding her friend, rendering his own help superfluous. But the duty of breaking the news was made doubly painful by the circumstance that the catastrophe which had befallen Mrs Downe was solely the result of her own and her husband's loving kindness towards himself.

He found Downe in his office. When the solicitor comprehended the intelligence he turned pale, stood up, and remained for a moment perfectly still, as if bereft of his faculties; then his shoulders heaved, he pulled out his handkerchief and began to cry like a child. His sobs might have been heard in the next room. He seemed to have no idea of going to the shore, or of doing anything; but when Barnet took him gently by the hand and proposed to start at once, he quietly acquiesced, neither uttering any further word nor making any effort to repress his tears.

Barnet accompanied him to the shore, where, finding that no trace had as yet been seen of Mrs Downe, and that his stay would be of no avail, he left Downe with his friends and the young doctor, and once more hastened back to his own house.

At the door he met Charlson. 'Well!' Barnet said.

'I have just come down,' said the doctor; 'we have done everything, but without result. I sympathize with you in your bereavement.'

Barnet did not much appreciate Charlson's sympathy, which sounded to his ears as something of a mockery from the lips of a man who knew what Charlson knew about his domestic relations. Indeed, there seemed an odd spark in Charlson's full black eye as he said the words; but that might have been imaginary.

'And, Mr Barnet,' Charlson resumed, 'that little matter between us – I hope to settle it finally in three weeks at least.'

'Never mind that now,' said Barnet abruptly. He directed the surgeon to go to the harbour in case his services might even now be necessary there: and himself entered the house.

The servants were coming from his wife's chamber, looking helplessly at each other and at him. He passed them by and entered the room, where he stood regarding the shape on the bed for a few minutes, after which he walked into his own dressing-room adjoining, and there paced up and down. In a minute or two he noticed what a strange and total silence had come over the upper part of the house; his own movements, muffled as they were by the carpet, seemed noisy, and his thoughts to disturb the air like articulate utterances. His eye glanced through the window. Far down the road to the harbour a roof detained his gaze: out of it rose a red chimney, and out of the red chimney a curl of smoke, as

from a fire newly kindled. He had often seen such a sight before. In that
house lived Lucy Savile; and the smoke was from the fire which was
regularly lighted at this time to make her tea.

After that he went back to the bedroom, and stood there some time
regarding his wife's silent form. She was a woman some years older than
himself, but had not by any means overpassed the maturity of good
looks and vigour. Her passionate features, well-defined, firm, and
statuesque in life, were doubly so now: her mouth and brow, beneath
her purplish-black hair, showed only too clearly that the turbulency of
character which had made a bear-garden of his house had been no
temporary phase of her existence. While he reflected, he suddenly said
to himself, I wonder if all has been done?

The thought was led up to by his having fancied that his wife's
features lacked in its completeness the expression which he had been
accustomed to associate with the faces of those whose spirits have fled
for ever. The effacement of life was not so marked but that, entering
uninformed, he might have supposed her sleeping. Her complexion
was that seen in the numerous faded portraits by Sir Joshua Reynolds;
it was pallid in comparison with life, but there was visible on a close
inspection the remnant of what had once been a flush; the keeping
between the cheeks and the hollows of the face being thus preserved,
although positive colour was gone. Long orange rays of evening sun
stole in through chinks in the blind, striking on the large mirror, and
being thence reflected upon the crimson hangings and woodwork of the
heavy bedstead, so that the general tone of light was remarkably warm;
and it was probable that something might be due to this circumstance.
Still the fact impressed him as strange. Charlson had been gone more
than a quarter of an hour: could it be possible that he had left too soon,
and that his attempts to restore her had operated so sluggishly as only
now to have made themselves felt? Barnet laid his hand upon her chest,
and fancied that ever and anon a faint flutter of palpitation, gentle as that
of a butterfly's wing, disturbed the stillness there – ceasing for a time,
then struggling to go on, then breaking down in weakness and ceasing
again.

Barnet's mother had been an active practitioner of the healing art
among her poorer neighbours, and her inspirations had all been derived
from an octavo volume of Domestic Medicine, which at this moment
was lying, as it had lain for many years, on a shelf in Barnet's dressing-
room. He hastily fetched it, and there read under the head 'Drowning': –

'Exertions for the recovery of any person who has not been immersed for a longer period than half-an-hour should be continued for at least four hours, as there have been many cases in which returning life has made itself visible even after a longer interval.

'Should, however, a weak action of any of the organs show itself when the case seems almost hopeless, our efforts must be redoubled; the feeble spark in this case requires to be solicited; it will certainly disappear under a relaxation of labour.'

Barnet looked at his watch; it was now barely two hours and a half from the time when he had first heard of the accident. He threw aside the book and turned quickly to reach a stimulant which had previously been used. Pulling up the blind for more light, his eye glanced out of the window. There he saw that red chimney still smoking cheerily, and that roof, and through the roof that somebody. His mechanical movements stopped, his hand remained on the blind-cord, and he seemed to become breathless, as if he had suddenly found himself treading a high rope.

While he stood a sparrow lighted on the window-sill, saw him, and flew away. Next a man and a dog walked over one of the green hills which bulged above the roofs of the town. But Barnet took no notice.

We may wonder what were the exact images that passed through his mind during those minutes of gazing upon Lucy Savile's house, the sparrow, the man and the dog, and Lucy Savile's house again. There are honest men who will not admit to their thoughts, even as idle hypotheses, views of the future that assume as done a deed which they would recoil from doing; and there are other honest men for whom morality ends at the surface of their own heads, who will deliberate what the first will not so much as suppose. Barnet had a wife whose presence distracted his home; she now lay as in death; by merely doing nothing – by letting the intelligence which had gone forth to the world lie undisturbed – he would effect such a deliverance for himself as he had never hoped for, and open up an opportunity of which till now he had never dreamed. Whether the conjuncture had arisen through any unscrupulous, ill-considered impulse of Charlson to help out of a strait the friend who was so kind as never to press him for what was due could not be told; there was nothing to prove it; and it was a question which could never be asked. The triangular situation – himself – his wife – Lucy Savile – was the one clear thing.

From Barnet's actions we may infer that he *supposed* such and such a result, for a moment, but did not deliberate. He withdrew his hazel eyes from the scene without, calmly turned, rang the bell for assistance, and vigorously exerted himself to learn if life still lingered in that motionless frame. In a short time another surgeon was in attendance; and then Barnet's surmise proved to be true. The slow life timidly heaved again; but much care and patience were needed to catch and retain it, and a considerable period elapsed before it could be said with certainty that Mrs Barnet lived. When this was the case, and there was no further room for doubt, Barnet left the chamber. The blue evening smoke from Lucy's chimney had died down to an imperceptible stream, and as he walked about downstairs he murmured to himself, 'My wife was dead, and she is alive again.'

It was not so with Downe. After three hours' immersion his wife's body had been recovered, life, of course, being quite extinct. Barnet, on descending, went straight to his friend's house, and there learned the result. Downe was helpless in his wild grief, occasionally even hysterical. Barnet said little, but finding that some guiding hand was necessary in the sorrow-stricken household, took upon him to supervise and manage till Downe should be in a state of mind to do so for himself.

VI

One September evening, four months later, when Mrs Barnet was in perfect health, and Mrs Downe but a weakening memory, an errand-boy paused to rest himself in front of Mr Barnet's old house, depositing his basket on one of the window-sills. The street was not yet lighted, but there were lights in the house, and at intervals a flitting shadow fell upon the blind at his elbow. Words also were audible from the same apartment, and they seemed to be those of persons in violent alter-cation. But the boy could not gather their purport, and he went on his way.

Ten minutes afterwards the door of Barnet's house opened, and a tall closely-veiled lady in a travelling-dress came out and descended the freestone steps. The servant stood in the doorway watching her as she went with a measured tread down the street. When she had been out of sight for some minutes Barnet appeared at the door from within.

'Did your mistress leave word where she was going?' he asked.

'No, sir.'

'Is the carriage ordered to meet her anywhere?'

'No, sir.'

'Did she take a latch-key?'

'No, sir.'

Barnet went in again, sat down in his chair, and leaned back. Then in solitude and silence he brooded over the bitter emotions that filled his heart. It was for this that he had gratuitously restored her to life, and made his union with another impossible! The evening drew on, and nobody came to disturb him. At bedtime he told the servants to retire, that he would sit up for Mrs Barnet himself; and when they were gone he leaned his head upon his hand and mused for hours.

The clock struck one, two; still his wife came not, and, with impatience added to depression, he went from room to room till another weary hour had passed. This was not altogether a new experience for Barnet; but she had never before so prolonged her absence. At last he sat down again and fell asleep.

He awoke at six o'clock to find that she had not returned. In searching about the rooms he discovered that she had taken a case of jewels which had been hers before her marriage. At eight a note was brought him; it was from his wife, in which she stated that she had gone by the coach to the house of a distant relative near London, and expressed a wish that certain boxes, articles of clothing, and so on, might be sent to her forthwith. The note was brought to him by a waiter at the Black-Bull Hotel, and had been written by Mrs Barnet immediately before she took her place in the stage.

By the evening this order was carried out, and Barnet, with a sense of relief, walked out into the town. A fair had been held during the day, and the large clear moon which rose over the most prominent hill flung its light upon the booths and standings that still remained in the street, mixing its rays curiously with those from the flaring naphtha lamps. The town was full of country-people who had come in to enjoy themselves, and on this account Barnet strolled through the streets unobserved. With a certain recklessness he made for the harbour-road, and presently found himself by the shore, where he walked on till he came to the spot near which his friend the kindly Mrs Downe had lost her life, and his own wife's life had been preserved. A tremulous pathway of bright moonshine now stretched over the water which had engulfed them, and not a living soul was near.

Here he ruminated on their characters, and next on the young girl in whom he now took a more sensitive interest than at the time when he had been free to marry her. Nothing, so far as he was aware, had ever

appeared in his own conduct to show that such an interest existed. He
had made it a point of the utmost strictness to hinder that feeling from
influencing in the faintest degree his attitude towards his wife; and this
was made all the more easy for him by the small demand Mrs Barnet
made upon his attentions, for which she ever evinced the greatest con-
tempt; thus unwittingly giving him the satisfaction of knowing that
their severance owed nothing to jealousy, or, indeed, to any personal
behaviour of his at all. Her concern was not with him or his feelings, as
she frequently told him; but that she had, in a moment of weakness,
thrown herself away upon a common burgher when she might have
aimed at, and possibly brought down, a peer of the realm. Her frequent
depreciation of Barnet in these terms had at times been so intense that he
was sorely tempted to retaliate on her egotism by owning that he loved
at the same low level on which he lived; but prudence had prevailed, for
which he was now thankful.

Something seemed to sound upon the shingle behind him over and
above the raking of the wave. He looked round, and a slight girlish
shape appeared quite close to him. He could not see her face because it
was in the direction of the moon.

'Mr Barnet?' the rambler said, in timid surprise. The voice was the
voice of Lucy Savile.

'Yes,' said Barnet. 'How can I repay you for this pleasure?'

'I only came because the night was so clear. I am now on my way
home.'

'I am glad we have met. I want to know if you will let me do something for you, to give me an occupation, as an idle man? I am sure I
ought to help you, for I know you are almost without friends.'

She hesitated. 'Why should you tell me that?' she said.

'In the hope that you will be frank with me.'

'I am not altogether without friends here. But I am going to make a
little change in my life – to go out as a teacher of freehand drawing and
practical perspective, of course I mean on a comparatively humble scale,
because I have not been specially educated for that profession. But I am
sure I shall like it much.'

'You have an opening?'

'I have not exactly got it, but I have advertised for one.'

'Lucy, you must let me help you!'

'Not at all.'

'You need not think it would compromise you, or that I am indifferent to delicacy. I bear in mind how we stand. It is very unlikely that you will succeed as teacher of the class you mention, so let me do something of a different kind for you. Say what you would like, and it shall be done.'

'No; if I can't be a drawing-mistress or governess, or something of that sort, I shall go to India and join my brother.'

'I wish I could go abroad, anywhere, everywhere with you, Lucy, and leave this place and its associations for ever!'

She played with the end of her bonnet-string, and hastily turned aside. 'Don't ever touch upon that kind of topic again,' she said, with a quick severity not free from anger. 'It simply makes it impossible for me to see you, much less receive any guidance from you. No, thank you, Mr Barnet; you can do nothing for me at present; and as I suppose my uncertainty will end in my leaving for India, I fear you never will. If ever I think you *can* do anything, I will take the trouble to ask you. Till then, good-bye.'

The tone of her latter words was equivocal, and while he remained in doubt whether a gentle irony was or was not inwrought with their sound, she swept lightly round and left him alone. He saw her form get smaller and smaller along the damp belt of sea-sand between ebb and flood, and when she had vanished round the cliff into the harbour-road he himself followed in the same direction.

That her hopes from an advertisement should be the single thread which held Lucy Savile in England was too much for Barnet. On reaching the town he went straight to the residence of Downe, now a widower with four children. The young motherless brood had been sent to bed about a quarter of an hour earlier, and when Barnet entered he found Downe sitting alone. It was the same room as that from which the family had been looking out for Downe at the beginning of the year, when Downe had slipped into the gutter and his wife had been so enviably tender towards him. The old neatness had gone from the house; articles lay in places which could show no reason for their presence, as if momentarily deposited there some months ago, and forgotten ever since; there were no flowers; things were jumbled together on the furniture which should have been in cupboards; and the place in general had that stagnant, unrenovated air which usually pervades the maimed home of the widower.

Downe soon renewed his customary full-worded lament over his wife, and even when he had worked himself up to tears, went on volubly, as if a listener were a luxury to be enjoyed whenever he could be caught.

'She was a treasure beyond compare, Mr Barnet! I shall never see such another. Nobody now to nurse me – nobody to console me in those daily troubles, you know, Barnet, which make consolation so necessary to a nature like mine. It would be unbecoming to repine, for her spirit's home was elsewhere – the tender light in her eyes always showed it; but it is a long dreary time that I have before me, and nobody else can ever fill the void left in my heart by her loss – nobody – nobody!' And Downe wiped his eyes again.

'She was a good woman in the highest sense,' gravely answered Barnet, who, though Downe's words drew genuine compassion from his heart, could not help feeling that a tender reticence would have been a finer tribute to Mrs Downe's really sterling virtues than such a second-class lament as this.

'I have something to show you,' Downe resumed, producing from a drawer a sheet of paper on which was an elaborate design for a canopied tomb. 'This has been sent me by the architect, but it is not exactly what I want.'

'You have got Jones to do it, I see, the man who is carrying out my house,' said Barnet, as he glanced at the signature to the drawing.

'Yes, but it is not quite what I want. I want something more striking – more like a tomb I have seen in St Paul's Cathedral. Nothing less will do justice to my feelings, and how far short of them that will fall!'

Barnet privately thought the design a sufficiently imposing one as it stood, even extravagantly ornate; but, feeling that he had no right to criticize, he said gently, 'Downe, should you not live more in your children's lives at the present time, and soften the sharpness of regret for your own past by thinking of their future?'

'Yes, yes; but what can I do more?' asked Downe, wrinkling his forehead hopelessly.

It was with anxious slowness that Barnet produced his reply – the secret object of his visit to-night. 'Did you not say one day that you ought by right to get a governess for the children?'

Downe admitted that he had said so, but that he could not see his way to it. 'The kind of woman I should like to have,' he said, 'would be rather beyond my means. No; I think I shall send them to school in the town when they are old enough to go out alone.'

'Now, I know of something better than that. The late Lieutenant Savile's daughter, Lucy, wants to do something for herself in the way of teaching. She would be inexpensive, and would answer your purpose as well as anybody for six or twelve months. She would probably come daily if you were to ask her, and so your housekeeping arrangements would not be much affected.'

'I thought she had gone away,' said the solicitor, musing. 'Where does she live?'

Barnet told him, and added that, if Downe should think of her as suitable, he would do well to call as soon as possible, or she might be on the wing. 'If you do see her,' he said, 'it would be advisable not to mention my name. She is rather stiff in her ideas of me, and it might prejudice her against a course if she knew that I recommended it.'

Downe promised to give the subject his consideration, and nothing more was said about it just then. But when Barnet rose to go, which was not till nearly bedtime, he reminded Downe of the suggestion and went up the street to his own solitary home with a sense of satisfaction at his promising diplomacy in a charitable cause.

VII

The walls of his new house were carried up nearly to their full height. By a curious though not infrequent reaction, Barnet's feelings about that unnecessary structure had undergone a change; he took considerable interest in its progress as a long-neglected thing, his wife before her departure having grown quite weary of it as a hobby. Moreover, it was an excellent distraction for a man in the unhappy position of having to live in a provincial town with nothing to do. He was probably the first of his line who had ever passed a day without toil, and perhaps something like an inherited instinct disqualifies such men for a life of pleasant inaction, such as lies in the power of those whose leisure is not a personal accident, but a vast historical accretion which has become part of their natures.

Thus Barnet got into a way of spending many of his leisure hours on the site of the new building, and he might have been seen on most days at this time trying the temper of the mortar by punching the joints with his stick, looking at the grain of a floor-board, and meditating where it grew, or picturing under what circumstances the last fire would be kindled in the at present sootless chimneys. One day when thus occupied he saw three children pass by in the company of a fair young woman, whose sudden appearance caused him to flush perceptibly.

'Ah, she is there,' he thought. 'That's a blessed thing.'

Casting an interested glance over the rising building and the busy workmen, Lucy Savile and the little Downes passed by; and after that time it became a regular though almost unconscious custom of Barnet to stand in the half-completed house and look from the ungarnished windows at the governess as she tripped towards the sea-shore with her young charges, which she was in the habit of doing on most fine afternoons. It was on one of these occasions, when he had been loitering on the first-floor landing, near the hole left for the staircase, not yet erected, that there appeared above the edge of the floor a little hat, followed by a little head.

Barnet withdrew through a doorway, and the child came to the top of the ladder, stepping on to the floor and crying to her sisters and Miss Savile to follow. Another head rose above the floor, and another, and then Lucy herself came into view. The troop ran hither and thither through the empty, shaving-strewn rooms, and Barnet came forward.

Lucy uttered a small exclamation: she was very sorry that she had intruded; she had not the least idea that Mr Barnet was there: the children had come up, and she had followed.

Barnet replied that he was only too glad to see them there. 'And now, let me show you the rooms,' he said.

She passively assented, and he took her round. There was not much to show in such a bare skeleton of a house, but he made the most of it, and explained the different ornamental fittings that were soon to be fixed here and there. Lucy made but few remarks in reply, though she seemed pleased with her visit, and stole away down the ladder, followed by her companions.

After this the new residence became yet more of a hobby for Barnet. Downe's children did not forget their first visit, and when the windows were glazed, and the handsome staircase spread its broad low steps into the hall, they came again, prancing in unwearied succession through every room from ground-floor to attics, while Lucy stood waiting for them at the door. Barnet, who rarely missed a day in coming to inspect progress, stepped out from the drawing-room.

'I could not keep them out,' she said, with an apologetic blush. 'I tried to do so very much; but they are rather wilful, and we are directed to walk this way for the sea air.'

'Do let them make the house their regular playground, and you yours,' said Barnet. 'There is no better place for children to romp and take their exercise in than an empty house, particularly in muddy or damp weather such as we shall get a good deal of now; and this place will not be furnished for a long long time – perhaps never. I am not at all decided about it.'

'O, but it must!' replied Lucy, looking round at the hall. 'The rooms are excellent, twice as high as ours, and the views from the windows are so lovely.'

'I daresay, I daresay,' he said absently.

'Will all the furniture be new?' she asked.

'All the furniture be new – that's a thing I have not thought of. In fact, I only come here and look on. My father's house would have been large enough for me, but another person had a voice in the matter, and it was settled that we should build. However, the place grows upon me; its recent associations are cheerful, and I am getting to like it fast.'

A certain uneasiness in Lucy's manner showed that the conversation was taking too personal a turn for her. 'Still, as modern tastes develop, people require more room to gratify them in,' she said, withdrawing to call the children; and serenely bidding him good-afternoon she went on her way.

Barnet's life at this period was singularly lonely, and yet he was happier than he could have expected. His wife's estrangement and absence, which promised to be permanent, left him free as a boy in his movements, and the solitary walks that he took gave him ample opportunity for chastened reflection on what might have been his lot if he had only shown wisdom enough to claim Lucy Savile when there was no bar between their lives, and she was to be had for the asking. He would occasionally call at the house of his friend Downe; but there was scarcely enough in common between their two natures to make them more than friends of that excellent sort whose personal knowledge of each other's history and character is always in excess of intimacy, whereby they are not so likely to be severed by a clash of sentiment as in cases where intimacy springs up in excess of knowledge. Lucy was never visible at these times, being either engaged in the school-room, or in taking an airing out of doors; but, knowing that she was now comfortable, and had given up the, to him, depressing idea of going off to the other side of the globe, he was quite content.

The new house had so far progressed that the gardeners were beginning to grass down the front. During an afternoon which he was passing in marking the curve for the carriage-drive, he beheld her coming

in boldly towards him from the road. Hitherto Barnet had only caught
her on the premises by stealth; and this advance seemed to show that at
last her reserve had broken down.

A smile gained strength upon her face as she approached, and it was
quite radiant when she came up, and said, without a trace of embarrassment, 'I find I owe you a hundred thanks – and it comes to me quite as a
surprise! It was through your kindness that I was engaged by Mr
Downe. Believe me, Mr Barnet, I did not know it until yesterday, or I
should have thanked you long and long ago!'

'I had offended you – just a trifle – at the time, I think?' said Barnet,
smiling, 'and it was best that you should not know.'

'Yes, yes,' she returned hastily. 'Don't allude to that; it is past and
over, and we will let it be. The house is finished almost, is it not? How
beautiful it will look when the evergreens are grown! Do you call the
style Palladian, Mr Barnet?'

'I – really don't quite know what it is. Yes, it must be Palladian,
certainly. But I'll ask Jones, the architect; for, to tell the truth, I had not
thought much about the style: I had nothing to do with choosing it, I
am sorry to say.'

She would not let him harp on this gloomy refrain, and talked on
bright matters till she said, producing a small roll of paper which he had
noticed in her hand all the while, 'Mr Downe wished me to bring you
this revised drawing of the late Mrs Downe's tomb, which the architect
has just sent him. He would like you to look it over.'

The children came up with their hoops, and she went off with them
down the harbour-road as usual. Barnet had been glad to get those
words of thanks; he had been thinking for many months that he would
like her to know of his share in finding her a home such as it was; and
what he could not do for himself, Downe had now kindly done for him.
He returned to his desolate house with a lighter tread; though in reason
he hardly knew why his tread should be light.

On examining the drawing, Barnet found that, instead of the vast
altar-tomb and canopy Downe had determined on at their last meeting,
it was to be a more modest memorial even than had been suggested by
the architect; a coped tomb of good solid construction, with no useless
elaboration at all. Barnet was truly glad to see that Downe had come to
reason of his own accord; and he returned the drawing with a note of
approval.

He followed up the house-work as before, and as he walked up and

down the rooms, occasionally gazing from the windows over the bulging
green hills and the quiet harbour that lay between them, he murmured
words and fragments of words which, if listened to, would have revealed
all the secrets of his existence. Whatever his reason in going there, Lucy
did not call again: the walk to the shore seemed to be abandoned: he
must have thought it as well for both that it should be so, for he did not
go anywhere out of his accustomed ways to endeavour to discover her.

VIII

The winter and the spring had passed, and the house was complete. It
was a fine morning in the early part of June, and Barnet, though not in
the habit of rising early, had taken a long walk before breakfast; returning by way of the new building. A sufficiently exciting cause of his
restlessness to-day might have been the intelligence which had reached
him the night before, that Lucy Savile was going to India after all, and
notwithstanding the representations of her friends that such a journey
was unadvisable in many ways for an unpractised girl, unless some more
definite advantage lay at the end of it than she could show to be the case.
Barnet's walk up the slope to the building betrayed that he was in a
dissatisfied mood. He hardly saw that the dewy time of day lent an
unusual freshness to the bushes and trees which had so recently put on
their summer habit of heavy leafage, and made his newly-laid lawn look
as well established as an old manorial meadow. The house had been so
adroitly placed between six tall elms which were growing on the site
beforehand, that they seemed like real ancestral trees; and the rooks,
young and old, cawed melodiously to their visitor.

   The door was not locked, and he entered. No workmen appeared to be
present, and he walked from sunny window to sunny window of the
empty rooms, with a sense of seclusion which might have been very
pleasant but for the antecedent knowledge that his almost paternal care of
Lucy Savile was to be thrown away by her wilfulness. Footsteps echoed
through an adjoining room; and bending his eyes in that direction, he
perceived Mr Jones, the architect. He had come to look over the building
before giving the contractor his final certificate. They walked over the
house together. Everything was finished except the papering: there
were the latest improvements of the period in bell-hanging, ventilating,
smoke-jacks, fire-grates, and French windows. The business was soon

ended, and Jones, having directed Barnet's attention to a book of wall-paper patterns which lay on a bench for his choice, was leaving to keep another engagement, when Barnet said, 'Is the tomb finished yet for Mrs Downe?'

'Well – yes: it is at last,' said the architect, coming back and speaking as if he were in a mood to make a confidence. 'I have had no end of trouble in the matter, and, to tell the truth, I am heartily glad it is over.'

Barnet expressed his surprise. 'I thought poor Downe had given up those extravagant notions of his? Then he has gone back to the altar and canopy after all? Well, he is to be excused, poor fellow!'

'O no – he has not at all gone back to them – quite the reverse,' Jones hastened to say. 'He has so reduced design after design that the whole thing has been nothing but waste labour for me; till in the end it has become a common headstone, which a mason put up in half a day.'

'A common headstone?' said Barnet.

'Yes. I held out for some time for the addition of a footstone at least. But he said, "O no – he couldn't afford it." '

'Ah, well – his family is growing up, poor fellow, and his expenses are getting serious.'

'Yes, exactly,' said Jones, as if the subject were none of his. And again directing Barnet's attention to the wall-papers, the bustling architect left him to keep some other engagement.

'A common headstone,' murmured Barnet, left again to himself. He mused a minute or two, and next began looking over and selecting from the patterns; but had not long been engaged in the work when he heard another footstep on the gravel without, and somebody enter the open porch.

Barnet went to the door – it was his manservant in search of him.

'I have been trying for some time to find you, sir,' he said. 'This letter has come by the post, and it is marked immediate. And there's this one from Mr Downe, who called just now wanting to see you.' He searched his pocket for the second.

Barnet took the first letter – it had a black border, and bore the London postmark. It was not in his wife's handwriting, or in that of any person he knew; but conjecture soon ceased as he read the page, wherein he was briefly informed that Mrs Barnet had died suddenly on the previous day, at the furnished villa she had occupied near London.

Barnet looked vaguely round the empty hall, at the blank walls, out of the doorway. Drawing a long palpitating breath, and with eyes down-

cast, he turned and climbed the stairs slowly, like a man who doubted
their stability. The fact of his wife having, as it were, died once already,
and lived on again, had entirely dislodged the possibility of her actual
death from his conjecture. He went to the landing, leant over the
balusters, and after a reverie, of whose duration he had but the faintest
notion, turned to the window and stretched his gaze to the cottage
further down the road, which was visible from his landing, and from
which Lucy still walked to the solicitor's house by a cross path. The
faint words that came from his moving lips were simply, 'At last!'

Then, almost involuntarily, Barnet fell down on his knees and murmured some incoherent words of thanksgiving. Surely his virtue in
restoring his wife to life had been rewarded! But, as if the impulse struck
uneasily on his conscience, he quickly rose, brushed the dust from his
trousers, and set himself to think of his next movements. He could not
start for London for some hours; and as he had no preparations to make
that could not be made in half-an-hour, he mechanically descended and
resumed his occupation of turning over the wall-papers. They had all got
brighter for him, those papers. It was all changed – who would sit in
the rooms that they were to line? He went on to muse upon Lucy's
conduct in so frequently coming to the house with the children; her
occasional blush in speaking to him; her evident interest in him. What
woman can in the long run avoid being interested in a man whom she
knows to be devoted to her? If human solicitation could ever effect
anything, there should be no going to India for Lucy now. All the papers
previously chosen seemed wrong in their shades, and he began from the
beginning to choose again.

While entering on the task he heard a forced 'Ahem!' from without the
porch, evidently uttered to attract his attention, and footsteps again
advancing to the door. His man, whom he had quite forgotten in his
mental turmoil, was still waiting there.

'I beg your pardon, sir,' the man said from round the doorway; 'but
here's the note from Mr Downe that you didn't take. He called just
after you went out, and as he couldn't wait, he wrote this on your study-
table.'

He handed in the letter – no black-bordered one now, but a practical-
looking note in the well-known writing of the solicitor.

'DEAR BARNET' – it ran – 'Perhaps you will be prepared for the
information I am about to give – that Lucy Savile and myself are
going to be married this morning. I have hitherto said nothing as

to my intention to any of my friends, for reasons which I am sure you will fully appreciate. The crisis has been brought about by her expressing her intention to join her brother in India. I then discovered that I could not do without her.

'It is to be quite a private wedding; but it is my particular wish that you come down here quietly at ten, and go to church with us; it will add greatly to the pleasure I shall experience in the ceremony, and, I believe, to Lucy's also. I have called on you very early to make the request, in the belief that I should find you at home; but you are beforehand with me in your early rising. – Yours sincerely,
C. DOWNE'

'Need I wait, sir?' said the servant after a dead silence.

'That will do, William. No answer,' said Barnet calmly.

When the man had gone Barnet re-read the letter. Turning eventually to the wall-papers, which he had been at such pains to select, he deliberately tore them into halves and quarters, and threw them into the empty fireplace. Then he went out of the house, locked the door, and stood in the front awhile. Instead of returning into the town, he went down the harbour-road and thoughtfully lingered about by the sea, near the spot where the body of Downe's late wife had been found and brought ashore.

Barnet was a man with a rich capacity for misery, and there is no doubt that he exercised it to its fullest extent now. The events that had, as it were, dashed themselves together into one half-hour of this day showed that curious refinement of cruelty in their arrangement which often proceeds from the bosom of the whimsical god at other times known as blind Circumstance. That his few minutes of hope, between the reading of the first and second letters, had carried him to extraordinary heights of rapture was proved by the immensity of his suffering now. The sun blazing into his face would have shown a close watcher that a horizontal line, which had never been seen before, but which was never to be gone thereafter, was somehow gradually forming itself in the smooth of his forehead. His eyes, of a light hazel, had a curious look which can only be described by the word bruised; the sorrow that looked from them being largely mixed with the surprise of a man taken unawares.

The secondary particulars of his present position, too, were odd enough, though for some time they appeared to engage little of his attention. Not a soul in the town knew, as yet, of his wife's death; and he almost owed Downe the kindness of not publishing it till the day was over: the conjuncture, taken with that which had accompanied the death of Mrs Downe, being so singular as to be quite sufficient to darken the pleasure of the impressionable solicitor to a cruel extent, if made known to him. But as Barnet could not set out on his journey to London, where his wife lay, for some hours (there being at this date no railway within a distance of many miles), no great reason existed why he should leave the town.

Impulse in all its forms characterized Barnet, and when he heard the distant clock strike the hour of ten his feet began to carry him up the harbour-road with the manner of a man who must do something to bring himself to life. He passed Lucy Savile's old house, his own new one, and came in view of the church. Now he gave a perceptible start, and his mechanical condition went away. Before the church-gate were a couple of carriages, and Barnet then could perceive that the marriage between Downe and Lucy was at that moment being solemnized within. A feeling of sudden, proud self-confidence, an indocile wish to walk unmoved in spite of grim environments, plainly possessed him, and when he reached the wicket-gate he turned in without apparent effort. Pacing up the paved footway he entered the church and stood for awhile in the nave passage. A group of people was standing round the vestry door; Barnet advanced through these and stepped into the vestry.

There they were, busily signing their names. Seeing Downe about to look round Barnet averted his somewhat disturbed face for a second or two; when he turned again front to front he was calm and quite smiling; it was a creditable triumph over himself, and deserved to be remembered in his native town. He greeted Downe heartily, offering his congratulations.

It seemed as if Barnet expected a half-guilty look upon Lucy's face; but no; save the natural flush and flurry engendered by the service just performed, there was nothing whatever in her bearing which showed a disturbed mind: her gray-brown eyes carried in them now as at other times the well-known expression of common-sensed rectitude which never went so far as to touch on hardness. She shook hands with him, and Downe said warmly, 'I wish you could have come sooner: I called on purpose to ask you. You'll drive back with us now?'

'No, no,' said Barnet; 'I am not at all prepared; but I thought I would look in upon you for a moment, even though I had not time to go home and dress. I'll stand back and see you pass out, and observe the effect of the spectacle upon myself as one of the public.'

Then Lucy and her husband laughed, and Barnet laughed and retired; and the quiet little party went gliding down the nave and towards the porch, Lucy's new silk dress sweeping with a smart rustle round the base-mouldings of the ancient font, and Downe's little daughters following in a state of round-eyed interest in their position, and that of Lucy, their teacher and friend.

So Downe was comforted after his Emily's death, which had taken place twelve months, two weeks, and three days before that time.

When the two flys had driven off and the spectators had vanished, Barnet followed to the door, and went out into the sun. He took no more trouble to preserve a spruce exterior; his step was unequal, hesitating, almost convulsive; and the slight changes of colour which went on in his face seemed refracted from some inward flame. In the churchyard he became pale as a summer cloud, and finding it not easy to proceed he sat down on one of the tombstones and supported his head with his hand.

Hard by was a sexton filling up a grave which he had not found time to finish on the previous evening. Observing Barnet, he went up to him, and recognizing him, said, 'Shall I help you home, sir?'

'O no, thank you,' said Barnet, rousing himself and standing up. The sexton returned to his grave, followed by Barnet, who, after watching him awhile, stepped into the grave, now nearly filled, and helped to tread in the earth.

The sexton apparently thought his conduct a little singular, but he made no observation, and when the grave was full, Barnet suddenly stopped, looked far away, and with a decided step proceeded to the gate and vanished. The sexton rested on his shovel and looked after him for a few moments, and then began banking up the mound.

In those short minutes of treading in the dead man Barnet had formed a design, but what it was the inhabitants of that town did not for some long time imagine. He went home, wrote several letters of business, called on his lawyer, an old man of the same place who had been the legal adviser of Barnet's father before him, and during the evening overhauled a large quantity of letters and other documents in his possession. By eleven o'clock the heap of papers in and before Barnet's grate had reached formidable dimensions, and he began to burn them. This, owing to their quantity, it was not so easy to do as he had expected, and he sat long into the night to complete the task.

The next morning Barnet departed for London, leaving a note for Downe to inform him of Mrs Barnet's sudden death, and that he was

gone to bury her; but when a thrice-sufficient time for that purpose had
elapsed, he was not seen again in his accustomed walks, or in his new
house, or in his old one. He was gone for good, nobody knew whither. It
was soon discovered that he had empowered his lawyer to dispose of all
his property, real and personal, in the borough, and pay in the proceeds
to the account of an unknown person at one of the large London banks.
The person was by some supposed to be himself under an assumed
name; but few, if any, had certain knowledge of that fact.

The elegant new residence was sold with the rest of his possessions;
and its purchaser was no other than Downe, now a thriving man in the
borough, and one whose growing family and new wife required more
roomy accommodation than was afforded by the little house up the
narrow side street. Barnet's old habitation was bought by the trustees of
the Congregational Baptist body in that town, who pulled down the
time-honoured dwelling and built a new chapel on its site. By the time
the last hour of that, to Barnet, eventful year had chimed, every vestige
of him had disappeared from the precincts of his native place, and the
name became extinct in the borough of Port-Bredy, after having been a
living force therein for more than two hundred years.

IX

Twenty-one years and six months do not pass without setting a mark
even upon durable stone and triple brass; upon humanity such a period
works nothing less than transformation. In Barnet's old birthplace
vivacious young children with bones like india-rubber had grown up to
be stable men and women, men and women had dried in the skin,
stiffened, withered, and sunk into decrepitude; while selections from
every class had been consigned to the outlying cemetery. Of inorganic
differences the greatest was that a railway had invaded the town, tying it
on to a main line at a junction a dozen miles off. Barnet's house on the
harbour-road, once so insistently new, had acquired a respectable
mellowness, with ivy, Virginia creepers, lichens, damp patches, and
even constitutional infirmities of its own like its elder fellows. Its
architecture, once so very improved and modern, had already become
stale in style, without having reached the dignity of being old-fashioned.
Trees about the harbour-road had increased in circumference or
disappeared under the saw; while the church had had such a tremendous

practical joke played upon it by some facetious restorer or other as to be scarce recognizable by its dearest old friends.

During this long interval George Barnet had never once been seen or heard of in the town of his fathers.

It was the evening of a market-day, and some half-dozen middle-aged farmers and dairymen were lounging round the bar of the Black-Bull Hotel, occasionally dropping a remark to each other, and less frequently to the two barmaids who stood within the pewter-topped counter in a perfunctory attitude of attention, these latter sighing and making a private observation to one another at odd intervals, on more interesting experiences than the present.

'Days get shorter,' said one of the dairymen, as he looked towards the street, and noticed that the lamplighter was passing by.

The farmers merely acknowledged by their countenances the propriety of this remark, and finding that nobody else spoke, one of the barmaids said 'yes', in a tone of painful duty.

'Come fair-day we shall have to light up before we start for home-along.'

'That's true,' his neighbour conceded, with a gaze of blankness.

'And after that we shan't see much further difference all's winter.'

The rest were not unwilling to go even so far as this.

The barmaid sighed again, and raised one of her hands from the counter on which they rested to scratch the smallest surface of her face with the smallest of her fingers. She looked towards the door, and presently remarked, 'I think I hear the 'bus coming in from station.'

The eyes of the dairymen and farmers turned to the glass door dividing the hall from the porch, and in a minute or two the omnibus drew up outside. Then there was a lumbering down of luggage, and then a man came into the hall, followed by a porter with a portmanteau on his poll, which he deposited on a bench.

The stranger was an elderly person, with curly ashen-white hair, a deeply-creviced outer corner to each eyelid, and a countenance baked by innumerable suns to the colour of terra-cotta, its hue and that of his hair contrasting like heat and cold respectively. He walked meditatively and gently, like one who was fearful of disturbing his own mental equilibrium. But whatever lay at the bottom of his breast had evidently made him so accustomed to its situation there that it caused him little practical inconvenience.

He paused in silence while, with his dubious eyes fixed on the barmaids, he seemed to consider himself. In a moment or two he addressed them, and asked to be accommodated for the night. As he waited he looked curiously round the hall, but said nothing. As soon as invited he disappeared up the staircase, preceded by a chambermaid and candle, and followed by a lad with his trunk. Not a soul had recognized him.

A quarter of an hour later, when the farmers and dairymen had driven off to their homesteads in the country, he came downstairs, took a biscuit and one glass of wine, and walked out into the town, where the radiance from the shop-windows had grown so in volume of late years as to flood with cheerfulness every standing cart, barrow, stall, and idler that occupied the wayside, whether shabby or genteel. His chief interest at present seemed to lie in the names painted over the shop-fronts and on doorways, as far as they were visible; these now differed to an ominous extent from what they had been one-and-twenty years before.

The traveller passed on till he came to the bookseller's, where he looked in through the glass door. A fresh-faced young man was standing behind the counter, otherwise the shop was empty. The gray-haired observer entered, asked for some periodical by way of paying for admission, and with his elbow on the counter began to turn over the pages he had bought, though that he read nothing was obvious.

At length he said, 'Is old Mr Watkins still alive?' in a voice which had a curious youthful cadence in it even now.

'My father is dead, sir,' said the young man.

'Ah, I am sorry to hear it,' said the stranger. 'But it is so many years since I last visited this town that I could hardly expect it should be otherwise.' After a short silence he continued – 'And is the firm of Barnet, Browse and Company still in existence? – they used to be large flax-merchants and twine-spinners here?'

'The firm is still going on, sir, but they have dropped the name of Barnet. I believe that was a sort of fancy name – at least, I never knew of any living Barnet. 'Tis now Browse and Co.'

'And does Andrew Jones still keep on as architect?'

'He's dead, sir.'

'And the vicar of St Mary's – Mr Melrose?'

'He's been dead a great many years.'

'Dear me!' He paused yet longer, and cleared his voice. 'Is Mr Downe, the solicitor, still in practice?'

'No, sir, he's dead. He died about seven years ago.'

Here it was a longer silence still; and an attentive observer would have noticed that the paper in the stranger's hand increased its imperceptible tremor to a visible shake. That gray-haired gentleman noticed it himself, and rested the paper on the counter. 'Is *Mrs* Downe still alive?' he asked, closing his lips firmly as soon as the words were out of his mouth, and dropping his eyes.

'Yes, sir, she's alive and well. She's living at the old place.'

'In East Street?'

'O no; at Château Ringdale. I believe it has been in the family for some generations.'

'She lives with her children, perhaps?'

'No; she has no children of her own. There were some Miss Downes; I think they were Mr Downe's daughters by a former wife; but they are married and living in other parts of the town. Mrs Downe lives alone.'

'Quite alone?'

'Yes, sir; quite alone.'

The newly-arrived gentleman went back to the hotel and dined; after which he made some change in his dress, shaved back his beard to the fashion that had prevailed twenty years earlier, when he was young and interesting, and once more emerging, bent his steps in the direction of the harbour-road. Just before getting to the point where the pavement ceased and the houses isolated themselves, he overtook a shambling, stooping, unshaven man, who at first sight appeared like a professional tramp, his shoulders having a perceptible greasiness as they passed under the gaslight. Each pedestrian momentarily turned and regarded the other, and the tramp-like gentleman started back.

'Good – why – is that Mr Barnet? 'Tis Mr Barnet, surely!'

'Yes; and you are Charlson?'

'Yes – ah – you notice my appearance. The Fates have rather ill-used me. By-the-bye, that fifty pounds. I never paid it, did I? . . . But I was not ungrateful!' Here the stooping man laid one hand emphatically on the palm of the other. 'I gave you a chance, Mr George Barnet, which many men would have thought full value received – the chance to marry your Lucy. As far as the world was concerned, your wife was a *drowned woman*, hey?'

'Heaven forbid all that, Charlson!'

'Well, well, 'twas a wrong way of showing gratitude, I suppose. And now a drop of something to drink for old acquaintance' sake! And, Mr

Barnet, she's again free – there's a chance now if you care for it – ha, ha!'
And the speaker pushed his tongue into his hollow cheek and slanted his
eye in the old fashion.

'I know all,' said Barnet quickly; and slipping a small present into the
hands of the needy, saddening man, he stepped ahead and was soon in
the outskirts of the town.

He reached the harbour-road, and paused before the entrance to a
well-known house. It was so highly bosomed in trees and shrubs
planted since the erection of the building that one would scarcely have
recognized the spot as that which had been a mere neglected slope till
chosen as a site for a dwelling. He opened the swing-gate, closed it
noiselessly, and gently moved into the semicircular drive, which remained exactly as it had been marked out by Barnet on the morning
when Lucy Savile ran in to thank him for procuring her the post of
governess to Downe's children. But the growth of trees and bushes
which revealed itself at every step was beyond all expectation; sun-
proof and moon-proof bowers vaulted the walks, and the walls of the
house were uniformly bearded with creeping plants as high as the first-
floor windows.

After lingering for a few minutes in the dusk of the bending boughs,
the visitor rang the door-bell, and on the servant appearing, he announced
himself as 'an old friend of Mrs Downe's'.

The hall was lighted, but not brightly, the gas being turned low, as if
visitors were rare. There was a stagnation in the dwelling; it seemed to
be waiting. Could it really be waiting for him? The partitions which had
been probed by Barnet's walking-stick when the mortar was green, were
now quite brown with the antiquity of their varnish, and the ornamental
woodwork of the staircase, which had glistened with a pale yellow new-
ness when first erected, was now of a rich wine-colour. During the
servant's absence the following colloquy could be dimly heard through
the nearly-closed door of the drawing-room.

'He didn't give his name?'

'He only said "an old friend", ma'am.'

'What kind of gentleman is he?'

'A staidish gentleman, with gray hair.'

The voice of the second speaker seemed to affect the listener greatly.
After a pause, the lady said, 'Very well, I will see him.'

And the stranger was shown in face to face with the Lucy who had
once been Lucy Savile. The round cheek of that formerly young lady

had, of course, alarmingly flattened its curve in her modern representative; a pervasive grayness overspread her once dark brown hair, like morning rime on heather. The parting down the middle was wide and jagged; once it had been a thin white line, a narrow crevice between two high banks of shade. But there was still enough left to form a handsome knob behind, and some curls beneath inwrought with a few hairs like silver wires were very becoming. In her eyes the only modification was that their originally mild rectitude of expression had become a little more stringent than heretofore. Yet she was still girlish – a girl who had been gratuitously weighted by destiny with a burden of five-and-forty years instead of her proper twenty.

'Lucy, don't you know me?' he said, when the servant had closed the door.

'I knew you the instant I saw you!' she returned cheerfully. 'I don't know why, but I always thought you would come back to your old town again.'

She gave him her hand, and then they sat down. 'They said you were dead,' continued Lucy, 'but I never thought so. We should have heard of it for certain if you had been.'

'It is a very long time since we met.'

'Yes; what you must have seen, Mr Barnet, in all these roving years, in comparison with what I have seen in this quiet place!' Her face grew more serious. 'You know my husband has been dead a long time? I am a lonely old woman now, considering what I have been; though Mr Downe's daughters – all married – manage to keep me pretty cheerful.'

'And I am a lonely old man, and have been any time these twenty years.'

'But where have you kept yourself? And why did you go off so mysteriously?'

'Well, Lucy, I have kept myself a little in America, and a little in Australia, a little in India, a little at the Cape, and so on; I have not stayed in any place for a long time, as it seems to me, and yet more than twenty years have flown. But when people get to my age two years go like one! – Your second question, why did I go away so mysteriously, is surely not necessary. You guessed why, didn't you?'

'No, I never once guessed,' she said simply; 'nor did Charles, nor did anybody as far as I know.'

'Well, indeed! Now think it over again, and then look at me, and say if you can't guess?'

She looked him in the face with an inquiring smile. 'Surely not because of me?' she said, pausing at the commencement of surprise.

Barnet nodded, and smiled again; but his smile was sadder than hers. 'Because I married Charles?' she asked.

'Yes; solely because you married him on the day I was free to ask you to marry me. My wife died four-and-twenty hours before you went to church with Downe. The fixing of my journey at that particular moment was because of her funeral; but once away I knew I should have no inducement to come back, and took my steps accordingly.'

Her face assumed an aspect of gentle reflection, and she looked up and down his form with great interest in her eyes. 'I never thought of it!' she said. 'I knew, of course, that you had once implied some warmth of feeling towards me, but I concluded that it passed off. And I have always been under the impression that your wife was alive at the time of my marriage. Was it not stupid of me! – But you will have some tea or something? I have never dined late, you know, since my husband's death. I have got into the way of making a regular meal of tea. You will have some tea with me, will you not?'

The travelled man assented quite readily, and tea was brought in. They sat and chatted over the tray, regardless of the flying hour. 'Well, well!' said Barnet presently, as for the first time he leisurely surveyed the room; 'how like it all is, and yet how different! Just where your piano stands was a board on a couple of trestles, bearing the patterns of wall-papers, when I was last here. I was choosing them – standing in this way, as it might be. Then my servant came in at the door, and handed me a note, so. It was from Downe, and announced that you were just going to be married to him. I chose no more wall-papers – tore up all those I had selected, and left the house. I never entered it again till now.'

'Ah, at last I understand it all,' she murmured.

They had both risen and gone to the fireplace. The mantel came almost on a level with her shoulder, which gently rested against it, and Barnet laid his hand upon the shelf close beside her shoulder. 'Lucy,' he said, 'better late than never. Will you marry me now?'

She started back, and the surprise which was so obvious in her wrought even greater surprise in him that it should be so. It was difficult to believe that she had been quite blind to the situation, and yet all reason and common sense went to prove that she was not acting.

'You take me quite unawares by such a question!' she said, with a forced laugh of uneasiness. It was the first time she had shown any embarrassment at all. 'Why,' she added, 'I couldn't marry you for the world.'

'Not after all this! Why not?'

'It is – I would – I really think I may say it – I would upon the whole rather marry you, Mr Barnet, than any other man I have ever met, if I ever dreamed of marriage again. But I don't dream of it – it is quite out of my thoughts; I have not the least intention of marrying again.'

'But – on my account – couldn't you alter your plans a little? Come!'

'Dear Mr Barnet,' she said with a little flutter, 'I would on your account if on anybody's in existence. But you don't know in the least what it is you are asking – such an impracticable thing – I won't say ridiculous, of course, because I see that you are really in earnest, and earnestness is never ridiculous to my mind.'

'Well, yes,' said Barnet more slowly, dropping her hand, which he had taken at the moment of pleading, 'I am in earnest. The resolve, two months ago, at the Cape, to come back once more was, it is true, rather sudden, and as I see now, not well considered. But I am in earnest in asking.'

'And I in declining. With all good feeling and all kindness, let me say that I am quite opposed to the idea of marrying a second time.'

'Well, no harm has been done,' he answered, with the same subdued and tender humorousness that he had shown on such occasions in early life. 'If you really won't accept me, I must put up with it, I suppose.' His eye fell on the clock as he spoke. 'Had you any notion that it was so late?' he asked. 'How absorbed I have been!'

She accompanied him to the hall, helped him to put on his overcoat, and let him out of the house herself.

'Good-night,' said Barnet, on the doorstep, as the lamp shone in his face. 'You are not offended with me?'

'Certainly not. Nor you with me?'

'I'll consider whether I am or not,' he pleasantly replied. 'Good-night.'

She watched him safely through the gate; and when his footsteps had died away upon the road, closed the door softly and returned to the room. Here the modest widow long pondered his speeches, with eyes dropped to an unusually low level. Barnet's urbanity under the blow of her refusal greatly impressed her. After having his long period of probation rendered useless by her decision, he had shown no anger, and had philosophically taken her words as if he deserved no better ones. It was very gentlemanly of him, certainly; it was more than gentlemanly: it was heroic and grand. The more she meditated, the more she questioned the virtue of her conduct in checking him so peremptorily; and went to her bedroom in a mood of dissatisfaction. On looking in the glass she was reminded that there was not so much remaining of her former beauty as to make his frank declaration an impulsive natural homage to her cheeks and eyes; it must undoubtedly have arisen from an old staunch feeling of his, deserving tenderest consideration. She recalled to her mind with much pleasure that he had told her he was staying at the Black-Bull Hotel; so that if, after waiting a day or two, he should not, in his modesty, call again, she might then send him a nice little note. To alter her views for the present was far from her intention; but she would allow herself to be induced to reconsider the case, as any generous woman ought to do.

The morrow came and passed, and Mr Barnet did not drop in. At every knock, light youthful hues flew across her cheek; and she was abstracted in the presence of her other visitors. In the evening she walked about the house, not knowing what to do with herself; the conditions of existence seemed totally different from those which ruled only four-and-twenty short hours ago. What had been at first a tantalizing, elusive sentiment was getting acclimatized within her as a definite hope, and her person was so informed by that emotion that she might almost have stood as its emblematical representative by the time the clock struck ten. In short, an interest in Barnet precisely resembling that of her early youth led her present heart to belie her yesterday's words to him, and she longed to see him again.

The next day she walked out early, thinking she might meet him in the street. The growing beauty of her romance absorbed her, and she went from the street to the fields, and from the fields to the shore, without any consciousness of distance, till reminded by her weariness that she could go no further. He had nowhere appeared. In the evening she took a step which under the circumstances seemed justifiable; she wrote a note to him at the hotel, inviting him to tea with her at six precisely, and signing her note 'Lucy'.

In a quarter of an hour the messenger came back. Mr Barnet had left the hotel early in the morning of the day before, but he had stated that he would probably return in the course of the week.

The note was sent back, to be given to him immediately on his arrival. There was no sign from the inn that this desired event had occurred, either on the next day or the day following. On both nights she had been restless, and had scarcely slept half-an-hour.

On the Saturday, putting off all diffidence, Lucy went herself to the Black-Bull, and questioned the staff closely.

Mr Barnet had cursorily remarked when leaving that he might return on the Thursday or Friday, but they were directed not to reserve a room for him unless he should write.

He had left no address.

Lucy sorrowfully took back her note, went home, and resolved to wait.

She did wait – years and years – but Barnet never reappeared.

April 1880

Interlopers at the Knap

THE north road from Casterbridge is tedious and lonely, especially in winter-time. Along a part of its course it connects with Long-Ash Lane, a monotonous track without a village or hamlet for many miles, and with very seldom a turning. Unapprized wayfarers who are too old, or too young, or in other respects too weak for the distance to be traversed, but who, nevertheless, have to walk it, say, as they look wistfully ahead, 'Once at the top of that hill, and I must surely see the end of Long-Ash Lane!' But they reach the hilltop, and Long-Ash Lane stretches in front as mercilessly as before.

Some few years ago a certain farmer was riding through this lane in the gloom of a winter evening. The farmer's friend, a dairyman, was riding beside him. A few paces in the rear rode the farmer's man. All three were well horsed on strong, round-barrelled cobs; and to be well horsed was to be in better spirits about Long-Ash Lane than poor pedestrians could attain to during its passage.

But the farmer did not talk much to his friend as he rode along. The enterprise which had brought him there filled his mind; for in truth it was important. Not altogether so important was it, perhaps, when estimated by its value to society at large; but if the true measure of a deed be proportionate to the space it occupies in the heart of him who undertakes it, Farmer Charles Darton's business to-night could hold its own with the business of kings.

He was a large farmer. His turnover, as it is called, was probably thirty thousand pounds a year. He had a great many draught horses, a great many milch cows, and of sheep a multitude. This comfortable position was, however, none of his own making. It had been created by his father, a man of a very different stamp from the present representative of the line.

Darton, the father, had been a one-idea'd character, with a buttoned-up pocket and a chink-like eye brimming with commercial subtlety. In Darton the son, this trade subtlety had become transmuted into emotional, and the harshness had disappeared; he would have been called a sad man but for his constant care not to divide himself from lively friends by piping notes out of harmony with theirs. Contemplative, he allowed his mind to be a quiet meeting-place for memories and hopes. So that, naturally enough, since succeeding to the agricultural calling, and up to his present age of thirty-two, he had neither advanced nor receded as a capitalist – a stationary result which did not agitate one of his unambitious, unstrategic nature, since he had all that he desired. The motive of his expedition to-night showed the same absence of anxious regard for Number One.

The party rode on in the slow, safe trot proper to night-time and bad roads, Farmer Darton's head jigging rather unromantically up and down against the sky, and his motions being repeated with bolder emphasis by his friend Japheth Johns; while those of the latter were travestied in jerks still less softened by art in the person of the lad who attended them. A pair of whitish objects hung one on each side of the latter, bumping against him at each step, and still further spoiling the grace of his seat. On close inspection they might have been perceived to be open rush baskets – one containing a turkey, and the other some bottles of wine.

'D'ye feel ye can meet your fate like a man, neighbour Darton?' asked Johns, breaking a silence which had lasted while five-and-twenty hedgerow trees had glided by.

Mr Darton with a half-laugh murmured, 'Ay – call it my fate! Hanging and wiving go by destiny.' And then they were silent again.

The darkness thickened rapidly, at intervals shutting down on the land in a perceptible flap, like the wave of a wing. The customary close of day was accelerated by a simultaneous blurring of the air. With the fall of night had come a mist just damp enough to incommode, but not sufficient to saturate them. Countrymen as they were – born, as may be said, with only an open door between them and the four seasons – they regarded the mist but as an added obscuration, and ignored its humid quality.

They were travelling in a direction that was enlivened by no modern current of traffic, the place of Darton's pilgrimage being an old-fashioned village – one of the Hintocks (several villages of that name, with a distinctive prefix or affix, lying thereabout) – where the people make the best cider and cider-wine in all Wessex, and where the dunghills smell of pomace instead of stable refuse as elsewhere. The lane was sometimes so narrow that the brambles of the hedge, which hung forward like anglers' rods over a stream, scratched their hats and hooked their whiskers as they passed. Yet this neglected lane had been a highway to Queen Elizabeth's subjects and the cavalcades of the past. Its day was over now, and its history as a national artery done for ever.

'Why I have decided to marry her,' resumed Darton (in a measured musical voice of confidence which revealed a good deal of his composition), as he glanced round to see that the lad was not too near, 'is not only that I like her, but that I can do no better, even from a fairly practical point of view. That I might ha' looked higher is possibly true, though it is really all nonsense. I have had experience enough in looking above me. "No more superior women for me," said I – you know when. Sally is a comely, independent, simple character, with no make-up about her, who'll think me as much a superior to her as I used to think – you know who I mean – was to me.'

'Ay,' said Johns. 'However, I shouldn't call Sally Hall simple. Primary, because no Sally is; secondary, because if some could be, this one wouldn't. 'Tis a wrong denomination to apply to a woman, Charles, and affects me, as your best man, like cold water. 'Tis like recommending a stage play by saying there's neither murder, villainy, nor harm of any sort in it, when that's what you've paid your half-crown to see.'

'Well; may your opinion do you good. Mine's a different one.' And turning the conversation from the philosophical to the practical, Darton expressed a hope that the said Sally had received what he'd sent on by the carrier that day.

Johns wanted to know what that was.

'It is a dress,' said Darton. 'Not exactly a wedding-dress; though she may use it as one if she likes. It is rather serviceable than showy – suitable for the winter weather.'

'Good,' said Johns. 'Serviceable is a wise word in a bridegroom. I commend 'ee, Charles.'

'For,' said Darton, 'why should a woman dress up like a rope-dancer because she's going to do the most solemn deed of her life except dying ?'

'Faith, why ? But she will, because she will, I suppose,' said Dairyman Johns.

'H'm,' said Darton.

The lane they followed had been nearly straight for several miles, but they now left it for a smaller one which after winding uncertainly for some distance forked into two. By night country roads are apt to reveal ungainly qualities which pass without observation during day; and though Darton had travelled this way before, he had not done so frequently, Sally having been wooed at the house of a relative near his own. He never remembered seeing at this spot a pair of alternative ways looking so equally probable as these two did now. Johns rode on a few steps.

'Don't be out of heart, sonny,' he cried. 'Here's a handpost. Ezra – come and climm this post, and tell us the way.'

The lad dismounted, and jumped into the hedge where the post stood under a tree.

'Unstrap the baskets, or you'll smash up that wine!' cried Darton, as the young man began spasmodically to climb the post, baskets and all.

'Was there ever less head in a brainless world?' said Johns. 'Here, simple Ezzy, I'll do it.' He leapt off, and with much puffing climbed the post, striking a match when he reached the top, and moving the light along the arm, the lad standing and gazing at the spectacle.

'I have faced tantalization these twenty years with a temper as mild as milk!' said Japheth; 'but such things as this don't come short of devilry!' And flinging the match away, he slipped down to the ground.

'What's the matter?' asked Darton.

'Not a letter, sacred or heathen – not so much as would tell us the way to the town of Smokeyhole – ever I should sin to say it! Either the moss and mildew have eat away the words, or we have arrived in a land where the natyves have lost the art o' writing, and should ha' brought our compass like Christopher Columbus.'

'Let us take the straightest road,' said Darton placidly; 'I shan't be sorry to get there – 'tis a tiresome ride. I would have driven if I had known.'

'Nor I neither, sir,' said Ezra. 'These straps plough my shoulder like a zull. If 'tis much further to your lady's home, Maister Darton, I shall ask to be let carry half of these good things in my innerds – hee, hee!'

'Don't you be such a reforming radical, Ezra,' said Johns sternly. 'Here, I'll take the turkey.'

This being done, they went forward by the right-hand lane, which ascended a hill, the left winding away under a plantation. The pit-a-pit of their horses' hoofs lessened up the slope; and the ironical directing-post stood in solitude as before, holding out its blank arms to the raw breeze, which brought a snore from the wood as if Skrymir the Giant were sleeping there.

II

Three miles to the left of the travellers, along the road they had not followed, rose an old house with mullioned windows of Ham-hill stone, and chimneys of lavish solidity. It stood at the top of a slope beside King's-Hintock village-street, only a mile or two from King's-Hintock Court, yet quite shut away from that mansion and its precincts. Immediately in front of it grew a large sycamore tree, whose bared roots formed a convenient staircase from the road below to the front door of the dwelling. Its situation gave the house what little distinctive name it possessed, namely, 'The Knap'. Some forty yards off a brook dribbled past, which, for its size, made a great deal of noise. At the back was a dairy barton, accessible for vehicles and live-stock by a side 'drong'. Thus much only of the character of the homestead could be divined out of doors at this shady evening-time.

But within there was plenty of light to see by, as plenty was construed at Hintock. Beside a Tudor fireplace, whose moulded four-centred arch was nearly hidden by a figured blue-cloth blower, were seated two women – mother and daughter – Mrs Hall, and Sarah, or Sally; for this was a part of the world where the latter modification had not as yet been effaced as a vulgarity by the march of intellect. The owner of the name was the young woman by whose means Mr Darton proposed to put an end to his bachelor condition on the approaching day.

The mother's bereavement had been so long ago as not to leave much mark of its occurrence upon her now, either in face or clothes. She had resumed the mob-cap of her early married life, enlivening its whiteness by a few rose-du-Barry ribbons. Sally required no such aids to pinkness. Roseate good-nature lit up her gaze; her features showed curves of decision and judgment; and she might have been regarded without much mistake as a warm-hearted, quick-spirited, handsome girl.

She did most of the talking, her mother listening with a half-absent air, as she picked up fragments of red-hot wood ember with the tongs, and piled them upon the brands. But the number of speeches that passed was very small in proportion to the meanings exchanged. Long experience together often enabled them to see the course of thought in each other's minds without a word being spoken. Behind them, in the centre of the room, the table was spread for supper, certain whiffs of air laden with fat vapours, which ever and anon entered from the kitchen, denoting its preparation there.

'The new gown he was going to send you stays about on the way like himself,' Sally's mother was saying.

'Yes, not finished, I daresay,' cried Sally independently. 'Lord, I shouldn't be amazed if it didn't come at all! Young men make such kind promises when they are near you, and forget 'em when they go away. But he doesn't intend it as a wedding-gown – he gives it to me merely as a gown to wear when I like – a travelling-dress is what it would be called by some. Come rathe or come late it don't much matter, as I have a dress of my own to fall back upon. But what time is it?'

She went to the family clock and opened the glass, for the hour was not otherwise discernible by night, and indeed at all times was rather a thing to be investigated than beheld, so much more wall than window was there in the apartment. 'It is nearly eight,' said she.

'Eight o'clock, and neither dress nor man,' said Mrs Hall.

'Mother, if you think to tantalize me by talking like that, you are much mistaken! Let him be as late as he will – or stay away altogether – I don't care,' said Sally. But a tender minute quaver in the negation showed that there was something forced in that statement.

Mrs Hall perceived it, and drily observed that she was not so sure about Sally not caring. 'But perhaps you don't care so much as I do, after all,' she said. 'For I see what you don't, that it is a good and flourishing match for you; a very honourable offer in Mr Darton. And I think I see a kind husband in him. So pray God 'twill go smooth, and wind up well.'

Sally would not listen to misgivings. Of course it would go smoothly, she asserted. 'How you are up and down, mother!' she went on. 'At this moment, whatever hinders him, we are not so anxious to see him as he is to be here, and his thought runs on before him, and settles down upon us like the star in the east. Hark!' she exclaimed, with a breath of relief, her eyes sparkling. 'I heard something. Yes – here they are!'

The next moment her mother's slower ear also distinguished the familiar reverberation occasioned by footsteps clambering up the roots of the sycamore.

'Yes, it sounds like them at last,' she said. 'Well, it is not so very late after all, considering the distance.'

The footfall ceased, and they arose, expecting a knock. They began to think it might have been, after all, some neighbouring villager under Bacchic influence, giving the centre of the road a wide berth, when their doubts were dispelled by the new-comer's entry into the passage. The door of the room was gently opened, and there appeared, not the pair of travellers with whom we have already made acquaintance, but a pale-faced man in the garb of extreme poverty – almost in rags.

'O, it's a tramp – gracious me!' said Sally, starting back.

His cheeks and eye-orbits were deep concaves – rather, it might be, from natural weakness of constitution than irregular living, though there were indications that he had led no careful life. He gazed at the two women fixedly for a moment: then with an abashed, humiliated demeanour, dropped his glance to the floor, and sank into a chair without uttering a word.

Sally was in advance of her mother, who had remained standing by the fire. She now tried to discern the visitor across the candles.

'Why – mother,' said Sally faintly, turning back to Mrs Hall. 'It is Phil, from Australia!'

Mrs Hall started, and grew pale, and a fit of coughing seized the man with the ragged clothes. 'To come home like this!' she said. 'O, Philip – are you ill?'

'No, no, mother,' replied he impatiently, as soon as he could speak.

'But for God's sake how do you come here – and just now, too?'

'Well, I am here,' said the man. 'How it is I hardly know. I've come home, mother, because I was driven to it. Things were against me out there, and went from bad to worse.'

'Then why didn't you let us know? – you've not writ a line for the last two or three years.'

The son admitted sadly that he had not. He said that he had hoped and thought he might fetch up again, and be able to send good news. Then he had been obliged to abandon that hope, and had finally come home from sheer necessity – previously to making a new start. 'Yes, things are very bad with me,' he repeated, perceiving their commiserating glances at his clothes.

They brought him nearer the fire, took his hat from his thin hand, which was so small and smooth as to show that his attempts to fetch up again had not been in a manual direction. His mother resumed her inquiries, and dubiously asked if he had chosen to come that particular night for any special reason.

For no reason, he told her. His arrival had been quite at random. Then Philip Hall looked round the room, and saw for the first time that the table was laid somewhat luxuriously, and for a larger number than themselves; and that an air of festivity pervaded their dress. He asked quickly what was going on.

'Sally is going to be married in a day or two,' replied the mother; and she explained how Mr Darton, Sally's intended husband, was coming there that night with the groomsman, Mr Johns, and other details. 'We thought it must be their step when we heard you,' said Mrs Hall.

The needy wanderer looked again on the floor. 'I see – I see,' he murmured. 'Why, indeed, should I have come to-night? Such folk as I are not wanted here at these times, naturally. And I have no business here – spoiling other people's happiness.'

'Phil,' said his mother, with a tear in her eye, but with a thinness of lip and severity of manner which were presumably not more than past events justified; 'since you speak like that to me, I'll speak honestly to you. For these three years you have taken no thought for us. You left home with a good supply of money, and strength and education, and you ought to have made good use of it all. But you come back like a beggar; and that you come in a very awkward time for us cannot be denied. Your return to-night may do us much harm. But mind – you are welcome to this home as long as it is mine. I don't wish to turn you adrift. We will make the best of a bad job; and I hope you are not seriously ill?'

'O no. I have only this infernal cough.'

She looked at him anxiously. 'I think you had better go to bed at once,' she said.

'Well – I shall be out of the way there,' said the son wearily. 'Having ruined myself, don't let me ruin you by being seen in these togs, for Heaven's sake. Who do you say Sally is going to be married to – a Farmer Darton?'

'Yes – a gentleman-farmer – quite a wealthy man. Far better in station than she could have expected. It is a good thing, altogether.'

'Well done, little Sal!' said her brother, brightening and looking up at her with a smile. 'I ought to have written; but perhaps I have thought of you all the more. But let me get out of sight. I would rather go and jump into the river than be seen here. But have you anything I can drink? I am confoundedly thirsty with my long tramp.'

'Yes, yes, we will bring something upstairs to you,' said Sally, with grief in her face.

'Ay, that will do nicely. But, Sally and mother—' He stopped, and they waited. 'Mother, I have not told you all,' he resumed slowly, still looking on the floor between his knees. 'Sad as what you see of me is, there's worse behind.'

His mother gazed upon him in grieved suspense, and Sally went and leant upon the bureau, listening for every sound, and sighing. Suddenly she turned round, saying, 'Let them come, I don't care! Philip, tell the worst, and take your time.'

'Well, then,' said the unhappy Phil, 'I am not the only one in this mess. Would to Heaven I were! But—'

'O, Phil!'

'I have a wife as destitute as I.'

'A wife?' said his mother.

'Unhappily!'

'A wife! Yes, that is the way with sons!'

'And besides—' said he.

'Besides! O, Philip, surely—'

'I have two little children.'

'Wife and children!' whispered Mrs Hall, sinking down confounded.

'Poor little things!' said Sally involuntarily.

His mother turned again to him. 'I suppose these helpless beings are left in Australia?'

'No. They are in England.'

'Well, I can only hope you've left them in a respectable place.'

'I have not left them at all. They are here – within a few yards of us. In short, they are in the stable.'

'Where?'

'In the stable. I did not like to bring them indoors till I had seen you, mother, and broken the bad news a bit to you. They were very tired, and are resting out there on some straw.'

Mrs Hall's fortitude visibly broke down. She had been brought up not without refinement, and was even more moved by such a collapse of genteel aims as this than a substantial dairyman's widow would in ordinary have been moved. 'Well, it must be borne,' she said, in a low voice, with her hands tightly joined. 'A starving son, a starving wife, starving children! Let it be. But why is this come to us now, to-day, to-night? Could no other misfortune happen to helpless women than this, which will quite upset my poor girl's chance of a happy life? Why have you done us this wrong, Philip? What respectable man will come here, and marry open-eyed into a family of vagabonds?'

'Nonsense, mother!' said Sally vehemently, while her face flushed. 'Charley isn't the man to desert me. But if he should be, and won't marry me because Phil's come, let him go and marry elsewhere. I won't be ashamed of my own flesh and blood for any man in England – not I!' And then Sally turned away and burst into tears.

'Wait till you are twenty years older and you will tell a different tale,' replied her mother.

The son stood up. 'Mother,' he said bitterly, 'as I have come, so I will go. All I ask of you is that you will allow me and mine to lie in your stable to-night. I give you my word that we'll be gone by break of day, and trouble you no further!'

Mrs Hall, the mother, changed at that. 'O no,' she answered hastily; 'never shall it be said that I sent any of my own family from my door. Bring 'em in, Philip, or take me out to them.'

'We will put 'em all into the large bedroom,' said Sally, brightening, 'and make up a large fire. Let's go and help them in, and call Rebekah.' (Rebekah was the woman who assisted at the dairy and housework; she lived in a cottage hard by with her husband, who attended to the cows.)

Sally went to fetch a lantern from the back-kitchen, but her brother said, 'You won't want a light. I lit the lantern that was hanging there.'

'What must we call your wife?' asked Mrs Hall.

'Helena,' said Philip.

With shawls over their heads they proceeded towards the back door. 'One minute before you go,' interrupted Philip. 'I – I haven't confessed all.'

'Then Heaven help us!' said Mrs Hall, pushing to the door and clasping her hands in calm despair.

'We passed through Evershead as we came,' he continued, 'and I just looked in at the "Sow-and-Acorn" to see if old Mike still kept on there as usual. The carrier had come in from Sherton Abbas at that moment, and guessing that I was bound for this place – for I think he knew me – he asked me to bring on a dressmaker's parcel for Sally that was marked "immediate". My wife had walked on with the children. 'Twas a flimsy parcel, and the paper was torn, and I found on looking at it that it was a thick warm gown. I didn't wish you to see poor Helena in a shabby state. I was ashamed that you should – 'twas not what she was born to. I untied the parcel in the road, took it on to her where she was waiting in the Lower Barn, and told her I had managed to get it for her, and that she was to ask no question. She, poor thing, must have supposed I obtained it on trust, through having reached a place where I was known, for she put it on gladly enough. She has it on now. Sally has other gowns, I daresay.'

Sally looked at her mother, speechless.

'You have others, I daresay!' repeated Phil, with a sick man's impatience. 'I thought to myself, "Better Sally cry than Helena freeze." Well, is the dress of great consequence ? 'Twas nothing very ornamental, as far as I could see.'

'No – no; not of consequence,' returned Sally sadly, adding in a gentle voice, 'You will not mind if I lend her another instead of that one, will you ?'

Philip's agitation at the confession had brought on another attack of the cough, which seemed to shake him to pieces. He was so obviously unfit to sit in a chair that they helped him upstairs at once; and having hastily given him a cordial and kindled the bedroom fire, they descended to fetch their unhappy new relations.

III

It was with strange feelings that the girl and her mother, lately so cheerful, passed out of the back door into the open air of the barton, laden with hay scents and the herby breath of cows. A fine sleet had begun to fall, and they trotted across the yard quickly. The stable-door was open; a light shone from it – from the lantern which always hung there, and which Philip had lighted, as he said. Softly nearing the door, Mrs Hall pronounced the name 'Helena!'

There was no answer for the moment. Looking in she was taken by surprise. Two people appeared before her. For one, instead of the drabbish woman she had expected, Mrs Hall saw a pale, dark-eyed, ladylike creature, whose personality ruled her attire rather than was ruled by it. She was in a new and handsome gown, Sally's own, and an old bonnet. She was standing up, agitated; her hand was held by her companion – none else than Sally's affianced, Farmer Charles Darton, upon whose fine figure the pale stranger's eyes were fixed, as his were fixed upon her. His other hand held the rein of his horse, which was standing saddled as if just led in.

At sight of Mrs Hall they both turned, looking at her in a way neither quite conscious nor unconscious, and without seeming to recollect that words were necessary as a solution to the scene. In another moment Sally entered also, when Mr Darton dropped his companion's hand, led the horse aside, and came to greet his betrothed and Mrs Hall.

'Ah!' he said, smiling – with something like forced composure – 'this is a roundabout way of arriving, you will say, my dear Mrs Hall. But we lost our way, which made us late. I saw a light here, and led in my horse at once – my friend Johns and my man have gone onward to the little inn with theirs, not to crowd you too much. No sooner had I entered than I saw that this lady had taken temporary shelter here – and found I was intruding.'

'She is my daughter-in-law,' said Mrs Hall calmly. 'My son, too, is in the house, but he has gone to bed unwell.'

Sally had stood staring wonderingly at the scene until this moment, hardly recognizing Darton's shake of the hand. The spell that bound her was broken by her perceiving the two little children seated on a heap of hay. She suddenly went forward, spoke to them, and took one on her arm and the other in her hand.

'And two children?' said Mr Darton, showing thus that he had not been there long enough as yet to understand the situation.

'My grandchildren,' said Mrs Hall, with as much affected ease as before.

Philip Hall's wife, in spite of this interruption to her first rencounter, seemed scarcely so much affected by it as to feel anyone's presence in addition to Mr Darton's. However, arousing herself by a quick re-flection, she threw a sudden critical glance of her sad eyes upon Mrs Hall, and, apparently finding her satisfactory, advanced to her in a meek initiative. Then Sally and the stranger spoke some friendly words to each other, and Sally went on with the children into the house. Mrs Hall and Helena followed, and Mr Darton followed these, looking at Helena's dress and outline, and listening to her voice like a man in a dream.

By the time the others reached the house Sally had already gone upstairs with the tired children. She rapped against the wall for Rebekah to come in and help to attend to them, Rebekah's house being a little 'spit-and-daub' cabin leaning against the substantial stonework of Mrs Hall's taller erection. When she came a bed was made up for the little ones, and some supper given to them. On descending the stairs after seeing this done Sally went to the sitting-room. Young Mrs Hall entered it just in advance of her, having in the interim retired with her mother-in-law to take off her bonnet, and otherwise make herself presentable. Hence it was evident that no further communication could have passed between her and Mr Darton since their brief interview in the stable.

Mr Japheth Johns now opportunely arrived, and broke up the restraint of the company, after a few orthodox meteorological commentaries had passed between him and Mrs Hall by way of introduction. They at once sat down to supper, the present of wine and turkey not being produced for consumption to-night, lest the premature display of those gifts should seem to throw doubt on Mrs Hall's capacities as a provider.

'Drink hearty, Mr Johns – drink hearty,' said that matron magnanimously. 'Such as it is there's plenty of. But perhaps cider-wine is not to your taste ? – though there's body in it.'

'Quite the contrairy, ma'am – quite the contrairy,' said the dairyman. 'For though I inherit the malt-liquor principle from my father, I am a cider-drinker on my mother's side. She came from these parts, you know. And there's this to be said for't – 'tis a more peaceful liquor, and don't lie about a man like your hotter drinks. With care, one may live on it a twelve-month without knocking down a neighbour, or getting a black eye from an old acquaintance.'

The general conversation thus begun was continued briskly, though it was in the main restricted to Mrs Hall and Japheth, who in truth required but little help from anybody. There being slight call upon Sally's tongue, she had ample leisure to do what her heart most desired, namely, watch her intended husband and her sister-in-law with a view of elucidating the strange momentary scene in which her mother and herself had surprised them in the stable. If that scene meant anything, it meant, at least, that they had met before. That there had been no time for explanations Sally could see, for their manner was still one of suppressed amazement at each other's presence there. Darton's eyes, too, fell continually on the gown worn by Helena as if this were an added riddle to his perplexity; though to Sally it was the one feature in the case which was no mystery. He seemed to feel that fate had impishly changed his *vis-à-vis* in the lover's jig he was about to foot; that while the gown had been expected to enclose a Sally, a Helena's face looked out from the bodice; that some long-lost hand met his own from the sleeves.

Sally could see that whatever Helena might know of Darton, she knew nothing of how the dress entered into his embarrassment. And at moments the young girl would have persuaded herself that Darton's looks at her sister-in-law were entirely the fruit of the clothes query. But surely at other times a more extensive range of speculation and sentiment was expressed by her lover's eye than that which the changed dress would account for.

Sally's independence made her one of the least jealous of women. But there was something in the relations of these two visitors which ought to be explained.

Japheth Johns continued to converse in his well-known style, interspersing his talk with some private reflections on the position of Darton and Sally, which, though the sparkle in his eye showed them to be highly entertaining to himself, were apparently not quite communicable to the company. At last he withdrew for the night, going off to the roadside inn half-a-mile ahead, whither Darton promised to follow him in a few minutes.

Half-an-hour passed, and then Mr Darton also rose to leave, Sally and her sister-in-law simultaneously wishing him good-night as they retired upstairs to their rooms. But on his arriving at the front door with Mrs Hall a sharp shower of rain began to come down, when the widow suggested that he should return to the fireside till the storm ceased.

Darton accepted her proposal, but insisted that, as it was getting late, and she was obviously tired, she should not sit up on his account, since he could let himself out of the house, and would quite enjoy smoking a pipe by the hearth alone. Mrs Hall assented; and Darton was left by himself. He spread his knees to the brands, lit up his tobacco as he had said, and sat gazing into the fire, and at the notches of the chimney-crook which hung above.

An occasional drop of rain rolled down the chimney with a hiss, and still he smoked on; but not like a man whose mind was at rest. In the long run, however, despite his meditations, early hours afield and a long ride in the open air produced their natural result. He began to doze.

How long he remained in this half-unconscious state he did not know. He suddenly opened his eyes. The back-brand had burnt itself in two, and ceased to flame; the light which he had placed on the mantelpiece had nearly gone out. But in spite of these deficiencies there was a light in the apartment, and it came from elsewhere. Turning his head he saw Philip Hall's wife standing at the entrance of the room with a bed-candle in one hand, a small brass tea-kettle in the other, and *his* gown, as it certainly seemed, still upon her.

'Helena!' said Darton, starting up.

Her countenance expressed dismay, and her first words were an apology. 'I – did not know you were here, Mr Darton,' she said, while a blush flashed to her cheek. 'I thought every one had retired – I was coming to make a little water boil; my husband seems to be worse. But perhaps the kitchen fire can be lighted up again.'

'Don't go on my account. By all means put it on here as you intended,' said Darton. 'Allow me to help you.' He went forward to take the kettle from her hand, but she did not allow him, and placed it on the fire herself.

They stood some way apart, one on each side of the fireplace, waiting till the water should boil, the candle on the mantel between them, and Helena with her eyes on the kettle. Darton was the first to break the silence. 'Shall I call Sally?' he said.

'O no,' she quickly returned. 'We have given trouble enough already. We have no right here. But we are the sport of fate, and were obliged to come.'

'No right here!' said he in surprise.

'None. I can't explain it now,' answered Helena. 'This kettle is very slow.'

There was another pause; the proverbial dilatoriness of watched pots was never more clearly exemplified.

Helena's face was of that sort which seems to ask for assistance without the owner's knowledge – the very antipodes of Sally's, which was self-reliance expressed. Darton's eyes travelled from the kettle to Helena's face, then back to the kettle, then to the face for rather a longer time. 'So I am not to know anything of the mystery that has distracted me all the evening?' he said. 'How is it that a woman, who refused me because (as I supposed) my position was not good enough for her taste, is found to be the wife of a man who certainly seems to be worse off than I?'

'He had the prior claim,' said she.

'What! you knew him at that time?'

'Yes, yes! And he went to Australia, and sent for me, and I joined him out there!'

'Ah – that was the mystery!'

'Please say no more,' she implored. 'Whatever my errors, I have paid for them during the last five years!'

The heart of Darton was subject to sudden overflowings. He was kind to a fault. 'I am sorry from my soul,' he said, involuntarily approaching her. Helena withdrew a step or two, at which he became conscious of his movement, and quickly took his former place. Here he stood without speaking, and the little kettle began to sing.

'Well, you might have been my wife if you had chosen,' he said at last. 'But that's all past and gone. However, if you are in any trouble or poverty I shall be glad to be of service, and as your relation by marriage I shall have a right to be. Does your uncle know of your distress?'

'My uncle is dead. He left me without a farthing. And now we have two children to maintain.'

'What, left you nothing? How could he be so cruel as that?'

'I disgraced myself in his eyes.'

'Now,' said Darton earnestly, 'let me take care of the children, at least while you are so unsettled. *You* belong to another, so I cannot take care of you.'

'Yes, you can,' said a voice; and suddenly a third figure stood beside them. It was Sally. 'You can, since you seem to wish to,' she repeated. 'She no longer belongs to another. . . . My poor brother is dead!'

Her face was red, her eyes sparkled, and all the woman came to the front. 'I have heard it!' she went on to him passionately. 'You can protect her now as well as the children!' She turned then to her agitated sister-in-law. 'I heard something,' said Sally (in a gentle murmur, differing much from her previous passionate words), 'and I went into his room. It must have been the moment you left. He went off so quickly, and weakly, and it was so unexpected, that I couldn't leave even to call you.'

Darton was just able to gather from the confused discourse which followed that, during his sleep by the fire, Sally's brother whom he had never seen had become worse; and that during Helena's absence for water the end had unexpectedly come. The two young women hastened upstairs, and he was again left alone.

After standing there a short time he went to the front door and looked out; till, softly closing it behind him, he advanced and stood under the large sycamore-tree. The stars were flickering coldly, and the dampness which had just descended upon the earth in rain now sent up a chill from it. Darton was in a strange position, and he felt it. The unexpected appearance, in deep poverty, of Helena – a young lady, daughter of a deceased naval officer, who had been brought up by her uncle, a solicitor, and had refused Darton in marriage years ago – the passionate, almost angry demeanour of Sally at discovering them, the abrupt announcement that Helena was a widow; all this coming together was a conjuncture difficult to cope with in a moment, and made him question whether he ought to leave the house or offer assistance. But for Sally's manner he would unhesitatingly have done the latter.

He was still standing under the tree when the door in front of him opened, and Mrs Hall came out. She went round to the garden-gate at the side without seeing him. Darton followed her, intending to speak. Pausing outside, as if in thought, she proceeded to a spot where the sun came earliest in spring-time, and where the north wind never blew; it was where the row of beehives stood under the wall. Discerning her object, he waited till she had accomplished it.

It was the universal custom thereabout to wake the bees by tapping at their hives whenever a death occurred in the household, under the belief that if this were not done the bees themselves would pine away and perish during the ensuing year. As soon as an interior buzzing responded to her tap at the first hive Mrs Hall went on to the second, and thus passed down the row. As soon as she came back he met her.

'What can I do in this trouble, Mrs Hall?' he said.

'O – nothing, thank you, nothing,' she said in a tearful voice, now just perceiving him. 'We have called Rebekah and her husband, and they will do everything necessary.' She told him in a few words the particulars of her son's arrival, broken in health – indeed, at death's very door, though they did not suspect it – and suggested, as the result of a conversation between her and her daughter, that the wedding should be postponed.

'Yes, of course,' said Darton. 'I think now to go straight to the inn and tell Johns what has happened.' It was not till after he had shaken hands with her that he turned hesitatingly and added, 'Will you tell the mother of his children that, as they are now left fatherless, I shall be glad to take the eldest of them, if it would be any convenience to her and to you?'

Mrs Hall promised that her son's widow should be told of the offer, and they parted. He retired down the rooty slope and disappeared in the direction of the inn, where he informed Johns of the circumstances. Meanwhile Mrs Hall had entered the house. Sally was downstairs in the sitting-room alone, and her mother explained to her that Darton had readily assented to the postponement.

'No doubt he has,' said Sally, with sad emphasis. 'It is not put off for a week, or a month, or a year. I shall never marry him, and she will!'

IV

Time passed, and the household on the Knap became again serene under the composing influences of daily routine. A desultory, very desultory, correspondence dragged on between Sally Hall and Darton, who, not quite knowing how to take her petulant words on the night of her brother's death, had continued passive thus long. Helena and her children remained at the dairy-house, almost of necessity, and Darton therefore deemed it advisable to stay away.

One day, seven months later on, when Mr Darton was as usual at his farm, twenty miles from King's-Hintock, a note reached him from Helena. She thanked him for his kind offer about her children, which her mother-in-law had duly communicated, and stated that she would be glad to accept it as regarded the eldest, the boy. Helena had, in truth, good need to do so, for her uncle had left her penniless, and all application to some relatives in the north had failed. There was, besides, as she said, no good school near Hintock to which she could send the child.

On a fine summer day the boy came. He was accompanied half-way by Sally and his mother – to the 'White Horse', the fine old Elizabethan inn at Chalk Newton,[1] where he was handed over to Darton's bailiff in a shining spring-cart, who met them there.

He was entered as a day-scholar at a popular school at Casterbridge, three or four miles from Darton's, having first been taught by Darton to ride a forest-pony, on which he cantered to and from the aforesaid fount of knowledge, and (as Darton hoped) brought away a promising headful of the same at each diurnal expedition. The thoughtful taciturnity into which Darton had latterly fallen was quite dissipated by the presence of this boy.

When the Christmas holidays came it was arranged that he should

[1] It is now pulled down, and its site occupied by a modern one in red brick (1912).

spend them with his mother. The journey was, for some reason or other, performed in two stages, as at his coming, except that Darton in person took the place of the bailiff, and that the boy and himself rode on horseback.

Reaching the renowned 'White Horse', Darton inquired if Miss and young Mrs Hall were there to meet little Philip (as they had agreed to be). He was answered by the appearance of Helena alone at the door.

'At the last moment Sally would not come,' she faltered.

That meeting practically settled the point towards which these long-severed persons were converging. But nothing was broached about it for some time yet. Sally Hall had, in fact, imparted the first decisive motion to events by refusing to accompany Helena. She soon gave them a second move by writing the following note: –

'[*Private.*]
'DEAR CHARLES, – Living here so long and intimately with Helena, I have naturally learnt her history, especially that of it which refers to you. I am sure she would accept you as a husband at the proper time, and I think you ought to give her the opportunity. You inquire in an old note if I am sorry that I showed temper (which it *wasn't*) that night when I heard you talking to her. No, Charles, I am not sorry at all for what I said then. – Yours sincerely,

SALLY HALL'

Thus set in train, the transfer of Darton's heart back to its original quarters proceeded by mere lapse of time. In the following July, Darton went to his friend Japheth to ask him at last to fulfil the bridal office which had been in abeyance since the previous January twelvemonths.

'With all my heart, man o' constancy!' said Dairyman Johns warmly. 'I've lost most of my genteel fair complexion haymaking this hot weather, 'tis true, but I'll do your business as well as them that look better. There be scents and good hair-oil in the world yet, thank God, and they'll take off the roughest o' my edge. I'll compliment her. "Better late than never, Sally Hall," I'll say.'

'It is not Sally,' said Darton hurriedly. 'It is young Mrs Hall.'

Japheth's face, as soon as he really comprehended, became a picture of reproachful dismay. 'Not Sally?' he said. 'Why not Sally? I can't believe it! Young Mrs Hall! Well, well – where's your wisdom?'

Darton shortly explained particulars; but Johns would not be reconciled. 'She was a woman worth having if ever woman was,' he cried. 'And now to let her go!'

'But I suppose I can marry where I like,' said Darton.

'H'm,' replied the dairyman, lifting his eyebrows expressively. 'This don't become you, Charles – it really do not. If I had done such a thing you would have sworn I was a curst no'thern fool to be drawn off the scent by such a red-herring doll-oll-oll.'

Farmer Darton responded in such sharp terms to this laconic opinion that the two friends finally parted in a way they had never parted before. Johns was to be no groomsman to Darton after all. He had flatly declined. Darton went off sorry, and even unhappy, particularly as Japheth was about to leave that side of the county, so that the words which had divided them were not likely to be explained away or softened down.

A short time after the interview Darton was united to Helena at a simple matter-of-fact wedding, and she and her little girl joined the boy who had already grown to look on Darton's house as home.

For some months the farmer experienced an unprecedented happiness and satisfaction. There had been a flaw in his life, and it was as neatly mended as was humanly possible. But after a season the stream of events followed less clearly, and there were shades in his reveries. Helena was a fragile woman, of little staying-power, physically or morally, and since the time that he had originally known her – eight or ten years before – she had been severely tried. She had loved herself out, in short, and was now occasionally given to moping. Sometimes she spoke regretfully of the gentilities of her early life, and instead of comparing her present state with her condition as the wife of the unlucky Hall, she mused rather on what it had been before she took the first fatal step of clandestinely marrying him. She did not care to please such people as those with whom she was thrown as a thriving farmer's wife. She allowed the pretty trifles of agricultural domesticity to glide by her as sorry details, and had it not been for the children Darton's house would have seemed but little brighter than it had been before.

This led to occasional unpleasantness, until Darton sometimes declared to himself that such endeavours as his to rectify early deviations of the heart by harking back to the old point mostly failed of success. 'Perhaps Johns was right,' he would say. 'I should have gone on with Sally. Better go with the tide and make the best of its course than stem it at the risk of a capsize.' But he kept these unmelodious thoughts to himself, and was outwardly considerate and kind.

This somewhat barren tract of his life had extended to less than a year and a half when his ponderings were cut short by the loss of the woman they concerned. When she was in her grave he thought better of her than when she had been alive; the farm was a worse place without her than with her, after all. No woman short of divine could have gone through such an experience as hers with her first husband without becoming a little soured. Her stagnant sympathies, her sometimes unreasonable manner, had covered a heart frank and well-meaning, and originally hopeful and warm. She left him a tiny red infant in white wrappings. To make life as easy as possible to this touching object became at once his care.

As this child learnt to walk and talk Darton learnt to see feasibility in a scheme which pleased him. Revolving the experiment which he had hitherto made upon life, he fancied he had gained wisdom from his mistakes and caution from his miscarriages.

What the scheme was needs no penetration to discover. Once more he had opportunity to recast and rectify his ill-wrought situations by returning to Sally Hall, who still lived quietly on under her mother's roof at Hintock. Helena had been a woman to lend pathos and refinement to a home; Sally was the woman to brighten it. She would not, as Helena did, despise the rural simplicities of a farmer's fireside. Moreover, she had a pre-eminent qualification for Darton's household; no other woman could make so desirable a mother to her brother's two children and Darton's one as Sally – while Darton, now that Helena had gone, was a more promising husband for Sally than he had ever been when liable to reminders from an uncured sentimental wound.

Darton was not a man to act rapidly, and the working out of his reparative designs might have been delayed for some time. But there came a winter evening precisely like the one which had darkened over that former ride to Hintock, and he asked himself why he should postpone longer, when the very landscape called for a repetition of that attempt.

He told his man to saddle the mare, booted and spurred himself with a younger horseman's nicety, kissed the two youngest children, and rode off. To make the journey a complete parallel to the first, he would fain have had his old acquaintance Japheth Johns with him. But Johns, alas! was missing. His removal to the other side of the county had left unrepaired the breach which had arisen between him and Darton; and though Darton had forgiven him a hundred times, as Johns had

probably forgiven Darton, the effort of reunion in present circumstances was one not likely to be made.

He screwed himself up to as cheerful a pitch as he could without his
former crony, and became content with his own thoughts as he rode,
instead of the words of a companion. The sun went down; the boughs
appeared scratched in like an etching against the sky; old crooked men
with faggots at their backs said 'Good-night, sir,' and Darton replied
'Good-night' right heartily.

By the time he reached the forking roads it was getting as dark as it
had been on the occasion when Johns climbed the directing-post.
Darton made no mistake this time. 'Nor shall I be able to mistake,
thank Heaven, when I arrive,' he murmured. It gave him peculiar
satisfaction to think that the proposed marriage, like his first, was of the
nature of setting in order things long awry, and not a momentary freak
of fancy.

Nothing hindered the smoothness of his journey, which seemed not
half its former length. Though dark, it was only between five and six
o'clock when the bulky chimneys of Mrs Hall's residence appeared in
view behind the sycamore tree. On second thoughts he retreated and put
up at the ale-house as in former time; and when he had plumed himself
before the inn mirror, called for something to drink, and smoothed out
the incipient wrinkles of care, he walked on to the Knap with a quick
step.

V

That evening Sally was making 'pinners' for the milkers, who were now
increased by two, for her mother and herself no longer joined in
milking the cows themselves. But upon the whole there was little
change in the household economy, and not much in its appearance,
beyond such minor particulars as that the crack over the window,
which had been a hundred years coming, was a trifle wider; that the
beams were a shade blacker; that the influence of modernism had
supplanted the open chimney-corner by a grate; that Rebekah, who
had worn a cap when she had plenty of hair, had left it off now she had
scarce any, because it was reported that caps were not fashionable; and
that Sally's face had naturally assumed a more womanly and experienced
cast.

Mrs Hall was actually lifting coals with the tongs, as she had used to do.

'Five years ago this very night, if I am not mistaken—' she said, laying on an ember.

'Not this very night – though 'twas one night this week,' said the correct Sally.

'Well, 'tis near enough. Five years ago Mr Darton came to marry you, and my poor boy Phil came home to die.' She sighed. 'Ah, Sally,' she presently said, 'if you had managed well Mr Darton would have had you, Helena or none.'

'Don't be sentimental about that, mother,' begged Sally. 'I didn't care to manage well in such a case. Though I liked him, I wasn't so anxious. I would never have married the man in the midst of such a hitch as that was,' she added with decision; 'and I don't think I would if he were to ask me now.'

'I am not sure about that, unless you have another in your eye.'

'I wouldn't; and I'll tell you why. I could hardly marry him for love at this time o' day. And as we've quite enough to live on if we give up the dairy to-morrow, I should have no need to marry for any meaner reason. . . . I am quite happy enough as I am, and there's an end of it.'

Now it was not long after this dialogue that there came a mild rap at the door, and in a moment there entered Rebekah, looking as though a ghost had arrived. The fact was that that accomplished skimmer and churner (now a resident in the house) had overheard the desultory observations between mother and daughter, and on opening the door to Mr Darton thought the coincidence must have a grisly meaning in it. Mrs Hall welcomed the farmer with warm surprise, as did Sally, and for a moment they rather wanted words.

'Can you push up the chimney-crook for me, Mr Darton? – the notches hitch,' said the matron. He did it, and the homely little act bridged over the awkward consciousness that he had been a stranger for four years.

Mrs Hall soon saw what he had come for, and left the principals together while she went to prepare him a late tea, smiling at Sally's recent hasty assertions of indifference, when she saw how civil Sally was. When tea was ready she joined them. She fancied that Darton did not look so confident as when he had arrived; but Sally was quite light-hearted, and the meal passed pleasantly.

About seven he took his leave of them. Mrs Hall went as far as the door to light him down the slope. On the doorstep he said frankly –

'I came to ask your daughter to marry me; chose the night and everything, with an eye to a favourable answer. But she won't.'

'Then she's a very ungrateful girl!' emphatically said Mrs Hall.

Darton paused to shape his sentence, and asked, 'I – I suppose there's nobody else more favoured?'

'I can't say that there is, or that there isn't,' answered Mrs Hall. 'She's private in some things. I'm on your side, however, Mr Darton, and I'll talk to her.'

'Thank 'ee, thank 'ee!' said the farmer in a gayer accent; and with this assurance the not very satisfactory visit came to an end. Darton descended the roots of the sycamore, the light was withdrawn, and the door closed. At the bottom of the slope he nearly ran against a man about to ascend.

'Can a jack-o'-lent believe his few senses on such a dark night, or can't he?' exclaimed one whose utterance Darton recognized in a moment, despite its unexpectedness. 'I dare not swear he can, though I fain would!' The speaker was Johns.

Darton said he was glad of this opportunity, bad as it was, of putting an end to the silence of years, and asked the dairyman what he was travelling that way for.

Japheth showed the old jovial confidence in a moment. 'I'm going to see your – relations – as they always seem to me,' he said – 'Mrs Hall and Sally. Well, Charles, the fact is I find the natural barbarousness of man is much increased by a bachelor life, and, as your leavings were always good enough for me, I'm trying civilization here.' He nodded towards the house.

'Not with Sally – to marry her?' said Darton, feeling something like a rill of ice water between his shoulders.

'Yes, by the help of Providence and my personal charms. And I think I shall get her. I am this road every week – my present dairy is only four miles off, you know, and I see her through the window. 'Tis rather odd that I was going to speak practical to-night to her for the first time. You've just called?'

'Yes, for a short while. But she didn't say a word about you.'

'A good sign, a good sign. Now that decides me. I'll swing the mallet and get her answer this very night as I planned.'

A few more remarks, and Darton, wishing his friend joy of Sally in a slightly hollow tone of jocularity, bade him good-bye. Johns promised to write particulars, and ascended, and was lost in the shade of the house and tree. A rectangle of light appeared when Johns was admitted, and all was dark again.

'Happy Japheth!' said Darton. 'This then is the explanation!'

He determined to return home that night. In a quarter of an hour he passed out of the village, and the next day went about his swede-lifting and storing as if nothing had occurred.

He waited and waited to hear from Johns whether the wedding-day was fixed: but no letter came. He learnt not a single particular till, meeting Johns one day at a horse-auction, Darton exclaimed genially – rather more genially than he felt – 'When is the joyful day to be ?'

To his great surprise a reciprocity of gladness was not conspicuous in Johns. 'Not at all,' he said, in a very subdued tone. ' 'Tis a bad job; she won't have me.'

Darton held his breath till he said with treacherous solicitude, 'Try again – 'tis coyness.'

'O no,' said Johns decisively. 'There's been none of that. We talked it over dozens of times in the most fair and square way. She tells me plainly, I don't suit her. 'Twould be simply annoying her to ask her again. Ah, Charles, you threw a prize away when you let her slip five years ago.'

'I did – I did,' said Darton.

He returned from that auction with a new set of feelings in play. He had certainly made a surprising mistake in thinking Johns his successful rival. It really seemed as if he might hope for Sally after all.

This time, being rather pressed by business, Darton had recourse to pen-and-ink, and wrote her as manly and straightforward a proposal as any woman could wish to receive. The reply came promptly: –

'DEAR MR DARTON, – I am as sensible as any woman can be of the goodness that leads you to make me this offer a second time. Better women than I would be proud of the honour, for when I read your nice long speeches on mangold-wurzel, and such-like topics, at the Casterbridge Farmers' Club, I do feel it an honour, I assure you. But my answer is just the same as before. I will not try to explain what, in truth, I cannot explain – my reasons; I will simply say that I must decline to be married to you. With good wishes as in former times, I am, your faithful friend,

SALLY HALL'

Darton dropped the letter hopelessly. Beyond the negative, there was

just a possibility of sarcasm in it – 'nice long speeches on mangold-
wurzel' had a suspicious sound. However, sarcasm or none, there was
the answer, and he had to be content.

He proceeded to seek relief in a business which at this time engrossed
much of his attention – that of clearing up a curious mistake just current
in the county, that he had been nearly ruined by the recent failure of a
local bank. A farmer named Darton had lost heavily, and the similarity
of name had probably led to the error. Belief in it was so persistent that
it demanded several days of letter-writing to set matters straight, and
persuade the world that he was as solvent as ever he had been in his life.
He had hardly concluded this worrying task when, to his delight,
another letter arrived in the handwriting of Sally.

Darton tore it open; it was very short.

'DEAR MR DARTON, – We have been so alarmed these last few
days by the report that you were ruined by the stoppage of ——'s
Bank, that, now it is contradicted, I hasten, by my mother's wish,
to say how truly glad we are to find there is no foundation for the
report. After your kindness to my poor brother's children, I can
do no less than write at such a moment. We had a letter from each
of them a few days ago. – Your faithful friend,
                                                          SALLY HALL'

'Mercenary little woman!' said Darton to himself with a smile. 'Then
that was the secret of her refusal this time – she thought I was ruined.'

Now, such was Darton, that as hours went on he could not help feeling
too generously towards Sally to condemn her in this. What did he want
in a wife? he asked himself. Love and integrity. What next? Worldly
wisdom. And was there really more than worldly wisdom in her refusal
to go aboard a sinking ship? She now knew it was otherwise. 'Begad,' he
said, 'I'll try her again.'

The fact was he had so set his heart upon Sally, and Sally alone, that
nothing was to be allowed to baulk him, and his reasoning was purely
formal.

Anniversaries having been unpropitious, he waited on till a bright day
late in May – a day when all animate nature was fancying, in its trusting,
foolish way, that it was going to bask under blue sky for evermore. As he
rode through Long-Ash Lane it was scarce recognizable as the track of
his two winter journeys. No mistake could be made now, even with his
eyes shut. The cuckoo's note was at its best, between April tentativeness
and midsummer decrepitude, and the reptiles in the sun behaved as

winningly as kittens on a hearth. Though afternoon, and about the same time as on the last occasion, it was broad day and sunshine when he entered Hintock, and the details of the Knap dairy-house were visible far up the road. He saw Sally in the garden, and was set vibrating. He had first intended to go on to the inn; but 'No,' he said; 'I'll tie my horse to the garden-gate. If all goes well it can soon be taken round; if not, I mount and ride away.'

The tall shade of the horseman darkened the room in which Mrs Hall sat, and made her start, for he had ridden by a side path to the top of the slope, where riders seldom came. In a few seconds he was in the garden with Sally.

Five – ay, three minutes – did the business at the back of that row of bees. Though spring had come and heavenly blue consecrated the scene, Darton succeeded not. '*No*,' said Sally firmly. 'I will never, never marry you, Mr Darton. I would have done it once; but now I never can.'

'But—!' implored Mr Darton. And with a burst of real eloquence he went on to declare all sorts of things that he would do for her. He would drive her to see her mother every week – take her to London – settle so much money upon her – Heaven knows what he did not promise, suggest, and tempt her with. But it availed nothing. She interposed with a stout negative which closed the course of his argument like an iron gate across a highway. Darton paused.

'Then,' said he simply, 'you hadn't heard of my supposed failure when you declined last time?'

'I had not,' she said. 'That you believed me capable of refusing you for such a reason does not help your cause.'

'And 'tis not because of any soreness from my slighting you years ago?'

'No. That soreness is long past.'

'Ah – then you despise me, Sally!'

'No,' she slowly answered. 'I don't altogether despise you. I don't think you quite such a hero as I once did – that's all. The truth is, I am happy enough as I am, and I don't mean to marry at all. Now, may *I* ask a favour, sir?' She spoke with an ineffable charm, which, whenever he thought of it, made him curse his loss of her as long as he lived.

'To any extent.'

'Please do not put this question to me any more. Friends as long as you like, but lovers and married never.'

'I never will,' said Darton. 'Not if I live a hundred years.'

And he never did. That he had worn out his welcome in her heart was only too plain.

When his step-children had grown up and were placed out in life all communication between Darton and the Hall family ceased. It was only by chance that, years after, he learnt that Sally, notwithstanding the solicitations her attractions drew down upon her, had refused several offers of marriage, and steadily adhered to her purpose of leading a single life.

May 1884

The Distracted Preacher

I. HOW HIS COLD WAS CURED

SOMETHING delayed the arrival of the Wesleyan minister, and a young
man came temporarily in his stead. It was on the thirteenth of January
183– that Mr Stockdale, the young man in question, made his humble
entry into the village, unknown, and almost unseen. But when those of
the inhabitants who styled themselves of his connection became
acquainted with him, they were rather pleased with the substitute than
otherwise, though he had scarcely as yet acquired ballast of character
sufficient to steady the consciences of the hundred-and-forty Methodists
of pure blood who, at this time, lived in Nether-Moynton, and to give in
addition supplementary support to the mixed race which went to church
in the morning and chapel in the evening, or when there was a tea – as
many as a hundred-and-ten people more, all told, and including the
parish-clerk in the winter-time, when it was too dark for the vicar to
observe who passed up the street at seven o'clock – which, to be just to
him, he was never anxious to do.

It was owing to this overlapping of creeds that the celebrated
population-puzzle arose among the denser gentry of the district around
Nether-Moynton: how could it be that a parish containing fifteen score
of strong full-grown Episcopalians, and nearly thirteen score of well-
matured Dissenters, numbered barely two-and-twenty score adults in
all?

The young man being personally interesting, those with whom he
came in contact were content to waive for a while the graver question of
his sufficiency. It is said that at this time of his life his eyes were
affectionate, though without a ray of levity; that his hair was curly, and
his figure tall; that he was, in short, a very lovable youth, who won upon
his female hearers as soon as they saw and heard him, and caused them
to say, 'Why didn't we know of this before he came, that we might have
gi'ed him a warmer welcome!'

The fact was that, knowing him to be only provisionally selected, and expecting nothing remarkable in his person or doctrine, they and the rest of his flock in Nether-Moynton had felt almost as indifferent about his advent as if they had been the soundest church-going parishioners in the country, and he their true and appointed parson. Thus when Stockdale set foot in the place nobody had secured a lodging for him, and though his journey had given him a bad cold in the head he was forced to attend to that business himself. On inquiry he learnt that the only possible accommodation in the village would be found at the house of one Mrs Lizzy Newberry, at the upper end of the street.

It was a youth who gave this information, and Stockdale asked him who Mrs Newberry might be.

The boy said that she was a widow-woman, who had got no husband, because he was dead. Mr Newberry, he added, had been a well-to-do man enough, as the saying was, and a farmer; but he had gone off in a decline. As regarded Mrs Newberry's serious side, Stockdale gathered that she was one of the trimmers who went to church and chapel both.

'I'll go there,' said Stockdale, feeling that, in the absence of purely sectarian lodgings, he could do no better.

'She's a little particular, and won't hae gover'ment folks, or curates, or the pa'son's friends, or such like,' said the lad dubiously.

'Ah, that may be a promising sign: I'll call. Or no; just you go up and ask first if she can find room for me. I have to see one or two persons on another matter. You will find me down at the carrier's.'

In a quarter of an hour the lad came back, and said that Mrs Newberry would have no objection to accommodate him, whereupon Stockdale called at the house. It stood within a garden-hedge, and seemed to be roomy and comfortable. He saw an elderly woman, with whom he made arrangements to come the same night, since there was no inn in the place, and he wished to house himself as soon as possible; the village being a local centre from which he was to radiate at once to the different small chapels in the neighbourhood. He forthwith sent his luggage to Mrs Newberry's from the carrier's, where he had taken shelter, and in the evening walked up to his temporary home.

As he now lived there, Stockdale felt it unnecessary to knock at the door, and entering quietly he had the pleasure of hearing footsteps scudding away like mice into the back quarters. He advanced to the parlour, as the front room was called, though its stone floor was scarcely disguised by the carpet, which only overlaid the trodden areas, leaving

sandy deserts under the furniture. But the room looked snug and cheerful. The firelight shone out brightly, trembling on the bulging mouldings
of the table-legs, playing with brass knobs and handles, and lurking in
great strength on the under surface of the chimney-piece. A deep arm-
chair, covered with horsehair, and studded with a countless throng of
brass nails, was pulled up on one side of the fireplace. The tea-things
were on the table, the teapot cover was open, and a little handbell had
been laid at that precise point towards which a person seated in the
great chair might be expected instinctively to stretch his hand.

Stockdale sat down, not objecting to his experience of the room thus
far, and began his residence by tinkling the bell. A little girl crept in at
the summons, and made tea for him. Her name, she said, was Marther
Sarer, and she lived out there, nodding towards the road and village
generally. Before Stockdale had got far with his meal a tap sounded on
the door behind him, and on his telling the inquirer to come in, a rustle
of garments caused him to turn his head. He saw before him a fine and
extremely well-made young woman, with dark hair, a wide, sensible,
beautiful forehead, eyes that warmed him before he knew it, and a mouth
that was in itself a picture to all appreciative souls.

'Can I get you anything else for tea ?' she said, coming forward a step
or two, an expression of liveliness on her features, and her hand waving
the door by its edge.

'Nothing, thank you,' said Stockdale, thinking less of what he replied
than of what might be her relation to the household.

'You are quite sure ?' said the young woman, apparently aware that he
had not considered his answer.

He conscientiously examined the tea-things, and found them all
there. 'Quite sure, Miss Newberry,' he said.

'It is Mrs Newberry,' she said. 'Lizzy Newberry. I used to be Lizzy
Simpkins.'

'O, I beg your pardon, Mrs Newberry.' And before he had occasion to
say more she left the room.

Stockdale remained in some doubt till Martha Sarah came to clear the
table. 'Whose house is this, my little woman ?' said he.

'Mrs Lizzy Newberry's, sir.'

'Then Mrs Newberry is not the old lady I saw this afternoon ?'

'No. That's Mrs Newberry's mother. It was Mrs Newberry who
comed in to you just by now, because she wanted to see if you was good-
looking.'

Later in the evening, when Stockdale was about to begin supper, she came again. 'I have come myself, Mr Stockdale,' she said. The minister stood up in acknowledgment of the honour. 'I am afraid little Marther might not make you understand. What will you have for supper? – there's cold rabbit, and there's a ham uncut.'

Stockdale said he could get on nicely with those viands, and supper was laid. He had no more than cut a slice when tap-tap came to the door again. The minister had already learnt that this particular rhythm in taps denoted the fingers of his enkindling landlady, and the doomed young fellow buried his first mouthful under a look of receptive blandness.

'We have a chicken in the house, Mr Stockdale – I quite forgot to mention it just now. Perhaps you would like Marther Sarer to bring it up?'

Stockdale had advanced far enough in the art of being a young man to say that he did not want the chicken, unless she brought it up herself; but when it was uttered he blushed at the daring gallantry of the speech, perhaps a shade too strong for a serious man and a minister. In three minutes the chicken appeared, but, to his great surprise, only in the hands of Martha Sarah. Stockdale was disappointed, which perhaps it was intended that he should be.

He had finished supper, and was not in the least anticipating Mrs Newberry again that night, when she tapped and entered as before. Stockdale's gratified look told that she had lost nothing by not appearing when expected. It happened that the cold in the head from which the young man suffered had increased with the approach of night, and before she had spoken he was seized with a violent fit of sneezing which he could not anyhow repress.

Mrs Newberry looked full of pity. 'Your cold is very bad to-night, Mr Stockdale.'

Stockdale replied that it was rather troublesome.

'And I've a good mind—' she added archly, looking at the cheerless glass of water on the table, which the abstemious minister was going to drink.

'Yes, Mrs Newberry?'

'I've a good mind that you should have something more likely to cure it than that cold stuff.'

'Well,' said Stockdale, looking down at the glass, 'as there is no inn here, and nothing better to be got in the village, of course it will do.'

To this she replied, 'There is something better, not far off, though not in the house. I really think you must try it, or you may be ill. Yes, Mr Stockdale, you shall.' She held up her finger, seeing that he was about to speak. 'Don't ask what it is; wait, and you shall see.'

Lizzy went away, and Stockdale waited in a pleasant mood. Presently she returned with her bonnet and cloak on, saying, 'I am so sorry, but you must help me to get it. Mother has gone to bed. Will you wrap yourself up, and come this way, and please bring that cup with you?'

Stockdale, a lonely young fellow, who had for weeks felt a great craving for somebody on whom to throw away superfluous interest, and even tenderness, was not sorry to join her, and followed his guide through the back door across the garden, to the bottom, where the boundary was a wall. This wall was low, and beyond it Stockdale discerned in the night shades several grey headstones, and the outlines of the church roof and tower.

'It is easy to get up this way,' she said, stepping upon a bank which abutted on the wall; then putting her foot on the top of the stonework, and descending by a spring inside, where the ground was much higher, as is the manner of graveyards to be. Stockdale did the same, and followed her in the dusk across the irregular ground till they came to the tower door, which, when they had entered, she softly closed behind them.

'You can keep a secret?' she said, in a musical voice.

'Like an iron chest!' said he fervently.

Then from under her cloak she produced a small lighted lantern, which the minister had not noticed that she carried at all. The light showed them to be close to the singing-gallery stairs, under which lay a heap of lumber of all sorts, but consisting mostly of decayed framework, pews, panels, and pieces of flooring, that from time to time had been removed from their original fixings in the body of the edifice and replaced by new.

'Perhaps you will drag some of those boards aside?' she said, holding the lantern over her head to light him better. 'Or will you take the lantern while I move them?'

'I can manage it,' said the young man, and acting as she ordered, he uncovered, to his surprise, a row of little barrels bound with wood hoops, each barrel being about as large as the nave of a heavy waggon-wheel. When they were laid open Lizzy fixed her eyes on him, as if she wondered what he would say.

'You know what they are ?' she asked, finding that he did not speak.

'Yes, barrels,' said Stockdale simply. He was an inland man, the son of highly respectable parents, and brought up with a single eye to the ministry, and the sight suggested nothing beyond the fact that such articles were there.

'You are quite right, they are barrels,' she said, in an emphatic tone of candour that was not without a touch of irony.

Stockdale looked at her with an eye of sudden misgiving. 'Not smugglers' liquor ?' he said.

'Yes,' said she. 'They are tubs of spirit that have accidentally floated over in the dark from France.'

In Nether-Moynton and its vicinity at this date people always smiled at the sort of sin called in the outside world illicit trading; and these little kegs of gin and brandy were as well known to the inhabitants as turnips. So that Stockdale's innocent ignorance, and his look of alarm when he guessed the sinister mystery, seemed to strike Lizzy first as ludicrous, and then as very awkward for the good impression that she wished to produce upon him.

'Smuggling is carried on here by some of the people,' she said in a gentle, apologetic voice. 'It has been their practice for generations, and they think it no harm. Now, will you roll out one of the tubs ?'

'What to do with it ?' said the minister.

'To draw a little from it to cure your cold,' she answered. 'It is so 'nation strong that it drives away that sort of thing in a jiffy. O, it is all right about our taking it. I may have what I like; the owner of the tubs says so. I ought to have had some in the house, and then I shouldn't ha' been put to this trouble; but I drink none myself, and so I often forget to keep it indoors.'

'You are allowed to help yourself, I suppose, that you may not inform where their hiding-place is ?'

'Well, no; not that particularly; but I may take any if I want it. So help yourself.'

'I will, to oblige you, since you have a right to it,' murmured the minister; and though he was not quite satisfied with his part in the performance, he rolled one of the 'tubs' out from the corner into the middle of the tower floor. 'How do you wish me to get it out – with a gimlet, I suppose ?'

'No, I'll show you,' said his interesting companion; and she held up with her other hand a shoemaker's awl and a hammer. 'You must never do these things with a gimlet, because the wood-dust gets in; and when the buyers pour out the brandy that would tell them that the tub had been broached. An awl makes no dust, and the hole nearly closes up again. Now tap one of the hoops forward.'

Stockdale took the hammer and did so.

'Now make the hole in the part that was covered by the hoop.'

He made the hole as directed. 'It won't run out,' he said.

'O yes it will,' said she. 'Take the tub between your knees, and squeeze the heads; and I'll hold the cup.'

Stockdale obeyed; and the pressure taking effect upon the tub, which seemed to be thin, the spirit spirted out in a stream. When the cup was full he ceased pressing, and the flow immediately stopped. 'Now we must fill up the keg with water,' said Lizzy, 'or it will cluck like forty hens when it is handled, and show that 'tis not full.'

'But they tell you you may take it?'

'Yes, the *smugglers*; but the *buyers* must not know that the smugglers have been kind to me at their expense.'

'I see,' said Stockdale doubtfully. 'I much question the honesty of this proceeding.'

By her direction he held the tub with the hole upwards, and while he went through the process of alternately pressing and ceasing to press, she produced a bottle of water, from which she took mouthfuls, conveying each to the keg by putting her pretty lips to the hole, where it was sucked in at each recovery of the cask from pressure. When it was again full he plugged the hole, knocked the hoop down to its place, and buried the tub in the lumber as before.

'Aren't the smugglers afraid that you will tell?' he asked, as they recrossed the churchyard.

'O no; they are not afraid of that. I couldn't do such a thing.'

'They have put you into a very awkward corner,' said Stockdale emphatically. 'You must, of course, as an honest person, sometimes feel that it is your duty to inform – really you must.'

'Well, I have never particularly felt it as a duty; and, besides, my first husband—' She stopped, and there was some confusion in her voice. Stockdale was so honest and unsophisticated that he did not at once discern why she paused: but at last he did perceive that the words were a slip, and that no woman would have uttered 'first husband' by accident unless she had thought pretty frequently of a second. He felt for her confusion, and allowed her time to recover and proceed. 'My husband,' she said, in a self-corrected tone, 'used to know of their doings, and so did my father, and kept the secret. I cannot inform, in fact, against anybody.'

'I see the hardness of it,' he continued, like a man who looked far into the moral of things. 'And it is very cruel that you should be tossed and tantalized between your memories and your conscience. I do hope, Mrs Newberry, that you will soon see your way out of this unpleasant position.'

'Well, I don't just now,' she murmured.

By this time they had passed over the wall and entered the house, where she brought him a glass and hot water, and left him to his own reflections. He looked after her vanishing form, asking himself whether he, as a respectable man, and a minister, and a shining light, even though as yet only of the halfpenny-candle sort, were quite justified in doing this thing. A sneeze settled the question; and he found that when the fiery liquid was lowered by the addition of twice or thrice the quantity of water, it was one of the prettiest cures for a cold in the head that he had ever known, particularly at this chilly time of the year.

Stockdale sat in the deep chair about twenty minutes sipping and meditating, till he at length took warmer views of things, and longed for the morrow, when he would see Mrs Newberry again. He then felt that, though chronologically at a short distance, it would in an emotional sense be very long before to-morrow came, and walked restlessly round the room. His eye was attracted by a framed and glazed sampler in which a running ornament of fir-trees and peacocks surrounded the following pretty bit of sentiment: –

> 'Rose-leaves smell when roses thrive,
> Here's my work while I'm alive;
> Rose-leaves smell when shrunk and shed,
> Here's my work when I am dead.

> 'Lizzy Simpkins. Fear God. Honour the King.
> Aged 11 years.'

' 'Tis hers,' he said to himself. 'Heavens, how I like that name!'

Before he had done thinking that no other name from Abigail to Zenobia would have suited his young landlady so well, tap-tap came again upon the door; and the minister started as her face appeared yet another time, looking so disinterested that the most ingenious would

have refrained from asserting that she had come to affect his feelings by
her seductive eyes.

'Would you like a fire in your room, Mr Stockdale, on account of your
cold?'

The minister, being still a little pricked in the conscience for counten-
ancing her in watering the spirits, saw here a way to self-chastisement.
'No, I thank you,' he said firmly; 'it is not necessary. I have never been
used to one in my life, and it would be giving way to luxury too far.'

'Then I won't insist,' she said, and disconcerted him by vanishing
instantly.

Wondering if she was vexed by his refusal, he wished that he had
chosen to have a fire, even though it should have scorched him out of
bed and endangered his self-discipline for a dozen days. However, he
consoled himself with what was in truth a rare consolation for a budding
lover, that he was under the same roof with Lizzy; her guest, in fact, to
take a poetical view of the term lodger; and that he would certainly see
her on the morrow.

The morrow came, and Stockdale rose early, his cold quite gone. He
had never in his life so longed for the breakfast-hour as he did that day,
and punctually at eight o'clock, after a short walk to reconnoitre the
premises, he re-entered the door of his dwelling. Breakfast passed, and
Martha Sarah attended, but nobody came voluntarily as on the night
before to inquire if there were other wants which he had not mentioned,
and which she would attempt to gratify. He was disappointed, and went
out, hoping to see her at dinner. Dinner-time came; he sat down to the
meal, finished it, lingered on for a whole hour, although two new teachers
were at that moment waiting at the chapel-door to speak to him by
appointment. It was useless to wait longer, and he slowly went his way
down the lane, cheered by the thought that, after all, he would see her
in the evening, and perhaps engage again in the delightful tub-broaching
in the neighbouring church tower, which proceeding he resolved to
render more moral by steadfastly insisting that no water should be
introduced to fill up, though the tub should cluck like all the hens in
Christendom. But nothing could disguise the fact that it was a queer
business; and his countenance fell when he thought how much more
his mind was interested in that matter than in his serious duties.

However, compunction vanished with the decline of day. Night came,
and his tea and supper; but no Lizzy Newberry, and no sweet tempta-
tions. At last the minister could bear it no longer, and said to his quaint

little attendant, 'Where is Mrs Newberry to-day?' judiciously handing
a penny as he spoke.

'She's busy,' said Martha.

'Anything serious happened?' he asked, handing another penny, and
revealing yet additional pennies in the background.

'O no – nothing at all!' said she, with breathless confidence. 'Nothing
ever happens to her. She's only biding upstairs in bed because 'tis her
way sometimes.'

Being a young man of some honour he would not question further,
and assuming that Lizzy must have a bad headache, or other slight
ailment, in spite of what the girl had said, he went to bed dissatisfied,
not even setting eyes on old Mrs Simpkins. 'I said last night that I
should see her to-morrow,' he reflected; 'but that was not to be!'

Next day he had better fortune, or worse, meeting her at the foot of
the stairs in the morning, and being favoured by a visit or two from her
during the day – once for the purpose of making kindly inquiries about
his comfort, as on the first evening, and at another time to place a bunch
of winter-violets on his table, with a promise to renew them when they
drooped. On these occasions there was something in her smile which
showed how conscious she was of the effect she produced, though it
must be said that it was rather a humorous than a designing consciousness, and savoured more of pride than of vanity.

As for Stockdale, he clearly perceived that he possessed unlimited
capacity for backsliding, and wished that tutelary saints were not denied
to Dissenters. He set a watch upon his tongue and eyes for the space of
one hour and a half, after which he found it was useless to struggle
further, and gave himself up to the situation. 'The other minister will
be here in a month,' he said to himself when sitting over the fire. 'Then I
shall be off, and she will distract my mind no more! . . . And then,
shall I go on living by myself for ever? No; when my two years of
probation are finished, I shall have a furnished house to live in, with a
varnished door and a brass knocker; and I'll march straight back to her,
and ask her flat, as soon as the last plate is on the dresser!'

Thus a titillating fortnight was passed by young Stockdale, during
which time things proceeded much as such matters have done ever
since the beginning of history. He saw the object of attachment several
times one day, did not see her at all the next, met her when he least
expected to do so, missed her when hints and signs as to where she
should be at a given hour almost amounted to an appointment. This

mild coquetry was perhaps fair enough under the circumstances of their being so closely lodged, and Stockdale put up with it as philosophically as he was able. Being in her own house she could, after vexing him or disappointing him of her presence, easily win him back by suddenly surrounding him with those little attentions which her position as his landlady put it in her power to bestow. When he had waited indoors half the day to see her, and on finding that she would not be seen, had gone off in a huff to the dreariest and dampest walk he could discover, she would restore equilibrium in the evening with 'Mr Stockdale, I have fancied you must feel draught o' nights from your bedroom window, and so I have been putting up thicker curtains this afternoon while you were out'; or, 'I noticed that you sneezed twice again this morning, Mr Stockdale. Depend upon it that cold is hanging about you yet; I am sure it is – I have thought of it continually; and you must let me make a posset for you.'

Sometimes in coming home he found his sitting-room rearranged, chairs placed where the table had stood, and the table ornamented with the few fresh flowers and leaves that could be obtained at this season, so as to add a novelty to the room. At times she would be standing on a chair outside the house, trying to nail up a branch of the monthly rose which the winter wind had blown down; and of course he stepped forward to assist her, when their hands got mixed in passing the shreds and nails. Thus they became friends again after a disagreement. She would utter on these occasions some pretty and deprecatory remark on the necessity of her troubling him anew; and he would straightway say that he would do a hundred times as much for her if she should so require.

II. HOW HE SAW TWO OTHER MEN

Matters being in this advancing state, Stockdale was rather surprised one cloudy evening, while sitting in his room, at hearing her speak in low tones of expostulation to some one at the door. It was nearly dark, but the shutters were not yet closed, nor the candles lighted; and Stockdale was tempted to stretch his head towards the window. He saw outside the door a young man in clothes of a whitish colour, and upon reflection judged their wearer to be the well-built and rather handsome miller who lived below. The miller's voice was alternately low and firm, and sometimes it reached the level of positive entreaty; but what the words were Stockdale could in no way hear.

Before the colloquy had ended, the minister's attention was attracted by a second incident. Opposite Lizzy's home grew a clump of laurels, forming a thick and permanent shade. One of the laurel boughs now quivered against the light background of sky, and in a moment the head of a man peered out, and remained still. He seemed to be also much interested in the conversation at the door, and was plainly lingering there to watch and listen. Had Stockdale stood in any other relation to Lizzy than that of a lover, he might have gone out and investigated the meaning of this: but being as yet but an unprivileged ally, he did nothing more than stand up and show himself against the firelight, whereupon the listener disappeared, and Lizzy and the miller spoke in lower tones.

Stockdale was made so uneasy by the circumstance, that as soon as the miller was gone, he said, 'Mrs Newberry, are you aware that you were watched just now, and your conversation heard?'

'When?' she said.

'When you were talking to that miller. A man was looking from the laurel-tree as jealously as if he could have eaten you.'

She showed more concern than the trifling event seemed to demand, and he added, 'Perhaps you were talking of things you did not wish to be overheard?'

'I was talking only on business,' she said.

'Lizzy, be frank!' said the young man. 'If it was only on business, why should anybody wish to listen to you?'

She looked curiously at him. 'What else do you think it could be, then?'

'Well – the only talk between a young woman and man that is likely to amuse an eavesdropper.'

'Ah yes,' she said, smiling in spite of her preoccupation. 'Well, my cousin Owlett has spoken to me about matrimony, every now and then, that's true; but he was not speaking of it then. I wish he had been speaking of it, with all my heart. It would have been much less serious for me.'

'O Mrs Newberry!'

'It would. Not that I should ha' chimed in with him, of course. I wish it for other reasons. I am glad, Mr Stockdale, that you have told me of that listener. It is a timely warning, and I must see my cousin again.'

'But don't go away till I have spoken,' said the minister. 'I'll out with it at once, and make no more ado. Let it be Yes or No between us, Lizzy; please do!' And he held out his hand, in which she freely allowed her own to rest, but without speaking.

'You mean Yes by that?' he asked, after waiting a while.

'You may be my sweetheart, if you will.'

'Why not say at once you will wait for me until I have a house and can come back to marry you.'

'Because I am thinking – thinking of something else,' she said with embarrassment. 'It all comes upon me at once, and I must settle one thing at a time.'

'At any rate, dear Lizzy, you can assure me that the miller shall not be allowed to speak to you except on business? You have never directly encouraged him?'

She parried the question by saying, 'You see, he and his party have been in the habit of leaving things on my premises sometimes, and as I have not denied him, it makes him rather forward.'

'Things – what things?'

'Tubs – they are called Things here.'

'But why don't you deny him, my dear Lizzy?'

'I cannot well.'

'You are too timid. It is unfair of him to impose so upon you, and get your good name into danger by his smuggling tricks. Promise me that the next time he wants to leave his tubs here you will let me roll them into the street?'

She shook her head. 'I would not venture to offend the neighbours so much as that,' said she, 'or do anything that would be so likely to put poor Owlett into the hands of the Customs-men.'

Stockdale sighed, and said that he thought hers a mistaken generosity when it extended to assisting those who cheated the king of his dues. 'At any rate, you will let me make him keep his distance as your lover, and tell him flatly that you are not for him?'

'Please not, at present,' she said. 'I don't wish to offend my old neighbours. It is not only Mr Owlett who is concerned.'

'This is too bad,' said Stockdale impatiently.

'On my honour, I won't encourage him as my lover,' Lizzy answered earnestly. 'A reasonable man will be satisfied with that.'

'Well, so I am,' said Stockdale, his countenance clearing.

III. THE MYSTERIOUS GREATCOAT

Stockdale now began to notice more particularly a feature in the life of his fair landlady, which he had casually observed but scarcely ever thought of before. It was that she was markedly irregular in her hours of rising. For a week or two she would be tolerably punctual, reaching the ground-floor within a few minutes of half-past seven. Then suddenly she would not be visible till twelve at noon, perhaps for three or four days in succession; and twice he had certain proof that she did not leave her room till half-past three in the afternoon. The second time that this extreme lateness came under his notice was on a day when he had particularly wished to consult with her about his future movements; and he concluded, as he always had done, that she had a cold, headache, or other ailment, unless she had kept herself invisible to avoid meeting and talking to him, which he could hardly believe. The former supposition was disproved, however, by her innocently saying, some days later, when they were speaking on a question of health, that she had never had a moment's heaviness, headache, or illness of any kind since the previous January twelvemonth.

'I am glad to hear it,' said he. 'I thought quite otherwise.'

'What, do I look sickly?' she asked, turning up her face to show the impossibility of his gazing on it and holding such a belief for a moment.

'Not at all; I merely thought so from your being sometimes obliged to keep your room through the best part of the day.'

'O, as for that – it means nothing,' she murmured, with a look which some might have called cold, and which was the worst look that he liked to see upon her. 'It is pure sleepiness, Mr Stockdale.'

'Never!'

'It is, I tell you. When I stay in my room till half-past three in the afternoon, you may always be sure that I slept soundly till three, or I shouldn't have stayed there.'

'It is dreadful,' said Stockdale, thinking of the disastrous effects of such indulgence upon the household of a minister, should it become a habit of everyday occurrence.

'But then,' she said, divining his good and prescient thoughts, 'it only happens when I stay awake all night. I don't go to sleep till five or six in the morning sometimes.'

'Ah, that's another matter,' said Stockdale. 'Sleeplessness to such an alarming extent is real illness. Have you spoken to a doctor?'

'O no – there is no need for doing that – it is all natural to me.' And she went away without further remark.

Stockdale might have waited a long time to know the real cause of her sleeplessness, had it not happened that one dark night he was sitting in his bedroom jotting down notes for a sermon, which occupied him perfunctorily for a considerable time after the other members of the household had retired. He did not get to bed till one o'clock. Before he had fallen asleep he heard a knocking at the front door, first rather timidly performed, and then louder. Nobody answered it, and the person knocked again. As the house still remained undisturbed, Stockdale got out of bed, went to his window, which overlooked the door, and opening it, asked who was there.

A young woman's voice replied that Susan Wallis was there, and that she had come to ask if Mrs Newberry could give her some mustard to make a plaster with, as her father was taken very ill on the chest.

The minister, having neither bell nor servant, was compelled to act in person. 'I will call Mrs Newberry,' he said. Partly dressing himself, he went along the passage and tapped at Lizzy's door. She did not answer, and, thinking of her erratic habits in the matter of sleep, he thumped the door persistently, when he discovered, by its moving ajar under his knocking, that it had only been gently pushed to. As there was now a sufficient entry for the voice, he knocked no longer, but said in firm tones, 'Mrs Newberry, you are wanted.'

The room was quite silent; not a breathing, not a rustle, came from any part of it. Stockdale now sent a positive shout through the open space of the door: 'Mrs Newberry!' – still no answer, or movement of any kind within. Then he heard sounds from the opposite room, that of Lizzy's mother, as if she had been aroused by his uproar though Lizzy had not, and was dressing herself hastily. Stockdale softly closed the younger woman's door and went on to the other, which was opened by Mrs Simpkins before he could reach it. She was in her ordinary clothes, and had a light in her hand.

'What's the person calling about?' she said in alarm.

Stockdale told the girl's errand, adding seriously, 'I cannot wake Mrs Newberry.'

'It is no matter,' said her mother. 'I can let the girl have what she wants as well as my daughter.' And she came out of the room and went downstairs.

Stockdale retired towards his own apartment, saying, however, to Mrs Simpkins from the landing, as if on second thoughts, 'I suppose there is nothing the matter with Mrs Newberry, that I could not wake her?'

'O no,' said the old lady hastily. 'Nothing at all.'

Still the minister was not satisfied. 'Will you go in and see?' he said. 'I should be much more at ease.'

Mrs Simpkins returned up the staircase, went to her daughter's room, and came out again almost instantly. 'There is nothing at all the matter with Lizzy,' she said; and descended again to attend to the applicant, who, having seen the light, had remained quiet during this interval.

Stockdale went into his room and lay down as before. He heard Lizzy's mother open the front door, admit the girl, and then the murmured discourse of both as they went to the store-cupboard for the medicament required. The girl departed, the door was fastened, Mrs Simpkins came upstairs, and the house was again in silence. Still the minister did not fall asleep. He could not get rid of a singular suspicion, which was all the more harassing in being, if true, the most unaccountable thing within his experience. That Lizzy Newberry was in her bedroom when he made such a clamour at the door he could not possibly convince himself, notwithstanding that he had heard her come upstairs at the usual time, go into her chamber, and shut herself up in the usual way. Yet all reason was so much against her being elsewhere, that he was constrained to go back again to the unlikely theory of a heavy sleep, though he had heard neither breath nor movement during a shouting and knocking loud enough to rouse the Seven Sleepers.

Before coming to any positive conclusion he fell asleep himself, and did not awake till day. He saw nothing of Mrs Newberry in the morning, before he went out to meet the rising sun, as he liked to do when the weather was fine; but as this was by no means unusual, he took no notice of it. At breakfast-time he knew that she was not far off by hearing her in the kitchen, and though he saw nothing of her person, that back apartment being rigorously closed against his eyes, she seemed to be talking, ordering, and bustling about among the pots and skimmers in so ordinary a manner, that there was no reason for his wasting more time in fruitless surmise.

The minister suffered from these distractions, and his extemporized sermons were not improved thereby. Already he often said Romans for

Corinthians in the pulpit, and gave out hymns in strange cramped metres, that hitherto had always been skipped, because the congregation could not raise a tune to fit them. He fully resolved that as soon as his few weeks of stay approached their end he would cut the matter short, and commit himself by proposing a definite engagement, repenting at leisure if necessary.

With this end in view, he suggested to her on the evening after her mysterious sleep that they should take a walk together just before dark, the latter part of the proposition being introduced that they might return home unseen. She consented to go; and away they went over a stile, to a shrouded footpath suited for the occasion. But, in spite of attempts on both sides, they were unable to infuse much spirit into the ramble. She looked rather paler than usual, and sometimes turned her head away.

'Lizzy,' said Stockdale reproachfully, when they had walked in silence a long distance.

'Yes,' said she.

'You yawned – much my company is to you!' He put it in that way, but he was really wondering whether her yawn could possibly have more to do with physical weariness from the night before than mental weariness of that present moment. Lizzy apologized, and owned that she was rather tired, which gave him an opening for a direct question on the point; but his modesty would not allow him to put it to her; and he uncomfortably resolved to wait.

The month of February passed with alternations of mud and frost, rain and sleet, east winds and north-westerly gales. The hollow places in the ploughed fields showed themselves as pools of water, which had settled there from the higher levels, and had not yet found time to soak away. The birds began to get lively, and a single thrush came just before sunset each evening, and sang hopefully on the large elm-tree which stood nearest to Mrs Newberry's house. Cold blasts and brittle earth had given place to an oozing dampness more unpleasant in itself than frost; but it suggested coming spring, and its unpleasantness was of a bearable kind.

Stockdale had been going to bring about a practical understanding with Lizzy at least half a dozen times; but, what with the mystery of her apparent absence on the night of the neighbour's call, and her curious way of lying in bed at unaccountable times, he felt a check within him whenever he wanted to speak out. Thus they still lived on as indefinitely

affianced lovers, each of whom hardly acknowledged the other's claim to
the name of chosen one. Stockdale persuaded himself that his hesitation
was owing to the postponement of the ordained minister's arrival, and
the consequent delay in his own departure, which did away with all
necessity for haste in his courtship; but perhaps it was only that his
discretion was reasserting itself, and telling him that he had better get
clearer ideas of Lizzy before arranging for the grand contract of his life
with her. She, on her part, always seemed ready to be urged further on
that question than he had hitherto attempted to go; but she was none
the less independent, and to a degree which would have kept from
flagging the passion of a far more mutable man.

On the evening of the first of March he went casually into his bedroom
about dusk, and noticed lying on a chair a greatcoat, hat, and breeches.
Having no recollection of leaving any clothes of his own in that spot, he
went and examined them as well as he could in the twilight, and found
that they did not belong to him. He paused for a moment to consider
how they might have got there. He was the only man living in the house;
and yet these were not his garments, unless he had made a mistake. No,
they were not his. He called up Martha Sarah.

'How did these things come in my room?' he said, flinging the
objectionable articles to the floor.

Martha said that Mrs Newberry had given them to her to brush, and
that she had brought them up there thinking they must be Mr Stockdale's,
as there was no other gentleman a-lodging there.

'Of course you did,' said Stockdale. 'Now take them down to your
mis'ess, and say they are some clothes I have found here and know
nothing about.'

As the door was left open he heard the conversation downstairs. 'How
stupid!' said Mrs Newberry, in a tone of confusion. 'Why, Marther
Sarer, I did not tell you to take 'em to Mr Stockdale's room!'

'I thought they must be his as they was so muddy,' said Martha
humbly.

'You should have left 'em on the clothes-horse,' said the young
mistress severely; and she came upstairs with the garments on her arm,
quickly passed Stockdale's room, and threw them forcibly into a closet at
the end of a passage. With this the incident ended, and the house was
silent again.

There would have been nothing remarkable in finding such clothes in
a widow's house had they been clean; or moth-eaten, or creased, or

mouldy from long lying by; but that they should be splashed with
recent mud bothered Stockdale a good deal. When a young pastor is in
the aspen stage of attachment, and open to agitation at the merest trifles,
a really substantial incongruity of this complexion is a disturbing thing.
However, nothing further occurred at that time; but he became
watchful, and given to conjecture, and was unable to forget the circumstance.

One morning, on looking from his window, he saw Mrs Newberry
herself brushing the tails of a long drab greatcoat, which, if he mistook
not, was the very same garment as the one that had adorned the chair
of his room. It was densely splashed up to the hollow of the back
with neighbouring Nether-Moynton mud, to judge by its colour, the
spots being distinctly visible to him in the sunlight. The previous day or
two having been wet, the inference was irresistible that the wearer had
quite recently been walking some considerable distance about the lanes
and fields. Stockdale opened the window and looked out, and Mrs
Newberry turned her head. Her face became slowly red; she never had
looked prettier, or more incomprehensible. He waved his hand affection-
ately, and said good-morning; she answered with embarrassment,
having ceased her occupation on the instant that she saw him, and rolled
up the coat half-cleaned.

Stockdale shut the window. Some simple explanation of her proceeding was doubtless within the bounds of possibility; but he himself
could not think of one; and he wished that she had placed the matter
beyond conjecture by voluntarily saying something about it there and
then.

But, though Lizzy had not offered an explanation at the moment, the
subject was brought forward by her at the next time of their meeting.
She was chatting to him concerning some other event, and remarked
that it happened about the time when she was dusting some old clothes
that had belonged to her poor husband.

'You keep them clean out of respect to his memory?' said Stockdale
tentatively.

'I air and dust them sometimes,' she said, with the most charming
innocence in the world.

'Do dead men come out of their graves and walk in mud?' murmured the minister, in a cold sweat at the deception that she was
practising.

'What did you say?' asked Lizzy.

'Nothing, nothing,' said he mournfully. 'Mere words – a phrase that will do for my sermon next Sunday.' It was too plain that Lizzy was unaware that he had seen fresh pedestrian splashes upon the skirts of the tell-tale overcoat, and that she imagined him to believe it had come direct from some chest or drawer.

The aspect of the case was now considerably darker. Stockdale was so much depressed by it that he did not challenge her explanation, or threaten to go off as a missionary to benighted islanders, or reproach her in any way whatever. He simply parted from her when she had done talking, and lived on in perplexity, till by degrees his natural manner became sad and constrained.

IV. AT THE TIME OF THE NEW MOON

The following Thursday was changeable, damp, and gloomy; and the night threatened to be windy and unpleasant. Stockdale had gone away to Knollsea in the morning, to be present at some commemoration service there, and on his return he was met by the attractive Lizzy in the passage. Whether influenced by the tide of cheerfulness which had attended him that day, or by the drive through the open air, or whether from a natural disposition to let bygones alone, he allowed himself to be fascinated into forgetfulness of the greatcoat incident, and upon the whole passed a pleasant evening; not so much in her society as within sound of her voice, as she sat talking in the back parlour to her mother, till the latter went to bed. Shortly after this Mrs Newberry retired, and then Stockdale prepared to go upstairs himself. But before he left the room he remained standing by the dying embers a while, thinking long of one thing and another; and was only aroused by the flickering of his candle in the socket as it suddenly declined and went out. Knowing that there were a tinder-box, matches, and another candle in his bedroom, he felt his way upstairs without a light. On reaching his chamber he laid his hand on every possible ledge and corner for the tinder-box, but for a long time in vain. Discovering it at length, Stockdale produced a spark, and was kindling the brimstone, when he fancied that he heard a movement in the passage. He blew harder at the lint, the match flared up, and looking by aid of the blue light through the door, which had been standing open all this time, he was surprised to see a male figure vanishing

round the top of the staircase with the evident intention of escaping unobserved. The personage wore the clothes which Lizzy had been
brushing, and something in the outline and gait suggested to the
minister that the wearer was Lizzy herself.

But he was not sure of this; and, greatly excited, Stockdale determined to investigate the mystery, and to adopt his own way for doing it.
He blew out the match without lighting the candle, went into the
passage, and proceeded on tiptoe towards Lizzy's room. A faint gray
square of light in the direction of the chamber-window as he approached
told him that the door was open, and at once suggested that the occupant
was gone. He turned and brought down his fist upon the handrail of the
staircase: 'It was she; in her late husband's coat and hat!'

Somewhat relieved to find that there was no intruder in the case, yet
none the less surprised, the minister crept down the stairs, softly put on
his boots, overcoat, and hat, and tried the front door. It was fastened as
usual; he went to the back door, found this unlocked, and emerged into
the garden. The night was mild and moonless, and rain had lately been
falling, though for the present it had ceased. There was a sudden dropping from the trees and bushes every now and then, as each passing wind
shook their boughs. Among these sounds Stockdale heard the faint fall
of feet upon the road outside, and he guessed from the step that it was
Lizzy's. He followed the sound, and, helped by the circumstance of the
wind blowing from the direction in which the pedestrian moved, he got
nearly close to her, and kept there, without risk of being overheard.
While he thus followed her up the street or lane, as it might indifferently
be called, there being more hedge than houses on either side, a figure
came forward to her from one of the cottage doors. Lizzy stopped; the
minister stepped upon the grass and stopped also.

'Is that Mrs Newberry?' said the man who had come out, whose
voice Stockdale recognized as that of one of the most devout members
of his congregation.

'It is,' said Lizzy.

'I be quite ready – I've been here this quarter-hour.'

'Ah, John,' said she, 'I have bad news; there is danger to-night for
our venture.'

'And d'ye tell o't! I dreamed there might be.'

'Yes,' she said hurriedly; 'and you must go at once round to where the
chaps are waiting, and tell them they will not be wanted till to-morrow
night at the same time. I go to burn the lugger off.'

'I will,' he said; and instantly went off through a gate, Lizzy continuing her way.

On she tripped at a quickening pace till the lane turned into the turnpike-road, which she crossed, and got into the track for Ringsworth. Here she ascended the hill without the least hesitation, passed the lonely hamlet of Holworth, and went down the vale on the other side. Stockdale had never taken any extensive walks in this direction, but he was aware that if she persisted in her course much longer she would draw near to the coast, which was here between two and three miles distant from Nether-Moynton; and as it had been about a quarter-past eleven o'clock when they set out, her intention seemed to be to reach the shore about midnight.

Lizzy soon ascended a small mound, which Stockdale at the same time adroitly skirted on the left; and a dull monotonous roar burst upon his ear. The hillock was about fifty yards from the top of the cliffs, and by day it apparently commanded a full view of the bay. There was light enough in the sky to show her disguised figure against it when she reached the top, where she paused, and afterwards sat down. Stockdale, not wishing on any account to alarm her at this moment, yet desirous of being near her, sank upon his hands and knees, crept a little higher up, and there stayed still.

The wind was chilly, the ground damp, and his position one in which he did not care to remain long. However, before he had decided to leave it, the young man heard voices behind him. What they signified he did not know; but, fearing that Lizzy was in danger, he was about to run forward and warn her that she might be seen, when she crept to the shelter of a little bush which maintained a precarious existence in that exposed spot; and her form was absorbed in its dark and stunted outline as if she had become part of it. She had evidently heard the men as well as he. They passed near him, talking in loud and careless tones, which could be heard above the uninterrupted washings of the sea, and which suggested that they were not engaged in any business at their own risk. This proved to be the fact; some of their words floated across to him, and caused him to forget at once the coldness of his situation.

'What's the vessel?'

'A lugger, about fifty tons.'

'From Cherbourg, I suppose?'

'Yes, 'a b'lieve.'

'But it don't all belong to Owlett?'

'O no. He's only got a share. There's another or two in it – a farmer and such like, but the names I don't know.'

The voices died away, and the heads and shoulders of the men diminished towards the cliff, and dropped out of sight.

'My darling has been tempted to buy a share by that unbeliever Owlett,' groaned the minister, his honest affection for Lizzy having quickened to its intensest point during these moments of risk to her person and name. 'That's why she's here,' he said to himself. 'O, it will be the ruin of her!'

His perturbation was interrupted by the sudden bursting out of a bright and increasing light from the spot where Lizzy was in hiding. A few seconds later, and before it had reached the height of a blaze, he heard her rush past him down the hollow like a stone from a sling, in the direction of home. The light now flared high and wide, and showed its position clearly. She had kindled a bough of furze and stuck it into the bush under which she had been crouching; the wind fanned the flame, which crackled fiercely, and threatened to consume the bush as well as the bough. Stockdale paused just long enough to notice thus much, and then followed rapidly the route taken by the young woman. His intention was to overtake her, and reveal himself as a friend; but run as he would he could see nothing of her. Thus he flew across the open country about Holworth, twisting his legs and ankles in unexpected fissures and descents, till, on coming to the gate between the downs and the road, he was forced to pause to get breath. There was no audible movement either in front or behind him, and he now concluded that she had not outrun him, but that, hearing him at her heels, and believing him one of the excise party, she had hidden herself somewhere on the way, and let him pass by.

He went on at a more leisurely pace towards the village. On reaching the house he found his surmise to be correct, for the gate was on the latch, and the door unfastened, just as he had left them. Stockdale closed the door behind him, and waited silently in the passage. In about ten minutes he heard the same light footstep that he had heard in going out; it paused at the gate, which opened and shut softly, and then the door-latch was lifted, and Lizzy came in.

Stockdale went forward and said at once, 'Lizzy, don't be frightened. I have been waiting up for you.'

She started, though she had recognized the voice. 'It is Mr Stockdale, isn't it?' she said.

'Yes,' he answered, becoming angry now that she was safe indoors, and not alarmed. 'And a nice game I've found you out in to-night. You are in man's clothes, and I am ashamed of you!'

Lizzy could hardly find a voice to answer this unexpected reproach.

'I am only partly in man's clothes,' she faltered, shrinking back to the wall. 'It is only his greatcoat and hat and breeches that I've got on, which is no harm, as he was my own husband; and I do it only because a cloak blows about so, and you can't use your arms. I have got my own dress under just the same – it is only tucked in! Will you go away upstairs and let me pass? I didn't want you to see me at such a time as this!'

'But I have a right to see you! How do you think there can be anything between us now?' Lizzy was silent. 'You are a smuggler,' he continued sadly.

'I have only a share in the run,' she said.

'That makes no difference. Whatever did you engage in such a trade as that for, and keep it such a secret from me all this time?'

'I don't do it always. I only do it in winter-time when 'tis new moon.'

'Well, I suppose that's because it can't be done anywhen else. . . . You have regularly upset me, Lizzy.'

'I am sorry for that,' Lizzy meekly replied.

'Well now,' said he more tenderly, 'no harm is done as yet. Won't you for the sake of me give up this blameable and dangerous practice altogether?'

'I must do my best to save this run,' said she, getting rather husky in the throat. 'I don't want to give you up – you know that; but I don't want to lose my venture. I don't know what to do now! Why I have kept it so secret from you is that I was afraid you would be angry if you knew.'

'I should think so! I suppose if I had married you without finding this out you'd have gone on with it just the same?'

'I don't know. I did not think so far ahead. I only went to-night to burn the folks off, because we found that the Preventive-men knew where the tubs were to be landed.'

'It is a pretty mess to be in altogether, is this,' said the distracted young minister. 'Well, what will you do now?'

Lizzy slowly murmured the particulars of their plan, the chief of which were that they meant to try their luck at some other point of the shore the next night; that three landing-places were always agreed upon

before the run was attempted, with the understanding that, if the vessel
was 'burnt off' from the first point, which was Ringsworth, as it had
been by her to-night, the crew should attempt to make the second,
which was Lulwind Cove, on the second night; and if there, too,
danger threatened, they should on the third night try the third place,
which was behind a headland further west.

'Suppose the officers hinder them landing there, too?' he said, his
attention to this interesting programme displacing for a moment his
concern at her share in it.

'Then we shan't try anywhere else all this dark – that's what we call
the time between moon and moon – and perhaps they'll string the tubs
to a stray-line, and sink 'em a little-ways from shore, and take the
bearings; and then when they have a chance they'll go to creep for 'em.'

'What's that?'

'O, they'll go out in a boat and drag a creeper – that's a grapnel –
along the bottom till it catch hold of the stray-line.'

The minister stood thinking; and there was no sound within doors
but the tick of the clock on the stairs, and the quick breathing of Lizzy,
partly from her walk and partly from agitation, as she stood close to the
wall, not in such complete darkness but that he could discern against its
whitewashed surface the greatcoat, breeches, and broad hat which
covered her.

'Lizzy, all this is very wrong,' he said. 'Don't you remember the
lesson of the tribute-money? "Render unto Cæsar the things that are
Cæsar's." Surely you have heard that read times enough in your
growing up?'

'He's dead,' she pouted.

'But the spirit of the text is in force just the same.'

'My father did it, and so did my grandfather, and almost everybody
in Nether-Moynton lives by it, and life would be so dull if it wasn't for
that, that I should not care to live at all.'

'I am nothing to live for, of course,' he replied bitterly. 'You would
not think it worth while to give up this wild business and live for me
alone?'

'I have never looked at it like that.'

'And you won't promise and wait till I am ready?'

'I cannot give you my word to-night.' And, looking thoughtfully
down, she gradually moved and moved away, going into the adjoining
room, and closing the door between them. She remained there in the

dark till he was tired of waiting, and had gone up to his own chamber.

Poor Stockdale was dreadfully depressed all the next day by the discoveries of the night before. Lizzy was unmistakably a fascinating young woman, but as a minister's wife she was hardly to be contemplated. 'If I had only stuck to father's little grocery business, instead of going in for the ministry, she would have suited me beautifully!' he said sadly, until he remembered that in that case he would never have come from his distant home to Nether-Moynton, and never have known her.

The estrangement between them was not complete, but it was sufficient to keep them out of each other's company. Once during the day he met her in the garden-path, and said, turning a reproachful eye upon her, 'Do you promise, Lizzy?' But she did not reply. The evening drew on, and he knew well enough that Lizzy would repeat her excursion at night – her half-offended manner had shown that she had not the slightest intention of altering her plans at present. He did not wish to repeat his own share of the adventure; but, act as he would, his uneasiness on her account increased with the decline of day. Supposing that an accident should befall her, he would never forgive himself for not being there to help, much as he disliked the idea of seeming to countenance such unlawful escapades.

V. HOW THEY WENT TO LULWIND COVE

As he had expected, she left the house at the same hour at night, this time passing his door without stealth, as if she knew very well that he would be watching, and were resolved to brave his displeasure. He was quite ready, opened the door quickly, and reached the back door almost as soon as she.

'Then you will go, Lizzy?' he said as he stood on the step beside her, who now again appeared as a little man with a face altogether unsuited to his clothes.

'I must,' she said, repressed by his stern manner.

'Then I shall go, too,' said he.

'And I am sure you will enjoy it!' she exclaimed in more buoyant tones. 'Everybody does who tries it.'

'God forbid that I should!' he said. 'But I must look after you.'

They opened the wicket and went up the road abreast of each other, but at some distance apart, scarcely a word passing between them. The evening was rather less favourable to smuggling enterprise than the last had been, the wind being lower, and the sky somewhat clear towards the north.

'It is rather lighter,' said Stockdale.

' 'Tis, unfortunately,' said she. 'But it is only from those few stars over there. The moon was new to-day at four o'clock, and I expected clouds. I hope we shall be able to do it this dark, for when we have to sink 'em for long it makes the stuff taste bleachy, and folks don't like it so well.'

Her course was different from that of the preceding night, branching off to the left over Lord's Barrow as soon as they had got out of the lane and crossed the highway. By the time they reached Chaldon Down, Stockdale, who had been in perplexed thought as to what he should say to her, decided that he would not attempt expostulation now, while she was excited by the adventure, but wait till it was over, and endeavour to keep her from such practices in future. It occurred to him once or twice, as they rambled on, that should they be surprised by the Preventive-guard, his situation would be more awkward than hers, for it would be difficult to prove his true motive in coming to the spot; but the risk was a slight consideration beside his wish to be with her.

They now arrived at a ravine which lay on the outskirts of Chaldon, a village two miles on their way towards the point of the shore they sought. Lizzy broke the silence this time: 'I have to wait here to meet the carriers. I don't know if they have come yet. As I told you, we go to Lulwind Cove to-night, and it is two miles further than Ringsworth.'

It turned out that the men had already come; for while she spoke two or three dozen heads broke the line of the slope, and a company of them at once descended from the bushes where they had been lying in wait. These carriers were men whom Lizzy and other proprietors regularly employed to bring the tubs from the boat to a hiding-place inland. They were all young fellows of Nether-Moynton, Chaldon, and the neighbourhood, quiet and inoffensive persons, even though some held heavy sticks, who simply engaged to carry the cargo for Lizzy and her cousin Owlett, as they would have engaged in any other labour for which they were fairly well paid.

At a word from her they closed in together. 'You had better take it now,' she said to them; and handed to each a packet. It contained six shillings, their remuneration for the night's undertaking, which was paid

beforehand without reference to success or failure; but, besides this,
they had the privilege of selling as agents when the run was successfully
made. As soon as it was done, she said to them, 'The place is the old one,
Dagger's Grave, near Lulwind Cove'; the men till that moment not
having been told whither they were bound, for obvious reasons. 'Mr
Owlett will meet you there,' added Lizzy. 'I shall follow behind, to see
that we are not watched.'

The carriers went on, and Stockdale and Mrs Newberry followed
at a distance of a stone's throw. 'What do these men do by day?' he
said.

'Twelve or fourteen of them are labouring men. Some are brick-
makers, some carpenters, some shoemakers, some thatchers. They are all
known to me very well. Nine of 'em are of your own congregation.'

'I can't help that,' said Stockdale.

'O, I know you can't. I only told you. The others are more church-
inclined, because they supply the pa'son with all the spirits he requires,
and they don't wish to show unfriendliness to a customer.'

'How do you choose 'em?' said Stockdale.

'We choose 'em for their closeness, and because they are strong and
surefooted, and able to carry a heavy load a long way without being
tired.'

Stockdale sighed as she enumerated each particular, for it proved how
far involved in the business a woman must be who was so well acquainted
with its conditions and needs. And yet he felt more tenderly towards her
at this moment than he had felt all the foregoing day. Perhaps it was that
her experienced manner and bold indifference stirred his admiration in
spite of himself.

'Take my arm, Lizzy,' he murmured.

'I don't want it,' she said. 'Besides, we may never be to each other
again what we once have been.'

'That depends upon you,' said he, and they went on again as before.

The hired carriers paced along over Chaldon Down with as little
hesitation as if it had been day, avoiding the cartway, and leaving the
village of East Chaldon on the left, so as to reach the crest of the hill at a
lonely trackless place not far from the ancient earthwork called Round
Pound. A quarter-hour more of brisk walking brought them within
sound of the sea, to the place called Dagger's Grave, not many hundred
yards from Lulwind Cove. Here they paused, and Lizzy and Stockdale
came up with them, when they went on together to the verge of the

cliff. One of the men now produced an iron bar, which he drove firmly into the soil a yard from the edge, and attached to it a rope that he had uncoiled from his body. They all began to descend, partly stepping, partly sliding down the incline, as the rope slipped through their hands.

'You will not go to the bottom, Lizzy?' said Stockdale anxiously.

'No. I stay here to watch,' she said. 'Mr Owlett is down there.'

The men remained quite silent when they reached the shore; and the next thing audible to the two at the top was the dip of heavy oars, and the dashing of waves against a boat's bow. In a moment the keel gently touched the shingle, and Stockdale heard the footsteps of the thirty-six carriers running forwards over the pebbles towards the point of landing.

There was a sousing in the water as of a brood of ducks plunging in, showing that the men had not been particular about keeping their legs, or even their waists, dry from the brine: but it was impossible to see what they were doing, and in a few minutes the shingle was trampled again. The iron bar sustaining the rope, on which Stockdale's hand rested, began to swerve a little, and the carriers one by one appeared climbing up the sloping cliff, dripping audibly as they came, and sustaining themselves by the guide-rope. Each man on reaching the top was seen to be carrying a pair of tubs, one on his back and one on his chest, the two being slung together by cords passing round the chine hoops, and resting on the carrier's shoulders. Some of the stronger men carried three by putting an extra one on the top behind, but the customary load was a pair, these being quite weighty enough to give their bearer the sensation of having chest and backbone in contact after a walk of four or five miles.

'Where is Mr Owlett?' said Lizzy to one of them.

'He will not come up this way,' said the carrier. 'He's to bide on shore till we be safe off.' Then, without waiting for the rest, the foremost men plunged across the down, and, when the last had ascended, Lizzy pulled up the rope, wound it round her arm, wriggled the bar from the sod, and turned to follow the carriers.

'You are very anxious about Owlett's safety,' said the minister.

'Was there ever such a man!' said Lizzy. 'Why, isn't he my cousin?'

'Yes. Well, it is a bad night's work,' said Stockdale heavily. 'But I'll carry the bar and rope for you.'

'Thank God, the tubs have got so far all right,' said she.

Stockdale shook his head, and, taking the bar, walked by her side towards the downs; and the moan of the sea was heard no more.

'Is this what you meant the other day when you spoke of having business with Owlett?' the young man asked.

'This is it,' she replied. 'I never see him on any other matter.'

'A partnership of that kind with a young man is very odd.'

'It was begun by my father and his, who were brother-laws.'

Her companion could not blind himself to the fact that where tastes and pursuits were so akin as Lizzy's and Owlett's, and where risks were shared, as with them, in every undertaking, there would be a peculiar appropriateness in her answering Owlett's standing question on matrimony in the affirmative. This did not soothe Stockdale, its tendency being rather to stimulate in him an effort to make the pair as inappropriate as possible, and win her away from this nocturnal crew to correctness of conduct and a minister's parlour in some far-removed inland county.

They had been walking near enough to the file of carriers for Stockdale to perceive that, when they got into the road to the village, they split up into two companies of unequal size, each of which made off in a direction of its own. One company, the smaller of the two, went towards the church, and by the time that Lizzy and Stockdale reached their own house these men had scaled the churchyard wall, and were proceeding noiselessly over the grass within.

'I see that Mr Owlett has arranged for one batch to be put in the church again,' observed Lizzy. 'Do you remember my taking you there the first night you came?'

'Yes, of course,' said Stockdale. 'No wonder you had permission to broach the tubs – they were his, I suppose?'

'No, they were not – they were mine; I had permission from myself. The day after that they went several miles inland in a waggon-load of manure, and sold very well.'

At this moment the group of men who had made off to the left some time before began leaping one by one from the hedge opposite Lizzy's house, and the first man, who had no tubs upon his shoulders, came forward.

'Mrs Newberry, isn't it?' he said hastily.

'Yes, Jim,' said she. 'What's the matter?'

'I find that we can't put any in Badger's Clump to-night, Lizzy,' said Owlett. 'The place is watched. We must sling the apple-tree in the orchet if there's time. We can't put any more under the church lumber than I have sent on there, and my mixen hev already more in en than is safe.'

'Very well,' she said. 'Be quick about it – that's all. What can I do ?'

'Nothing at all, please. Ah, it is the minister! – you two that can't do anything had better get indoors and not be zeed.'

While Owlett thus conversed, in a tone so full of contraband anxiety and so free from lover's jealousy, the men who followed him had been descending one by one from the hedge; and it unfortunately happened that when the hindmost took his leap, the cord slipped which sustained his tubs; the result was that both the kegs fell into the road, one of them being stove in by the blow.

' 'Od drown it all!' said Owlett, rushing back.

'It is worth a good deal, I suppose ?' said Stockdale.

'O no – about two guineas and half to us now,' said Lizzy excitedly. 'It isn't that – it is the smell! It is so blazing strong before it has been lowered by water, that it smells dreadfully when spilt in the road like that! I do hope Latimer won't pass by till it is gone off.'

Owlett and one or two others picked up the burst tub and began to scrape and trample over the spot, to disperse the liquor as much as possible; and then they all entered the gate of Owlett's orchard, which adjoined Lizzy's garden on the right. Stockdale did not care to follow them, for several on recognizing him had looked wonderingly at his presence, though they said nothing. Lizzy left his side and went to the bottom of the garden, looking over the hedge into the orchard, where the men could be dimly seen bustling about, and apparently hiding the tubs. All was done noiselessly, and without a light; and when it was over they dispersed in different directions, those who had taken their cargoes to the church having already gone off to their homes.

Lizzy returned to the garden-gate, over which Stockdale was still abstractedly leaning. 'It is all finished: I am going indoors now,' she said gently. 'I will leave the door ajar for you.'

'O no – you needn't,' said Stockdale; 'I am coming too.'

But before either of them had moved, the faint clatter of horses' hoofs broke upon the ear, and it seemed to come from the point where the track across the down joined the hard road.

'They are just too late!' cried Lizzy exultingly.

'Who ?' said Stockdale.

'Latimer, the riding-officer, and some assistant of his. We had better go indoors.'

They entered the house, and Lizzy bolted the door. 'Please don't get a light, Mr Stockdale,' she said.

'Of course I will not,' said he.

'I thought you might be on the side of the king,' said Lizzy, with faintest sarcasm.

'I am,' said Stockdale. 'But, Lizzy Newberry, I love you, and you know it perfectly well, and you ought to know, if you do not, what I have suffered in my conscience on your account these last few days!'

'I guess very well,' she said hurriedly. 'Yet I don't see why. Ah, you are better than I!'

The trotting of the horses seemed to have again died away, and the pair of listeners touched each other's fingers in the cold 'Good-night' of those whom something seriously divided. They were on the landing, but before they had taken three steps apart, the tramp of the horsemen suddenly revived, almost close to the house. Lizzy turned to the staircase window, opened the casement about an inch, and put her face close to the aperture. 'Yes, one of 'em is Latimer,' she whispered. 'He always rides a white horse. One would think it was the last colour for a man in that line.'

Stockdale looked, and saw the white shape of the animal as it passed by; but before the riders had gone another ten yards Latimer reined in his horse, and said something to his companion which neither Stockdale nor Lizzy could hear. Its drift was, however, soon made evident, for the other man stopped also; and sharply turning the horses' heads they cautiously retraced their steps. When they were again opposite Mrs Newberry's garden, Latimer dismounted, and the man on the dark horse did the same.

Lizzy and Stockdale, intently listening and observing the proceedings, naturally put their heads as close as possible to the slit formed by the slightly opened casement; and thus it occurred that at last their cheeks came positively into contact. They went on listening, as if they did not know of the singular incident which had happened to their faces, and the pressure of each to each rather increased than lessened with the lapse of time.

They could hear the Customs-men sniffing the air like hounds as they paced slowly along. When they reached the spot where the tub had burst, both stopped on the instant.

'Ay, ay, 'tis quite strong here,' said the second officer. 'Shall we knock at the door?'

'Well, no,' said Latimer. 'Maybe this is only a trick to put us off the scent. They wouldn't kick up this stink anywhere near their hiding-place. I have known such things before.'

'Anyhow, the things, or some of 'em, must have been brought this way,' said the other.

'Yes,' said Latimer musingly. 'Unless 'tis all done to tole us the wrong way. I have a mind that we go home for to-night without saying a word, and come the first thing in the morning with more hands. I know they have storages about here, but we can do nothing by this owl's light. We will look round the parish and see if everybody is in bed, John; and if all is quiet, we will do as I say.'

They went on, and the two inside the window could hear them passing leisurely through the whole village, the street of which curved round at the bottom and entered the turnpike road at another junction. This way the officers followed, and the amble of their horses died quite away.

'What will you do?' said Stockdale, withdrawing from his position.

She knew that he alluded to the coming search by the officers to divert her attention from their own tender incident by the casement, which he wished to be passed over as a thing rather dreamt of than done. 'O, nothing,' she replied, with as much coolness as she could command under her disappointment at his manner. 'We often have such storms as this. You would not be frightened if you knew what fools they are. Fancy riding o' horseback through the place; of course they will hear and see nobody while they make that noise; but they are always afraid to get off, in case some of our fellows should burst out upon 'em, and tie them up to the gate-post, as they have done before now. Good-night, Mr Stockdale.'

She closed the window and went to her room, where a tear fell from her eyes; and that not because of the alertness of the riding-officers.

VI. THE GREAT SEARCH AT NETHER-MOYNTON

Stockdale was so excited by the events of the evening, and the dilemma that he was placed in between conscience and love, that he did not sleep, or even doze, but remained as broadly awake as at noonday. As soon as the gray light began to touch ever so faintly the whiter objects in his bedroom he arose, dressed himself, and went downstairs into the road.

The village was already astir. Several of the carriers had heard the well-known canter of Latimer's horse while they were undressing in the dark that night, and had already communicated with each other and Owlett on the subject. The only doubt seemed to be about the safety of those tubs which had been left under the church gallery-stairs, and after a short discussion at the corner of the mill, it was agreed that these should be removed before it got lighter, and hidden in the middle of a double hedge bordering the adjoining field. However, before anything could be carried into effect, the footsteps of many men were heard coming down the lane from the highway.

'Damn it, here they be,' said Owlett, who, having already drawn the hatch and started his mill for the day, stood stolidly at the mill-door covered with flour, as if the interest of his whole soul was bound up in the shaking walls around him.

The two or three with whom he had been talking dispersed to their usual work, and when the Customs-officers, and the formidable body of men they had hired, reached the village cross, between the mill and Mrs Newberry's house, the village wore the natural aspect of a place beginning its morning labours.

'Now,' said Latimer to his associates, who numbered thirteen men in all, 'what I know is that the things are somewhere in this here place. We have got the day before us, and 'tis hard if we can't light upon 'em and get 'em to Budmouth Custom-house before night. First we will try the fuel-houses, and then we'll work our way into the chimmers, and then to the ricks and stables, and so creep round. You have nothing but your noses to guide ye, mind, so use 'em to-day if you never did in your lives before.'

Then the search began. Owlett, during the early part, watched from his mill-window, Lizzy from the door of her house, with the greatest self-possession. A farmer down below, who also had a share in the run, rode about with one eye on his fields and the other on Latimer and his myrmidons, prepared to put them off the scent if he should be asked a question. Stockdale, who was no smuggler at all, felt more anxiety than the worst of them, and went about his studies with a heavy heart, coming frequently to the door to ask Lizzy some question or other on the consequences to her of the tubs being found.

'The consequences,' she said quietly, 'are simply that I shall lose 'em. As I have none in the house or garden, they can't touch me personally.'

'But you have some in the orchard?'

'Mr Owlett rents that of me, and he lends it to others. So it will be hard to say who put any tubs there if they should be found.'

There was never such a tremendous sniffing known as that which took place in Nether-Moynton parish and its vicinity this day. All was done methodically, and mostly on hands and knees. At different hours of the day they had different plans. From daybreak to breakfast-time the officers used their sense of smell in a direct and straightforward manner only, pausing nowhere but at such places as the tubs might be supposed to be secreted in at that very moment, pending their removal on the following night. Among the places tested and examined were: –

Hollow trees	Cupboards	Culverts
Potato-graves	Clock-cases	Hedgerows
Fuel-houses	Chimney-flues	Faggot-ricks
Bedrooms	Rainwater-butts	Haystacks
Apple-lofts	Pigsties	Coppers and ovens

After breakfast they recommenced with renewed vigour, taking a new line; that is to say, directing their attention to clothes that might be supposed to have come in contact with the tubs in their removal from the shore, such garments being usually tainted with the spirit, owing to its oozing between the staves. They now sniffed at –

Smock-frocks	Smiths' and shoemakers' aprons
Old shirts and waistcoats	Knee-naps and hedging-gloves
Coats and hats	Tarpaulins
Breeches and leggings	Market-cloaks
Women's shawls and gowns	Scarecrows

And as soon as the midday meal was over, they pushed their search into places where the spirits might have been thrown away in alarm: –

Horse-ponds	Mixens	Sinks in yards
Stable-drains	Wet ditches	Road-scrapings, and
Cinder-heaps	Cesspools	Back-door gutters

But still these indefatigable Custom-house men discovered nothing more than the original tell-tale smell in the road opposite Lizzy's house, which even yet had not passed off.

'I'll tell ye what it is, men,' said Latimer, about three o'clock in the afternoon, 'we must begin over again. Find them tubs I will.'

The men, who had been hired for the day, looked at their hands and knees, muddy with creeping on all fours so frequently, and rubbed their noses, as if they had almost had enough of it; for the quantity of bad air which had passed into each one's nostril had rendered it nearly as insensible as a flue. However, after a moment's hesitation, they prepared to start anew, except three, whose power of smell had quite succumbed under the excessive wear and tear of the day.

By this time not a male villager was to be seen in the parish. Owlett was not at his mill, the farmers were not in their fields, the parson was not in his garden, the smith had left his forge, and the wheelwright's shop was silent.

'Where the divil are the folk gone?' said Latimer, waking up to the fact of their absence, and looking round. 'I'll have 'em up for this! Why don't they come and help us? There's not a man about the place but the Methodist parson, and he's an old woman. I demand assistance in the king's name!'

'We must find the jineral public afore we can demand that,' said his lieutenant.

'Well, well, we shall do better without 'em,' said Latimer, who changed his moods at a moment's notice. 'But there's great cause of suspicion in this silence and this keeping out of sight, and I'll bear it in mind. Now we will go across to Owlett's orchard and see what we can find there.'

Stockdale, who heard this discussion from the garden-gate, over which he had been leaning, was rather alarmed, and thought it a mistake of the villagers to keep so completely out of the way. He himself, like the Preventives, had been wondering for the last half-hour what could have become of them. Some labourers were of necessity engaged in distant fields, but the master-workmen should have been at home; though one and all, after just showing themselves at their shops, had apparently gone off for the day. He went in to Lizzy, who sat at a back window sewing, and said, 'Lizzy, where are the men?'

Lizzy laughed. 'Where they mostly are when they're run so hard as this.' She cast her eyes to heaven. 'Up there,' she said.

Stockdale looked up. 'What – on the top of the church tower?' he asked, seeing the direction of her glance.

'Yes.'

'Well, I expect they will soon have to come down,' said he gravely. 'I have been listening to the officers, and they are going to search the orchard over again, and then every nook in the church.'

Lizzy looked alarmed for the first time. 'Will you go and tell our
folk?' she said. 'They ought to be let know.' Seeing his conscience
struggling within him like a boiling pot, she added, 'No, never mind,
I'll go myself.'

She went out, descended the garden, and climbed over the churchyard wall at the same time that the Preventive-men were ascending the
road to the orchard. Stockdale could do no less than follow her. By the
time that she reached the tower entrance he was at her side, and they
entered together.

Nether-Moynton church-tower was, as in many villages, without a
turret, and the only way to the top was by going up to the singers'
gallery, and thence ascending by a ladder to a square trap-door in the
floor of the bell-loft, above which a permanent ladder was fixed, passing
through the bells to a hole in the roof. When Lizzy and Stockdale
reached the gallery and looked up, nothing but the trap-door and the
five holes for the bell-ropes appeared. The ladder was gone.

'There's no getting up,' said Stockdale.

'O yes, there is,' said she. 'There's an eye looking at us at this moment
through a knot-hole in that trap-door.'

And as she spoke the trap opened, and the dark line of the ladder was
seen descending against the whitewashed wall. When it touched the
bottom Lizzy dragged it to its place, and said, 'If you'll go up, I'll
follow.'

The young man ascended, and presently found himself among
consecrated bells for the first time in his life, nonconformity having been
in the Stockdale blood for some generations. He eyed them uneasily,
and looked round for Lizzy. Owlett stood here, holding the top of the
ladder.

'What, be you really one of us?' said the miller.

'It seems so,' said Stockdale sadly.

'He's not,' said Lizzy, who overheard. 'He's neither for nor against us.
He'll do us no harm.'

She stepped up beside them, and then they went on to the next stage,
which, when they had clambered over the dusty bell-carriages, was of
easy ascent, leading towards the hole through which the pale sky
appeared, and into the open air. Owlett remained behind for a moment,
to pull up the lower ladder.

'Keep down your heads,' said a voice, as soon as they set foot on the
flat.

Stockdale here beheld all the missing parishioners, lying on their stomachs on the tower roof, except a few who, elevated on their hands and knees, were peeping through the embrasures of the parapet. Stockdale did the same, and saw the village lying like a map below him, over which moved the figures of the Customs-men, each foreshortened to a crablike object, the crown of his hat forming a circular disc in the centre of him. Some of the men had turned their heads when the young preacher's figure arose among them.

'What, Mr Stockdale?' said Matt Grey, in a tone of surprise.

'I'd as lief that it hadn't been,' said Jim Clarke. 'If the pa'son should see him a-trespassing here in his tower, 'twould be none the better for we, seeing how 'a do hate chapel-members. He'd never buy a tub of us again, and he's as good a customer as we have got this side o' Warm'll.'

'Where is the pa'son?' said Lizzy.

'In his house, to be sure, that he mid see nothing of what's going on – where all good folks ought to be, and this young man likewise.'

'Well, he has brought some news,' said Lizzy. 'They are going to search the orchard and church; can we do anything if they should find?'

'Yes,' said her cousin Owlett. 'That's what we've been talking o', and we have settled our line. Well, be dazed!'

The exclamation was caused by his perceiving that some of the searchers, having got into the orchard, and begun stooping and creeping hither and thither, were pausing in the middle, where a tree smaller than the rest was growing. They drew closer, and bent lower than ever upon the ground.

'O, my tubs!' said Lizzy faintly, as she peered through the parapet at them.

'They have got 'em, 'a b'lieve,' said Owlett.

The interest in the movements of the officers was so keen that not a single eye was looking in any other direction; but at that moment a shout from the church beneath them attracted the attention of the smugglers, as it did also of the party in the orchard, who sprang to their feet and went towards the churchyard wall. At the same time those of the Government men who had entered the church unperceived by the smugglers cried aloud, 'Here be some of 'em at last.'

The smugglers remained in a blank silence, uncertain whether 'some of 'em' meant tubs or men; but again peeping cautiously over the edge

of the tower they learnt that tubs were the things descried; and soon
these fated articles were brought one by one into the middle of the
churchyard from their hiding-place under the gallery-stairs.

'They are going to put 'em on Hinton's vault till they find the rest!'
said Lizzy hopelessly. The Customs-men had, in fact, begun to pile up
the tubs on a large stone slab which was fixed there; and when all were
brought out from the tower, two or three of the men were left standing
by them, the rest of the party again proceeding to the orchard.

The interest of the smugglers in the next manœuvres of their enemies
became painfully intense. Only about thirty tubs had been secreted in
the lumber of the tower, but seventy were hidden in the orchard, making
up all that they had brought ashore as yet, the remainder of the cargo
having been tied to a sinker and dropped overboard for another night's
operations. The Preventives, having re-entered the orchard, acted as if
they were positive that here lay hidden the rest of the tubs, which they
were determined to find before nightfall. They spread themselves out
round the field, and advancing on all fours as before, went anew round
every apple-tree in the enclosure. The young tree in the middle again led
them to pause, and at length the whole company gathered there in a way
which signified that a second chain of reasoning had led to the same
results as the first.

When they had examined the sod hereabouts for some minutes, one
of the men rose, ran to a disused part of the church where tools were
kept, and returned with the sexton's pickaxe and shovel, with which
they set to work.

'Are they really buried there?' said the minister, for the grass was so
green and uninjured that it was difficult to believe it had been disturbed.
The smugglers were too interested to reply, and presently they saw, to
their chagrin, the officers stand several on each side of the tree; and,
stooping and applying their hands to the soil, they bodily lifted the
tree and the turf around it. The apple-tree now showed itself to be
growing in a shallow box, with handles for lifting at each of the four
sides. Under the site of the tree a square hole was revealed, and an
officer went and looked down.

'It is all up now,' said Owlett quietly. 'And now all of ye get down
before they notice we are here; and be ready for our next move. I had
better bide here till dark, or they may take me on suspicion, as 'tis on
my ground. I'll be with ye as soon as daylight begins to pink in.'

'And I!' said Lizzy.

'You please look to the linch-pins and screws; then go indoors and know nothing at all. The chaps will do the rest.'

The ladder was replaced, and all but Owlett descended, the men passing off one by one at the back of the church, and vanishing on their respective errands. Lizzy walked boldly along the street, followed closely by the minister.

'You are going indoors, Mrs Newberry?' he said.

She knew from the words 'Mrs Newberry' that the division between them had widened yet another degree.

'I am not going home,' she said. 'I have a little thing to do before I go in. Martha Sarah will get your tea.'

'O, I don't mean on that account,' said Stockdale. 'What *can* you have to do further in this unhallowed affair?'

'Only a little,' she said.

'What is that? I'll go with you.'

'No, I shall go by myself. Will you please go indoors? I shall be there in less than an hour.'

'You are not going to run any danger, Lizzy?' said the young man, his tenderness reasserting itself.

'None whatever – worth mentioning,' answered she, and went down towards the Cross.

Stockdale entered the garden-gate, and stood behind it looking on. The Preventive-men were still busy in the orchard, and at last he was tempted to enter and watch their proceedings. When he came closer he found that the secret cellar, of whose existence he had been totally unaware, was formed by timbers placed across from side to side about a foot under the ground, and grassed over.

The officers looked up at Stockdale's fair and downy countenance, and evidently thinking him above suspicion, went on with their work again. As soon as all the tubs were taken out they began tearing up the turf, pulling out the timbers, and breaking in the sides, till the cellar was wholly dismantled and shapeless, the apple-tree lying with its roots high to the air. But the hole which had in its time held so much contra-band merchandize was never completely filled up, either then or afterwards, a depression in the greensward marking the spot to this day.

VII. THE WALK TO WARM'ELL CROSS
AND AFTERWARDS

As the goods had all to be carried to Budmouth that night, the next object of the Custom-house officers was to find horses and carts for the journey, and they went about the village for that purpose. Latimer strode hither and thither with a lump of chalk in his hand, marking broad-arrows so vigorously on every vehicle and set of harness that he came across, that it seemed as if he would chalk broad-arrows on the very hedges and roads. The owner of every conveyance so marked was bound to give it up for Government purposes. Stockdale, who had had enough of the scene, turned indoors thoughtful and depressed. Lizzy was already there, having come in at the back, though she had not yet taken off her bonnet. She looked tired, and her mood was not much brighter than his own. They had but little to say to each other; and the minister went away and attempted to read; but at this he could not succeed, and he shook the little bell for tea.

Lizzy herself brought in the tray, the girl having run off into the village during the afternoon, too full of excitement at the proceedings to remember her state of life. However, almost before the sad lovers had said anything to each other, Martha came in in a steaming state.

'O, there's such a stoor, Mrs Newberry and Mr Stockdale! The king's officers can't get the carts ready nohow at all! They pulled Thomas Artnell's, and William Rogers's, and Stephen Sprake's carts into the road, and off came the wheels, and down fell the carts; and they found there was no linch-pins in the arms; and then they tried Samuel Shane's waggon, and found that the screws were gone from he, and at last they looked at the dairyman's cart, and he's got none neither! They have gone now to the blacksmith's to get some made, but he's nowhere to be found!'

Stockdale looked at Lizzy, who blushed very slightly, and went out of the room, followed by Martha Sarah. But before they had got through the passage there was a rap at the front door, and Stockdale recognized Latimer's voice addressing Mrs Newberry, who had turned back.

'For God's sake, Mrs Newberry, have you seen Hardman the blacksmith up this way? If we could get hold of him, we'd e'en a'most drag him by the hair of his head to his anvil, where he ought to be.'

'He's an idle man, Mr Latimer,' said Lizzy archly. 'What do you
want him for?'

'Why, there isn't a horse in the place that has got more than three
shoes on, and some have only two. The waggon-wheels be without
strakes, and there's no linch-pins to the carts. What with that, and the
bother about every set of harness being out of order, we shan't be off
before nightfall – upon my soul we shan't. 'Tis a rough lot, Mrs
Newberry, that you've got about you here; but they'll play at this game
once too often, mark my words they will! There's not a man in the
parish that don't deserve to be whipped.'

It happened that Hardman was at that moment a little further up the
lane, smoking his pipe behind a holly-bush. When Latimer had done
speaking he went on in this direction, and Hardman, hearing the
riding-officer's steps, found curiosity too strong for prudence. He
peeped out from the bush at the very moment that Latimer's glance was
on it. There was nothing left for him to do but to come forward with
unconcern.

'I've been looking for you for the last hour!' said Latimer with a
glare in his eye.

'Sorry to hear that,' said Hardman. 'I've been out for a stroll, to look
for more hid tubs, to deliver 'em up to Gover'ment.'

'O yes, Hardman, we know it,' said Latimer, with withering sarcasm.
'We know that you'll deliver 'em up to Gover'ment. We know that all
the parish is helping us, and have been all day! Now you please walk
along with me down to your shop, and kindly let me hire ye in the
king's name.'

They went down the lane together, and presently there resounded
from the smithy the ring of a hammer not very briskly swung. However,
the carts and horses were got into some sort of travelling condition, but
it was not until after the clock had struck six, when the muddy roads
were glistening under the horizontal light of the fading day. The
smuggled tubs were soon packed into the vehicles, and Latimer, with
three of his assistants, drove slowly out of the village in the direction of
the port of Budmouth, some considerable number of miles distant, the
other men of the Preventive-guard being left to watch for the remainder
of the cargo, which they knew to have been sunk somewhere between
Ringsworth and Lulwind Cove, and to unearth Owlett, the only person
clearly implicated by the discovery of the cave.

Women and children stood at the doors as the carts, each chalked with the Government pitchfork, passed in the increasing twilight; and as they stood they looked at the confiscated property with a melancholy expression that told only too plainly the relation which they bore to the trade.

'Well, Lizzy,' said Stockdale, when the crackle of the wheels had nearly died away. 'This is a fit finish to your adventure. I am truly thankful that you have got off without suspicion, and the loss only of the liquor. Will you sit down and let me talk to you?'

'By and by,' she said. 'But I must go out now.'

'Not to that horrid shore again?' he said blankly.

'No, not there. I am only going to see the end of this day's business.'

He did not answer to this, and she moved towards the door slowly, as if waiting for him to say something more.

'You don't offer to come with me,' she added at last. 'I suppose that's because you hate me after all this!'

'Can you say it, Lizzy, when you know I only want to save you from such practices? Come with you! – of course I will, if it is only to take care of you. But why will you go out again?'

'Because I cannot rest indoors. Something is happening, and I must know what. Now, come!' And they went into the dusk together.

When they reached the turnpike-road she turned to the right, and he soon perceived that they were following the direction of the Preventive-men and their load. He had given her his arm, and every now and then she suddenly pulled it back, to signify that he was to halt a moment and listen. They had walked rather quickly along the first quarter of a mile, and on the second or third time of standing still she said, 'I hear them ahead – don't you?'

'Yes,' he said; 'I hear the wheels. But what of that?'

'I only want to know if they get clear away from the neighbourhood.'

'Ah,' said he, a light breaking upon him. 'Something desperate is to be attempted! – and now I remember there was not a man about the village when we left.'

'Hark!' she murmured. The noise of the cart-wheels had stopped, and given place to another sort of sound.

' 'Tis a scuffle!' said Stockdale. 'There'll be murder! Lizzy, let go my arm; I am going on. On my conscience, I must not stay here and do nothing!'

'There'll be no murder, and not even a broken head,' she said. 'Our men are thirty to four of them: no harm will be done at all.'

'Then there *is* an attack!' exclaimed Stockdale; 'and you knew it was to be. Why should you side with men who break the laws like this ?'

'Why should you side with men who take from country traders what they have honestly bought wi' their own money in France ?' said she firmly.

'They are not honestly bought,' said he.

'They are,' she contradicted. 'I and Mr Owlett and the others paid thirty shillings for every one of the tubs before they were put on board at Cherbourg, and if a king who is nothing to us sends his people to steal our property we have a right to steal it back again.'

Stockdale did not stop to argue the matter but went quickly in the direction of the noise, Lizzy keeping at his side. 'Don't you interfere, will you, dear Richard ?' she said anxiously, as they drew near. 'Don't let us go any closer: 'tis at Warm'ell Cross where they are seizing 'em. You can do no good, and you may meet with a hard blow!'

'Let us see first what is going on,' he said. But before they had got much further the noise of the cart-wheels began again; and Stockdale soon found that they were coming towards him. In another minute the three carts came up, and Stockdale and Lizzy stood in the ditch to let them pass.

Instead of being conducted by four men, as had happened when they went out of the village, the horses and carts were now accompanied by a body of from twenty to thirty, all of whom, as Stockdale perceived to his astonishment, had blackened faces. Among them walked six or eight huge female figures, whom, from their wide strides, Stockdale guessed to be men in disguise. As soon as the party discerned Lizzy and her companion four or five fell back, and when the carts had passed, came close to the pair.

'There is no walking up this way for the present,' said one of the gaunt women, who wore curls a foot long, dangling down the sides of her face, in the fashion of the time. Stockdale recognized this lady's voice as Owlett's.

'Why not ?' said Stockdale. 'This is the public highway.'

'Now look here, youngster,' said Owlett. 'O, 'tis the Methodist parson! – what, and Mrs Newberry! Well, you'd better not go up that way, Lizzy. They've all run off, and folks have got their own again.'

The miller then hastened on and joined his comrades. Stockdale and Lizzy also turned back. 'I wish all this hadn't been forced upon us,' she said regretfully. 'But if those Coast-men had got off with the tubs, half the people in the parish would have been in want for the next month or two.'

Stockdale was not paying much attention to her words, and he said, 'I don't think I can go back like this. Those four poor Preventives may be murdered for all I know.'

'Murdered!' said Lizzy impatiently. 'We don't do murder here.'

'Well, I shall go as far as Warm'ell Cross to see,' said Stockdale decisively; and, without wishing her safe home or anything else, the minister turned back. Lizzy stood looking at him till his form was absorbed in the shades; and then, with sadness, she went in the direction of Nether-Moynton.

The road was lonely, and after nightfall at this time of the year there was often not a passer for hours. Stockdale pursued his way without hearing a sound beyond that of his own footsteps; and in due time he passed beneath the trees of the plantation which surrounded the Warm'ell Cross-road. Before he had reached the point of intersection he heard voices from the thicket.

'Hoi-hoi-hoi! Help, help!'

The voices were not at all feeble or despairing, but they were un-mistakably anxious. Stockdale had no weapon, and before plunging into the pitchy darkness of the plantation he pulled a stake from the hedge, to use in case of need. When he got among the trees he shouted – 'What's the matter – where are you?'

'Here,' answered the voices; and, pushing through the brambles in that direction, he came near the objects of his search.

'Why don't you come forward?' said Stockdale.

'We be tied to the trees!'

'Who are you?'

'Poor Will Latimer the Customs-officer!' said one plaintively. 'Just come and cut these cords, there's a good man. We were afraid nobody would pass by to-night.'

Stockdale soon loosened them, upon which they stretched their limbs and stood at their ease.

'The rascals!' said Latimer, getting now into a rage, though he had seemed quite meek when Stockdale first came up. ' 'Tis the same set of fellows. I know they were Moynton chaps to a man.'

'But we can't swear to 'em,' said another. 'Not one of 'em spoke.'

'What are you going to do?' said Stockdale.

'I'd fain go back to Moynton, and have at 'em again!' said Latimer.

'So would we!' said his comrades.

'Fight till we die!' said Latimer.

'We will, we will!' said his men.

'But,' said Latimer, more frigidly, as they came out of the plantation, 'we don't *know* that these chaps with black faces were Moynton men? And proof is a hard thing.'

'So it is,' said the rest.

'And therefore we won't do nothing at all,' said Latimer, with complete dispassionateness. 'For my part, I'd sooner be them than we. The clitches of my arms are burning like fire from the cords those two strapping women tied round 'em. My opinion is, now I have had time to think o't, that you may serve your Gover'ment at too high a price. For these two nights and days I have not had an hour's rest; and, please God, here's for home-along.'

The other officers agreed heartily to this course; and, thanking Stockdale for his timely assistance, they parted from him at the Cross, taking themselves the western road, and Stockdale going back to Nether-Moynton.

During that walk the minister was lost in reverie of the most painful kind. As soon as he got into the house, and before entering his own rooms, he advanced to the door of the little back parlour in which Lizzy usually sat with her mother. He found her there alone. Stockdale went forward, and, like a man in a dream, looked down upon the table that stood between him and the young woman, who had her bonnet and cloak still on. As he did not speak, she looked up from her chair at him, with misgiving in her eye.

'Where are they gone?' he then said listlessly.

'Who? – I don't know. I have seen nothing of them since. I came straight in here.'

'If your men can manage to get off with those tubs, it will be a great profit to you, I suppose?'

'A share will be mine, a share my cousin Owlett's, a share to each of the two farmers, and a share divided amongst the men who helped us.'

'And you still think,' he went on slowly, 'that you will not give this business up?'

Lizzy rose, and put her hand upon his shoulder. 'Don't ask that,' she whispered. 'You don't know what you are asking. I must tell you, though I meant not to do it. What I make by that trade is all I have to keep my mother and myself with.'

He was astonished. 'I did not dream of such a thing,' he said. 'I would rather have scraped the roads, had I been you. What is money compared with a clear conscience?'

'My conscience is clear. I know my mother, but the king I have never seen. His dues are nothing to me. But it is a great deal to me that my mother and I should live.'

'Marry me, and promise to give it up. I will keep your mother.'

'It is good of you,' she said, moved a little. 'Let me think of it by myself. I would rather not answer now.'

She reserved her answer till the next day, and came into his room with a solemn face. 'I cannot do what you wished!' she said passionately. 'It is too much to ask. My whole life ha' been passed in this way.' Her words and manner showed that before entering she had been struggling with herself in private, and that the contention had been strong.

Stockdale turned pale, but he spoke quietly. 'Then, Lizzy, we must part. I cannot go against my principles in this matter, and I cannot make my profession a mockery. You know how I love you, and what I would do for you; but this one thing I cannot do.'

'But why should you belong to that profession?' she burst out. 'I have got this large house; why can't you marry me, and live here with us, and not be a Methodist preacher any more? I assure you, Richard, it is no harm, and I wish you could only see it as I do! We only carry it on in winter: in summer it is never done at all. It stirs up one's dull life at this time o' the year, and gives excitement, which I have got so used to now that I should hardly know how to do 'ithout it. At nights, when the wind blows, instead of being dull and stupid, and not noticing whether it do blow or not, your mind is afield, even if you are not afield yourself; and you are wondering how the chaps are getting on; and you walk up and down the room, and look out o' window, and then you go out yourself, and know your way about as well by night as by day, and have hair-breadth escapes from old Latimer and his fellows, who are too stupid ever to really frighten us, and only make us a bit nimble.'

'He frightened you a little last night, anyhow: and I would advise you to drop it before it is worse.'

She shook her head. 'No, I must go on as I have begun. I was born to it. It is in my blood, and I can't be cured. O, Richard, you cannot think what a hard thing you have asked, and how sharp you try me when you put me between this and my love for 'ee!'

Stockdale was leaning with his elbow on the mantelpiece, his hands over his eyes. 'We ought never to have met, Lizzy,' he said. 'It was an ill day for us! I little thought there was anything so hopeless and impossible in our engagement as this. Well, it is too late now to regret consequences in this way. I have had the happiness of seeing you and knowing you at least.'

'You dissent from Church, and I dissent from State,' she said. 'And I don't see why we are not well matched.'

He smiled sadly, while Lizzy remained looking down, her eyes beginning to overflow.

That was an unhappy evening for both of them, and the days that followed were unhappy days. Both she and he went mechanically about their employments, and his depression was marked in the village by more than one of his denomination with whom he came in contact. But Lizzy, who passed her days indoors, was unsuspected of being the cause: for it was generally understood that a quiet engagement to marry existed between her and her cousin Owlett, and had existed for some time.

Thus uncertainly the week passed on; till one morning Stockdale said to her: 'I have had a letter, Lizzy. I must call you that till I am gone.'

'Gone?' said she blankly.

'Yes,' he said. 'I am going from this place. I felt it would be better for us both that I should not stay after what has happened. In fact, I couldn't stay here, and look on you from day to day, without becoming weak and faltering in my course. I have just heard of an arrangement by which the other minister can arrive here in about a week; and let me go elsewhere.'

That he had all this time continued so firmly fixed in his resolution came upon her as a grievous surprise. 'You never loved me!' she said bitterly.

'I might say the same,' he returned; 'but I will not. Grant me one favour. Come and hear my last sermon on the day before I go.'

Lizzy, who was a church-goer on Sunday mornings, frequently attended Stockdale's chapel in the evening with the rest of the double-minded; and she promised.

It became known that Stockdale was going to leave, and a good many people outside his own sect were sorry to hear it. The intervening days flew rapidly away, and on the evening of the Sunday which preceded the morning of his departure Lizzy sat in the chapel to hear him for the last time. The little building was full to overflowing, and he took up the

subject which all had expected, that of the contraband trade so extensively practised among them. His hearers, in laying his words to their
own hearts, did not perceive that they were most particularly directed
against Lizzy, till the sermon waxed warm, and Stockdale nearly broke
down with emotion. In truth his own earnestness, and her sad eyes
looking up at him, were too much for the young man's equanimity. He
hardly knew how he ended. He saw Lizzy, as through a mist, turn and go
away with the rest of the congregation; and shortly afterwards followed
her home.

She invited him to supper, and they sat down alone, her mother
having, as was usual with her on Sunday nights, gone to bed early.

'We will part friends, won't we?' said Lizzy, with forced gaiety, and
never alluding to the sermon: a reticence which rather disappointed him.

'We will,' he said, with a forced smile on his part; and they sat down.

It was the first meal that they had ever shared together in their lives,
and probably the last that they would so share. When it was over, and
the indifferent conversation could no longer be continued, he arose
and took her hand. 'Lizzy,' he said, 'do you say we must part – do
you?'

'You do,' she said solemnly. 'I can say no more.'

'Nor I,' said he. 'If that is your answer, good-bye!'

Stockdale bent over her and kissed her, and she involuntarily
returned his kiss. 'I shall go early,' he said hurriedly. 'I shall not see you
again.'

And he did leave early. He fancied, when stepping forth into the gray
morning light, to mount the van which was to carry him away, that he
saw a face between the parted curtains of Lizzy's window, but the light
was faint, and the panes glistened with wet; so he could not be sure.
Stockdale mounted the vehicle, and was gone; and on the following
Sunday the new minister preached in the chapel of the Moynton
Wesleyans.

One day, two years after the parting, Stockdale, now settled in a midland
town, came into Nether-Moynton by carrier in the original way.
Jogging along in the van that afternoon he had put questions to the
driver, and the answers that he received interested the minister deeply.
The result of them was that he went without the least hesitation to the
door of his former lodging. It was about six o'clock in the evening, and
the same time of year as when he had left; now, too, the ground was

damp and glistening, the west was bright, and Lizzy's snowdrops were raising their heads in the border under the wall.

Lizzy must have caught sight of him from the window, for by the time that he reached the door she was there holding it open: and then, as if she had not sufficiently considered her act of coming out, she drew herself back, saying with some constraint, 'Mr Stockdale!'

'You knew it was,' said Stockdale, taking her hand. 'I wrote to say I should call.'

'Yes, but you did not say when,' she answered.

'I did not. I was not quite sure when my business would lead me to these parts.'

'You only came because business brought you near?'

'Well, that is the fact; but I have often thought I should like to come on purpose to see you. . . . But what's all this that has happened? I told you how it would be, Lizzy, and you would not listen to me.'

'I would not,' she said sadly. 'But I had been brought up to that life; and it was second nature to me. However, it is all over now. The officers have blood-money for taking a man dead or alive, and the trade is going to nothing. We were hunted down like rats.'

'Owlett is quite gone, I hear.'

'Yes. He is in America. We had a dreadful struggle that last time, when they tried to take him. It is a perfect miracle that he lived through it; and it is a wonder that I was not killed. I was shot in the hand. It was not by aim; the shot was really meant for my cousin; but I was behind, looking on as usual, and the bullet came to me. It bled terribly, but I got home without fainting; and it healed after a time. You know how he suffered?'

'No,' said Stockdale. 'I only heard that he just escaped with his life.'

'He was shot in the back; but a rib turned the ball. He was badly hurt. We would not let him be took. The men carried him all night across the meads to Kingsbere, and hid him in a barn, dressing his wound as well as they could, till he was so far recovered as to be able to get about. Then he was caught, and tried with the others at the assizes; but they all got off.[1] He had given up his mill for some time; and at last he went to Bristol, and took a passage to America, where he's settled.'

'What do you think of smuggling now?' said the minister gravely.

'I own that we were wrong,' said she. 'But I have suffered for it. I am

---

[1] See the Preface to *Wessex Tales*.

very poor now, and my mother has been dead these twelve months. . . .
But won't you come in, Mr Stockdale?'

Stockdale went in; and it is to be supposed that they came to an
understanding; for a fortnight later there was a sale of Lizzy's furniture,
and after that a wedding at a chapel in a neighbouring town.

He took her away from her old haunts to the home that he had made
for himself in his native county, where she studied her duties as a
minister's wife with praiseworthy assiduity. It is said that in after years
she wrote an excellent tract called *Render unto Cæsar; or, The Repentant
Villagers*, in which her own experience was anonymously used as the
introductory story. Stockdale got it printed, after making some correc-
tions, and putting in a few powerful sentences of his own; and many
hundreds of copies were distributed by the couple in the course of their
married life.

April 1879

NOTE. – The ending of this story with the marriage of Lizzy and
the minister was almost *de rigueur* in an English magazine at the
time of writing. But at this late date, thirty years after, it may not
be amiss to give the ending that would have been preferred by the
writer to the convention used above. Moreover it corresponds more
closely with the true incidents of which the tale is a vague and
flickering shadow. Lizzy did not, in fact, marry the minister, but –
much to her credit in the author's opinion – stuck to Jim the smuggler,
and emigrated with him after their marriage, an expatrial step
rather forced upon him by his adventurous antecedents. They
both died in Wisconsin between 1850 and 1860. (*May 1912*)

A GROUP OF NOBLE DAMES

'. . . Store of ladies, whose bright eyes
Rain influence.' – L'ALLEGRO

Preface to
'A Group of Noble Dames'

THE pedigrees of our county families, arranged in diagrams on the pages of county histories, mostly appear at first sight to be as barren of any touch of nature as a table of logarithms. But given a clue – the faintest tradition of what went on behind the scenes, and this dryness as of dust may be transformed into a palpitating drama. More, the careful comparison of dates alone – that of birth with marriage, of marriage with death, of one marriage, birth, or death with a kindred marriage, birth, or death – will often effect the same transformation, and anybody practised in raising images from such genealogies finds himself un-consciously filling into the framework the motives, passions, and personal qualities which would appear to be the single explanation possible of some extraordinary conjunction in times, events, and personages that occasionally marks these reticent family records.

Out of such pedigrees and supplementary material most of the following stories have arisen and taken shape.

I would make this preface an opportunity of expressing my sense of the courtesy and kindness of several bright-eyed Noble Dames yet in the flesh, who, since the first publication of these tales in periodicals, six or seven years ago, have given me interesting comments and conjectures on such of the narratives as they have recognized to be connected with their own families, residences, or traditions; in which they have shown a truly philosophic absence of prejudice in their regard of those incidents whose relation has tended more distinctly to dramatize than to eulogize their ancestors. The outlines they have also given of other singular events in their family histories for use in a second 'Group of Noble Dames' will, I fear, never reach the printing-press through me; but I shall store them up in memory of my informants' good nature.

The tales were first collected and published in their present form in 1891.

T.H.

June 1896

PART FIRST
BEFORE DINNER

Dame the First
The First Countess of Wessex

By the Local Historian

KING'S-HINTOCK COURT (said the narrator, turning over his memoranda for reference) – King's-Hintock Court is, as we know, one of the most imposing of the mansions that overlook our beautiful Blackmoor or Blakemore Vale. On the particular occasion of which I have to speak this building stood, as it had often stood before, in the perfect silence of a calm clear night, lighted only by the cold shine of the stars. The season was winter, in days long ago, the eighteenth century having run but little more than a third of its length. North, south, and west, not a casement was unfastened, not a curtain undrawn; eastward, one window on the upper floor was open, and a girl of twelve or thirteen was leaning over the sill. That she had not taken up the position for purposes of observation was apparent at a glance, for she kept her eyes covered with her hands.

The room occupied by the girl was an inner one of a suite, to be reached only by passing through a large bedchamber adjoining. From this apartment voices in altercation were audible, everything else in the building being so still. It was to avoid listening to these voices that the girl had left her little cot, thrown a cloak round her head and shoulders, and stretched into the night air.

But she could not escape the conversation, try as she would. The words reached her in all their painfulness, one sentence in masculine tones, those of her father, being repeated many times.

'I tell 'ee there shall be no such betrothal! I tell 'ee there shan't! A child like her!'

She knew the subject of dispute to be herself. A cool feminine voice, her mother's, replied:

'Have done with you, and be wise. He is willing to wait a good five or six years before the marriage takes place, and there's not a man in the county to compare with him.'

'It shall not be! He is over thirty. It is wickedness.'

'He is just thirty, and the best and finest man alive – a perfect match for her.'

'He is poor!'

'But his father and elder brothers are made much of at Court – none so constantly at the palace as they; and with her fortune, who knows? He may be able to get a barony.'

'I believe you are in love with en yourself!'

'How can you insult me so, Thomas! And is it not monstrous for you to talk of my wickedness when you have a like scheme in your own head? You know you have. Some bumpkin of your own choosing – some petty gentleman who lives down at that outlandish place of yours, Falls-Park – one of your pot-companions' sons—'

There was an outburst of imprecation on the part of her husband in lieu of further argument. As soon as he could utter a connected sentence he said: 'You crow and you domineer, mistress, because you are heiress-general here. You are in your own house; you are on your own land. But let me tell 'ee that if I did come here to you instead of taking you to me, it was done at the dictates of convenience merely. Hell! I'm no beggar! Han't I a place of my own? Han't I an avenue as long as thine? Han't I beeches that will more than match thy oaks? I should have lived in my own quiet house and land, contented, if you had not called me off with your airs and graces. Faith, I'll go back there; I'll not stay with thee longer! If it had not been for our Betty I should have gone long ago!'

After this there were no more words; but presently, hearing the sound of a door opening and shutting below, the girl again looked from the window. Footsteps crunched on the gravel-walk, and a shape in a drab greatcoat, easily distinguishable as her father, withdrew from the house. He moved to the left, and she watched him diminish down the long east front till he had turned the corner and vanished. He must have gone round to the stables.

She closed the window and shrank into bed, where she cried herself to sleep. This child, their only one, Betty, beloved ambitiously by her mother, and with uncalculating passionateness by her father, was frequently made wretched by such episodes as this; though she was too young to care very deeply, for her own sake, whether her mother betrothed her to the gentleman discussed or not.

The Squire had often gone out of the house in this manner, declaring that he would never return, but he had always reappeared in the morning. The present occasion, however, was different in the issue: next day she was told that her father had ridden to his estate at Falls-Park early in the morning on business with his agent, and might not come back for some days.

Falls-Park was over twenty miles from King's-Hintock Court, and was altogether a more modest centre-piece to a more modest possession than the latter. But as Squire Dornell came in view of it that February morning, he thought that he had been a fool ever to leave it, though it was for the sake of the greatest heiress in Wessex. Its Palladian front, of the period of the first Charles, derived from its regular features a dignity which the great, many-gabled, heterogeneous mansion of his wife could not eclipse. Altogether he was sick at heart, and the gloom which the densely-timbered park threw over the scene did not tend to remove the depression of this rubicund man of eight-and-forty, who sat so heavily upon his gelding. The child, his darling Betty: there lay the root of his trouble. He was unhappy when near his wife, he was unhappy when away from his little girl; and from this dilemma there was no practicable escape. As a consequence he indulged rather freely in the pleasures of the table, became what was called a three-bottle man, and, in his wife's estimation, less and less presentable to her polite friends from town.

He was received by the two or three old servants who were in charge of the lonely place, where a few rooms only were kept habitable for his use or that of his friends when hunting; and during the morning he was made more comfortable by the arrival of his faithful servant Tupcombe from King's-Hintock. But after a day or two spent here in solitude he began to feel that he had made a mistake in coming. By leaving King's-Hintock in his anger he had thrown away his best opportunity of counter-acting his wife's preposterous notion of promising his poor little Betty's hand to a man she had hardly seen. To protect her from such a repugnant bargain he should have remained on the spot. He felt it almost as a misfortune that the child would inherit so much wealth. She would be a mark for all the adventurers in the kingdom. Had she been only the heiress to his own unassuming little place at Falls, how much better would have been her chances of happiness!

His wife had divined truly when she insinuated that he himself had a lover in view for this pet child. The son of a dear deceased friend of his, who lived not two miles from where the Squire now was, a lad a couple of years his daughter's senior, seemed in her father's opinion the one person in the world likely to make her happy. But as to breathing such a scheme to either of the young people with the indecent haste that his wife had shown, he would not dream of it; years hence would be soon enough for that. They had already seen each other, and the Squire fancied that he noticed a tenderness on the youth's part which promised well. He was strongly tempted to profit by his wife's example, and forestall her match-making by throwing the two young people together there at Falls. The girl, though marriageable in the views of those days, was too young to be in love, but the lad was fifteen, and already felt an interest in her.

Still better than keeping watch over her at King's-Hintock, where she was necessarily much under her mother's influence, would it be to get the child to stay with him at Falls for a time, under his exclusive control. But how accomplish this without using main force? The only possible chance was that his wife might, for appearance' sake, as she had done before, consent to Betty paying him a day's visit, when he might find means of detaining her till Reynard, the suitor whom his wife favoured, had gone abroad, which he was expected to do the following week. Squire Dornell determined to return to King's-Hintock and attempt the enterprise. If he were refused, it was almost in him to pick up Betty bodily and carry her off.

The journey back, vague and Quixotic as were his intentions, was performed with a far lighter heart than his setting forth. He would see Betty, and talk to her, come what might of his plan.

So he rode along the dead level which stretches between the hills skirting Falls-Park and those bounding the town of Ivell, trotted through that borough, and out by the King's-Hintock highway, till, passing the village, he entered the mile-long drive through the park to the Court. The drive being open, without an avenue, the Squire could discern the north front and door of the Court a long way off, and was himself visible from the windows on that side; for which reason he hoped that Betty might perceive him coming, as she sometimes did on his return from an outing, and run to the door or wave her handkerchief.

But there was no sign. He inquired for his wife as soon as he set foot to earth.

'Mistress is away. She was called to London, sir.'

'And Mistress Betty?' said the Squire blankly.

'Gone likewise, sir, for a little change. Mistress has left a letter for you.'

The note explained nothing, merely stating that she had posted to London on her own affairs, and had taken the child to give her a holiday. On the fly-leaf were some words from Betty herself to the same effect, evidently written in a state of high jubilation at the idea of her jaunt. Squire Dornell murmured a few expletives, and submitted to his disappointment. How long his wife meant to stay in town she did not say; but on investigation he found that the carriage had been packed with sufficient luggage for a sojourn of two or three weeks.

King's-Hintock Court was in consequence as gloomy as Falls-Park had been. He had lost all zest for hunting of late, and had hardly attended a meet that season. Dornell read and re-read Betty's scrawl, and hunted up some other such notes of hers to look over, this seeming to be the only pleasure there was left for him. That they were really in London he learnt in a few days by another letter from Mrs Dornell, in which she explained that they hoped to be home in about a week, and that she had had no idea he was coming back to King's-Hintock so soon, or she would not have gone away without telling him.

Squire Dornell wondered if, in going or returning, it had been her plan to call at the Reynards' place near Melchester, through which city their journey lay. It was possible that she might do this in furtherance of her project, and the sense that his own might become the losing game was harassing.

He did not know how to dispose of himself, till it occurred to him that, to get rid of his intolerable heaviness, he would invite some friends to dinner and drown his cares in grog and wine. No sooner was the carouse decided upon than he put it in hand; those invited being mostly neighbouring landholders, all smaller men than himself, members of the hunt; also the doctor from Evershead, and the like – some of them rollicking blades whose presence his wife would not have countenanced had she been at home. 'When the cat's away—!' said the Squire.

They arrived, and there were indications in their manner that they meant to make a night of it. Baxby of Sherton Castle was late, and they waited a quarter of an hour for him, he being one of the liveliest of Dornell's friends; without whose presence no such dinner as this would be considered complete, and, it may be added, with whose presence no dinner which included both sexes could be conducted with strict propriety. He had just returned from London, and the Squire was anxious to talk to him – for no definite reason; but he had lately breathed the atmosphere in which Betty was.

At length they heard Baxby driving up to the door, whereupon the host and the rest of his guests crossed over to the dining-room. In a moment Baxby came hastily in at their heels, apologizing for his lateness.

'I only came back last night, you know,' he said; 'and the truth o't is, I had as much as I could carry.' He turned to the Squire. 'Well, Dornell – so cunning reynard has stolen your little ewe lamb? Ha, ha!'

'What?' said Squire Dornell vacantly, across the dining-table, round which they were all standing, the cold March sunlight streaming in upon his full, clean-shaven face.

'Surely th'st know what all the town knows? – you've had a letter by this time? – that Stephen Reynard has married your Betty? Yes, as I'm a living man. It was a carefully-arranged thing: they parted at once, and are not to meet for five or six years. But, Lord, you must know!'

A thud on the floor was the only reply of the Squire. They quickly turned. He had fallen down like a log behind the table, and lay motionless on the oak boards.

Those at hand hastily bent over him, and the whole group were in confusion. They found him to be quite unconscious, though puffing and panting like a blacksmith's bellows. His face was livid, his veins swollen, and beads of perspiration stood upon his brow.

'What's happened to him?' said several.

'An apoplectic fit,' said the doctor from Evershead, gravely.

He was only called in at the Court for small ailments, as a rule, and felt the importance of the situation. He lifted the Squire's head, loosened his cravat and clothing, and rang for the servants, who took the Squire upstairs.

There he lay as if in a drugged sleep. The surgeon drew a basinful of blood from him, but it was nearly six o'clock before he came to himself. The dinner was completely disorganized, and some had gone home long ago; but two or three remained.

'Bless my soul,' Baxby kept repeating, 'I didn't know things had come to this pass between Dornell and his lady! I thought the feast he was spreading to-day was in honour of the event, though privately kept for the present! His little maid married without his knowledge!'

As soon as the Squire recovered consciousness he gasped: ' 'Tis

abduction! 'Tis a capital felony! He can be hung! Where is Baxby? I
am very well now. What items have ye heard, Baxby?'

The bearer of the untoward news was extremely unwilling to agitate
Dornell further, and would say little more at first. But an hour after,
when the Squire had partially recovered and was sitting up, Baxby told
as much as he knew, the most important particular being that Betty's
mother was present at the marriage, and showed every mark of approval.
'Everything appeared to have been done so regularly that I, of course,
thought you knew all about it,' he said.

'I knew no more than the underground dead that such a step was in
the wind! A child just gone thirteen! How Sue hath outwitted me! Did
Reynard go up to Lon'on with 'em, d'ye know?'

'I can't say. All I know is that your lady and daughter were walking
along the street, with the footman behind 'em; that they entered a
jeweller's shop, where Reynard was standing; and that there, in the
presence o' the shopkeeper and your man, who was called in on purpose,
your Betty said to Reynard – so the story goes: 'pon my soul I don't
vouch for the truth of it – she said, "Will you marry me?" or, "I want to
marry you: will you have me – now or never?" she said.'

'What she said means nothing,' murmured the Squire, with wet eyes.
'Her mother put the words into her mouth to avoid the serious consequences that would attach to any suspicion of force. The words be not
the child's – she didn't dream of marriage – how should she, poor little
maid! Go on.'

'Well, be that as it will, they were all agreed apparently. They bought
the ring on the spot, and the marriage took place at the nearest church
within half-an-hour.'

A day or two later there came a letter from Mrs Dornell to her husband,
written before she knew of his stroke. She related the circumstances of
the marriage in the gentlest manner, and gave cogent reasons and
excuses for consenting to the premature union, which was now an
accomplished fact indeed. She had no idea, till sudden pressure was put
upon her, that the contract was expected to be carried out so soon, but
being taken half unawares she had consented, having learned that
Stephen Reynard, now their son-in-law, was becoming a great favourite
at Court, and that he would in all likelihood have a peerage granted him
before long. No harm could come to their dear daughter by this early
marriage-contract, seeing that her life would be continued under their

own eyes, exactly as before, for some years. In fine, she had felt that no other such fair opportunity for a good marriage with a shrewd courtier and wise man of the world, who was at the same time noted for his excellent personal qualities, was within the range of probability, owing to the rusticated lives they led at King's-Hintock. Hence she had yielded to Stephen's solicitation, and hoped her husband would forgive her. She wrote, in short, like a woman who, having had her way as to the deed, is prepared to make any concession as to words and subsequent behaviour.

All this Dornell took at its true value, or rather, perhaps, at less than its true value. As his life depended upon his not getting into a passion, he controlled his perturbed emotions as well as he was able, going about the house sadly and utterly unlike his former self. He took every pre-caution to prevent his wife knowing of the incidents of his sudden illness, from a sense of shame at having a heart so tender; a ridiculous quality, no doubt, in her eyes, now that she had become so imbued with town ideas. But rumours of his seizure somehow reached her, and she let him know that she was about to return to nurse him. He thereupon packed up and went off to his own place at Falls-Park.

Here he lived the life of a recluse for some time. He was still too un-well to entertain company, or to ride to hounds or elsewhither; but more than this, his aversion to the faces of strangers and acquaintances who knew by that time of the trick his wife had played him, operated to hold him aloof.

Nothing could influence him to censure Betty for her share in the exploit. He never once believed that she had acted voluntarily. Anxious to know how she was getting on, he despatched the trusty servant Tupcombe to Evershead village, close to King's-Hintock, timing his journey so that he should reach the place under cover of dark. The emissary arrived without notice, being out of livery, and took a seat in the chimney-corner of the Sow-and-Acorn.

The conversation of the droppers-in was always of the nine days' wonder – the recent marriage. The smoking listener learnt that Mrs Dornell and the girl had returned to King's-Hintock for a day or two, that Reynard had set out for the Continent, and that Betty had since been packed off to school. She did not realize her position as Reynard's child-wife – so the story went – and though somewhat awe-stricken at first by the ceremony, she had soon recovered her spirits on finding that her freedom was in no way to be interfered with.

After that, formal messages began to pass between Dornell and his wife, the latter being now as persistently conciliating as she was formerly masterful. But her rustic, simple, blustering husband still held personally aloof. Her wish to be reconciled – to win his forgiveness for her stratagem – moreover, a genuine tenderness and desire to soothe his sorrow, which welled up in her at times, brought her at last to his door at Falls-Park one day.

They had not met since that night of altercation, before her departure for London and his subsequent illness. She was shocked at the change in him. His face had become expressionless, as blank as that of a puppet, and what troubled her still more was that she found him living in one room, and indulging freely in stimulants, in absolute disobedience to the physician's order. The fact was obvious that he could no longer be allowed to live thus uncouthly.

So she sympathized, and begged his pardon, and coaxed. But though after this date there was no longer such a complete estrangement as before, they only occasionally saw each other, Dornell for the most part making Falls his headquarters still.

Three or four years passed thus. Then she came one day, with more animation in her manner, and at once moved him by the simple statement that Betty's schooling had ended; she had returned, and was grieved because he was away. She had sent a message to him in these words: 'Ask father to come home to his dear Betty.'

'Ah! Then she is very unhappy!' said Squire Dornell.

His wife was silent.

' 'Tis that accursed marriage!' continued the Squire.

Still his wife would not dispute with him. 'She is outside in the carriage,' said Mrs Dornell gently.

'What – Betty?'

'Yes.'

'Why didn't you tell me?' Dornell rushed out, and there was the girl awaiting his forgiveness, for she supposed herself, no less than her mother, to be under his displeasure.

Yes, Betty had left school, and had returned to King's-Hintock. She was nearly seventeen, and had developed to quite a young woman. She looked not less a member of the household for her early marriage-contract, which she seemed, indeed, to have almost forgotten. It was like a dream to her; that clear cold March day, the London church, with its gorgeous pews, and green-baize linings, and the great organ in the west gallery – so different from their own little church in the shrubbery

of King's-Hintock Court – the man of thirty, to whose face she had
looked up with so much awe, and with a sense that he was rather ugly
and formidable; the man whom, though they corresponded politely, she
had never seen since; one to whose existence she was now so indifferent
that if informed of his death, and that she would never see him more, she
would merely have replied, 'Indeed!' Betty's passions as yet still slept.

'Hast heard from thy husband lately?' said Squire Dornell, when they
were indoors, with an ironical laugh of fondness which demanded no
answer.

The girl winced, and he noticed that his wife looked appealingly at him.
As the conversation went on, and there were signs that Dornell would
express sentiments that might do harm to a position which they could
not alter, Mrs Dornell suggested that Betty should leave the room till
her father and herself had finished their private conversation; and this
Betty obediently did.

Dornell renewed his animadversions freely. 'Did you see how the
sound of his name frightened her?' he presently added. 'If you didn't, I
did. Zounds! what a future is in store for that poor little unfortunate
wench o' mine! I tell 'ee, Sue, 'twas not a marriage at all, in morality,
and if I were a woman in such a position, I shouldn't feel it as one. She
might, without a sign of sin, love a man of her choice as well now as if
she were chained up to no other at all. There, that's my mind, and I can't
help it. Ah, Sue, my man was best! He'd ha' suited her.'

'I don't believe it,' she replied incredulously.

'You should see him; then you would. He's growing up a fine fellow,
I can tell 'ee.'

'Hush! not so loud!' she answered, rising from her seat and going to
the door of the next room, whither her daughter had betaken herself. To
Mrs Dornell's alarm, there sat Betty in a reverie, her round eyes fixed on
vacancy, musing so deeply that she did not perceive her mother's
entrance. She had heard every word, and was digesting the new knowledge.

Her mother felt that Falls-Park was dangerous ground for a young
girl of the susceptible age, and in Betty's peculiar position, while
Dornell talked and reasoned thus. She called Betty to her, and they took
leave. The Squire would not clearly promise to return and make King's-
Hintock Court his permanent abode; but Betty's presence there, as at
former times, was sufficient to make him agree to pay them a visit soon.

All the way home Betty remained preoccupied and silent. It was too

plain to her anxious mother that Squire Dornell's free views had been a
sort of awakening to the girl.

The interval before Dornell redeemed his pledge to come and see
them was unexpectedly short. He arrived one morning about twelve
o'clock, driving his own pair of black-bays in the curricle-phaeton with
yellow panels and red wheels, just as he had used to do, and his faithful
old Tupcombe on horseback behind. A young man sat beside the
Squire in the carriage, and Mrs Dornell's consternation could scarcely
be concealed when, abruptly entering with his companion, the Squire
announced him as his friend Phelipson of Elm-Cranlynch.

Dornell passed on to Betty in the background and tenderly kissed her.
'Sting your mother's conscience, my maid!' he whispered. 'Sting her
conscience by pretending you are struck with Phelipson, and would ha'
loved him, as your old father's choice, much more than him she has
forced upon 'ee.'

The simple-souled speaker fondly imagined that it was entirely in
obedience to this direction that Betty's eyes stole interested glances at
the frank and impulsive Phelipson that day at dinner, and he laughed
grimly within himself to see how this joke of his, as he imagined it to be,
was disturbing the peace of mind of the lady of the house. 'Now Sue
sees what a mistake she has made!' said he.

Mrs Dornell was verily greatly alarmed, and as soon as she could
speak a word with him alone she upbraided him. 'You ought not to have
brought him here. O Thomas, how could you be so thoughtless! Lord,
don't you see, dear, that what is done cannot be undone, and how all this
foolery jeopardizes her happiness with her husband? Until you interfered, and spoke in her hearing about this Phelipson, she was as patient
and as willing as a lamb, and looked forward to Mr Reynard's return
with real pleasure. Since her visit to Falls-Park she has been monstrous
close-mouthed and busy with her own thoughts. What mischief will you
do? How will it end?'

'Own, then, that my man was best suited to her. I only brought him
to convince you.'

'Yes, yes; I do admit it. But O! do take him back again at once!
Don't keep him here! I fear she is even attracted by him already.'

'Nonsense, Sue. 'Tis only a little trick to tease 'ee!'

Nevertheless her motherly eye was not so likely to be deceived as his,
and if Betty were really only playing at being love-struck that day, she
played at it with the perfection of a Rosalind, and would have deceived

the best professors into a belief that it was no counterfeit. The Squire, having obtained his victory, was quite ready to take back the too attractive youth, and early in the afternoon they set out on their return journey.

A silent figure who rode behind them was as interested as Dornell in that day's experiment. It was the staunch Tupcombe, who, with his eyes on the Squire's and young Phelipson's backs, thought how well the latter would have suited Betty, and how greatly the former had changed for the worse during these last two or three years. He cursed his mistress as the cause of the change.

After this memorable visit to prove his point, the lives of the Dornell couple flowed on quietly enough for the space of a twelvemonth, the Squire for the most part remaining at Falls, and Betty passing and repassing between them now and then, once or twice alarming her mother by not driving home from her father's house till midnight.

The repose of King's-Hintock was broken by the arrival of a special messenger. Squire Dornell had had an access of gout so violent as to be serious. He wished to see Betty again: why had she not come for so long?

Mrs Dornell was extremely reluctant to take Betty in that direction too frequently; but the girl was so anxious to go, her interests latterly seeming to be so entirely bound up in Falls-Park, and its neighbourhood, that there was nothing to be done but to let her set out and accompany her mother.

Squire Dornell had been impatiently awaiting her arrival. They found him very ill and irritable. It had been his habit to take powerful medicines to drive away his enemy, and they had failed in their effect on this occasion.

The presence of his daughter, as usual, calmed him much, even while, as usual, too, it saddened him; for he could never forget that she had disposed of herself for life in opposition to his wishes, though she had secretly assured him that she would never have consented had she been as old as she was now.

As on a former occasion, his wife wished to speak to him alone about the girl's future, the time now drawing nigh at which Reynard was expected to come and claim her. He would have done so already, but he had been put off by the earnest request of the young woman herself, which accorded with that of her parents, on the score of her youth. Reynard had deferentially submitted to their wishes in this respect, the understanding between them having been that he would not visit her before she was eighteen, except by the mutual consent of all parties. But this could not go on much longer, and there was no doubt, from the tenor of his last letter, that he would soon take possession of her whether or no.

To be out of the sound of this delicate discussion Betty was accordingly sent downstairs, and they soon saw her walking away into the shrubberies, looking very pretty in her sweeping green gown, and flapping broad-brimmed hat overhung with a feather.

On returning to the subject, Mrs Dornell found her husband's reluctance to reply in the affirmative to Reynard's letter to be as great as ever.

'She is three months short of eighteen!' he exclaimed. ' 'Tis too soon. I won't hear of it! If I have to keep him off sword in hand, he shall not have her yet.'

'But, my dear Thomas,' she expostulated, 'consider if anything should happen to you or to me, how much better it would be that she should be settled in her home with him!'

'I say it is too soon!' he argued, the veins of his forehead beginning to swell. 'If he gets her this side o' Candlemas I'll challenge en – I'll take my oath on't! I'll be back to King's-Hintock in two or three days, and I'll not lose sight of her day or night!'

She feared to agitate him further, and gave way, assuring him, in obedience to his demand, that if Reynard should write again before he got back, to fix a time for joining Betty, she would put the letter in her husband's hands, and he should do as he chose. This was all that required discussion privately, and Mrs Dornell went to call in Betty, hoping that she had not heard her father's loud tones.

She had certainly not done so this time. Mrs Dornell followed the path along which she had seen Betty wandering, but went a considerable distance without perceiving anything of her. The Squire's wife then turned round to proceed to the other side of the house by a short cut across the grass, when to her surprise and consternation, she beheld the object of her search sitting on the horizontal bough of a cedar, beside her being a young man, whose arm was round her waist. He moved a little, and she recognized him as young Phelipson.

Alas, then, she was right. The so-called counterfeit love was real. What Mrs Dornell called her husband at that moment, for his folly in originally throwing the young people together, it is not necessary to mention. She decided in a moment not to let the lovers know that she had seen them. She accordingly retreated, reached the front of the house by another route, and called at the top of her voice from a window, 'Betty!'

For the first time since her strategic marriage of the child, Susan Dornell doubted the wisdom of that step. Her husband had, as it were, been assisted by destiny to make his objection, originally trivial, a valid one. She saw the outlines of trouble in the future. Why had Dornell interfered? Why had he insisted upon producing his man? This, then, accounted for Betty's pleading for postponement whenever the subject of her husband's return was broached; this accounted for her attachment to Falls-Park. Possibly this very meeting that she had witnessed had been arranged by letter.

Perhaps the girl's thoughts would never have strayed for a moment if her father had not filled her head with ideas of repugnance to her early union, on the ground that she had been coerced into it before she knew her own mind; and she might have rushed to meet her husband with open arms on the appointed day.

Betty at length appeared in the distance in answer to the call, and came up pale, but looking innocent of having seen a living soul. Mrs Dornell groaned in spirit at such duplicity in the child of her bosom. This was the simple creature for whose development into womanhood they had all been so tenderly waiting – a forward minx, old enough not only to have a lover, but to conceal his existence as adroitly as any woman of the world! Bitterly did the Squire's lady regret that Stephen Reynard had not been allowed to come to claim her at the time he first proposed.

The two sat beside each other almost in silence on their journey back to King's-Hintock. Such words as were spoken came mainly from Betty, and their formality indicated how much her mind and heart were occupied with other things.

Mrs Dornell was far too astute a mother to openly attack Betty on the matter. That would be only fanning flame. The indispensable course seemed to her to be that of keeping the treacherous girl under lock and key till her husband came to take her off her mother's hands. That he would disregard Dornell's opposition, and come soon, was her devout wish.

It seemed, therefore, a fortunate coincidence that on her arrival at King's-Hintock a letter from Reynard was put into Mrs Dornell's

hands. It was addressed to both her and her husband, and courteously
informed them that the writer had landed at Bristol, and proposed to
come on to King's-Hintock in a few days, at last to meet and carry off
his darling Betty, if she and her parents saw no objection.

Betty had also received a letter of the same tenor. Her mother had
only to look at her face to see how the girl received the information. She
was as pale as a sheet.

'You must do your best to welcome him this time, my dear Betty,' her
mother said gently.

'But – but – I—'

'You are a woman now,' added her mother severely, 'and these
postponements must come to an end.'

'But my father – O, I am sure he will not allow this! I am not ready.
If he could only wait a year longer – if he could only wait a few months
longer! O, I wish – I wish my dear father were here! I will send to him
instantly.' She broke off abruptly, and falling upon her mother's neck,
burst into tears, saying, 'O my mother, have mercy upon me – I do not
love this man, my husband!'

The agonized appeal went too straight to Mrs Dornell's heart for her
to hear it unmoved. Yet, things having come to this pass, what could she
do? She was distracted, and for a moment was on Betty's side. Her
original thought had been to write an affirmative reply to Reynard, allow
him to come on to King's-Hintock, and keep her husband in ignorance
of the whole proceeding till he should arrive from Falls on some fine day
after his recovery, and find everything settled, and Reynard and Betty
living together in harmony. But the events of the day, and her daughter's
sudden outburst of feeling, had overthrown this intention. Betty was
sure to do as she had threatened, and communicate instantly with her
father, possibly attempt to fly to him. Moreover, Reynard's letter was
addressed to Mr Dornell and herself conjointly, and she could not in
conscience keep it from her husband.

'I will send the letter on to your father speedily,' she replied soothingly.
'He shall act entirely as he chooses, and you know that will not be in
opposition to your wishes. He would ruin you rather than thwart you. I
only hope he may be well enough to bear the agitation of this news. Do
you agree to this?'

Poor Betty agreed, on condition that she should actually witness the
despatch of the letter. Her mother had no objection to offer to this; but
as soon as the horseman had cantered down the drive towards the

highway, Mrs Dornell's sympathy with Betty's recalcitration began to die
out. The girl's secret affection for young Phelipson could not possibly
be condoned. Betty might communicate with him, might even try to
reach him. Ruin lay that way. Stephen Reynard must be speedily
installed in his proper place by Betty's side.

She sat down and penned a private letter to Reynard, which threw
light upon her plan.

> 'It is Necessary that I should now tell you,' she said, 'what I have
> never Mentioned before – indeed I may have signified the Contrary
> – that her Father's Objection to your joining her has not as yet
> been overcome. As I personally Wish to delay you no longer –
> am indeed as anxious for your Arrival as you can be yourself,
> having the good of my Daughter at Heart – no course is left open
> to me but to assist your Cause without my Husband's Knowledge.
> He, I am sorry to say, is at present ill at Falls-Park, but I felt it
> my Duty to forward him your Letter. He will therefore be like
> to reply with a peremptory Command to you to go back again, for
> some Months, whence you came, till the Time he originally stipulated
> has expir'd. My Advice is, if you get such a Letter, to take no
> Notice of it, but to come on hither as you had proposed, letting me
> know the Day and Hour (after dark, if possible) at which we may
> expect you. Dear Betty is with me, and I warrant ye that she shall
> be in the House when you arrive.'

Mrs Dornell, having sent away this epistle unsuspected of anybody,
next took steps to prevent her daughter leaving the Court, avoiding if
possible to excite the girl's suspicions that she was under restraint. But,
as if by divination, Betty had seemed to read the husband's approach in
the aspect of her mother's face.

'He is coming!' exclaimed the maiden.

'Not for a week,' her mother assured her.

'He is then – for certain?'

'Well, yes.'

Betty hastily retired to her room, and would not be seen.

To lock her up, and hand over the key to Reynard when he should
appear in the hall, was a plan charming in its simplicity, till her mother
found, on trying the door of the girl's chamber softly, that Betty had
already locked and bolted it on the inside, and had given directions to
have her meals served where she was, by leaving them on a dumb-waiter
outside the door.

Thereupon Mrs Dornell noiselessly sat down in her boudoir, which,
as well as her bed-chamber, was a passage-room to the girl's apartment,

and she resolved not to vacate her post night or day till her daughter's husband should appear, to which end she too arranged to breakfast, dine, and sup on the spot. It was impossible now that Betty should escape without her knowledge, even if she had wished, there being no other door to the chamber, except one admitting to a small inner dressing-room inaccessible by any second way.

But it was plain that the young girl had no thought of escape. Her ideas ran rather in the direction of intrenchment: she was prepared to stand a siege, but scorned flight. This, at any rate, rendered her secure. As to how Reynard would contrive a meeting with her coy daughter while in such a defensive humour, that, thought her mother, must be left to his own ingenuity to discover.

Betty had looked so wild and pale at the announcement of her husband's approaching visit that Mrs Dornell, somewhat uneasy, could not leave her to herself. She peeped through the keyhole an hour later. Betty lay on the sofa, staring listlessly at the ceiling.

'You are looking ill, child,' cried her mother. 'You've not taken the air lately. Come with me for a drive.'

Betty made no objection. Soon they drove through the park towards the village, the daughter still in the strained, strung-up silence that had fallen upon her. They left the park to return by another route, and on the open road passed a cottage.

Betty's eye fell upon the cottage-window. Within it she saw a young girl about her own age, whom she knew by sight, sitting in a chair and propped by a pillow. The girl's face was covered with scales, which glistened in the sun. She was a convalescent from smallpox – a disease whose prevalence at that period was a terror of which we at present can hardly form a conception.

An idea suddenly energized Betty's apathetic features. She glanced at her mother; Mrs Dornell had been looking in the opposite direction. Betty said that she wished to go back to the cottage for a moment to speak to a girl in whom she took an interest. Mrs Dornell appeared suspicious, but observing that the cottage had no back door, and that Betty could not escape without being seen, she allowed the carriage to be stopped. Betty ran back and entered the cottage, emerging again in about a minute, and resuming her seat in the carriage. As they drove on she fixed her eyes upon her mother and said, 'There, I have done it now!' Her pale face was stormy, and her eyes full of waiting tears.

'What have you done?' said Mrs Dornell.

'Nanny Priddle is sick of the smallpox, and I saw her at the window, and I went in and kissed her, so that I might take it; and now I shall have it, and *he* won't be able to come near me!'

'Wicked girl!' cries her mother. 'O, what am I to do! What – bring a distemper on yourself, and usurp the sacred prerogative of God, because you can't palate the man you've wedded!'

The alarmed woman gave orders to drive home as rapidly as possible, and on arriving, Betty, who was by this time also somewhat frightened at her own enormity, was put into a bath, and fumigated, and treated in every way that could be thought of to ward off the dreadful malady that in a rash moment she had tried to acquire.

There was now a double reason for isolating the rebellious daughter and wife in her own chamber, and there she accordingly remained for the rest of the day and the days that followed; till no ill results seemed likely to arise from her wilfulness.

Meanwhile the first letter from Reynard, announcing to Mrs Dornell and her husband jointly that he was coming in a few days, had sped on its way to Falls-Park. It was directed under cover to Tupcombe, the confidential servant, with instructions not to put it into his master's hands till he had been refreshed by a good long sleep. Tupcombe much regretted this commission, letters sent in this way always disturbing the Squire; but guessing that it would be infinitely worse in the end to withhold the news than to reveal it, he chose his time, which was early the next morning, and delivered the missive.

The utmost effect that Mrs Dornell had anticipated from the message was a peremptory order from her husband to Reynard to hold aloof a few months longer. What the Squire really did was to declare that he would go himself and confront Reynard at Bristol, and have it out with him there by word of mouth.

'But, master,' said Tupcombe, 'you can't. You cannot get out of bed.'

'You leave the room, Tupcombe, and don't say "can't" before me! Have Jerry saddled in an hour.'

The long-tried Tupcombe thought his employer demented, so utterly helpless was his appearance just then, and he went out reluctantly. No sooner was he gone than the Squire, with great difficulty, stretched himself over to a cabinet by the bedside, unlocked it, and took out a small bottle. It contained a gout specific, against whose use he had been repeatedly warned by his regular physician, but whose warning he now cast to the winds.

He took a double dose, and waited half an hour. It seemed to produce no effect. He then poured out a treble dose, swallowed it, leant back upon his pillow, and waited. The miracle he anticipated had been worked at last. It seemed as though the second draught had not only operated with its own strength, but had kindled into power the latent forces of the first. He put away the bottle, and rang up Tupcombe.

Less than an hour later one of the housemaids, who of course was quite aware that the Squire's illness was serious, was surprised to hear a bold and decided step descending the stairs from the direction of Mr Dornell's room, accompanied by the humming of a tune. She knew that the doctor had not paid a visit that morning, and that it was too heavy to be the valet or any other man-servant. Looking up, she saw Squire Dornell fully dressed, descending toward her in his drab caped riding-coat and boots, with the swinging easy movement of his prime. Her face expressed her amazement.

'What the devil beest looking at?' said the Squire. 'Did you never see a man walk out of his house before, wench?'

Resuming his humming – which was of a defiant sort – he proceeded to the library, rang the bell, asked if the horses were ready, and directed them to be brought round. Ten minutes later he rode away in the direction of Bristol, Tupcombe behind him, trembling at what these movements might portend.

They rode on over the airy uplands and through the monotonous straight lanes at an equal pace. The distance traversed might have been about fifteen miles when Tupcombe could perceive that the Squire was getting tired – as weary as he would have been after riding three times the distance ten years before. However, they reached Bristol without any mishap, and put up at the Squire's accustomed inn. Dornell almost immediately proceeded on foot to the inn which Reynard had given as his address, it being now about four o'clock.

Reynard had already dined – for people dined early then – and he was staying indoors. He had already received Mrs Dornell's reply to his letter; but before acting upon her advice and starting for King's-Hintock he made up his mind to wait another day, that Betty's father might at least have time to write to him if so minded. The returned traveller much desired to obtain the Squire's assent, as well as his wife's, to the proposed visit to his bride, that nothing might seem harsh or forced in his method of taking his position as one of the family. But though he anticipated some sort of objection from his father-in-law, in consequence of Mrs Dornell's warning, he was surprised at the announcement of the Squire in person.

Stephen Reynard formed the completest of possible contrasts to Dornell as they stood confronting each other in the best parlour of the Bristol tavern. The Squire, hot-tempered, gouty, impulsive, generous, reckless; the younger man, pale, tall, sedate, self-possessed – a man of the world, fully bearing out at least one couplet in his epitaph, still extant in King's-Hintock church, which places in the inventory of his good qualities

> Engaging Manners, cultivated Mind,
> Adorn'd by Letters, and in Courts refin'd.

He was at this time about five-and-thirty, though careful living and an even, unemotional temperament caused him to look much younger than his years.

Squire Dornell plunged into his errand without much ceremony or preface.

'I am your humble servant, sir,' he said. 'I have read your letter writ to my wife and myself, and considered that the best way to answer it would be to do so in person.'

'I am vastly honoured by your visit, sir,' said Mr Stephen Reynard, bowing.

'Well, what's done can't be undone,' said Dornell, 'though it was mighty early, and was no doing of mine. She's your wife; and there's an end on't. But in brief, sir, she's too young for you to claim yet; we mustn't reckon by years; we must reckon by nature. She's still a girl; 'tis onpolite of 'ee to come yet; next year will be full soon enough for you to take her to you.'

Now, courteous as Reynard could be, he was a little obstinate when his resolution had once been formed. She had been promised him by her eighteenth birthday at latest – sooner if she were in robust health. Her mother had fixed the time on her own judgment, without a word of interference on his part. He had been hanging about foreign courts till he was weary. Betty was now a woman, if she would ever be one, and there was not, in his mind, the shadow of an excuse for putting him off longer. Therefore, fortified as he was by the support of her mother, he blandly but firmly told the Squire that he had been willing to waive his rights, out of deference to her parents, to any reasonable extent, but must now, in justice to himself and her, insist on maintaining them. He therefore, since she had not come to meet him, should proceed to King's-Hintock in a few days to fetch her.

This announcement, in spite of the urbanity with which it was delivered, set Dornell in a passion.

'O dammy, sir; you talk about rights, you do, after stealing her away, a mere child, against my will and knowledge! If we'd begged and prayed 'ee to take her, you could say no more.'

'Upon my honour, your charge is quite baseless, sir,' said his son-in-law. 'You must know by this time – or if you do not, it has been a monstrous cruel injustice to me that I should have been allowed to remain in your mind with such a stain upon my character – you must know that I used no seductiveness or temptation of any kind. Her mother assented; she assented. I took them at their word. That you was really opposed to the marriage was not known to me till afterwards.'

Dornell professed to believe not a word of it. 'You shan't have her till she's dree sixes full – no maid ought to be married till she's dree sixes! – and my daughter shan't be treated out of nater!' So he stormed on till Tupcombe, who had been alarmedly listening in the next room, entered suddenly, declaring to Reynard that his master's life was in danger if the interview were prolonged, he being subject to apoplectic strokes at these crises. Reynard immediately said that he would be the last to wish to injure Squire Dornell, and left the room, and as soon as the Squire had recovered breath and equanimity, he went out of the inn, leaning on the arm of Tupcombe.

Tupcombe was for sleeping in Bristol that night, but Dornell, whose energy seemed as invincible as it was sudden, insisted upon mounting and getting back as far as Falls-Park, to continue the journey to King's-Hintock on the following day. At five they started, and took the southern road towards the Mendip Hills. The evening was dry and windy, and, excepting that the sun did not shine, strongly reminded Tupcombe of the evening of that March month, nearly five years earlier, when news had been brought to King's-Hintock Court of the child Betty's marriage in London – news which had produced upon Dornell such a marked effect for the worse ever since, and indirectly upon the household of which he was the head. Before that time the winters were lively at Falls-Park, as well as at King's-Hintock, although the Squire had ceased to make it his regular residence. Hunting-guests and shooting-

guests came and went, and open house was kept. Tupcombe disliked the
clever courtier who had put a stop to this by taking away from the
Squire the only treasure he valued.

It grew darker with their progress along the lanes, and Tupcombe
discovered from Mr Dornell's manner of riding that his strength was
giving way; and spurring his own horse close alongside, he asked him
how he felt.

'Oh, bad; damn bad, Tupcombe! I can hardly keep my seat. I shall
never be any better, I fear! Have we passed Three-Man-Gibbet
yet?'

'Not yet by a long ways, sir.'

'I wish we had. I can hardly hold on.' The Squire could not repress
a groan now and then, and Tupcombe knew he was in great pain. 'I wish
I was underground – that's the place for such fools as I! I'd gladly be
there if it were not for Mistress Betty. He's coming on to King's-
Hintock to-morrow – he won't put it off any longer; he'll set out and
reach there to-morrow night, without stopping at Falls; and he'll take
her unawares, and I want to be there before him.'

'I hope you may be well enough to do it, sir. But really—'

'I *must*, Tupcombe! You don't know what my trouble is; it is not so
much that she is married to this man without my agreeing – for, after all,
there's nothing to say against him, so far as I know; but that she don't
take to him at all, seems to fear him – in fact, cares nothing about him;
and if he comes forcing himself into the house upon her, why, 'twill be
rank cruelty. Would to the Lord something would happen to prevent
him!'

How they reached home that night Tupcombe hardly knew. The
Squire was in such pain that he was obliged to recline upon his horse,
and Tupcombe was afraid every moment lest he would fall into the road.
But they did reach home at last, and Mr Dornell was instantly assisted
to bed.

Next morning it was obvious that he could not possibly go to King's-
Hintock for several days at least, and there on the bed he lay, cursing his
inability to proceed on an errand so personal and so delicate that no
emissary could perform it. What he wished to do was to ascertain from
Betty's own lips if her aversion to Reynard was so strong that his
presence would be positively distasteful to her. Were that the case, he
would have borne her away bodily on the saddle behind him.

But all that was hindered now, and he repeated a hundred times in Tupcombe's hearing, and in that of the nurse and other servants, 'I wish to God something would happen to him!'

This sentiment, reiterated by the Squire as he tossed in the agony induced by the powerful drugs of the day before, entered sharply into the soul of Tupcombe and of all who were attached to the house of Dornell, as distinct from the house of his wife at King's-Hintock. Tupcombe, who was an excitable man, was hardly less disquieted by the thought of Reynard's return than the Squire himself was. As the morning drew on, and the afternoon advanced at which Reynard would in all probability be passing near Falls on his way to the Court, the Squire's feelings became acuter, and the responsive Tupcombe could hardly bear to come near him. Having left him in the hands of the doctor, the former went out upon the lawn, for he could hardly breathe in the contagion of excitement caught from the employer who had virtually made him his confidant. He had lived with the Dornells from his boy-hood, had been born under the shadow of their walls; his whole life was annexed and welded to the life of the family in a degree which has no counterpart in these latter days.

He was summoned indoors, and learnt that it had been decided to send for Mrs Dornell: her husband was in great danger. There were two or three who could have acted as messenger, but Dornell wished Tupcombe to go, the reason showing itself when, Tupcombe being ready to start, Squire Dornell summoned him to his chamber and leaned down so that he could whisper in his ear:

'Put Peggy along smart, Tupcombe, and get there before him, you know – before him. This is the day he fixed. He has not passed Falls Cross-roads yet. If you can do that you will be able to get Betty to come – d'ye see? – after her mother has started; whom my illness will hinder waiting for him. Bring her by the lower road – he'll go by the upper. Your business is to make 'em miss each other – d'ye see? – but that's a thing I couldn't write down.'

Five minutes after, Tupcombe was astride the horse and on his way – the way he had followed so many times since his master, a florid young countryman, had first gone wooing to King's-Hintock Court. As soon as he had crossed the hills in the immediate neighbourhood of the manor, the road lay over a plain, where it ran in long straight stretches for several miles. In the best of times, when all had been gay in the united houses, that part of the road had seemed tedious. It was gloomy in the extreme now that he pursued it, at night and alone, on such an errand.

He rode and brooded. If the Squire were to die, he, Tupcombe, would be alone in the world and friendless, for he was no favourite with Mrs Dornell; and to find himself baffled, after all, in what he had set his mind on, would probably kill the Squire. Thinking thus, Tupcombe stopped his horse every now and then, and listened for the coming husband. The time was drawing on to the moment when Reynard might be expected to pass along this very route. He had watched the road well during the afternoon, and had inquired of the tavern-keepers as he came up to each, and he was convinced that the premature descent of the stranger-husband upon his young mistress had not been made by this highway as yet.

Besides the girl's mother, Tupcombe was the only member of the household who suspected Betty's tender feelings towards young Phelipson, so unhappily generated on her return from school; and he could therefore imagine, even better than her fond father, what would be her emotions on the sudden announcement of Reynard's advent that evening at King's-Hintock Court.

So he rode and rode, desponding and hopeful by turns. He felt assured that, unless in the unfortunate event of the almost immediate arrival of her son-in-law at his own heels, Mrs Dornell would not be able to hinder Betty from following to her father's bedside.

It was about nine o'clock that, having put twenty miles of country behind him, he turned in at the lodge-gate nearest to Ivell and King's-Hintock village, and pursued the long north drive – itself much like a turnpike road – which led thence through the park to the Court. Though there were so many trees in King's-Hintock park, few bordered the carriage roadway; he could see it stretching ahead in the pale night light like an unrolled deal shaving. Presently the irregular frontage of the house came in view, of great extent, but low, except where it rose into the outlines of a broad square tower.

As Tupcombe approached he rode aside upon the grass, to make sure, if possible, that he was the first comer, before letting his presence be known. The Court was dark and sleepy, in no respect as if a bride-groom were about to arrive.

While pausing he distinctly heard the tread of a horse upon the track behind him, and for a moment despaired of arriving in time: here, surely, was Reynard! Pulling up closer to the densest tree at hand he waited, and found he had retreated nothing too soon, for the second rider avoided the gravel also, and passed quite close to him. In the profile he recognized young Phelipson.

Before Tupcombe could think what to do, Phelipson had gone on; but not to the door of the house. Swerving to the left, he passed round to the east angle, where, as Tupcombe knew, were situated Betty's apartments. Dismounting, Tupcombe left the horse tethered to a hanging bough, and followed behind.

Suddenly his eye caught sight of an object which explained the position immediately. It was a ladder stretching from beneath the trees, which there came pretty close to the house, up to a first-floor window – one which lighted Miss Betty's rooms. Yes, it was Betty's chamber; he knew every room in the house well.

The young horseman who had passed him, having evidently left his steed somewhere under the trees also, was perceptible at the top of the ladder, immediately outside Betty's window. While Tupcombe watched, a cloaked female figure stepped timidly over the sill, and the two cautiously descended, one before the other, the young man's arms enclosing the young woman between his grasp of the ladder, so that she could not fall. As soon as they reached the bottom, young Phelipson quickly removed the ladder and hid it under the bushes. The pair disappeared; till, in a few minutes, Tupcombe could discern a horse emerging from a remoter part of the umbrage. The horse carried double, the girl being on a pillion behind her lover.

Tupcombe hardly knew what to do or think; yet, though this was not exactly the kind of flight that had been intended, she had certainly escaped. He went back to his own animal, and rode round to the servants' door, where he delivered the letter for Mrs Dornell. To leave a verbal message for Betty was now impossible.

The Court servants desired him to stay over the night, but he would not do so, desiring to get back to the Squire as soon as possible and tell what he had seen. Whether he ought not to have intercepted the young people, and carried off Betty himself to her father, he did not know. However, it was too late to think of that now, and without wetting his lips or swallowing a crumb, Tupcombe turned his back upon King's-Hintock Court.

It was not till he had advanced a considerable distance on his way homeward that, halting under the lantern of a roadside inn while the horse was watered, there came a traveller from the opposite direction in a hired coach; the lantern lit the stranger's face as he passed along and dropped into the shade. Tupcombe exulted for the moment, though he could hardly have justified his exultation. The belated traveller was Reynard; and another had stepped in before him.

You may now be willing to know of the fortunes of Miss Betty. Left much to herself through the intervening days, she had ample time to brood over her desperate attempt at the stratagem of infection – thwarted, apparently, by her mother's promptitude. In what other way to gain time she could not think. Thus drew on the day and the hour of the evening on which her husband was expected to announce himself.

At some period after dark, when she could not tell, a tap at the window, twice and thrice repeated, became audible. It caused her to start up, for the only visitant in her mind was the one whose advances she had so feared as to risk health and life to repel them. She crept to the window, and heard a whisper without.

'It is I – Charley,' said the voice.

Betty's face fired with excitement. She had latterly begun to doubt her admirer's staunchness, fancying his love to be going off in mere attentions which neither committed him nor herself very deeply. She opened the window, saying in a joyous whisper, 'O Charley; I thought you had deserted me quite!'

He assured her he had not done that, and that he had a horse in waiting, if she would ride off with him. 'You must come quickly,' he said; 'for Reynard's on the way!'

To throw a cloak round herself was the work of a moment, and assuring herself that her door was locked against a surprise, she climbed over the window-sill and descended with him as we have seen.

Her mother meanwhile, having received Tupcombe's note, found the news of her husband's illness so serious as to displace her thoughts of the coming son-in-law, and she hastened to tell her daughter of the Squire's dangerous condition, thinking it might be desirable to take her to her father's bedside. On trying the door of the girl's room, she found it still locked. Mrs Dornell called, but there was no answer. Full of misgivings, she privately fetched the old house-steward and bade him burst open the door – an order by no means easy to execute, the joinery of the Court being massively constructed. However, the lock sprang open at last, and she entered Betty's chamber only to find the window unfastened and the bird flown.

For a moment Mrs Dornell was staggered. Then it occurred to her that Betty might have privately obtained from Tupcombe the news of her father's serious illness, and, fearing she might be kept back to meet her husband, have gone off with that obstinate and biassed servitor to Falls-Park. The more she thought it over the more probable did the supposition appear; and binding her own head-man to secrecy as to Betty's movements, whether as she conjectured, or otherwise, Mrs Dornell herself prepared to set out.

She had no suspicion how grievously her husband's malady had been aggravated by his ride to Bristol, and thought more of Betty's affairs than of her own. That Betty's husband should arrive by some other road to-night, and find neither wife nor mother-in-law to receive him, and no explanation of their absence, was possible; but never forgetting chances, Mrs Dornell as she journeyed kept her eyes fixed upon the highway on the off-side, where, before she had reached the town of Ivell, the hired coach containing Stephen Reynard flashed into the lamp-light of her own carriage.

Mrs Dornell's coachman pulled up, in obedience to a direction she had given him at starting; the other coach was hailed, a few words passed, and Reynard alighted and came to Mrs Dornell's carriage-window.

'Come inside,' says she. 'I want to speak privately to you. Why are you so late?'

'One hindrance and another,' says he. 'I meant to be at the Court by eight at latest. My gratitude for your letter. I hope—'

'You must not try to see Betty yet,' said she. 'There be far other and newer reasons against your seeing her now than there were when I wrote.'

The circumstances were such that Mrs Dornell could not possibly conceal them entirely; nothing short of knowing some of the facts would prevent his blindly acting in a manner which might be fatal to the future. Moreover, there are times when deeper intriguers than Mrs Dornell feel that they must let out a few truths, if only in self-indulgence. So she told so much of recent surprises as that Betty's heart had been attracted by another image than his, and that his insisting on visiting her now might drive the girl to desperation. 'Betty has, in fact, rushed off to her father to avoid you,' she said. 'But if you wait she will soon forget this young man, and you will have nothing to fear.'

As a woman and a mother she could go no further, and Betty's desperate attempt to infect herself the week before as a means of repelling him, together with the alarming possibility that, after all, she had not gone to her father, but to her lover, was not revealed.

'Well,' sighed the diplomatist, in a tone unexpectedly quiet, 'such things have been known before. After all, she may prefer me to him some day, when she reflects how very differently I might have acted than I am going to act towards her. But I'll say no more about that now. I can have a bed at your house for to-night?'

'To-night, certainly. And you leave to-morrow morning early?' She spoke anxiously, for on no account did she wish him to make further discoveries. 'My husband is so woefully ill,' she continued, 'that my absence and Betty's on your arrival is naturally accounted for.'

He promised to leave early, and to write to her soon. 'And when I think the time is ripe,' he said, 'I'll write to her. I may have something to tell her that will bring her to graciousness.'

It was about one o'clock in the morning when Mrs Dornell reached Falls-Park. A double blow awaited her there. Betty had not arrived; her flight had been elsewhither; and her stricken mother divined with whom. She ascended to the bedside of her husband, where to her concern she found that the physician had given up all hope. The Squire was sinking, and his extreme weakness had almost changed his character, except in the particular that his old obstinacy sustained him in a refusal to see a clergyman. He shed tears at the least word, and sobbed at the sight of his wife. He asked for Betty, and it was with a heavy heart that Mrs Dornell told him that the girl had not accompanied her.

'He is not keeping her away?'

'No, no. He is going back – he is not coming to her for some time.'

'Then what is detaining her – cruel, neglectful maid!'

'No, no, Thomas; she is— She could not come.'

'How's that?'

Somehow the solemnity of these last moments of his gave him inquisitorial power, and the too cold wife could not conceal from him the flight which had taken place from King's-Hintock that night.

To her amazement, the effect upon him was electrical.

'What – Betty – a trump after all? Hurrah! She's her father's own maid! She's game! She knew he was her father's own choice! She vowed that my man should win! Well done, Bet! – haw! haw! Hurrah!'

He had raised himself in bed by starts as he spoke, and now fell back exhausted. He never uttered another word, and died before the dawn. People said there had not been such an ungenteel death in a good county family for years.

*

Now I will go back to the time of Betty's riding off on the pillion behind her lover. They left the park by an obscure gate to the east, and presently found themselves in the lonely and solitary length of the old Roman road now called Long-Ash Lane.

By this time they were rather alarmed at their own performance, for they were both young and inexperienced. Hence they proceeded almost in silence till they came to a mean roadside inn which was not yet closed; when Betty, who had held on to him with much misgivings all this while, felt dreadfully unwell, and said she thought she would like to get down.

They accordingly dismounted from the jaded animal that had brought them, and were shown into a small dark parlour, where they stood side by side awkwardly, like the fugitives they were. A light was brought, and when they were left alone Betty threw off the cloak which had enveloped her. No sooner did young Phelipson see her face than he uttered an alarmed exclamation.

'Why, Lord, Lord, you are sickening for the smallpox!' he cried.

'O – I forgot!' faltered Betty. And then she informed him that, on hearing of her husband's approach the week before, in a desperate attempt to keep him from her side, she had tried to imbibe the infection – an act which till this moment she had supposed to have been ineffectual, imagining her feverishness to be the result of her excitement.

The effect of this discovery upon young Phelipson was overwhelming. Better-seasoned men than he would not have been proof against it, and he was only a little over her own age. 'And you've been holding on to me!' he said. 'And suppose you get worse, and we both have it, what shall we do? Won't you be a fright in a month or two, poor, poor Betty!'

In his horror he attempted to laugh, but the laugh ended in a weakly giggle. She was more woman than girl by this time, and realized his feeling.

'What – in trying to keep off him, I keep off you?' she said miserably. 'Do you hate me because I am going to be ugly and ill?'

'O no, no!' he said soothingly. 'But I – I am thinking if it is quite right for us to do this. You see, dear Betty, if you was not married it would be different. You are not in honour married to him, we've often said; still you are his by law, and you can't be mine whilst he's alive. And with this terrible sickness coming on, perhaps you had better let me take you back, and – climb in at the window again.'

'Is *this* your love?' said Betty reproachfully. 'O, if you was sickening for the plague itself, and going to be as ugly as the Ooser in the church-vestry, I wouldn't—'

'No, no, you mistake, upon my soul!'

But Betty with a swollen heart had rewrapped herself and gone out of the door. The horse was still standing there. She mounted by the help of the upping-stock, and when he had followed her she said, 'Do not come near me, Charley; but please lead the horse, so that if you've not caught anything already you'll not catch it going back. After all, what keeps off you may keep off him. Now onward.'

He did not resist her command, and back they went by the way they had come, Betty shedding bitter tears at the retribution she had already brought upon herself; for though she had reproached Phelipson, she was staunch enough not to blame him in her secret heart for showing that his love was only skin-deep. The horse was stopped in the planta-tion, and they walked silently to the lawn, reaching the bushes wherein the ladder still lay.

'Will you put it up for me?' she asked mournfully.

He re-erected the ladder without a word; but when she approached to ascend he said, 'Good-bye, Betty!'

'Good-bye!' said she; and involuntarily turned her face towards his. He hung back from imprinting the expected kiss: at which Betty started as if she had received a poignant wound. She moved away so suddenly that he hardly had time to follow her up the ladder to prevent her falling.

'Tell your mother to get the doctor at once!' he said anxiously.

She stepped in without looking behind; he descended, withdrew the ladder, and went away.

Alone in her chamber, Betty flung herself upon her face on the bed, and burst into shaking sobs. Yet she would not admit to herself that her lover's conduct was unreasonable; only that her rash act of the previous week had been wrong. No one had heard her enter, and she was too worn out, in body and mind, to think or care about medical aid. In an hour or so she felt yet more unwell, positively ill; and nobody coming to her at the usual bedtime, she looked towards the door. Marks of the lock having been forced were visible, and this made her chary of summoning a servant. She opened the door cautiously and sallied forth downstairs.

In the dining-parlour, as it was called, the now sick and sorry Betty was startled to see at that late hour not her mother, but a man sitting, calmly finishing his supper. There was no servant in the room. He turned, and she recognized her husband.

'Where's my mamma?' she demanded without preface.

'Gone to your father's. Is that—' He stopped, aghast.

'Yes, sir. This spotted object is your wife! I've done it because I don't want you to come near me!'

He was sixteen years her senior; old enough to be compassionate. 'My poor child, you must get to bed directly! Don't be afraid of me – I'll carry you upstairs, and send for a doctor instantly.'

'Ah, you don't know what I am!' she cried. 'I had a lover once; but now he's gone! 'Twasn't I who deserted him. He has deserted me; because I am ill he wouldn't kiss me, though I wanted him to!'

'Wouldn't he? Then he was a very poor slack-twisted sort of fellow. Betty, *I've* never kissed you since you stood beside me as my little wife, barely thirteen years old! May I kiss you now?'

Though Betty by no means desired his kisses, she had enough of the spirit of Cunigonde in Schiller's ballad to test his daring. 'If you have courage to venture, yes, sir!' said she. 'But you may die for it, mind!'

He came up to her and imprinted a deliberate kiss full upon her mouth, saying, 'May many others follow!'

She shook her head, and hastily withdrew, though secretly pleased at his hardihood. The excitement had supported her for the few minutes she had passed in his presence, and she could hardly drag herself back to her room. Her husband summoned the servants, and, sending them to her assistance, went off himself for a doctor.

The next morning Reynard waited at the Court till he had learnt from the medical man that Betty's attack promised to be a very light one – or, as it was expressed, 'very fine'; and in taking his leave sent up a note to her: –

Now I must be Gone. I promised your Mother I would not see You yet, and she may be anger'd if she finds me here. Promise to see me as Soon as you are well?

He was of all men then living one of the best able to cope with such an untimely situation as this. A contriving, sagacious, gentle-mannered man, a philosopher who saw that the only constant attribute of life is change, he held that, as long as she lives, there is nothing finite in the most impassioned attitude a woman may take up. In twelve months his girl-wife's recent infatuation might be as distasteful to her mind as it was now to his own. In a few years her very flesh would change – so said the scientific; – her spirit, so much more ephemeral, was capable of changing in one. Betty was his, and it became a mere question of means how to effect that change.

During the day Mrs Dornell, having closed her husband's eyes, returned to the Court. She was truly relieved to find Betty there, even though on a bed of sickness. The disease ran its course, and in due time Betty became convalescent, without having suffered deeply for her rashness, one little pit beneath her ear, and one beneath her chin, being all the marks she retained.

The Squire's body was not brought back to King's-Hintock. Where he was born, and where he had lived before wedding his Sue, there he had wished to be buried. No sooner had she lost him than Mrs Dornell, like certain other wives, though she had never shown any great affection for him while he lived, awoke suddenly to his many virtues, and zealously embraced his opinion about delaying Betty's union with her husband, which she had formerly combated strenuously. 'Poor man! how right he was, and how wrong was I!' Eighteen was certainly the lowest age at which Mr Reynard should claim her child – nay, it was too low! Far too low!

So desirous was she of honouring her lamented husband's sentiments in this respect, that she wrote to her son-in-law suggesting that, partly on account of Betty's sorrow for her father's loss, and out of consideration for his known wishes for delay, Betty should not be taken from her till her nineteenth birthday.

However much or little Stephen Reynard might have been to blame in his marriage, the patient man now almost deserved to be pitied. First Betty's skittishness; now her mother's remorseful *volte-face*: it was enough to exasperate anybody; and he wrote to the widow in a tone which led to a little coolness between those hitherto firm friends. However, knowing that he had a wife not to claim but to win, and that young Phelipson had been packed off to sea by his parents, Stephen was complaisant to a degree, returning to London, and holding quite aloof from Betty and her mother, who remained for the present in the country. In town he had a mild visitation of the distemper he had taken from Betty, and in writing to her he took care not to dwell upon its mildness. It was now that Betty began to pity him for what she had inflicted upon him by the kiss, and her correspondence acquired a distinct flavour of kindness thenceforward.

Owing to his rebuffs, Reynard had grown to be truly in love with Betty in his mild, placid, durable way – in that way which perhaps, upon the whole, tends most generally to the woman's comfort under the institution of marriage, if not particularly to her ecstasy. Mrs Dornell's exaggeration of her husband's wish for delay in their living together was inconvenient, but he would not openly infringe it. He wrote tenderly to Betty, and soon announced that he had a little surprise in store for her. The secret was that the King had been graciously pleased to inform him privately, through a relation, that His Majesty was about to offer him a Barony. Would she like the title to be Ivell? Moreover, he had reason for knowing that in a few years the dignity would be raised to that of an Earl, for which creation he thought the title of Wessex would be eminently suitable, considering the position of much of their property. As Lady Ivell, therefore, and future Countess of Wessex, he should beg leave to offer her his heart a third time.

He did not add, as he might have added, how greatly the consideration of the enormous estates at King's-Hintock and elsewhere which Betty would inherit, and her children after her, had conduced to this desirable honour.

Whether the impending titles had really any effect upon Betty's regard for him I cannot state, for she was one of those close characters who never let their minds be known upon anything. That such honour was absolutely unexpected by her from such a quarter is, however, certain; and she could not deny that Stephen had shown her kindness, forbearance, even magnanimity; had forgiven her for an errant passion which he might with some reason have denounced, notwithstanding her cruel position as a child entrapped into marriage ere able to understand its bearings.

Her mother, in her grief and remorse for the loveless life she had led with her rough, though open-hearted, husband, made now a creed of his merest whim; and continued to insist that, out of respect to his known desire, her son-in-law should not reside with Betty till the girl's father had been dead a year at least, at which time the girl would still be under nineteen. Letters must suffice for Stephen till then.

'It is rather long for him to wait,' Betty hesitatingly said one day.

'What!' said her mother. 'From *you*? not to respect your dear dead father—'

'Of course it is quite proper,' said Betty hastily. 'I don't gainsay it. I was but thinking that – that—'

In the long slow months of the stipulated interval her mother tended and trained Betty carefully for her duties. Fully awake now to the many

virtues of her dear departed one, she, among other acts of pious devotion
to his memory, rebuilt the church of King's-Hintock village, and
established valuable charities in all the villages of that name, as far as to
Little-Hintock, several miles eastward.

In superintending these works, particularly that of the church-
building, her daughter Betty was her constant companion, and the
incidents of their execution were doubtless not without a soothing
effect upon the young creature's heart. She had sprung from girl to
woman by a sudden bound, and few would have recognized in the
thoughtful face of Betty now the same person who, the year before, had
seemed to have absolutely no idea whatever of responsibility, moral or
other. Time passed thus till the Squire had been nearly a year in his
vault; and Mrs Dornell was duly asked by letter by the patient Reynard
if she were willing for him to come soon. He did not wish to take Betty
away if her mother's sense of loneliness would be too great, but would
willingly live at King's-Hintock a while with them.

Before the widow had replied to this communication, she one day
happened to observe Betty walking on the south terrace in the full
sunlight, without hat or mantle, and was struck by her child's figure.
Mrs Dornell called her in, and said suddenly: 'Have you seen your
husband since the time of your poor father's death?'

'Well – yes, mamma,' says Betty, colouring.

'What – against my wishes and those of the dear deceased! I am
shocked at your disobedience!'

'But my father said eighteen, ma'am, and you made it much longer—'

'Why, of course – out of consideration for you! When have ye seen
him?'

'Well,' stammered Betty, 'in the course of his letters to me he said
that I belonged to him, and if nobody knew that we met it would make
no difference. And that I need not hurt your feelings by telling you.'

'Well?'

'So I went to Casterbridge that time you went to London about five
months ago—'

'And met him there? When did you come back?'

'Dear mamma, it grew very late, and he said it was safer not to go
back till next day, as the roads were bad; and as you were away from
home—'

'I don't want to hear any more! This is your respect for your father's
memory,' groaned the widow. 'When did you meet him again?'

'Oh – not for more than a fortnight.'

'A fortnight! How many times have ye seen him altogether?'

'I'm sure, mamma, I've not seen him altogether a dozen times – I mean quite alone, and not reckoning—'

'A dozen! And eighteen and a half years old barely!'

'Twice we met by accident,' pleaded Betty. 'Once at Abbot's-Cernel in the ruined chamber over the gate-house, and another time at the Red Lion, Melchester.'

'O thou deceitful girl!' cried Mrs Dornell. 'An *accident* took you to the Red Lion tavern whilst I was staying at the White Hart! I remember – I wondered what could have happened, and then you came in at twelve o'clock at night, and said you'd been to see the cathedral by the light o' the moon!'

'My ever-honoured mamma, so I had! I only went to the Red Lion with him afterwards.'

'O Betty, Betty! That my child should have deceived me even in my widowed days!'

'But, my dearest mamma, you made me marry him!' says Betty with spirit, 'and of course I've to obey him more than you now!'

Mrs Dornell sighed. 'All I have to say is, that you'd better get your husband to join you as soon as possible,' she remarked. 'To go on playing the maiden like this – I'm ashamed to see you!'

She wrote instantly to Stephen Reynard: 'I wash my hands of the whole matter as between you two; though I should advise you to *openly* join each other as soon as you can – if you wish to avoid scandal.'

He came, though not till the promised title had been granted, and he could call Betty archly 'My Lady'.

People said in after years that she and her husband were very happy. However that may be, they had a numerous family; and she became in due course first Countess of Wessex, as he had foretold.

The little figured frock in which she had been married to him at the tender age of thirteen was carefully preserved among the relics at King's-Hintock Court, where it may still be seen by the curious – a yellowing, pathetic testimony to the small count taken of the happiness of an innocent child in the social strategy of those days, which might have led, but providentially did not lead, to great unhappiness.

When the Earl died Betty wrote him an epitaph, in which she described him as the best of husbands, fathers, and friends, and called herself his disconsolate widow.

Such is woman; or rather (not to give offence by so sweeping an assertion), such was Betty Dornell.

It was at a meeting of one of the Wessex Field and Antiquarian Clubs that the foregoing story, partly told, partly read from a manuscript, was made to do duty for the regulation papers on deformed butterflies, fossil ox-horns, prehistoric dung-mixens, and such-like, that usually occupied the more serious attention of the members.

This Club was of an inclusive and intersocial character; to a degree, indeed, remarkable for the part of England in which it had its being – dear, delightful Wessex, whose statuesque dynasties are even now only just beginning to feel the shaking of the new and strange spirit without, like that which entered the lonely valley of Ezekiel's vision and made the dry bones move: where the honest squires, tradesmen, parsons, clerks, and people still praise the Lord with one voice for His best of all possible worlds.

The present meeting, which was to extend over two days, had opened its proceedings at the museum of the town whose buildings and environs were to be visited by the members. Lunch had ended and the afternoon excursion had been about to be undertaken, when the rain came down in an obstinate spatter, which revealed no sign of cessation. As the members waited they grew chilly, although it was only autumn, and a fire was lighted, which threw a cheerful shine upon the varnished skulls, urns, penates, tesseræ, costumes, coats of mail, weapons, and missals, animated the fossilized ichthyosaurus and iguanodon; while the dead eyes of the stuffed birds – those never-absent familiars in such collections, though murdered to extinction out of doors – flashed as they had flashed to the rising sun above the neighbouring moors on the fatal morning when the trigger was pulled which ended their little flight. It was then that the historian produced his manuscript, which he had prepared, he said, with a view to publication. His delivery of the story having concluded as aforesaid, the speaker expressed his hope that the constraint of the weather, and the paucity of more scientific papers, would excuse any inappropriateness in his subject.

Several members observed that a storm-bound club could not presume to be selective, and they were all very much obliged to him for such a curious chapter from the domestic histories of the county.

The President looked gloomily from the window at the descending rain, and broke a short silence by saying that though the Club had met, there seemed little probability of its being able to visit the objects of interest set down among the *agenda*.

The Treasurer observed that they had at least a roof over their heads; and they had also a second day before them.

A sentimental member, leaning back in his chair, declared that he was in no hurry to go out, and that nothing would please him so much as another county story, with or without manuscript.

The Colonel added that the subject should be a lady, like the former, to which a gentleman known as the Spark said 'Hear, hear!'

Though these had spoken in jest, a rural dean who was present observed blandly that there was no lack of materials. Many, indeed, were the legends and traditions of gentle and noble dames, renowned in times past in that part of England, whose actions and passions were now, but for men's memories, buried under the brief inscription on a tomb or an entry of dates in a dry pedigree.

Another member, an old surgeon, a somewhat grim though sociable personage, was quite of the speaker's opinion, and felt fully sure that the memory of the reverend gentleman must abound with such curious tales of fair dames, of their loves and hates, their joys and their misfortunes, their beauty and their fate.

The parson, a trifle confused, retorted that their friend the surgeon, the son of a surgeon, seemed to him, as a man who had seen much and heard more during the long course of his own and his father's practice, the member of all others most likely to be acquainted with such lore.

The bookworm, the Colonel, the historian, the Vice-president, the churchwarden, the two curates, the gentleman-tradesman, the sentimental member, the crimson maltster, the quiet gentleman, the man of family, the Spark, and several others, quite agreed, and begged that he would recall something of the kind. The old surgeon said that, though a meeting of the South-Wessex Field and Antiquarian Club was the last place at which he should have expected to be called upon in this way, he had no objection; and the parson said he would come next. The surgeon then reflected, and decided to relate the history of a lady named Barbara, who lived towards the end of the last century, apologizing for his tale as being perhaps a little too professional. The crimson maltster winked to the Spark at hearing the nature of the apology, and the surgeon began.

Dame the Second
Barbara of the House of Grebe

By the Old Surgeon

I T was apparently an idea, rather than a passion, that inspired Lord Uplandtowers' resolve to win her. Nobody ever knew when he formed it, or whence he got his assurance of success in the face of her manifest dislike of him. Possibly not until after that first important act of her life which I shall presently mention. His matured and cynical doggedness at the age of nineteen, when impulse mostly rules calculation, was remarkable, and might have owed its existence as much to his succession to the earldom and its accompanying local honours in childhood, as to the family character; an elevation which jerked him into maturity, so to speak, without his having known adolescence. He had only reached his twelfth year when his father, the fourth Earl, died, after a course of the Bath waters.

Nevertheless, the family character had a great deal to do with it. Determination was hereditary in the bearers of that escutcheon; sometimes for good, sometimes for evil.

The seats of the two families were about ten miles apart, the way between them lying along the now old, then new, turnpike-road connecting Havenpool and Warborne with the city of Melchester; a road which, though only a branch from what was known as the Great Western Highway, is probably, even at present, as it has been for the last hundred years, one of the finest examples of a macadamized turnpike-track that can be found in England.

The mansion of the Earl, as well as that of his neighbour, Barbara's father, stood back about a mile from the highway, with which each was connected by an ordinary drive and lodge. It was along this particular highway that the young Earl drove on a certain evening at Christmastide some twenty years before the end of the last century, to attend a ball at Chene Manor, the home of Barbara, and her parents Sir John and Lady

Grebe. Sir John's was a baronetcy created a few years before the breaking out of the Civil War, and his lands were even more extensive than those of Lord Uplandtowers himself, comprising this Manor of Chene, another on the coast near, half the Hundred of Cockdene, and well-enclosed lands in several other parishes, notably Warborne and those contiguous. At this time Barbara was barely seventeen, and the ball is the first occasion on which we have any tradition of Lord Upland-towers attempting tender relations with her; it was early enough, God knows.

An intimate friend – one of the Drenkhards – is said to have dined with him that day, and Lord Uplandtowers had, for a wonder, com-municated to his guest the secret design of his heart.

'You'll never get her – sure; you'll never get her!' this friend had said at parting. 'She's not drawn to your lordship by love: and as for thought of a good match, why, there's no more calculation in her than in a bird.'

'We'll see,' said Lord Uplandtowers impassively.

He no doubt thought of his friend's forecast as he travelled along the highway in his chariot; but the sculptural repose of his profile against the vanishing daylight on his right hand would have shown his friend that the Earl's equanimity was undisturbed. He reached the solitary wayside tavern called Lornton Inn – the rendezvous of many a daring poacher for operations in the adjoining forest; and he might have observed, if he had taken the trouble, a strange post-chaise standing in the halting-space before the inn. He duly sped past it, and half-an-hour after through the little town of Warborne. Onward, a mile further, was the house of his entertainer.

At this date it was an imposing edifice – or, rather, congeries of edifices – as extensive as the residence of the Earl himself, though far less regular. One wing showed extreme antiquity, having huge chimneys, whose sub-structures projected from the external walls like towers; and a kitchen of vast dimensions, in which (it was said) breakfasts had been cooked for John of Gaunt. Whilst he was yet in the forecourt he could hear the rhythm of French horns and clarionets, the favourite instru-ments of those days at such entertainments.

Entering the long parlour, in which the dance had just been opened by Lady Grebe with a minuet – it being now seven o'clock, according to the tradition – he was received with a welcome befitting his rank, and looked round for Barbara. She was not dancing, and seemed to be pre-occupied – almost, indeed, as though she had been waiting for him.

Barbara at this time was a good and pretty girl, who never spoke ill of
anyone, and hated other pretty women the very least possible. She did
not refuse him for the country-dance which followed, and soon after was
his partner in a second.

The evening wore on, and the horns and clarionets tootled merrily.
Barbara evinced towards her lover neither distinct preference nor
aversion; but old eyes would have seen that she pondered something.
However, after supper she pleaded a headache, and disappeared. To pass
the time of her absence, Lord Uplandtowers went into a little room
adjoining the long gallery, where some elderly ones were sitting by the
fire, – for he had a phlegmatic dislike of dancing for its own sake, – and,
lifting the window-curtains, he looked out of the window into the park
and wood, dark now as a cavern. Some of the guests appeared to be
leaving even so soon as this, two lights showing themselves as turning
away from the door and sinking to nothing in the distance.

His hostess put her head into the room to look for partners for the
ladies, and Lord Uplandtowers came out. Lady Grebe informed him
that Barbara had not returned to the ball-room: she had gone to bed in
sheer necessity.

'She has been so excited over the ball all day,' her mother continued,
'that I feared she would be worn out early. . . . But sure, Lord Uplandtowers, you won't be leaving yet?'

He said that it was near twelve o'clock, and that some had already
left.

'I protest nobody has gone yet,' said Lady Grebe.

To humour her he stayed till midnight, and then set out. He had
made no progress in his suit; but he had assured himself that Barbara
gave no other guest the preference, and nearly everybody in the neighbourhood was there.

' 'Tis only a matter of time,' said the calm young philosopher.

The next morning he lay till near ten o'clock, and he had only just
come out upon the head of the staircase when he heard hoofs upon the
gravel without; in a few moments the door had been opened, and Sir
John Grebe met him in the hall, as he set foot on the lowest stair.

'My lord – where's Barbara – my daughter?'

Even the Earl of Uplandtowers could not repress amazement. 'What's
the matter, my dear Sir John?' says he.

The news was startling, indeed. From the Baronet's disjointed
explanation Lord Uplandtowers gathered that after his own and the

other guests' departure Sir John and Lady Grebe had gone to rest without seeing any more of Barbara; it being understood by them that she
had retired to bed when she sent word to say that she could not join the
dancers again. Before then she had told her maid that she would dispense
with her services for this night; and there was evidence to show that the
young lady had never lain down at all, the bed remaining unpressed.
Circumstances seemed to prove that the deceitful girl had feigned
indisposition to get an excuse for leaving the ball-room, and that she had
left the house within ten minutes, presumably during the first dance
after supper.

'I saw her go,' said Lord Uplandtowers.

'The devil you did!' says Sir John.

'Yes.' And he mentioned the retreating carriage-lights, and how he
was assured by Lady Grebe that no guest had departed.

'Surely that was it!' said the father. 'But she's not gone alone, d'ye
know!'

'Ah – who is the young man?'

'I can on'y guess. My worst fear is my most likely guess. I'll say no
more. I thought – yet I would not believe – it possible that you was the
sinner. Would that you had been! But 'tis t'other, 'tis t'other, by
Heaven! I must e'en up and after 'em!'

'Whom do you suspect?'

Sir John would not give a name, and, stultified rather than agitated,
Lord Uplandtowers accompanied him back to Chene. He again asked
upon whom were the Baronet's suspicions directed; and the impulsive
Sir John was no match for the insistence of Uplandtowers.

He said at length, 'I fear 'tis Edmond Willowes.'

'Who's he?'

'A young fellow of Shottsford-Forum – a widow-woman's son,' the
other told him, and explained that Willowes's father, or grandfather,
was the last of the old glass-painters in that place, where (as you may
know) the art lingered on when it had died out in every other part of
England.

'By God, that's bad – mighty bad!' said Lord Uplandtowers, throwing
himself back in the chaise in frigid despair.

They despatched emissaries in all directions; one by the Melchester
Road, another by Shottsford-Forum, another coastwards.

But the lovers had a ten-hours' start; and it was apparent that sound
judgment had been exercised in choosing as their time of flight the

particular night when the movements of a strange carriage would not be noticed, either in the park or on the neighbouring highway, owing to the general press of vehicles. The chaise which had been seen waiting at Lornton Inn was, no doubt, the one they had escaped in; and the pair of heads which had planned so cleverly thus far had probably contrived marriage ere now.

The fears of her parents were realized. A letter sent by special messenger from Barbara, on the evening of that day, briefly informed them that her lover and herself were on the way to London, and before this communication reached her home they would be united as husband and wife. She had taken this extreme step because she loved her dear Edmond as she could love no other man, and because she had seen closing round her the doom of marriage with Lord Uplandtowers, unless she put that threatened fate out of possibility by doing as she had done. She had well considered the step beforehand, and was prepared to live like any other country-townsman's wife if her father repudiated her for her action.

'Damn her!' said Lord Uplandtowers, as he drove homeward that night. 'Damn her for a fool!' – which shows the kind of love he bore her.

Well; Sir John had already started in pursuit of them as a matter of duty, driving like a wild man to Melchester, and thence by the direct highway to the capital. But he soon saw that he was acting to no purpose; and by and by, discovering that the marriage had actually taken place, he forebore all attempts to unearth them in the City, and returned and sat down with his lady to digest the event as best they could.

To proceed against this Willowes for the abduction of our heiress was, possibly, in their power; yet, when they considered the now unalterable facts, they refrained from violent retribution. Some six weeks passed, during which time Barbara's parents, though they keenly felt her loss, held no communication with the truant, either for reproach or condonation. They continued to think of the disgrace she had brought upon herself; for, though the young man was an honest fellow, and the son of an honest father, the latter had died so early, and his widow had had such struggles to maintain herself, that the son was very imperfectly educated. Moreover, his blood was, as far as they knew, of no distinction whatever, whilst hers, through her mother, was compounded of the best juices of ancient baronial distillation, containing tinctures of Maundeville, and Mohun, and Syward, and Peverell, and Culliford, and Talbot, and Plantagenet, and York, and Lancaster, and God knows what besides, which it was a thousand pities to throw away.

The father and mother sat by the fireplace that was spanned by the four-centred arch bearing the family shields on its haunches, and groaned aloud – the lady more than Sir John.

'To think this should have come upon us in our old age!' said he.

'Speak for yourself!' she snapped through her sobs, 'I am only one-and-forty! . . . Why didn't ye ride faster and overtake 'em!'

In the meantime the young married lovers, caring no more about their blood than about ditch-water, were intensely happy – happy, that is, in the descending scale which, as we all know, Heaven in its wisdom has ordained for such rash cases; that is to say, the first week they were in the seventh heaven, the second in the sixth, the third week temperate, the fourth reflective, and so on; a lover's heart after possession being comparable to the earth in its geologic stages, as described to us sometimes by our worthy President; first a hot coal, then a warm one, then a cooling cinder, then chilly – the simile shall be pursued no further. The long and the short of it was that one day a letter, sealed with their daughter's own little seal, came into Sir John and Lady Grebe's hands; and, on opening it, they found it to contain an appeal from the young couple to Sir John to forgive them for what they had done, and they would fall on their naked knees and be most dutiful children for evermore.

Then Sir John and his lady sat down again by the fireplace with the four-centred arch, and consulted, and re-read the letter. Sir John Grebe, if the truth must be told, loved his daughter's happiness far more, poor man, than he loved his name and lineage; he recalled to his mind all her little ways, gave vent to a sigh; and, by this time acclimatized to the idea of the marriage, said that what was done could not be undone, and that he supposed they must not be too harsh with her. Perhaps Barbara and her husband were in actual need; and how could they let their only child starve?

A slight consolation had come to them in an unexpected manner. They had been credibly informed that an ancestor of plebeian Willowes was once honoured with intermarriage with a scion of the aristocracy who had gone to the dogs. In short, such is the foolishness of distinguished parents, and sometimes of others also, that they wrote that very day to the address Barbara had given them, informing her that she might return home and bring her husband with her; they would not object to see him, would not reproach her, and would endeavour to welcome both, and to discuss with them what could best be arranged for their future.

In three or four days a rather shabby post-chaise drew up at the door of Chene Manor-house, at sound of which the tender-hearted baronet and his wife ran out as if to welcome a prince and princess of the blood. They were overjoyed to see their spoilt child return safe and sound – though she was only Mrs Willowes, wife of Edmond Willowes of nowhere. Barbara burst into penitential tears, and both husband and wife were contrite enough, as well they might be, considering that they had not a guinea to call their own.

When the four had calmed themselves, and not a word of chiding had been uttered to the pair, they discussed the position soberly, young Willowes sitting in the background with great modesty till invited forward by Lady Grebe in no frigid tone.

'How handsome he is!' she said to herself. 'I don't wonder at Barbara's craze for him.'

He was, indeed, one of the handsomest men who ever set his lips on a maid's. A blue coat, murrey waistcoat, and breeches of drab set off a figure that could scarcely be surpassed. He had large dark eyes, anxious now, as they glanced from Barbara to her parents and tenderly back again to her; observing whom, even now in her trepidation, one could see why the *sang froid* of Lord Uplandtowers had been raised to more than lukewarmness. Her fair young face (according to the tale handed down by old women) looked out from under a gray conical hat, trimmed with white ostrich-feathers, and her little toes peeped from a buff petticoat worn under a puce gown. Her features were not regular: they were almost infantine, as you may see from miniatures in possession of the family, her mouth showing much sensitiveness, and one could be sure that her faults would not lie on the side of bad temper unless for urgent reasons.

Well, they discussed their state as became them, and the desire of the young couple to gain the goodwill of those upon whom they were literally dependent for everything induced them to agree to any temporizing measure that was not too irksome. Therefore, having been nearly two months united, they did not oppose Sir John's proposal that he should furnish Edmond Willowes with funds sufficient for him to travel a year on the Continent in the company of a tutor, the young man undertaking to lend himself with the utmost diligence to the tutor's instructions, till he became polished outwardly and inwardly to the degree required in the husband of such a lady as Barbara. He was to apply himself to the study of languages, manners, history, society, ruins and everything else that came under his eyes, till he should return to take his place without blushing by Barbara's side.

'And by that time,' said worthy Sir John, 'I'll get my little place out at Yewsholt ready for you and Barbara to occupy on your return. The house is small and out of the way; but it will do for a young couple for a while.'

'If 'twere no bigger than a summer-house it would do!' says Barbara.

'If 'twere no bigger than a sedan-chair!' says Willowes. 'And the more lonely the better.'

'We can put up with the loneliness,' said Barbara, with less zest. 'Some friends will come, no doubt.'

All this being laid down, a travelled tutor was called in – a man of many gifts and great experience, – and on a fine morning away tutor and pupil went. A great reason urged against Barbara accompanying her youthful husband was that his attentions to her would naturally be such as to prevent his zealously applying every hour of his time to learning and seeing – an argument of wise prescience, and unanswerable. Regular days for letter-writing were fixed, Barbara and her Edmond exchanged their last kisses at the door, and the chaise swept under the archway into the drive.

He wrote to her from Le Havre, as soon as he reached that port, which was not for seven days, on account of adverse winds; he wrote from Rouen, and from Paris; described to her his sight of the King and Court at Versailles, and the wonderful marble-work and mirrors in that palace; wrote next from Lyons; then, after a comparatively long interval, from Turin, narrating his fearful adventures in crossing Mont Cenis on mules, and how he was overtaken with a terrific snowstorm, which had well-nigh been the end of him, and his tutor, and his guides. Then he wrote glowingly of Italy; and Barbara could see the development of her husband's mind reflected in his letters month by month; and she much admired the forethought of her father in suggesting this education for Edmond. Yet she sighed sometimes – her husband being no longer in evidence to fortify her in her choice of him – and timidly dreaded what mortifications might be in store for her by reason of this *mésalliance*. She went out very little; for on the one or two occasions on which she had shown herself to former friends she noticed a distinct difference in their manner, as though they should say, 'Ah, my happy swain's wife; you're caught!'

Edmond's letters were as affectionate as ever; even more affectionate, after a while, than hers were to him. Barbara observed this growing coolness in herself; and like a good and honest lady was horrified and grieved, since her only wish was to act faithfully and uprightly. It troubled her so much that she prayed for a warmer heart, and at last wrote to her husband to beg him now that he was in the land of Art, to send her his portrait, ever so small, that she might look at it all day and every day, and never for a moment forget his features.

Willowes was nothing loth, and replied that he would do more than she wished: he had made friends with a sculptor in Pisa, who was much interested in him and his history; and he had commissioned this artist to make a bust of himself in marble, which when finished he would send her. What Barbara had wanted was something immediate; but she expressed no objection to the delay; and in his next communication Edmond told her that the sculptor, of his own choice, had decided to extend the bust to a full-length statue, so anxious was he to get a specimen of his skill introduced to the notice of the English aristocracy. It was progressing well, and rapidly.

Meanwhile, Barbara's attention began to be occupied at home with Yewsholt Lodge, the house that her kind-hearted father was preparing for her residence when her husband returned. It was a small place on the plan of a large one – a cottage built in the form of a mansion, having a central hall with a wooden gallery running round it, and rooms no bigger than closets to support this introduction. It stood on a slope so solitary, and surrounded by trees so dense, that the birds who inhabited the boughs sang at strange hours, as if they hardly could distinguish night from day.

During the progress of repairs at this bower Barbara frequently visited it. Though so secluded by the dense growth, it was near the high road, and one day while looking over the fence she saw Lord Upland-towers riding past. He saluted her courteously, yet with mechanical stiffness, and did not halt. Barbara went home, and continued to pray that she might never cease to love her husband. After that she sickened, and did not come out of doors again for a long time.

The year of education had extended to fourteen months, and the house was in order for Edmond's return to take up his abode there with Barbara, when, instead of the accustomed letter for her, came one to Sir

John Grebe in the handwriting of the said tutor, informing him of a terrible catastrophe that had occurred to them at Venice. Mr Willowes and himself had attended the theatre one night during the Carnival of the preceding week, to witness the Italian comedy, when, owing to the carelessness of one of the candle-snuffers, the theatre had caught fire, and been burnt to the ground. Few persons had lost their lives, owing to the superhuman exertions of some of the audience in getting out the senseless sufferers; and, among them all, he who had risked his own life the most heroically was Mr Willowes. In re-entering for the fifth time to save his fellow-creatures some fiery beams had fallen upon him, and he had been given up for lost. He was, however, by the blessing of Providence, recovered, with the life still in him, though he was fearfully burnt; and by almost a miracle he seemed likely to survive, his constitution being wondrously sound. He was, of course, unable to write, but he was receiving the attention of several skilful surgeons. Further report would be made by the next mail or by private hand.

The tutor said nothing in detail of poor Willowes's sufferings, but as soon as the news was broken to Barbara she realized how intense they must have been, and her immediate instinct was to rush to his side, though, on consideration, the journey seemed impossible to her. Her health was by no means what it had been, and to post across Europe at that season of the year, or to traverse the Bay of Biscay in a sailing-craft, was an undertaking that would hardly be justified by the result. But she was anxious to go till, on reading to the end of the letter, her husband's tutor was found to hint very strongly against such a step if it should be contemplated, this being also the opinion of the surgeons. And though Willowes's comrade refrained from giving his reasons, they disclosed themselves plainly enough in the sequel.

The truth was that the worst of the wounds resulting from the fire had occurred to his head and face – that handsome face which had won her heart from her, – and both the tutor and the surgeons knew that for a sensitive young woman to see him before his wounds had healed would cause more misery to her by the shock than happiness to him by her ministrations.

Lady Grebe blurted out what Sir John and Barbara had thought, but had had too much delicacy to express.

'Sure, 'tis mighty hard for you, poor Barbara, that the one little gift he had to justify your rash choice of him – his wonderful good looks – should be taken away like this, to leave 'ee no excuse at all for your

conduct in the world's eyes. . . . Well, I wish you'd married t'other –
that do I!' And the lady sighed.

'He'll soon get right again,' said her father soothingly.

Such remarks as the above were not often made; but they were
frequent enough to cause Barbara an uneasy sense of self-stultification.
She determined to hear them no longer; and the house at Yewsholt
being ready and furnished, she withdrew thither with her maids, where
for the first time she could feel mistress of a home that would be hers
and her husband's exclusively, when he came.

After long weeks Willowes had recovered sufficiently to be able to
write himself, and slowly and tenderly he enlightened her upon the full
extent of his injuries. It was a mercy, he said, that he had not lost his
sight entirely; but he was thankful to say that he still retained full vision
in one eye, though the other was dark for ever. The sparing manner in
which he meted out particulars of his condition told Barbara how
appalling had been his experience. He was grateful for her assurance
that nothing could change her; but feared she did not fully realize that
he was so sadly disfigured as to make it doubtful if she would recognize
him. However, in spite of all, his heart was as true to her as it ever had
been.

Barbara saw from his anxiety how much lay behind. She replied that
she submitted to the decrees of Fate, and would welcome him in any
shape as soon as he could come. She told him of the pretty retreat in
which she had taken up her abode, pending their joint occupation of
it, and did not reveal how much she had sighed over the information that
all his good looks were gone. Still less did she say that she felt a certain
strangeness in awaiting him, the weeks they had lived together having
been so short by comparison with the length of his absence.

Slowly drew on the time when Willowes found himself well enough to
come home. He landed at Southampton, and posted thence towards
Yewsholt. Barbara arranged to go out to meet him as far as Lornton Inn
– the spot between the Forest and the Chase at which he had waited for
night on the evening of their elopement. Thither she drove at the
appointed hour in a little pony-chaise, presented her by her father on her
birthday for her especial use in her new house; which vehicle she sent
back on arriving at the inn, the plan agreed upon being that she should
perform the return journey with her husband in his hired coach.

There was not much accommodation for a lady at this wayside tavern;
but, as it was a fine evening in early summer, she did not mind –

walking about outside, and straining her eyes along the highway for the expected one. But each cloud of dust that enlarged in the distance and drew near was found to disclose a conveyance other than his post-chaise. Barbara remained till the appointment was two hours passed, and then began to fear that owing to some adverse wind in the Channel he was not coming that night.

While waiting she was conscious of a curious trepidation that was not entirely solicitude, and did not amount to dread; her tense state of incertitude bordered both on disappointment and on relief. She had lived six or seven weeks with an imperfectly educated yet handsome husband whom now she had not seen for seventeen months, and who was so changed physically by an accident that she was assured she would hardly know him. Can we wonder at her compound state of mind ?

But her immediate difficulty was to get away from Lornton Inn, for her situation was becoming embarrassing. Like too many of Barbara's actions, this drive had been undertaken without much reflection. Expecting to wait no more than a few minutes for her husband in his post-chaise, and to enter it with him, she had not hesitated to isolate herself by sending back her own little vehicle. She now found that, being so well known in this neighbourhood, her excursion to meet her long-absent husband was exciting great interest. She was conscious that more eyes were watching her from the inn-windows than met her own gaze. Barbara had decided to get home by hiring whatever kind of conveyance the tavern afforded, when, straining her eyes for the last time over the now darkening highway, she perceived yet another dust-cloud drawing near. She paused; a chariot ascended to the inn, and would have passed had not its occupant caught sight of her standing expectantly. The horses were checked on the instant.

'You here – and alone, my dear Mrs Willowes ?' said Lord Upland-towers, whose carriage it was.

She explained what had brought her into this lonely situation; and, as he was going in the direction of her own home, she accepted his offer of a seat beside him. Their conversation was embarrassed and fragmentary at first; but when they had driven a mile or two she was surprised to find herself talking earnestly and warmly to him: her impulsiveness was in truth but the natural consequence of her late existence – a somewhat desolate one by reason of the strange marriage she had made; and there is no more indiscreet mood than that of a woman surprised into talk who has long been imposing upon herself a policy of reserve. Therefore her ingenuous heart rose with a bound into her throat when, in response to his leading questions, or rather hints, she allowed her troubles to leak out of her. Lord Uplandtowers took her quite to her own door, although he had driven three miles out of his way to do so; and in handing her down she heard from him a whisper of stern reproach: 'It need not have been thus if you had listened to me!'

She made no reply, and went indoors. There, as the evening wore away, she regretted more and more that she had been so friendly with Lord Uplandtowers. But he had launched himself upon her so unexpectedly: if she had only foreseen the meeting with him, what a careful line of conduct she would have marked out! Barbara broke into a perspiration of disquiet when she thought of her unreserve, and, in self-chastisement, resolved to sit up till midnight on the bare chance of Edmond's return; directing that supper should be laid for him, improbable as his arrival till the morrow was.

The hours went past, and there was dead silence in and round about Yewsholt Lodge, except for the soughing of the trees; till, when it was near upon midnight, she heard the noise of hoofs and wheels approaching the door. Knowing that it could only be her husband, Barbara instantly went into the hall to meet him. Yet she stood there not without a sensation of faintness, so many were the changes since their parting! And owing to her casual encounter with Lord Uplandtowers, his voice and image still remained with her, excluding Edmond, her husband, from the inner circle of her impressions.

But she went to the door, and the next moment a figure stepped inside, of which she knew the outline, but little besides. Her husband was attired in a flapping black cloak and slouched hat, appearing altogether as a foreigner, and not as the young English burgess who had left her side. When he came forward into the light of the lamp, she perceived with surprise, and almost with fright, that he wore a mask. At first she had not noticed this – there being nothing in its colour which would lead a casual observer to think he was looking on anything but a real countenance.

He must have seen her start of dismay at the unexpectedness of his appearance, for he said hastily: 'I did not mean to come in to you like this – I thought you would have been in bed. How good you are, dear Barbara!' He put his arm round her, but he did not attempt to kiss her.

'O Edmond – it *is* you? – it must be?' she said, with clasped hands, for though his figure and movement were almost enough to prove it and the tones were not unlike the old tones, the enunciation was so altered as to seem that of a stranger.

'I am covered like this to hide myself from the curious eyes of the inn-servants and others,' he said, in a low voice. 'I will send back the carriage and join you in a moment.'

'You are quite alone?'

'Quite. My companion stopped at Southampton.'

The wheels of the post-chaise rolled away as she entered the dining-room, where the supper was spread; and presently he rejoined her there. He had removed his cloak and hat, but the mask was still retained; and she could now see that it was of special make, of some flexible material like silk, coloured so as to represent flesh; it joined naturally to the front hair, and was otherwise cleverly executed.

'Barbara - you look ill,' he said, removing his glove, and taking her hand.

'Yes - I have been ill,' said she.

'Is this pretty little house ours?'

'O - yes.' She was hardly conscious of her words, for the hand he had ungloved in order to take hers was contorted, and had one or two of its fingers missing; while through the mask she discerned the twinkle of one eye only.

'I would give anything to kiss you, dearest, now at this moment!' he continued, with mournful passionateness. 'But I cannot - in this guise. The servants are abed, I suppose?'

'Yes,' said she. 'But I can call them? You will have some supper?'

He said he would have some, but that it was not necessary to call anybody at that hour. Thereupon they approached the table, and sat down, facing each other.

Despite Barbara's scared state of mind, it was forced upon her notice that her husband trembled, as if he feared the impression he was producing, or was about to produce, as much as, or more than, she. He drew nearer, and took her hand again.

'I had this mask made at Venice,' he began, in evident embarrassment. 'My darling Barbara - my dearest wife - do you think you - will mind when I take it off? You will not dislike me - will you?'

'O Edmond, of course I shall not mind,' said she. 'What has happened to you is our misfortune; but I am prepared for it.'

'Are you sure you are prepared?'

'O yes! You are my husband.'

'You really feel quite confident that nothing external can affect you?' he said again, in a voice rendered uncertain by his agitation.

'I think I am – quite,' she answered faintly.

He bent his head. 'I hope, I hope you are,' he whispered.

In the pause which followed, the ticking of the clock in the hall seemed to grow loud; and he turned a little aside to remove the mask. She breathlessly awaited the operation, which was one of some tediousness, watching him one moment, averting her face the next; and when it was done she shut her eyes at the dreadful spectacle that was revealed. A quick spasm of horror had passed through her; but though she quailed she forced herself to regard him anew, repressing the cry that would naturally have escaped from her ashy lips. Unable to look at him longer, Barbara sank down on the floor beside her chair, covering her eyes.

'You cannot look at me!' he groaned in a hopeless way. 'I am too terrible an object even for you to bear! I knew it; yet I hoped against it. O, this is a bitter fate – curse the skill of those Venetian surgeons who saved me alive!... Look up, Barbara,' he continued beseechingly; 'view me completely; say you loathe me, if you do loathe me, and settle the case between us for ever!'

His unhappy wife pulled herself together for a desperate strain. He was her Edmond; he had done her no wrong; he had suffered. A momentary devotion to him helped her, and lifting her eyes as bidden she regarded this human remnant, this *écorché*, a second time. But the sight was too much. She again involuntarily looked aside and shuddered.

'Do you think you can get used to this?' he said. 'Yes or no! Can you bear such a thing of the charnel-house near you? Judge for yourself, Barbara. Your Adonis, your matchless man, has come to this!'

The poor lady stood beside him motionless, save for the restlessness of her eyes. All her natural sentiments of affection and pity were driven clean out of her by a sort of panic; she had just the same sense of dismay and fearfulness that she would have had in the presence of an apparition. She could nohow fancy this to be her chosen one – the man she had loved; he was metamorphosed to a specimen of another species. 'I do not loathe you,' she said with trembling. 'But I am so horrified – so overcome! Let me recover myself. Will you sup now? And while you do so may I go to my room to – regain my old feeling for you? I will try, if I may leave you awhile? Yes, I will try!'

Without waiting for an answer from him, and keeping her gaze carefully averted, the frightened woman crept to the door and out of the room. She heard him sit down to the table, as if to begin supper; though, Heaven knows, his appetite was slight enough after a reception which had confirmed his worst surmises. When Barbara had ascended the stairs and arrived in her chamber she sank down, and buried her face in the coverlet of the bed.

Thus she remained for some time. The bed-chamber was over the dining-room, and presently as she knelt Barbara heard Willowes thrust back his chair, and rise to go into the hall. In five minutes that figure would probably come up the stairs and confront her again; it, – this new and terrible form, that was not her husband's. In the loneliness of this night, with neither maid nor friend beside her, she lost all self-control, and at the first sound of his footstep on the stairs, without so much as flinging a cloak round her, she flew from the room, ran along the gallery to the back staircase, which she descended, and, unlocking the back door, let herself out. She scarcely was aware what she had done till she found herself in the greenhouse, crouching on a flower-stand.

Here she remained, her great timid eyes strained through the glass upon the garden without, and her skirts gathered up, in fear of the field-mice which sometimes came there. Every moment she dreaded to hear footsteps which she ought by law to have longed for, and a voice that should have been as music to her soul. But Edmond Willowes came not that way. The nights were getting short at this season, and soon the dawn appeared, and the first rays of the sun. By daylight she had less fear than in the dark. She thought she could meet him, and accustom herself to the spectacle.

So the much-tried young woman unfastened the door of the hothouse, and went back by the way she had emerged a few hours ago. Her poor husband was probably in bed and asleep, his journey having been long; and she made as little noise as possible in her entry. The house was just as she had left it, and she looked about in the hall for his cloak and hat, but she could not see them; nor did she perceive the small trunk which had been all that he brought with him, his heavier baggage having been left at Southampton for the road-waggon. She summoned courage to mount the stairs; the bedroom-door was open as she had left it. She fearfully peeped round; the bed had not been pressed. Perhaps he had lain down on the dining-room sofa. She descended and entered; he was not there. On the table beside his unsoiled plate lay a note, hastily written on the leaf of a pocket-book. It was something like this: –

MY EVER-BELOVED WIFE, – The effect that my forbidding appearance has produced upon you was one which I foresaw as quite
possible. I hoped against it, but foolishly so. I was aware that no
human love could survive such a catastrophe. I confess I thought
yours *divine*; but, after so long an absence, there could not be left
sufficient warmth to overcome the too natural first aversion. It was
an experiment, and it has failed. I do not blame you; perhaps,
even, it is better so. Good-bye. I leave England for one year. You
will see me again at the expiration of that time, if I live. Then I will
ascertain your true feeling; and, if it be against me, go away for ever.
                                                                    E.W.

On recovering from her surprise, Barbara's remorse was such that she
felt herself absolutely unforgivable. She should have regarded him as an
afflicted being, and not have been this slave to mere eyesight, like a
child. To follow him and entreat him to return was her first thought.
But on making inquiries she found that nobody had seen him: he had
silently disappeared.

More than this, to undo the scene of last night was impossible. Her
terror had been too plain, and he was a man unlikely to be coaxed back
by her efforts to do her duty. She went and confessed to her parents all
that had occurred; which, indeed, soon became known to more persons
than those of her own family.

The year passed, and he did not return; and it was doubted if he were
alive. Barbara's contrition for her unconquerable repugnance was now
such that she longed to build a church-aisle, or erect a monument, and
devote herself to deeds of charity for the remainder of her days. To that
end she made inquiry of the excellent parson under whom she sat on
Sundays, at a vertical distance of a dozen feet. But he could only adjust
his wig and tap his snuff-box; for such was the lukewarm state of
religion in those days, that not an aisle, steeple, porch, east window,
Ten-Commandment board, lion-and-unicorn, or brass candlestick, was
required anywhere at all in the neighbourhood as a votive offering from
a distracted soul – the last century contrasting greatly in this respect with
the happy times in which we live, when urgent appeals for contributions
to such objects pour in by every morning's post, and nearly all churches
have been made to look like new pennies. As the poor lady could not
ease her conscience this way, she determined at least to be charitable,
and soon had the satisfaction of finding her porch thronged every

morning by the raggedest, idlest, most drunken, hypocritical, and worthless tramps in Christendom.

But human hearts are as prone to change as the leaves of the creeper on the wall, and in the course of time, hearing nothing of her husband, Barbara could sit unmoved whilst her mother and friends said in her hearing, 'Well, what has happened is for the best.' She began to think so herself, for even now she could not summon up that lopped and mutilated form without a shiver, though whenever her mind flew back to her early wedded days, and the man who had stood beside her then, a thrill of tenderness moved her, which if quickened by his living presence might have become strong. She was young and inexperienced, and had hardly on his late return grown out of the capricious fancies of girlhood.

But he did not come again, and when she thought of his word that he would return once more, if living, and how unlikely he was to break his word, she gave him up for dead. So did her parents; so also did another person – that man of silence, of irresistible incisiveness, of still countenance, who was as awake as seven sentinels when he seemed to be as sound asleep as the figures on his family monument. Lord Uplandtowers, though not yet thirty, had chuckled like a caustic fogey of threescore when he heard of Barbara's terror and flight at her husband's return, and of the latter's prompt departure. He felt pretty sure, however, that Willowes, despite his hurt feelings, would have reappeared to claim his bright-eyed property if he had been alive at the end of the twelve months.

As there was no husband to live with her, Barbara had relinquished the house prepared for them by her father, and taken up her abode anew at Chene Manor, as in the days of her girlhood. By degrees the episode with Edmond Willowes seemed but a fevered dream, and as the months grew to years Lord Uplandtowers' friendship with the people at Chene – which had somewhat cooled after Barbara's elopement – revived considerably, and he again became a frequent visitor there. He could not make the most trivial alteration or improvement at Knollingwood Hall, where he lived, without riding off to consult with his friend Sir John at Chene; and thus putting himself frequently under her eyes, Barbara grew accustomed to him, and talked to him as freely as to a brother. She even began to look up to him as a person of authority, judgment, and prudence; and though his severity on the bench towards poachers, smugglers, and turnip-stealers was matter of common notoriety, she trusted that much of what was said might be misrepresentation.

Thus they lived on till her husband's absence had stretched to years, and there could be no longer any doubt of his death. A passionless manner of renewing his addresses seemed no longer out of place in Lord Uplandtowers. Barbara did not love him, but hers was essentially one of those sweet-pea or with-wind natures which require a twig of stouter fibre than its own to hang upon and bloom. Now, too, she was older, and admitted to herself that a man whose ancestor had run scores of Saracens through and through in fighting for the site of the Holy Sepulchre was a more desirable husband, socially considered, than one who could only claim with certainty to know that his father and grandfather were respectable burgesses.

Sir John took occasion to inform her that she might legally consider herself a widow; and, in brief, Lord Uplandtowers carried his point with her, and she married him, though he could never get her to own that she loved him as she had loved Willowes. In my childhood I knew an old lady whose mother saw the wedding, and she said that when Lord and Lady Uplandtowers drove away from her father's house in the evening it was in a coach-and-four, and that my lady was dressed in green and silver, and wore the gayest hat and feather that ever were seen; though whether it was that the green did not suit her complexion, or otherwise, the Countess looked pale, and the reverse of blooming. After their marriage her husband took her to London, and she saw the gaieties of a season there; then they returned to Knollingwood Hall, and thus a year passed away.

Before their marriage her husband had seemed to care but little about her inability to love him passionately. 'Only let me win you,' he had said, 'and I will submit to all that.' But now her lack of warmth seemed to irritate him, and he conducted himself towards her with a resentfulness which led to her passing many hours with him in painful silence. The heir-presumptive to the title was a remote relative, whom Lord Uplandtowers did not exclude from the dislike he entertained towards many persons and things besides, and he had set his mind upon a lineal successor. He blamed her much that there was no promise of this, and asked her what she was good for.

On a particular day in her gloomy life a letter, addressed to her as Mrs Willowes, reached Lady Uplandtowers from an unexpected quarter. A sculptor in Pisa, knowing nothing of her second marriage, informed her that the long-delayed life-size statue of Mr Willowes, which, when her husband left that city, he had been directed to retain till it was sent for, was still in his studio. As his commission had not wholly been paid, and the statue was taking up room he could ill spare, he should be glad to have the debt cleared off, and directions where to forward the figure. Arriving at a time when the Countess was beginning to have little secrets (of a harmless kind, it is true) from her husband, by reason of their growing estrangement, she replied to this letter without saying a word to Lord Uplandtowers, sending off the balance that was owing to the sculptor, and telling him to despatch the statue to her without delay.

It was some weeks before it arrived at Knollingwood Hall, and, by a singular coincidence, during the interval she received the first absolutely conclusive tidings of her Edmond's death. It had taken place years before, in a foreign land, about six months after their parting, and had been induced by the sufferings he had already undergone, coupled with much depression of spirit, which had caused him to succumb to a slight ailment. The news was sent her in a brief and formal letter from some relative of Willowes's in another part of England.

Her grief took the form of passionate pity for his misfortunes, and of reproach to herself for never having been able to conquer her aversion to his latter image by recollection of what Nature had originally made him. The sad spectacle that had gone from earth had never been her Edmond at all to her. O that she could have met him as he was at first! Thus Barbara thought. It was only a few days later that a waggon with two horses, containing an immense packing-case, was seen at breakfast-time both by Barbara and her husband to drive round to the back of the house, and by-and-by they were informed that a case labelled 'Sculpture' had arrived for her ladyship.

'What can that be?' said Lord Uplandtowers.

'It is the statue of poor Edmond, which belongs to me, but has never been sent till now,' she answered.

'Where are you going to put it?' asked he.

'I have not decided,' said the Countess. 'Anywhere, so that it will not annoy you.'

'Oh, it won't annoy me,' says he.

When it had been unpacked in a back room of the house, they went to examine it. The statue was a full-length figure, in the purest Carrara marble, representing Edmond Willowes in all his original beauty, as he had stood at parting from her when about to set out on his travels; a specimen of manhood almost perfect in every line and contour. The work had been carried out with absolute fidelity.

'Phœbus-Apollo, sure,' said the Earl of Uplandtowers, who had never seen Willowes, real or represented, till now.

Barbara did not hear him. She was standing in a sort of trance before the first husband, as if she had no consciousness of the other husband at her side. The mutilated features of Willowes had disappeared from her mind's eye; this perfect being was really the man she had loved, and not that later pitiable figure; in whom tenderness and truth should have seen this image always, but had not done so.

It was not till Lord Uplandtowers said roughly, 'Are you going to stay here all the morning worshipping him?' that she roused herself.

Her husband had not till now the least suspicion that Edmond Willowes originally looked thus, and he thought how deep would have been his jealousy years ago if Willowes had been known to him. Returning to the Hall in the afternoon he found his wife in the gallery, whither the statue had been brought.

She was lost in reverie before it, just as in the morning.

'What are you doing?' he asked.

She started and turned. 'I am looking at my husb— my statue, to see if it is well done,' she stammered. 'Why should I not?'

'There's no reason why,' he said. 'What are you going to do with the monstrous thing? It can't stand here for ever.'

'I don't wish it,' she said. 'I'll find a place.'

In her boudoir there was a deep recess, and while the Earl was absent from home for a few days in the following week, she hired joiners from the village, who under her directions enclosed the recess with a panelled door. Into the tabernacle thus formed she had the statue placed, fastening the door with a lock, the key of which she kept in her pocket.

When her husband returned he missed the statue from the gallery, and, concluding that it had been put away out of deference to his feelings, made no remark. Yet at moments he noticed something on his lady's face which he had never noticed there before. He could not construe it; it was a sort of silent ecstasy, a reserved beatification. What had become of the statue he could not divine, and growing more and more curious, looked about here and there for it till, thinking of her private room, he went towards that spot. After knocking he heard the shutting of a door, and the click of a key; but when he entered his wife was sitting at work, on what was in those days called knotting. Lord Uplandtowers' eye fell upon the newly-painted door where the recess had formerly been.

'You have been carpentering in my absence then, Barbara,' he said carelessly.

'Yes, Uplandtowers.'

'Why did you go putting up such a tasteless enclosure as that – spoiling the handsome arch of the alcove?'

'I wanted more closet-room; and I thought that as this was my own apartment—'

'Of course,' he returned. Lord Uplandtowers knew now where the statue of young Willowes was.

One night, or rather in the smallest hours of the morning, he missed the Countess from his side. Not being a man of nervous imaginings he fell asleep again before he had much considered the matter, and the next morning had forgotten the incident. But a few nights later the same circumstances occurred. This time he fully roused himself; but before he had moved to search for her she returned to the chamber in her dressing-gown, carrying a candle, which she extinguished as she approached, deeming him asleep. He could discover from her breathing that she was strangely moved; but not on this occasion either did he reveal that he had seen her. Presently, when she had lain down, affecting to wake, he asked her some trivial questions. 'Yes, *Edmond*,' she replied absently.

Lord Uplandtowers became convinced that she was in the habit of leaving the chamber in this queer way more frequently than he had observed, and he determined to watch. The next midnight he feigned deep sleep, and shortly after perceived her stealthily rise and let herself out of the room in the dark. He slipped on some clothing and followed. At the further end of the corridor, where the clash of flint and steel would be out of the hearing of one in the bed-chamber, she struck a light. He stepped aside into an empty room till she had lit a taper and had passed on to her boudoir. In a minute or two he followed. Arrived at the door of the boudoir, he beheld the door of the private recess open, and Barbara within it, standing with her arms clasped tightly round the neck of her Edmond, and her mouth on his. The shawl which she had thrown round her nightclothes had slipped from her shoulders, and her long white robe and pale face lent her the blanched appearance of a second statue embracing the first. Between her kisses, she apostrophized it in a low murmur of infantine tenderness:

'My only love – how could I be so cruel to you, my perfect one – so good and true – I am ever faithful to you, despite my seeming infidelity! I always think of you – dream of you – during the long hours of the day, and in the night-watches! O Edmond, I am always yours!' Such words as these, intermingled with sobs, and streaming tears, and dishevelled hair, testified to an intensity of feeling in his wife which Lord Upland-towers had not dreamed of her possessing.

'Ha, ha!' says he to himself. 'This is where we evaporate – this is where my hopes of a successor in the title dissolve – ha! ha! This must be seen to, verily!'

Lord Uplandtowers was a subtle man when once he set himself to strategy; though in the present instance he never thought of the simple stratagem of constant tenderness. Nor did he enter the room and surprise his wife as a blunderer would have done, but went back to his chamber as silently as he had left it. When the Countess returned thither, shaken by spent sobs and sighs, he appeared to be soundly sleeping as usual. The next day he began his countermoves by making inquiries as to the whereabouts of the tutor who had travelled with his wife's first husband; this gentleman, he found, was now master of a grammar-school at no great distance from Knollingwood. At the first convenient moment Lord Uplandtowers went thither and obtained an interview with the said gentleman. The schoolmaster was much gratified by a visit from such an influential neighbour, and was ready to communicate anything that his lordship desired to know.

After some general conversation on the school and its progress, the visitor observed that he believed the schoolmaster had once travelled a good deal with the unfortunate Mr Willowes, and had been with him on the occasion of his accident. He, Lord Uplandtowers, was interested in knowing what had really happened at that time, and had often thought of inquiring. And then the Earl not only heard by word of mouth as much as he wished to know, but, their chat becoming more intimate, the schoolmaster drew upon paper a sketch of the disfigured head, explaining with bated breath various details in the representation.

'It was very strange and terrible!' said Lord Uplandtowers, taking the sketch in his hand. 'Neither nose nor ears, nor lips scarcely!'

A poor man in the town nearest to Knollingwood Hall, who combined the art of sign-painting with ingenious mechanical occupations, was sent for by Lord Uplandtowers to come to the Hall on a day in that week when the Countess had gone on a short visit to her parents. His employer made the man understand that the business in which his assistance was demanded was to be considered private, and money insured the observance of this request. The lock of the cupboard was picked, and the ingenious mechanic and painter, assisted by the schoolmaster's sketch, which Lord Uplandtowers had put in his pocket, set to work upon the god-like countenance of the statue under my lord's direction. What the fire had maimed in the original the chisel maimed in the copy. It was a fiendish disfigurement, ruthlessly carried out, and was rendered still more shocking by being tinted to the hues of life, as life had been after the wreck.

Six hours after, when the workman was gone, Lord Uplandtowers looked upon the result, and smiled grimly, and said:

'A statue should represent a man as he appeared in life, and that's as he appeared. Ha! ha! But 'tis done to good purpose, and not idly.'

He locked the door of the closet with a skeleton key, and went his way to fetch the Countess home.

That night she slept, but he kept awake. According to the tale, she murmured soft words in her dream; and he knew that the tender converse of her imaginings was held with one whom he had supplanted but in name. At the end of her dream the Countess of Uplandtowers awoke and arose, and then the enactment of former nights was repeated. Her husband remained still and listened. Two strokes sounded from the clock in the pediment without, when, leaving the chamber-door ajar, she passed along the corridor to the other end, where, as usual, she obtained a light. So deep was the silence that he could even from his bed hear her softly blowing the tinder to a glow after striking the steel. She moved on into the boudoir, and he heard, or fancied he heard, the turning of the key in the closet-door. The next moment there came from that direction a loud and prolonged shriek, which resounded to the furthest corners of the house. It was repeated, and there was the noise of a heavy fall.

Lord Uplandtowers sprang out of bed. He hastened along the dark corridor to the door of the boudoir, which stood ajar, and, by the light of the candle within, saw his poor young Countess lying in a heap in her nightdress on the floor of the closet. When he reached her side he found that she had fainted, much to the relief of his fears that matters were worse. He quickly shut up and locked in the hated image which had done the mischief, and lifted his wife in his arms, where in a few instants she opened her eyes. Pressing her face to his without saying a word, he carried her back to her room, endeavouring as he went to disperse her

terrors by a laugh in her ear, oddly compounded of causticity, predilec-
tion, and brutality.

'Ho – ho – ho!' says he. 'Frightened, dear one, hey? What a baby 'tis!
Only a joke, sure, Barbara – a splendid joke! But a baby should not go to
closets at midnight to look for the ghost of the dear departed! If it do it
must expect to be terrified at his aspect – ho – ho – ho!'

When she was in her bed-chamber, and had quite come to herself,
though her nerves were still much shaken, he spoke to her more sternly.
'Now, my lady, answer me: do you love him – eh?'

'No – no!' she faltered, shuddering, with her expanded eyes fixed on
her husband. 'He is too terrible – no, no!'

'You are sure?'

'Quite sure!' replied the poor broken-spirited Countess.

But her natural elasticity asserted itself. Next morning he again
inquired of her: 'Do you love him now?' She quailed under his gaze,
but did not reply.

'That means that you do still, by God!' he continued.

'It means that I will not tell an untruth, and do not wish to incense
my lord,' she answered, with dignity.

'Then suppose we go and have another look at him?' As he spoke, he
suddenly took her by the wrist, and turned as if to lead her towards the
ghastly closet.

'No – no! O – no!' she cried, and her desperate wriggle out of his hand
revealed that the fright of the night had left more impression upon her
delicate soul than superficially appeared.

'Another dose or two, and she will be cured,' he said to himself.

It was now so generally known that the Earl and Countess were not in
accord, that he took no great trouble to disguise his deeds in relation to
this matter. During the day he ordered four men with ropes and rollers
to attend him in the boudoir. When they arrived, the closet was open,
and the upper part of the statue tied up in canvas. He had it taken to the
sleeping-chamber. What followed is more or less matter of conjecture.
The story, as told to me, goes on to say that, when Lady Uplandtowers
retired with him that night, she saw facing the foot of the heavy oak four-
poster, a tall dark wardrobe, which had not stood there before; but she
did not ask what its presence meant.

'I have had a little whim,' he explained when they were in the dark.

'Have you?' says she.

'To erect a little shrine, as it may be called.'

'A little shrine?'

'Yes; to one whom we both equally adore – eh? I'll show you what it contains.'

He pulled a cord which hung covered by the bed-curtains, and the doors of the wardrobe slowly opened, disclosing that the shelves within had been removed throughout, and the interior adapted to receive the ghastly figure, which stood there as it had stood in the boudoir, but with a wax candle burning on each side of it to throw the cropped and distorted features into relief. She clutched him, uttered a low scream, and buried her head in the bedclothes. 'O, take it away – please take it away!' she implored.

'All in good time; namely, when you love me best,' he returned calmly. 'You don't quite yet – eh?'

'I don't know – I think – O Uplandtowers, have mercy – I cannot bear it – O, in pity, take it away!'

'Nonsense; one gets accustomed to anything. Take another gaze.'

In short, he allowed the doors to remain unclosed at the foot of the bed, and the wax-tapers burning; and such was the strange fascination of the grisly exhibition that a morbid curiosity took possession of the Countess as she lay, and, at his repeated request, she did again look out from the coverlet, shuddered, hid her eyes, and looked again, all the while begging him to take it away, or it would drive her out of her senses. But he would not do so yet, and the wardrobe was not locked till dawn.

The scene was repeated the next night. Firm in enforcing his ferocious correctives, he continued the treatment till the nerves of the poor lady were quivering in agony under the virtuous tortures inflicted by her lord, to bring her truant heart back to faithfulness.

The third night, when the scene had opened as usual, and she lay staring with immense wild eyes at the horrid fascination, on a sudden she gave an unnatural laugh; she laughed more and more, staring at the image, till she literally shrieked with laughter: then there was silence, and he found her to have become insensible. He thought she had fainted, but soon saw that the event was worse: she was in an epileptic fit. He started up, dismayed by the sense that, like many other subtle personages, he had been too exacting for his own interests. Such love as he was capable of, though rather a selfish gloating than a cherishing solicitude, was fanned into life on the instant. He closed the wardrobe with the pulley, clasped her in his arms, took her gently to the window, and did all he could to restore her.

It was a long time before the Countess came to herself, and when she did so, a considerable change seemed to have taken place in her emotions. She flung her arms around him, and with gasps of fear abjectly kissed him many times, at last bursting into tears. She had never wept in this scene before.

'You'll take it away, dearest – you will!' she begged plaintively.

'If you love me.'

'I do – oh, I do!'

'And hate him, and his memory?'

'Yes – yes!'

'Thoroughly?'

'I cannot endure recollection of him!' cried the poor Countess slavishly. 'It fills me with shame – how could I ever be so depraved! I'll never behave badly again, Uplandtowers; and you will never put the hated statue again before my eyes?'

He felt that he could promise with perfect safety. 'Never,' said he.

'And then I'll love you,' she returned eagerly, as if dreading lest the scourge should be applied anew. 'And I'll never, never dream of thinking a single thought that seems like faithlessness to my marriage vow.'

The strange thing now was that this fictitious love wrung from her by terror took on, through mere habit of enactment, a certain quality of reality. A servile mood of attachment to the Earl became distinctly visible in her contemporaneously with an actual dislike for her late husband's memory. The mood of attachment grew and continued when the statue was removed. A permanent revulsion was operant in her, which intensified as time wore on. How fright could have effected such a change of idiosyncrasy learned physicians alone can say; but I believe such cases of reactionary instinct are not unknown.

The upshot was that the cure became so permanent as to be itself a new disease. She clung to him so tightly that she would not willingly be out of his sight for a moment. She would have no sitting-room apart from his, though she could not help starting when he entered suddenly to her. Her eyes were wellnigh always fixed upon him. If he drove out, she wished to go with him; his slightest civilities to other women made her frantically jealous; till at length her very fidelity became a burden to him, absorbing his time, and curtailing his liberty, and causing him to curse and swear. If he ever spoke sharply to her now, she did not revenge herself by flying off to a mental world of her own; all that affection for another, which had provided her with a resource, was now a cold black cinder.

From that time the life of this scared and enervated lady – whose existence might have been developed to so much higher purpose but for the ignoble ambition of her parents and the conventions of the time – was one of obsequious amativeness towards a perverse and cruel man. Little personal events came to her in quick succession – half a dozen, eight, nine, ten such events, – in brief, she bore him no less than eleven children in the nine following years, but half of them came prematurely into the world, or died a few days old; only one, a girl, attained to maturity; she in after years became the wife of the Honourable Mr Beltonleigh, who was created Lord d'Almaine, as may be remembered.

There was no living son and heir. At length, completely worn out in mind and body, Lady Uplandtowers was taken abroad by her husband, to try the effect of a more genial climate upon her wasted frame. But nothing availed to strengthen her, and she died at Florence, a few months after her arrival in Italy.

Contrary to expectation, the Earl of Uplandtowers did not marry again. Such affection as existed in him – strange, hard, brutal as it was – seemed untransferable, and the title, as is known, passed at his death to his nephew. Perhaps it may not be so generally known that, during the enlargement of the Hall for the sixth Earl, while digging in the grounds for the new foundations, the broken fragments of a marble statue were unearthed. They were submitted to various antiquaries, who said that, so far as the damaged pieces would allow them to form an opinion, the statue seemed to be that of a mutilated Roman satyr; or, if not, an allegorical figure of Death. Only one or two old inhabitants guessed whose statue those fragments had composed.

I should have added that, shortly after the death of the Countess, an excellent sermon was preached by the Dean of Melchester, the subject of which, though names were not mentioned, was unquestionably suggested by the aforesaid events. He dwelt upon the folly of indulgence in sensuous love for a handsome form merely; and showed that the only rational and virtuous growths of that affection were those based upon intrinsic worth. In the case of the tender but somewhat shallow lady whose life I have related, there is no doubt that an infatuation for the person of young Willowes was the chief feeling that induced her to marry him; which was the more deplorable in that his beauty, by all

tradition, was the least of his recommendations, every report bearing out
the inference that he must have been a man of steadfast nature, bright
intelligence, and promising life.

The company thanked the old surgeon for his story, which the rural dean
declared to be a far more striking one than anything he could hope to tell.
An elderly member of the Club, who was mostly called the Bookworm,
said that a woman's natural instinct of fidelity would, indeed, send back
her heart to a man after his death in a truly wonderful manner sometimes – if anything occurred to put before her forcibly the original
affection between them, and his original aspect in her eyes, – whatever
his inferiority may have been, social or otherwise; and then a general
conversation ensued upon the power that a woman has of seeing the
actual in the representation, the reality in the dream – a power which
(according to the sentimental member) men have no faculty of equalling.
    The rural dean thought that such cases as that related by the surgeon
were rather an illustration of passion electrified back to life than of a
latent, true affection. The story had suggested that he should try to
recount to them one which he had used to hear in his youth, and which
afforded an instance of the latter and better kind of feeling, his heroine
being also a lady who had married beneath her, though he feared his
narrative would be of a much slighter kind than the surgeon's. The
Club begged him to proceed, and the parson began.

Dame the Third
The Marchioness of Stonehenge

By the Rural Dean

I WOULD have you know, then, that a great many years ago there lived in a classical mansion with which I used to be familiar, standing not a hundred miles from the city of Melchester, a lady whose personal charms were so rare and unparalleled that she was courted, flattered, and spoilt by almost all the young noblemen and gentlemen in that part of Wessex. For a time these attentions pleased her well. But as, in the words of good Robert South (whose sermons might be read much more than they are), the most passionate lover of sport, if tied to follow his hawks and hounds every day of his life, would find the pursuit the greatest torment and calamity, and would fly to the mines and galleys for his recreation, so did this lofty and beautiful lady after a while become satiated with the constant iteration of what she had in its novelty enjoyed; and by an almost natural revulsion turned her regards absolutely netherward, socially speaking. She perversely and passionately centred her affection on quite a plain-looking young man of humble birth and no position at all; though it is true that he was gentle and delicate in nature, of good address, and guileless heart. In short, he was the parish-clerk's son, acting as assistant to the land-steward of her father the Earl of Avon, with the hope of becoming some day a land-steward himself. It should be said that perhaps the Lady Caroline (as she was called) was a little stimulated in this passion by the discovery that a young girl of the village already loved the young man fondly, and that he had paid some attentions to her, though merely of a casual and good-natured kind.

Since his occupation brought him frequently to the manor-house and its environs, Lady Caroline could make ample opportunities of seeing and speaking to him. She had, in Chaucer's phrase, 'all the craft of fine loving' at her fingers' ends, and the young man, being of a readily-kindling heart, was quick to notice the tenderness in her eyes and voice.

He could not at first believe in his good fortune, having no understanding of her weariness of more artificial men; but a time comes when the stupidest sees in an eye the glance of his other half; and it came to him, who was quite the reverse of dull. As he gained confidence accidental encounters led to encounters by design; till at length when they were alone together there was no reserve on the matter. They whispered tender words as other lovers do, and were as devoted a pair as ever was seen. But not a ray or symptom of this attachment was allowed to show itself to the outer world.

Now, as she became less and less scrupulous towards him under the influence of her affection, and he became more and more reverential under the influence of his, and they looked the situation in the face together, their condition seemed intolerable in its hopelessness. That she could ever ask to be allowed to marry him, or could hold her tongue and quietly renounce him, was equally beyond conception. They resolved upon a third course, possessing neither of the disadvantages of these two: to wed secretly, and live on in outward appearance the same as before. In this they differed from the lovers of my friend's story.

Not a soul in the parental mansion guessed, when Lady Caroline came coolly into the hall one day after a visit to her aunt, that, during the visit, her lover and herself had found an opportunity of uniting themselves till death should part them. Yet such was the fact; the young woman who rode fine horses, and drove in pony-chaises, and was saluted deferentially by every one, and the young man who trudged about, and directed the tree-felling, and the laying out of fish-ponds in the park, were husband and wife.

As they had planned, so they acted to the letter for the space of a month and more, clandestinely meeting when and where they best could do so; both being supremely happy and content. To be sure, towards the latter part of that month, when the first wild warmth of her love had gone off, the Lady Caroline sometimes wondered within herself how she, who might have chosen a peer of the realm, baronet, knight; or, if serious-minded, a bishop or judge of the more gallant sort who prefer young wives, could have brought herself to do a thing so rash as to make this marriage; particularly when, in their private meetings, she perceived that though her young husband was full of ideas, and fairly well read, they had not a single social experience in common. It was his custom to visit her after nightfall, in her own house, when he could find no opportunity for an interview elsewhere; and to further this course she would contrive to leave unfastened a window on the ground-floor overlooking the lawn, by entering which a back staircase was accessible; so that he could climb up to her apartments, and gain audience of his lady when the house was still.

One dark midnight, when he had not been able to see her during the day, he made use of this secret method, as he had done many times before; and when they had remained in company about an hour he declared that it was time for him to descend.

He would have stayed longer but that the interview had been a somewhat painful one. What she had said to him that night had much excited and angered him, for it had revealed a change in her; cold reason had come to his lofty wife; she was beginning to have more anxiety about her own position and prospects than ardour for him. Whether from the agitation of this perception or not, he was seized with a spasm; he gasped, rose, and in moving towards the window for air he uttered in a short thick whisper, 'O, my heart!'

With his hand upon his chest he sank down to the floor before he had gone another step. By the time that she had relighted the candle, which had been extinguished in case any eye in the opposite grounds should witness his egress, she found that his poor heart had ceased to beat; and there rushed upon her mind what his cottage-friends had once told her, that he was liable to attacks of heart-failure, one of which, the doctor had informed them, might some day carry him off.

Accustomed as she was to doctoring the other parishioners, nothing that she could effect upon him in that kind made any difference whatever; and his stillness, and the increasing coldness of his feet and hands, disclosed too surely to the affrighted young woman that her husband was dead indeed. For more than an hour, however, she did not abandon her efforts to restore him; when she fully realized the fact that he was a corpse she bent over his body, distracted and bewildered as to what step she next should take.

Her first feelings had undoubtedly been those of passionate grief at the loss of him; her second thoughts were concern at her own position as the daughter of an earl. 'O, why, why, my unfortunate husband, did you die in my chamber at this hour!' she said piteously to the corpse. 'Why not have died in your own cottage if you would die! Then nobody would ever have known of our imprudent union, and no syllable would have been breathed of how I mismated myself for love of you!'

The clock in the courtyard striking the solitary hour of one aroused Lady Caroline from the stupor into which she had fallen, and she stood up, and went towards the door. To awaken and tell her mother seemed her only way out of this terrible situation; yet when she put her hand on the key to unlock it she withdrew herself again. It would be impossible to call even her mother's assistance without risking a revelation to all the world through the servants; while if she could remove the body unassisted to a distance she might avert suspicion of their union even now. This thought of immunity from the social consequences of her rash act, of renewed freedom, was indubitably a relief to her, for, as has been said, the constraint and riskiness of her position had begun to tell upon the Lady Caroline's nerves.

She braced herself for the effort, and hastily dressed herself, and then dressed him. Tying his dead hands together with a handkerchief, she laid his arms round her shoulders, and bore him to the landing and down the narrow stairs. Reaching the bottom by the window, she let his body slide slowly over the sill till it lay on the ground without. She then climbed over the window-sill herself, and, leaving the sash open, dragged him on to the lawn with a rustle not louder than the rustle of a broom. There she took a securer hold, and plunged with him under the trees, still dragging him by his tied hands.

Away from the precincts of the house she could apply herself more vigorously to her task, which was a heavy one enough for her, robust as she was; and the exertion and fright she had already undergone began to tell upon her by the time she reached the corner of a beech-plantation which intervened between the manor-house and the village. Here she was so nearly exhausted that she feared she might have to leave him on the spot. But she plodded on after a while, and keeping upon the grass at every opportunity she stood at last opposite the poor young man's garden-gate, where he lived with his father, the parish-clerk. How she accomplished the end of her task Lady Caroline never quite knew; but, to avoid leaving traces in the road, she carried him bodily across the gravel, and laid him down at the door. Perfectly aware of his ways of coming and going, she searched behind the shutter for the cottage door-key, which she placed in his cold hand. Then she kissed his face for the last time, and with silent little sobs bade him farewell.

Lady Caroline retraced her steps, and reached the mansion without hindrance; and to her great relief found the window open just as she had left it. When she had climbed in she listened attentively, fastened the window behind her, and ascending the stairs noiselessly to her room, set everything in order, and returned to bed.

The next morning it was speedily echoed around that the amiable and gentle young villager had been found dead outside his father's door, which he had apparently been in the act of unlocking when he fell. The circumstances were sufficiently exceptional to justify an inquest, at which syncope from heart-disease was ascertained to be beyond doubt the explanation of his death, and no more was said about the matter then. But, after the funeral, it was rumoured that some man who had been returning late from a distant horse-fair had seen in the gloom of night a person, apparently a woman, dragging a heavy body of some sort towards the cottage-gate, which, by the light of after events, would seem to have been the corpse of the young fellow. His clothes were thereupon examined more particularly than at first, with the result that marks of friction were visible upon them here and there, precisely resembling such as would be left by dragging on the ground.

Our beautiful and ingenious Lady Caroline was now in great consternation; and began to think that, after all, it might have been better to honestly confess the truth. But having reached this stage without discovery or suspicion, she determined to make another effort towards concealment; and a bright idea struck her as a means of securing it. I think I mentioned that, before she cast eyes on the unfortunate steward's clerk, he had been the beloved of a certain village damsel, the woodman's daughter, his neighbour, to whom he had paid some attentions; and possibly he was beloved of her still. At any rate, the Lady Caroline's influence on the estates of her father being considerable, she resolved to seek an interview with the young girl in furtherance of her plan to save her reputation, about which she was now exceedingly anxious; for by this time, the fit being over, she began to be ashamed of her mad passion for her late husband, and almost wished she had never seen him.

In the course of her parish-visiting she lighted on the young girl without much difficulty, and found her looking pale and sad, and wearing a simple black gown, which she had put on out of respect for the young man's memory, whom she had tenderly loved, though he had not loved her.

'Ah, you have lost your lover, Milly,' said Lady Caroline.

The young woman could not repress her tears. 'My lady, he was not quite my lover,' she said. 'But I was his – and now he is dead I don't care to live any more!'

'Can you keep a secret about him?' asks the lady; 'one in which his honour is involved – which is known to me alone, but should be known to you?'

The girl readily promised, and, indeed, could be safely trusted on such a subject, so deep was her affection for the youth she mourned.

'Then meet me at his grave to-night, half-an-hour after sunset, and I will tell it to you,' says the other.

In the dusk of that spring evening the two shadowy figures of the young women converged upon the assistant-steward's newly-turfed mound; and at that solemn place and hour, which she had chosen on purpose, the one of birth and beauty unfolded her tale: how she had loved him and married him secretly; how he had died in her chamber; and how, to keep her secret, she had dragged him to his own door.

'Married him, my lady!' said the rustic maiden, starting back.

'I have said so,' replied Lady Caroline. 'But it was a mad thing, and a mistaken course. He ought to have married you. You, Milly, were peculiarly his. But you lost him.'

'Yes,' said the poor girl; 'and for that they laughed at me. "Ha – ha, you mid love him, Milly," they said; "but he will not love you!" '

'Victory over such unkind jeerers would be sweet,' said Lady Caroline. 'You lost him in life; but you may have him in death *as if* you had had him in life; and so turn the tables upon them.'

'How?' said the breathless girl.

The young lady then unfolded her plan, which was that Milly should go forward and declare that the young man had contracted a secret marriage (as he truly had done); that it was with her, Milly, his sweetheart; that he had been visiting her in her cottage on the evening of his death; when, on finding he was a corpse, she had carried him to his house to prevent discovery by her parents, and that she had meant to keep the whole matter a secret till the rumours afloat had forced it from her.

'And how shall I prove this?' said the woodman's daughter, amazed at the boldness of the proposal.

'Quite sufficiently. You can say, if necessary, that you were married to him at the church of St Something, in Bath City, in my name, as the first that occurred to you, to escape detection. That was where he married me. I will support you in this.'

'O – I don't quite like—'

'If you will do so,' said the lady peremptorily, 'I will always be your father's friend and yours; if not, it will be otherwise. And I will give you my wedding-ring, which you shall wear as yours.'

'Have you worn it, my lady?'

'Only at night.'

There was not much choice in the matter, and Milly consented. Then this noble lady took from her bosom the ring she had never been able openly to exhibit, and, grasping the young girl's hand, slipped it upon her finger as she stood upon her lover's grave.

Milly shivered, and bowed her head, saying, 'I feel as if I had become a corpse's bride!'

But from that moment the maiden was heart and soul in the substitution. A blissful repose came over her spirit. It seemed to her that she had secured in death him whom in life she had vainly idolized; and she was almost content. After that the lady handed over to the young man's new wife all the little mementoes and trinkets he had given herself, even to a brooch containing his hair.

The next day the girl made her so-called confession, which the simple mourning she had already worn, without stating for whom, seemed to bear out; and soon the story of the little romance spread through the village and country-side, almost as far as Melchester. It was a curious psychological fact that, having once made the avowal, Milly seemed possessed with a spirit of ecstasy at her position. With the liberal sum of money supplied to her by Lady Caroline she now purchased the garb of a widow, and duly appeared at church in her weeds, her simple face looking so sweet against its margin of crape that she was almost envied her state by the other village-girls of her age. And when a woman's sorrow for her beloved can maim her young life so obviously as it had done Milly's there was, in truth, little subterfuge in the case. Her explanation tallied so well with the details of her lover's latter movements – those strange absences and sudden returnings, which had occasionally puzzled his friends – that nobody supposed for a moment that the second actor in these secret nuptials was other than she. The actual and whole truth would indeed have seemed a preposterous assertion beside this plausible one, by reason of the lofty demeanour of the Lady Caroline and the unassuming habits of the late villager. There being no inheritance in question, not a soul took the trouble to go to the city church, forty miles off, and search the registers for marriage signatures bearing out so humble a romance.

In a short time Milly caused a decent tombstone to be erected over her nominal husband's grave, whereon appeared the statement that it was placed there by his heartbroken widow, which, considering that the payment for it came from Lady Caroline and the grief from Milly, was as truthful as such inscriptions usually are, and only required pluralizing to render it yet more nearly so.

The impressionable and complaisant Milly, in her character of widow, took delight in going to his grave every day, and indulging in sorrow which was a positive luxury to her. She placed fresh flowers on his grave, and so keen was her emotional imaginativeness that she almost believed herself to have been his wife indeed as she walked to and fro in her garb of woe. One afternoon, Milly being busily engaged in this labour of love at the grave, Lady Caroline passed outside the churchyard wall with some of her visiting friends, who, seeing Milly there, watched her actions with interest, remarked upon the pathos of the scene, and upon the intense affection the young man must have felt for such a tender creature as Milly. A strange light, as of pain, shot from the Lady Caroline's eye, as if for the first time she begrudged to the young girl the position she had been at such pains to transfer to her; it showed that a slumbering affection for her husband still had life in Lady Caroline, obscured and stifled as it was by social considerations.

An end was put to this smooth arrangement by the sudden appearance in the churchyard one day of the Lady Caroline, when Milly had come there on her usual errand of laying flowers. Lady Caroline had been anxiously awaiting her behind the chancel, and her countenance was pale and agitated.

'Milly!' she said, 'come here! I don't know how to say to you what I am going to say. I am half dead!'

'I am sorry for your ladyship,' says Milly, wondering.

'Give me that ring!' says the lady, snatching at the girl's left hand. Milly drew it quickly away.

'I tell you give it to me!' repeated Caroline, almost fiercely. 'O – but you don't know why? I am in a grief and a trouble I did not expect!' And Lady Caroline whispered a few words to the girl.

'O my lady!' said the thunderstruck Milly. 'What *will* you do?'

'You must say that your statement was a wicked lie, an invention, a scandal, a deadly sin – that I told you to make it to screen me! That it was I whom he married at Bath. In short, we must tell the truth, or I am ruined – body, mind, and reputation – for ever!'

But there is a limit to the flexibility of gentle-souled women. Milly by this time had so grown to the idea of being one flesh with this young man, of having the right to bear his name as she bore it; had so thoroughly come to regard him as her husband, to dream of him as her husband, to speak of him as her husband, that she could not relinquish him at a moment's peremptory notice.

'No, no,' she said desperately, 'I cannot, I will not give him up! Your ladyship took him away from me alive, and gave him back to me only when he was dead. Now I will keep him! I am truly his widow. More truly than you, my lady! for I love him and mourn for him, and call myself by his dear name, and your ladyship does neither!'

'I *do* love him!' cries Lady Caroline with flashing eyes, 'and I cling to him, and won't let him go to such as you! How can I, when he is the father of this poor child that's coming to me? I must have him back again! Milly, Milly, can't you pity and understand me, perverse girl that you are, and the miserable plight that I am in? O, this precipitancy – it is the ruin of women! Why did I not consider, and wait! Come, give me back all that I have given you, and assure me you will support me in confessing the truth!'

'Never, never!' persisted Milly, with woe-begone passionateness. 'Look at this headstone! Look at my gown and bonnet of crape – this ring: listen to the name they call me by! My character is worth as much to me as yours is to you! After declaring my Love mine, myself his, taking his name, making his death my own particular sorrow, how can I say it was not so? No such dishonour for me! I will outswear you, my lady; and I shall be believed. My story is so much the more likely that yours will be thought false. But, O please, my lady, do not drive me to this! In pity let me keep him!'

The poor nominal widow exhibited such anguish at a proposal which would have been truly a bitter humiliation to her, that Lady Caroline was warmed to pity in spite of her own condition.

'Yes, I see your position,' she answered. 'But think of mine! What can I do? Without your support it would seem an invention to save me from disgrace; even if I produced the register, the love of scandal in the world is such that the multitude would slur over the fact, say it was a fabrication, and believe your story. I do not know who were the witnesses, or the name of the church, or anything!'

In a few minutes these two poor young women felt, as so many in a strait have felt before, that union was their greatest strength, even now;

and they consulted calmly together. The result of their deliberations
was that Milly went home as usual, and Lady Caroline also, the latter
confessing that very night to the Countess her mother of the marriage,
and to nobody else in the world. And, some time after, Lady Caroline
and her mother went away to London, where a little while later still
they were joined by Milly, who was supposed to have left the village to
proceed to a watering-place in the North for the benefit of her health, at
the expense of the ladies of the Manor, who had been much interested in
her state of lonely and defenceless widowhood.

Early the next year the ostensible widow Milly came home with an
infant in her arms, the family at the Manor House having meanwhile
gone abroad. They did not return from their tour till the autumn
ensuing, by which time Milly and the child had again departed from the
cottage of her father the woodman, Milly having attained to the dignity
of dwelling in a cottage of her own, many miles to the eastward of her
native village; a comfortable little allowance had moreover been settled
on her and the child for life, through the instrumentality of Lady
Caroline and her mother.

Two or three years passed away, and the Lady Caroline married a
nobleman – the Marquis of Stonehenge – considerably her senior, who
had wooed her long and phlegmatically. He was not rich, but she led a
placid life with him for many years, though there was no child of the
marriage. Meanwhile Milly's boy, as the youngster was called, and as
Milly herself considered him, grew up, and throve wonderfully, and
loved her as she deserved to be loved for her devotion to him, in whom
she every day traced more distinctly the lineaments of the man who had
won her girlish heart, and kept it even in the tomb.

She educated him as well as she could with the limited means at
her disposal, for the allowance had never been increased, Lady Caroline,
or the Marchioness of Stonehenge as she now was, seeming by degrees
to care little what had become of them. Milly became extremely
ambitious on the boy's account; she pinched herself almost of neces-
saries to send him to the Grammar School in the town to which they
retired, and at twenty he enlisted in a cavalry regiment, joining it with a
deliberate intent of making the Army his profession, and not in a freak
of idleness. His exceptional attainments, his manly bearing, his steady
conduct, speedily won him promotion, which was furthered by the
serious war in which this country was at that time engaged. On his
return to England after the peace he had risen to the rank of riding-

master, and was soon after advanced another stage, and made quarter-master, though still a young man.

His mother – his corporeal mother, that is, the Marchioness of Stonehenge – heard tidings of this unaided progress; it reawakened her maternal instincts, and filled her with pride. She became keenly interested in her successful soldier-son; and as she grew older much wished to see him again, particularly when, the Marquis dying, she was left a solitary and childless widow. Whether or not she would have gone to him of her own impulse I cannot say; but one day, when she was driving in an open carriage in the outskirts of a neighbouring town, the troops lying at the barracks hard by passed her in marching order. She eyed them narrowly, and in the finest of the horsemen recognized her son from his likeness to her first husband.

This sight of him doubly intensified the motherly emotions which had lain dormant in her for so many years, and she wildly asked herself how she could so have neglected him? Had she possessed the true courage of affection she would have owned to her first marriage, and have reared him as her own! What would it have mattered if she had never obtained this precious coronet of pearls and gold leaves, by comparison with the gain of having the love and protection of such a noble and worthy son? These and other sad reflections cut the gloomy and solitary lady to the heart; and she repented of her pride in disclaiming her first husband more bitterly than she had ever repented of her infatuation in marrying him.

Her yearning was so strong that at length it seemed to her that she could not live without announcing herself to him as his mother. Come what might, she would do it: late as it was, she would have him away from that woman whom she began to hate with the fierceness of a deserted heart for having taken her place as the mother of her only child. She felt confidently enough that her son would only too gladly exchange a cottage-mother for one who was a peeress of the realm. Being now, in her widowhood, free to come and go as she chose, without question from anybody, Lady Stonehenge started next day for the little town where Milly yet lived, still in her robes of sable for the lost lover of her youth.

'He is *my* son,' said the Marchioness, as soon as she was alone in the cottage with Milly. 'You must give him back to me, now that I am in a position in which I can defy the world's opinion. I suppose he comes to see you continually?'

'Every month since he returned from the war, my lady. And some-times he stays two or three days, and takes me about seeing sights everywhere!' She spoke with quiet triumph.

'Well, you will have to give him up,' said the Marchioness calmly. 'It shall not be the worse for you – you may see him when you choose. I am going to avow my first marriage, and have him with me.'

'You forget that there are two to be reckoned with, my lady. Not only me, but himself.'

'That can be arranged. You don't suppose that he wouldn't—' But not wishing to insult Milly by comparing their positions, she said, 'He is my own flesh and blood, not yours.'

'Flesh and blood's nothing!' said Milly, flashing with as much scorn as a cottager could show to a peeress, which, in this case, was not so little as may be supposed. 'But I will agree to put it to him, and let him settle it for himself.'

'That's all I require,' said Lady Stonehenge. 'You must ask him to come, and I will meet him here.'

The soldier was written to, and the meeting took place. He was not so much astonished at the disclosure of his parentage as Lady Stonehenge had been led to expect, having known for years that there was a little mystery about his birth. His manner towards the Marchioness, though respectful, was less warm than she could have hoped. The alternatives as to his choice of a mother were put before him. His answer amazed and stupefied her.

'No, my lady,' said the quartermaster. 'Thank you much, but I prefer to let things be as they have been. My father's name is mine in any case. You see, my lady, you cared little for me when I was weak and helpless; why should I come to you now I am strong? She, dear devoted soul [pointing to Milly], tended me from my birth, watched over me, nursed me when I was ill, and deprived herself of many a little comfort to push me on. I cannot love another mother as I love her. She *is* my mother, and I will always be her son!' As he spoke he put his manly arm round Milly's neck, and kissed her with the tenderest affection.

The agony of the poor Marchioness was pitiable. 'You kill me!' she said, between her shaking sobs. 'Cannot you – love – me – too?'

'No, my lady. If I must say it, you were once ashamed of my poor father, who was a sincere and honest man; therefore, I am now ashamed of you.'

Nothing would move him; and the suffering woman at last gasped,

'Cannot – O, cannot you give one kiss to me – as you did to her ? It is not much – it is all I ask – all!'

'Certainly,' he replied.

He kissed her, but with a difference – quite coldly; and the painful scene came to an end. That day was the beginning of death to the unfortunate Marchioness of Stonehenge. It was in the perverseness of her human heart that his denial of her should add fuel to the fire of her craving for his love. How long afterwards she lived I do not know with any exactness, but it was no great length of time. That anguish that is sharper than a serpent's tooth wore her out soon. Utterly reckless of the world, its ways, and its opinions, she allowed her story to become known; and when the welcome end supervened (which, I grieve to say, she refused to lighten by the consolations of religion), a broken heart was the truest phrase in which to sum up its cause.

The rural dean having concluded, some observations upon his tale were made in due course. The sentimental member said that Lady Caroline's history afforded a sad instance of how an honest human affection will become shamefaced and mean under the frost of class-division and social prejudices. She probably deserved some pity; though her off-spring, before he grew up to man's estate, had deserved more. There was no pathos like the pathos of childhood, when a child found itself in a world where it was not wanted, and could not understand the reason why. A tale by the speaker, further illustrating the same subject, though with different results from the last, naturally followed.

Dame the Fourth
Lady Mottisfont

By the Sentimental Member

OF all the romantic towns in Wessex, Wintoncester is probably the most convenient for meditative people to live in; since there you have a cathedral with a nave so long that it affords space in which to walk and summon your remoter moods without continually turning on your heel, or seeming to do more than take an afternoon stroll under cover from the rain or sun. In an uninterrupted course of nearly three hundred steps eastward, and again nearly three hundred steps westward amid those magnificent tombs, you can, for instance, compare in the most leisurely way the dry dustiness which ultimately pervades the persons of kings and bishops with the damper dustiness that is usually the final shape of commoners, curates, and others who take their last rest out of doors. Then, if you are in love, you can, by sauntering in the chapels and behind the episcopal chantries with the bright-eyed one, so steep and mellow your ecstasy in the solemnities around, that it will assume a rarer and finer tincture, even more grateful to the understanding, if not to the senses, than that form of the emotion which arises from such companionship in spots where all is life, and growth, and fecundity.

It was in this solemn place, whither they had withdrawn from the sight of relatives on one cold day in March, that Sir Ashley Mottisfont asked in marriage, as his second wife, Philippa, the gentle daughter of plain Squire Okehall. Her life had been an obscure one thus far; while Sir Ashley, though not a rich man, had a certain distinction about him; so that everybody thought what a convenient, elevating, and, in a word, blessed match it would be for such a supernumerary as she. Nobody thought so more than the amiable girl herself. She had been smitten with such affection for him that, when she walked the cathedral aisles at his side on the before-mentioned day, she did not know that her feet touched hard pavement; it seemed to her rather that she was floating in space. Philippa was an ecstatic, heart-thumping maiden, and could not understand how she had deserved to have sent to her such an illustrious lover, such a travelled personage, such a handsome man.

When he put the question, it was in no clumsy language, such as the ordinary bucolic county landlords were wont to use on like quivering occasions, but as elegantly as if he had been taught it in Enfield's *Speaker*. Yet he hesitated a little – for he had something to add.

'My pretty Philippa,' he said (she was not very pretty by the way), 'I have, you must know, a little girl dependent upon me: a little waif I found one day in a patch of wild oats [such was this worthy baronet's humour] when I was riding home: a little nameless creature, whom I wish to take care of till she is old enough to take care of herself, and to educate in a plain way. She is only fifteen months old, and is at present in the hands of a kind villager's wife in my parish. Will you object to give some attention to the little thing in her helplessness ?'

It need hardly be said that our innocent young lady, loving him so deeply and joyfully as she did, replied that she would do all she could for the nameless child; and, shortly afterwards, the pair were married in the same cathedral that had echoed the whispers of his declaration, the officiating minister being the Bishop himself, a venerable and experienced man, so well accomplished in uniting people who had a mind for that sort of experiment, that the couple, with some sense of surprise, found themselves one while they were still vaguely gazing at each other as two independent beings.

After this operation they went home to Deansleigh Park, and made a beginning of living happily ever after. Lady Mottisfont, true to her promise, was always running down to the village during the following weeks to see the baby whom her husband had so mysteriously lighted on during his ride home – concerning which interesting discovery she had her own opinion; but being so extremely amiable and affectionate that she could have loved stocks and stones if there had been no living creatures to love, she uttered none of her thoughts. The little thing, who had been christened Dorothy, took to Lady Mottisfont as if the baronet's young wife had been her mother; and at length Philippa grew so fond of the child that she ventured to ask her husband if she might have Dorothy in her own home, and bring her up carefully, just as if she were her own. To this he answered that, though remarks might be made thereon, he had no objection; a fact which was obvious, Sir Ashley seeming rather pleased than otherwise with the proposal.

After this they lived quietly and uneventfully for two or three years at Sir Ashley Mottisfont's residence in that part of England, with as near an approach to bliss as the climate of this country allows. The child had been a godsend to Philippa, for there seemed no great probability of her having one of her own: and she wisely regarded the possession of Dorothy as a special kindness of Providence, and did not worry her mind at all as to Dorothy's possible origin. Being a tender and impulsive creature, she loved her husband without criticism, exhaustively and religiously, and the child not much otherwise. She watched the little foundling as if she had been her own by nature, and Dorothy became a great solace to her when her husband was absent on pleasure or business; and when he came home he looked pleased to see how the two had won each other's hearts. Sir Ashley would kiss his wife, and his wife would kiss little Dorothy, and little Dorothy would kiss Sir Ashley, and after this triangular burst of affection Lady Mottisfont would say, 'Dear me – I forget she is not mine!'

'What does it matter?' her husband would reply. 'Providence is fore-knowing. He has sent this one because he is not intending to send us one by any other channel.'

Their life was of the simplest. Since his travels the baronet had taken to sporting and farming; while Philippa was a pattern of domesticity. Their pleasures were all local. They retired early to rest, and rose with the cart-horses and whistling waggoners. They knew the names of every bird and tree not exceptionally uncommon, and could foretell the weather almost as well as anxious farmers and old people with corns.

One day Sir Ashley Mottisfont received a letter, which he read, and musingly laid down on the table without remark.

'What is it, dearest?' asked his wife, glancing at the sheet.

'Oh, it is from an old lawyer at Bath whom I used to know. He reminds me of something I said to him four or five years ago – some little time before we were married – about Dorothy.'

'What about her?'

'It was a casual remark I made to him, when I thought you might not take kindly to her, that if he knew a lady who was anxious to adopt a child, and could insure a good home to Dorothy, he was to let me know.'

'But that was when you had nobody to take care of her,' she said quickly. 'How absurd of him to write now! Does he know you are married? He must, surely.'

'O yes!'

He handed her the letter. The solicitor stated that a widow lady of position, who did not at present wish her name to be disclosed, had lately become a client of his while taking the waters, and had mentioned to him that she would like a little girl to bring up as her own, if she could be certain of finding one of good and pleasing disposition; and, the better to insure this, she would not wish the child to be too young for judging her qualities. He had remembered Sir Ashley's observation to him a long while ago, and therefore brought the matter before him. It would be an excellent home for the little girl – of that he was positive – if she had not already found such a home.

'But it is absurd of the man to write so long after!' said Lady Mottisfont, with a lumpiness about the back of her throat as she thought how much Dorothy had become to her. 'I suppose it was when you first – found her – that you told him this?'

'Exactly – it was then.'

He fell into thought, and neither Sir Ashley nor Lady Mottisfont took the trouble to answer the lawyer's letter; and so the matter ended for the time.

One day at dinner, on their return from a short absence in town, whither they had gone to see what the world was doing, hear what it was saying, and to make themselves generally fashionable after rusticating for so long – on this occasion, I say, they learnt from some friend who had joined them at dinner that Fernell Hall – the manorial house of the estate next their own, which had been offered on lease by reason of the impecuniosity of its owner – had been taken for a term by a widow lady, an Italian Contessa, whose name I will not mention for certain reasons which may by and by appear. Lady Mottisfont expressed her surprise and interest at the probability of having such a neighbour. 'Though, if I had been born in Italy, I think I should have liked to remain there,' she said.

'She is not Italian, though her husband was,' said Sir Ashley.

'O; you have heard about her before now?'

'Yes; they were talking of her at Grey's the other evening. She is English.' And then, as her husband said no more about the lady, the friend who was dining with them told Lady Mottisfont that the Countess's father had speculated largely in East-India Stock, in which immense fortunes were being made at that time: through this his daughter had found herself enormously wealthy at his death, which had occurred only a few weeks after the death of her husband. It was supposed that the marriage of an enterprising English speculator's daughter to a poor foreign nobleman had been matter of arrangement merely. As soon as the Countess's widowhood was a little further advanced she would, no doubt, be the mark of all the schemers who came near her, for she was still quite young. But at present she seemed to desire quiet, and avoided society and town.

Some weeks after this time Sir Ashley Mottisfont sat looking fixedly at his lady for many moments. He said:

'It might have been better for Dorothy if the Countess had taken her. She is so wealthy in comparison with ourselves, and could have ushered the girl into the great world more effectually than we ever shall be able to do.'

'The Contessa take Dorothy?' said Lady Mottisfont with a start. 'What – was she the lady who wished to adopt her?'

'Yes; she was staying at Bath when Lawyer Gayton wrote to me.'

'But how do you know all this, Ashley?'

He showed a little hesitation. 'Oh, I've seen her,' he says. 'You know, she drives to the meet sometimes, though she does not ride; and she has informed me that she was the lady who inquired of Gayton.'

'You have talked to her as well as seen her, then?'

'O yes, several times; everybody has.'

'Why didn't you tell me?' says his lady. 'I had quite forgotten to call upon her. I'll go to-morrow, or soon. . . . But I can't think, Ashley, how you can say that it might have been better for Dorothy to have gone to her; she is so much our own now that I cannot admit any such conjectures as those, even in jest.' Her eyes reproached him so eloquently that Sir Ashley Mottisfont did not answer.

Lady Mottisfont did not hunt any more than the Anglo-Italian Countess did; indeed, she had become so absorbed in household matters and in Dorothy's well-being that she had no mind to waste a minute on mere enjoyments. As she had said, to talk coolly of what might have been the best destination in days past for a child to whom they had become so attached seemed quite barbarous, and she could not understand how her husband should consider the point so abstractedly; for, as will probably have been guessed, Lady Mottisfont long before this time, if she had not done so at the very beginning, divined Sir Ashley's true relation to Dorothy. But the baronet's wife was so discreetly meek and mild that she never told him of her surmise, and took what Heaven had sent her without cavil, her generosity in this respect having been bountifully rewarded by the new life she found in her love for the little girl.

Her husband recurred to the same uncomfortable subject, when, a few days later, they were speaking of travelling abroad. He said that it was almost a pity, if they thought of going, that they had not fallen in with the Countess's wish. That lady had told him that she had met Dorothy walking with her nurse, and that she had never seen a child she liked so well.

'What - she covets her still? How impertinent of the woman!' said Lady Mottisfont.

'She seems to do so. . . . You see, dearest Philippa, the advantage to Dorothy would have been that the Countess would have adopted her legally, and have made her as her own daughter; while we have not done that - we are only bringing up and educating a poor child in charity.'

'But I'll adopt her fully - make her mine legally!' cried his wife in an anxious voice. 'How is it to be done?'

'H'm.' He did not inform her, but fell into thought; and, for reasons of her own, his lady was restless and uneasy.

The very next day Lady Mottisfont drove to Fernell Hall to pay the neglected call upon her neighbour. The Countess was at home, and received her graciously. But poor Lady Mottisfont's heart died within her as soon as she set eyes on her new acquaintance. Such wonderful beauty, of the fully-developed kind, had never confronted her before inside the lines of a human face. She seemed to shine with every light and grace that woman can possess. Her finished Continental manners, her expanded mind, her ready wit, composed a study that made the other poor lady sick; for she, and latterly Sir Ashley himself, were rather rural in manners, and she felt abashed by new sounds and ideas from without. She hardly knew three words in any language but her own, while this divine creature, though truly English, had, apparently, whatever she wanted in the Italian and French tongues to suit every impression; which was considered a great improvement to speech in those days, and, indeed, is by many considered as such in these.

'How very strange it was about the little girl!' the Contessa said to Lady Mottisfont, in her gay tones. 'I mean, that the child the lawyer recommended should, just before then, have been adopted by you, who are now my neighbour. How is she getting on? I must come and see her.'

'Do you still want her?' asks Lady Mottisfont suspiciously.

'O, I should like to have her!'

'But you can't! She's mine!' said the other greedily.

A drooping manner appeared in the Countess from that moment.

Lady Mottisfont, too, was in a wretched mood all the way home that day. The Countess was so charming in every way that she had charmed her gentle ladyship; how should it be possible that she had failed to charm Sir Ashley? Moreover, she had awakened a strange thought in Philippa's mind. As soon as she reached home she rushed to the nursery, and there, seizing Dorothy, frantically kissed her; then, holding her at arm's length, she gazed with a piercing inquisitiveness into the girl's lineaments. She sighed deeply, abandoned the wondering Dorothy, and hastened away.

She had seen there not only her husband's traits, which she had often beheld before, but others, of the shade, shape, and expression which characterized those of her new neighbour.

Then this poor lady perceived the whole perturbing sequence of things, and asked herself how she could have been such a walking piece of simplicity as not to have thought of this before. But she did not stay long upbraiding herself for her shortsightedness, so overwhelmed was she with misery at the spectacle of herself as an intruder between these. To be sure she could not have foreseen such a conjuncture; but that did not lessen her grief. The woman who had been both her husband's bliss and his backsliding had reappeared free when he was no longer so, and she evidently was dying to claim her own in the person of Dorothy, who had meanwhile grown to be, to Lady Mottisfont, almost the only source of each day's happiness, supplying her with something to watch over, inspiring her with the sense of maternity, and so largely reflecting her husband's nature as almost to deceive her into the pleasant belief that the girl reflected her own also.

If there was a single direction in which this devoted and virtuous lady erred, it was in the direction of over-submissiveness. When all is said and done, and the truth told, men seldom show much self-sacrifice in their conduct as lords and masters to helpless women bound to them for life, and perhaps (though I say it with all uncertainty) if she had blazed up in his face like a furze-faggot, directly he came home, she might have helped herself a little. But God knows whether this is a true supposition; at any rate she did no such thing, and waited and prayed that she might never do despite to him who, she was bound to admit, had always been tender and courteous towards her; and hoped that little Dorothy might never be taken away.

By degrees the two households became friendly, and very seldom did a week pass without their seeing something of each other. Try as she might, and dangerous as she assumed the acquaintanceship to be, Lady Mottisfont could detect no fault or flaw in her new friend. It was obvious that Dorothy had been the magnet which had drawn the Contessa hither, and not Sir Ashley. Such beauty, united with such understanding and brightness, Philippa had never before known in one of her own sex, and she tried to think (whether she succeeded I do not know) that she did not mind the propinquity; since a woman so rich, so fair, and with such a command of suitors, could not desire to wreck the happiness of so inoffensive a person as herself.

The season drew on when it was the custom for families of distinction to go off to The Bath, and Sir Ashley Mottisfont persuaded his wife to accompany him thither with Dorothy. Everybody of any note was there this year. From their own part of England came many that they knew; among the rest, Lord and Lady Purbeck, the Earl and Countess of Wessex, Sir John Grebe, the Drenkhards, Lady Stourvale, the old Duke of Hamptonshire, the Bishop of Melchester, the Dean of Exonbury, and other lesser lights of Court, pulpit and field. Thither also came the fair Contessa, whom, as soon as Philippa saw how much she was sought after by younger men, she could not conscientiously suspect of renewed designs upon Sir Ashley.

But the Countess had finer opportunities than ever with Dorothy; for Lady Mottisfont was often indisposed, and even at other times could not honestly hinder an intercourse which gave bright ideas to the child. Dorothy welcomed her new acquaintance with a strange and instinctive readiness that intimated the wonderful subtlety of the threads which bind flesh and flesh together.

At last the crisis came: it was precipitated by an accident. Dorothy and her nurse had gone out one day for an airing, leaving Lady Mottisfont alone indoors. While she sat gloomily thinking that in all likelihood the Countess would contrive to meet the child somewhere, and exchange a few tender words with her, Sir Ashley Mottisfont rushed in and informed her that Dorothy had just had the narrowest possible escape from death. Some workmen were undermining a house to pull it down for rebuilding, when, without warning, the front wall inclined slowly outwards for its fall, the nurse and child passing beneath it at the same

moment. The fall was temporarily arrested by the scaffolding, while in
the meantime the Countess had witnessed their imminent danger from
the other side of the street. Springing across, she snatched Dorothy
from under the wall, and pulled the nurse after her, the middle of the
way being barely reached before they were enveloped in the dense dust
of the descending mass, though not a stone touched them.

'Where is Dorothy?' says the excited Lady Mottisfont.

'She has her – she won't let her go for a time—'

'Has her? But she's *mine* – she's mine!' cries Lady Mottisfont.

Then her quick and tender eyes perceived that her husband had
almost forgotten her intrusive existence in contemplating the oneness of
Dorothy's, the Countess's, and his own: he was in a dream of exaltation
which recognized nothing necessary to his well-being outside that
welded circle of three lives.

Dorothy was at length brought home; she was much fascinated by the
Countess, and saw nothing tragic, but rather all that was truly delightful,
in what had happened. In the evening, when the excitement was over,
and Dorothy was put to bed, Sir Ashley said, 'She has saved Dorothy,
and I have been asking myself what I can do for her as a slight acknowledgment of her heroism. Surely we ought to let her have Dorothy to
bring up, since she still desires to do it? It would be so much to Dorothy's
advantage. We ought to look at it in that light, and not selfishly.'

Philippa seized his hand. 'Ashley, Ashley! You don't mean it – that I
must lose my pretty darling – the only one I have?' She met his gaze with
her piteous mouth and wet eyes so painfully strained, that he turned
away his face.

The next morning, before Dorothy was awake, Lady Mottisfont stole
to the girl's bedside, and sat regarding her. When Dorothy opened her
eyes, she fixed them for a long time upon Philippa's features.

'Mamma – you are not so pretty as the Contessa, are you?' she said at
length.

'I am not, Dorothy.'

'Why are you not, mamma?'

'Dorothy – where would you rather live, always; with me, or with
her?'

The little girl looked troubled. 'I am sorry, mamma; I don't mean to
be unkind; but I would rather live with her; I mean, if I might without
trouble, and you did not mind, and it could be just the same to us all,
you know.'

'Has she ever asked you the same question?'

'Never, mamma.'

There lay the sting of it: the Countess seemed the soul of honour and fairness in this matter, test her as she might. That afternoon Lady Mottisfont went to her husband with singular firmness upon her gentle face.

'Ashley, we have been married nearly five years, and I have never challenged you with what I know perfectly well – the parentage of Dorothy.'

'Never have you, Philippa dear. Though I have seen that you knew from the first.'

'From the first as to her father, not as to her mother. Her I did not know for some time; but I know now.'

'Ah! you have discovered that too?' says he, without much surprise.

'Could I help it? Very well, that being so, I have thought it over; and I have spoken to Dorothy. I agree to her going. I can do no less than grant to the Countess her wish, after her kindness to my – your – her – child.'

Then this self-sacrificing woman went hastily away that he might not see that her heart was bursting; and thereupon, before they left the city, Dorothy changed her mother and her home. After this, the Countess went away to London for a while, taking Dorothy with her; and the baronet and his wife returned to their lonely place at Deansleigh Park without her.

To renounce Dorothy in the bustle of Bath was a different thing from living without her in this quiet home. One evening Sir Ashley missed his wife from the supper-table; her manner had been so pensive and woeful of late that he immediately became alarmed. He said nothing, but looked about outside the house narrowly, and discerned her form in the park, where recently she had been accustomed to walk alone. In its lower levels there was a pool fed by a trickling brook, and he reached this spot in time to hear a splash. Running forward, he dimly perceived her light gown floating in the water. To pull her out was the work of a few instants, and bearing her indoors to her room, he undressed her, nobody in the house knowing of the incident but himself. She had not been immersed long enough to lose her senses, and soon recovered. She owned that she had done it because the Contessa had taken away her child, as she persisted in calling Dorothy. Her husband spoke sternly to

her, and impressed upon her the weakness of giving way thus, when all
that had happened was for the best. She took his reproof meekly, and
admitted her fault.

After that she became more resigned, but he often caught her in tears
over some doll, shoe, or ribbon of Dorothy's, and decided to take her to
the North of England for change of air and scene. This was not without
its beneficial effect, corporeally no less than mentally, as later events
showed, but she still evinced a preternatural sharpness of ear at the most
casual mention of the child. When they reached home, the Countess and
Dorothy were still absent from the neighbouring Fernell Hall, but in a
month or two they returned, and a little later Sir Ashley Mottisfont
came into his wife's room full of news.

'Well – would you think it, Philippa! After being so desperate, too,
about getting Dorothy to be with her!'

'Ah – what?'

'Our neighbour, the Countess, is going to be married again! It is to
somebody she has met in London.'

Lady Mottisfont was much surprised; she had never dreamt of such
an event. The conflict for the possession of Dorothy's person had
obscured the possibility of it; yet what more likely, the Countess being
still under thirty, and so good-looking?

'What is of still more interest to us, or to you,' continued her husband, 'is a kind offer she has made. She is willing that you should have
Dorothy back again. Seeing what a grief the loss of her has been to you,
she will try to do without her.'

'It is not for that; it is not to oblige me,' said Lady Mottisfont
quickly. 'One can see well enough what it is for!'

'Well, never mind; beggars mustn't be choosers. The reason or
motive is nothing to us, so that you obtain your desire.'

'I am not a beggar any longer,' said Lady Mottisfont, with proud
mystery.

'What do you mean by that?'

Lady Mottisfont hesitated. However, it was only too plain that she
did not now jump at a restitution of one for whom some months before
she had been breaking her heart.

The explanation of this change of mood became apparent some little
time farther on. Lady Mottisfont, after five years of wedded life, was
expecting to become a mother, and the aspect of many things was
greatly altered in her view. Among the more important changes was that

of no longer feeling Dorothy to be absolutely indispensable to her existence.

Meanwhile, in view of her coming marriage, the Countess decided to abandon the remainder of her term at Fernell Hall, and return to her pretty little house in town. But she could not do this quite so quickly as she had expected, and half a year or more elapsed before she finally quitted the neighbourhood, the interval being passed in alternations between the country and London. Prior to her last departure she had an interview with Sir Ashley Mottisfont, and it occurred three days after his wife had presented him with a son and heir.

'I wanted to speak to you,' said the Countess, looking him luminously in the face, 'about the dear foundling I have adopted temporarily, and thought to have adopted permanently. But my marriage makes it too risky!'

'I thought it might be that,' he answered, regarding her steadfastly back again, and observing two tears come slowly into her eyes as she heard her own voice describe Dorothy in those words.

'Don't criticize me,' she said hastily; and recovering herself, went on. 'If Lady Mottisfont could take her back again, as I suggested, it would be better for me, and certainly no worse for Dorothy. To every one but ourselves she is but a child I have taken a fancy to, and Lady Mottisfont coveted her so much, and was very reluctant to let her go. . . . I am sure she will adopt her again?' she added anxiously.

'I will sound her afresh,' said the baronet. 'You leave Dorothy behind for the present?'

'Yes; although I go away, I do not give up the house for another month.'

He did not speak to his wife about the proposal till some few days after, when Lady Mottisfont had nearly recovered, and news of the Countess's marriage in London had just reached them. He had no sooner mentioned Dorothy's name than Lady Mottisfont showed symptoms of disquietude.

'I have not acquired any dislike of Dorothy,' she said, 'but I feel that there is one nearer to me now. Dorothy chose the alternative of going to the Countess, you must remember, when I put it to her as between the Countess and myself.'

'But, my dear Philippa, how can you argue thus about a child, and that child our Dorothy?'

'Not *ours*,' said his wife, pointing to the cot. 'Ours is here.'

'What, then, Philippa,' he said, surprised, 'you won't have her back, after nearly dying of grief at the loss of her?'

'I cannot argue, dear Ashley. I should prefer not to have the responsibility of Dorothy again. Her place is filled now.'

Her husband sighed, and went out of the chamber. There had been a previous arrangement that Dorothy should be brought to the house on a visit that day, but instead of taking her up to his wife, he did not inform Lady Mottisfont of the child's presence. He entertained her himself as well as he could, and accompanied her into the park, where they had a ramble together. Presently he sat down on the root of an elm and took her upon his knee.

'Between this husband and this baby, little Dorothy, you who had two homes are left out in the cold,' he said.

'Can't I go to London with my pretty mamma?' said Dorothy, perceiving from his manner that there was a hitch somewhere.

'I am afraid not, my child. She only took you to live with her because she was lonely, you know.'

'Then can't I stay at Deansleigh Park with my other mamma and you?'

'I am afraid that cannot be done either,' said he sadly. 'We have a baby in the house now.' He closed the reply by stooping down and kissing her, there being a tear in his eye.

'Then nobody wants me!' said Dorothy pathetically.

'O yes, somebody wants you,' he assured her. 'Where would you like to live besides?'

Dorothy's experiences being rather limited, she mentioned the only other place in the world that she was acquainted with, the cottage of the villager who had taken care of her before Lady Mottisfont had removed her to the Manor House.

'Yes; that's where you'll be best off, and most independent,' he answered. 'And I'll come to see you, my dear girl, and bring you pretty things; and perhaps you'll be just as happy there.'

Nevertheless, when the change came, and Dorothy was handed over to the kind cottage-woman, the poor child missed the luxurious roominess of Fernell Hall and Deansleigh; and for a long time her little feet, which had been accustomed to carpets and oak floors, suffered from the cold of the stone flags on which it was now her lot to live and to play; while chilblains came upon her fingers with washing at the pump. But thicker shoes with nails in them somewhat remedied the cold feet, and her complaints and tears on this and other scores diminished to silence as she became inured anew to the hardships of the farm-cottage, and she grew up robust if not handsome. She was never altogether lost sight of by Sir Ashley, though she was deprived of the systematic education which had been devised and begun for her by Lady Mottisfont, as well as by her real mother, the enthusiastic Countess. The latter soon had other Dorothys to think of, who occupied her time and affection as fully as Lady Mottisfont's were occupied by her precious boy. In the course of time the doubly-desired and doubly-rejected Dorothy married, I believe, a respectable road-contractor – the same, if I mistake not, who repaired and improved the old highway running from Winton-cester south-westerly through the New Forest – and in the heart of this worthy man of business the poor girl found the nest which had been denied her by her own flesh and blood of higher degree.

Several of the listeners wished to hear another story from the senti-mental member after this, but he said that he could recall nothing else at the moment, and that it seemed to him as if his friend on the other side of the fireplace had something to say from the look of his face.

The member alluded to was a respectable churchwarden, with a sly chink to one eyelid – possibly the result of an accident – and a regular attendant at the Club meetings. He replied that his looks had been mainly caused by his interest in the two ladies of the last story, apparently women of strong motherly instincts, even though they were not genu-inely staunch in their tenderness. The tale had brought to his mind an instance of a firmer affection of that sort on the paternal side, in a nature otherwise culpable. As for telling the story, his manner was much against him, he feared; but he would do his best, if they wished.

Here the President interposed with a suggestion that as it was getting late in the afternoon it would be as well to adjourn to their respective inns and lodgings for dinner, after which those who cared to do so could return and resume these curious domestic traditions for the remainder of the evening, which might otherwise prove irksome enough. The curator had told him that the room was at their service. The church-warden, who was beginning to feel hungry himself, readily acquiesced, and the Club separated for an hour and a half. Then the faithful ones began to drop in again – among whom were not the President; neither came the rural dean, nor the two curates, though the Colonel, and the man of family, cigars in mouth, were good enough to return, having

found their hotel dreary. The museum had no regular means of illumination, and a solitary candle, less powerful than the rays of the fire, was
placed on the table; also bottles and glasses, provided by some thoughtful
member. The chink-eyed churchwarden, now thoroughly primed,
proceeded to relate in his own terms what was in substance as follows,
while many of his listeners smoked.

PART SECOND
AFTER DINNER

Dame the Fifth
The Lady Icenway

By the Churchwarden

IN the reign of His Most Excellent Majesty King George the Third, Defender of the Faith and of the American Colonies, there lived in 'a faire maner-place' (so Leland called it in his day, as I have been told), in one o' the greenest bits of woodland between Bristol and the city of Exonbury, a young lady who resembled some aforesaid ones in having many talents and exceeding great beauty. With these gifts she combined a somewhat imperious temper and arbitrary mind, though her experience of the world was not actually so large as her conclusive manner would have led the stranger to suppose. Being an orphan she resided with her uncle, who, though he was fairly considerate as to her welfare, left her pretty much to herself.

Now it chanced that when this lovely young lady was about nineteen, she (being a fearless horsewoman) was riding, with only a young lad as an attendant, in one o' the woods near her uncle's house, and, in trotting along, her horse stumbled over the root of a felled tree. She slipped to the ground, not seriously hurt, and was assisted home by a gentleman who came in view at the moment of her mishap. It turned out that this gentleman, a total stranger to her, was on a visit at the house of a neighbouring landowner. He was of Dutch extraction, and occasionally came to England on business or pleasure from his plantations in Guiana, on the north coast of South America, where he usually resided.

On this account he was naturally but little known in Wessex, and was but a slight acquaintance of the gentleman at whose mansion he was a guest. However, the friendship between him and the Heymeres – as the uncle and niece were named – warmed and warmed by degrees, there being but few folk o' note in the vicinity at that time, which made a newcomer, if he were at all sociable and of good credit, always sure of a welcome. A tender feeling (as it is called by the romantic) sprang up between the two young people, which ripened into intimacy. Anderling, the foreign gentleman, was of an amorous temperament; and, though he endeavoured to conceal his feeling, it could be seen that Miss Maria Heymere had impressed him rather more deeply than would be represented by a scratch upon a stone. He seemed absolutely unable to free himself from her fascination; and his inability to do so, much as he tried – evidently thinking he had not the ghost of a chance with her – gave her the pleasure of power; though she more than sympathized when she overheard him heaving his deep-drawn sighs – privately to himself, as he supposed.

After prolonging his visit by every conceivable excuse in his power, he summoned courage, and offered her his hand and his heart. Being in no way disinclined to him, though not so fervid as he, and her uncle making no objection to the match, she consented to share his fate, for better or otherwise, in the distant colony where, as he assured her, his rice, and coffee, and maize, and timber, produced him ample means – a statement which was borne out by his friend, her uncle's neighbour. In short, a day for their marriage was fixed, earlier in the engagement than is usual or desirable between comparative strangers, by reason of the necessity he was under of returning to look after his properties.

The wedding took place, and Maria left her uncle's mansion with her husband, going in the first place to London, and about a fortnight after sailing with him across the great ocean for their distant home – which, however, he assured her, should not be her home for long, it being his intention to dispose of his interests in this part of the world as soon as the war was over, and he could do so advantageously; when they could come to Europe, and reside in some favourite capital.

As they advanced on the slow voyage she observed that he grew more and more constrained; and, by the time they had drawn near the Line, he was quite depressed, just as he had been before proposing to her. A day or two before landing at Paramaribo he embraced her in a very tearful and passionate manner, and said he wished to make a confession. It had been his misfortune, he said, to marry at Quebec in early life a woman whose reputation proved to be in every way bad and scandalous. The discovery had nearly killed him; but he had ultimately separated from her, and had never seen her since. He had hoped and prayed she might be dead; but recently in London, when they were starting on this journey, he had discovered that she was still alive. At first he had decided to keep this dark intelligence from her beloved ears; but he had felt that he could not do it. All he hoped was that such a condition of things would make no difference in her feelings for him, as it need make no difference in the course of their lives.

Thereupon the spirit of this proud and masterful lady showed itself in violent turmoil, like the raging of a nor'-west thunderstorm – as well it might, God knows. But she was of too stout a nature to be broken down by his revelation, as many ladies of my acquaintance would have been – so far from home, and right under the tropical blaze o' the sun. Of the two, indeed, he was the more wretched and shattered in spirit, for he loved her deeply, and (there being a foreign twist in his make) had been tempted to this crime by her exceeding beauty, against which he had struggled day and night, till he had no further resistance left in him. It was she who came first to a decision as to what should be done – whether a wise one I do not attempt to judge.

'I put it to you,' says she, when many useless self-reproaches and protestations on his part had been uttered – 'I put it to you whether, if any manliness is left in you, you ought not to do exactly what I consider the best thing for me in this strait to which you have reduced me?'

He promised to do anything in the whole world. She then requested him to allow her to return, and announce him as having died of malignant ague immediately on their arrival at Paramaribo; that she should consequently appear in weeds as his widow in her native place; that he would never molest her, or come again to that part of the world during the whole course of his life – a good reason for which would be that the legal consequences might be serious.

He readily acquiesced in this, as he would have acquiesced in anything for the restitution of one he adored so deeply – even to the yielding of life itself. To put her in an immediate state of independence he gave her, in bonds and jewels, a considerable sum (for his worldly means had been in no way exaggerated); and by the next ship she sailed again for England, having travelled no further than to Paramaribo. At parting he declared it to be his intention to turn all his landed possessions into personal property, and to be a wanderer on the face of the earth in remorse for his conduct towards her.

Maria duly arrived in England, and immediately on landing apprised her uncle of her return, duly appearing at his house in the garb of a

widow. She was commiserated by all the neighbours as soon as her
story was told; but only to her uncle did she reveal the real state of
affairs, and her reason for concealing it. For, though she had been
innocent of wrong, Maria's pride was of that grain which could not
brook the least appearance of having been fooled, or deluded, or non-
plussed in her worldly aims.

For some time she led a quiet life with her relative, and in due
course a son was born to her. She was much respected for her dignity
and reserve, and the portable wealth which her temporary husband had
made over to her enabled her to live in comfort in a wing of the mansion,
without assistance from her uncle at all. But, knowing that she was not
what she seemed to be, her life was an uneasy one, and she often said to
herself: 'Suppose his continued existence should become known here,
and people should discern the pride of my motive in hiding my humiliation? It would be worse than if I had been frank at first, which I
should have been but for the credit of this child.'

Such grave reflections as these occupied her with increasing force;
and during their continuance she encountered a worthy man of noble
birth and title – Lord Icenway his name – whose seat was beyond
Wintoncester, quite at t'other end of Wessex. He being anxious to pay
his addresses to her, Maria willingly accepted them, though he was a
plain man, older than herself; for she discerned in a second marriage a
method of fortifying her position against mortifying discoveries. In a
few months their union took place, and Maria lifted her head as Lady
Icenway, and left with her husband and child for his home as aforesaid,
where she was quite unknown.

A justification, or a condemnation, of her step (according as you view
it) was seen when, not long after, she received a note from her former
husband Anderling. It was a hasty and tender epistle, and perhaps it
was fortunate that it arrived during the temporary absence of Lord
Icenway. His worthless wife, said Anderling, had just died in Quebec;
he had gone there to ascertain particulars, and had seen the unfortunate
woman buried. He now was hastening to England to repair the wrong
he had done his Maria. He asked her to meet him at Southampton, his
port of arrival; which she need be in no fear of doing, as he had changed
his name, and was almost absolutely unknown in Europe. He would remarry her immediately, and live with her in any part of the Continent,
as they had originally intended, where, for the great love he still bore
her, he would devote himself to her service for the rest of his days.

Lady Icenway, self-possessed as it was her nature to be, was yet much disturbed at this news, and set off to meet him, unattended, as soon as she heard that the ship was in sight. As soon as they stood face to face she found that she still possessed all her old influence over him, though his power to fascinate her had quite departed. In his sorrow for his offence against her he had become a man of strict religious habits, self-denying as a lenten saint, though formerly he had been a free and joyous liver. Having first got him to swear to make her any amends she should choose (which he was imagining must be by a true marriage), she informed him that she had already wedded another husband, an excellent man of ancient family and possessions, who had given her a title, in which she much rejoiced.

At this the countenance of the poor foreign gentleman became cold as clay, and his heart withered within him; for as it had been her beauty and bearing which had led him to sin to obtain her, so, now that her beauty was in fuller bloom, and her manner more haughty by her success, did he feel her fascination to be almost more than he could bear. Nevertheless, having sworn his word, he undertook to obey her commands, which were simply a renewal of her old request - that he would depart for some foreign country, and never reveal his existence to her friends, or husband, or any person in England; never trouble her more, seeing how great a harm it would do her in the high position which she at present occupied.

He bowed his head. 'And the child - our child?' he said.

'He is well,' says she. 'Quite well.'

With this the unhappy gentleman departed, much sadder in his heart than on his voyage to England; for it had never occurred to him that a woman who rated her honour so highly as Maria had done, and who was the mother of a child of his, would have adopted such means as this for the restoration of that honour, and at so surprisingly early a date. He had fully calculated on making her his wife in law and truth, and on living in cheerful unity with her and his offspring, for whom he felt a deep and growing tenderness, though he had never once seen the child.

The lady returned to her mansion beyond Wintoncester, and told nothing of the interview to her noble husband, who had fortunately gone that day to do a little cocking and ratting out by Weydon Priors, and knew nothing of her movements. She had dismissed her poor Anderling peremptorily enough; yet she would often after this look in the face of the child of her so-called widowhood, to discover what and how many traits of his father were to be seen in his lineaments. For this she had ample opportunity during the following autumn and winter months, her husband being a matter-of-fact nobleman, who spent the greater part of his time in field-sports and agriculture.

One winter day, when he had started for a meet of the hounds a long way from the house – it being his custom to hunt three or four times a week at this season of the year – she had walked into the sunshine upon the terrace before the windows, where there fell at her feet some little white object that had come over a boundary wall hard by. It proved to be a tiny note wrapped round a stone. Lady Icenway opened it and read it, and immediately (no doubt, with a stern fixture of her queenly countenance) walked hastily along the terrace, and through the door into the shrubbery, whence the note had come. The man who had first married her stood under the bushes before her. It was plain from his appearance that something had gone wrong with him.

'You notice a change in me, my best-beloved,' he said. 'Yes, Maria – I have lost all the wealth I once possessed – mainly by reckless gambling in the Continental hells to which you banished me. But one thing in the world remains to me – the child – and it is for him that I have intruded here. Don't fear me, darling! I shall not inconvenience you long; I love you too well! But I think of the boy day and night – I cannot help it – I cannot keep my feeling for him down; and I long to see him, and speak a word to him once in my lifetime!'

'But your oath?' says she. 'You promised never to reveal by word or sign—'

'I will reveal nothing. Only let me see the child. I know what I have sworn to you, cruel mistress, and I respect my oath. Otherwise I might have seen him by some subterfuge. But I preferred the frank course of asking your permission.'

She demurred, with the haughty severity which had grown part of her character, and which her elevation to the rank of a peeress had rather intensified than diminished. She said that she would consider, and would give him an answer the day after the next, at the same hour and place, when her husband would again be absent with his pack of hounds.

The gentleman waited patiently. Lady Icenway, who had now no conscious love left for him, well considered the matter, and felt that it would be advisable not to push to extremes a man of so passionate a heart. On the day and hour she met him as she had promised to do.

'You shall see him,' she said, 'of course on the strict condition that you do not reveal yourself, and hence, though you see him, he must not see you, or your manner might betray you and me. I will lull him into a nap in the afternoon, and then I will come to you here, and fetch you indoors by a private way.'

The unfortunate father, whose misdemeanour had recoiled upon his own head in a way he could not have foreseen, promised to adhere to her instructions, and waited in the shrubberies till the moment when she should call him. This she duly did about three o'clock that day, leading him in by a garden door, and upstairs to the nursery where the child lay. He was in his little cot, breathing calmly, his arm thrown over his head, and his silken curls crushed into the pillow. His father, now almost to be pitied, bent over him, and a tear from his eye wetted the coverlet.

She held up a warning finger as he lowered his mouth to the lips of the boy.

'But O, why not?' implored he.

'Very well, then,' said she, relenting. 'But as gently as possible.'

He kissed the child without waking him, turned, gave him a last look, and followed her out of the chamber, when she conducted him off the premises by the way he had come.

But this remedy for his sadness of heart at being a stranger to his own son had the effect of intensifying the malady; for while originally, not knowing or having ever seen the boy, he had loved him vaguely and imaginatively only, he now became attached to him in flesh and bone, as any parent might; and the feeling that he could at best only see his child at the rarest and most cursory moments, if at all, drove him into a state of distraction which threatened to overthrow his promise to the boy's mother to keep out of his sight. But such was his chivalrous respect for Lady Icenway, and his regret at having ever deceived her, that he schooled his poor heart into submission. Owing to his loneliness, all the fervour of which he was capable — and that was much — flowed now in the channel of parental and marital love — for a child who did not know him, and a woman who had ceased to love him.

At length this singular punishment became such a torture to the poor foreigner that he resolved to lessen it at all hazards, compatible with punctilious care for the name of the lady his former wife, to whom his attachment seemed to increase in proportion to her punitive treatment of him. At one time of his life he had taken great interest in tulip-culture, as well as gardening in general; and since the ruin of his fortunes, and his arrival in England, he had made of his knowledge a precarious income in the hot-houses of nurserymen and others. With the new idea in his head he applied himself zealously to the business, till he acquired in a few months great skill in horticulture. Waiting till the noble lord, his lady's husband, had room for an under-gardener of a general sort, he offered himself for the place, and was engaged immediately by reason of his civility and intelligence before Lady Icenway knew anything of the matter. Much therefore did he surprise her when she found him in the conservatories of her mansion a week or two after his arrival. The punishment of instant dismissal, with which at first she haughtily threatened him, my lady thought fit, on reflection, not to enforce. While he served her thus she knew he would not harm her by a word, while, if he were expelled, chagrin might induce him to reveal in a moment of exasperation what kind treatment would assist him to conceal.

So he was allowed to remain on the premises, and had for his residence a little cottage by the garden-wall which had been the domicile of some of his predecessors in the same occupation. Here he lived absolutely alone, and spent much of his leisure in reading, but the greater part in watching the windows and lawns of his lady's house for glimpses of the form of the child. It was for that child's sake that he abandoned the tenets of the Roman Catholic Church in which he had been reared, and became the most regular attendant at the services in the parish place of worship hard by, where, sitting behind the pew of my lady, my lord, and my lord's stepson, the gardener could pensively study the traits and movements of the youngster at only a few feet distance, without suspicion or hindrance.

He filled his post for more than two years with a pleasure to himself which, though mournful, was soothing, his lady never forgiving him, or allowing him to be anything more than 'the gardener' to her child, though once or twice the boy said, 'That gardener's eyes are so sad! Why does he look so sadly at me?' He sunned himself in her scornfulness as if it were love, and his ears drank in her curt monosyllables as though they were rhapsodies of endearment. Strangely enough, the coldness with which she treated her foreigner began to be the conduct of Lord Icenway towards herself. It was a matter of great anxiety to him that there should be a lineal successor to the barony, yet no sign of that successor had as yet appeared. One day he complained to her quite roughly of his fate. 'All will go to that dolt of a cousin!' he cried. 'I'd sooner see my name and place at the bottom of the sea!'

The lady soothed him and fell into thought, and did not recriminate. But one day, soon after, she went down to the cottage of the gardener to inquire how he was getting on, for he had been ailing of late, though, as was supposed, not seriously. Though she often visited the poor, she had never entered her under-gardener's home before, and was much surprised – even grieved and dismayed – to find that he was too ill to rise from his bed. She went back to her mansion and returned with some delicate soup, that she might have a reason for seeing him.

His condition was so feeble and alarming, and his face so thin, that it quite shocked her softening heart, and gazing upon him she said, 'You must get well – you must! *There's a reason.* I have been hard with you hitherto – I know it. I will not be so again.'

The sick and dying man – for he was dying indeed – took her hand and pressed it to his lips. 'Too late, my darling, too late!' he murmured.

'But you *must not* die! O, you must not!' she said. And on an impulse she bent down and whispered some words to him, blushing as she had blushed in her maiden days.

He replied by a faint wan smile. 'Ah – why did you not say so sooner? Time was . . . but that's past!' he said. 'I must die!'

And die he did, a few days later, as the sun was going down behind the garden-wall. Her harshness seemed to come trebly home to her then, and she remorsefully exclaimed against herself in secret and alone. Her one desire now was to erect some tribute to his memory without its being recognized as her handiwork. In the completion of this scheme there arrived a few months later a handsome stained-glass window for the church; and when it was unpacked and in course of erection Lord Icenway strolled into the building with his wife.

' "*Erected to his memory by his grieving widow*," ' he said, reading the legend on the glass. 'I didn't know that he had a wife; I've never seen her.'

'O yes, you must have, Icenway; only you forget,' replied his lady blandly. 'But she didn't live with him, and was never seen visiting him, because there were differences between them; which, as is usually the case, makes her all the more sorry now.'

'And go ruining herself by this expensive ruby-and-azure glass-design.'

'She is not poor, they say.'

As Lord Icenway grew older he became crustier and crustier, and
whenever he set eyes on his wife's boy by her other husband he would
burst out morosely, saying,

' 'Tis a very odd thing, my lady, that you could oblige your first
husband, and couldn't oblige me.'

'Ah! if I had only thought of it sooner!' she murmured.

'What?' said he.

'Nothing, dearest,' replied Lady Icenway.

The Colonel was the first to comment upon the churchwarden's tale, by
saying that the fate of the poor fellow was rather a hard one.

The gentleman-tradesman could not see that his fate was at all too
hard for him. He was legally nothing to her, and he had served her
shamefully. If he had been really her husband it would have stood
differently.

The Bookworm remarked that Lord Icenway seemed to have been a
very unsuspicious man, with which view a fat member with a crimson
face agreed. It was true his wife was a very close-mouthed personage,
which made a difference. If she had spoken out recklessly her lord
might have been suspicious enough, as in the case of that lady who lived
at Stapleford Park in their great-grandfathers' time. Though there, to be
sure, considerations arose which made her husband view matters with
much philosophy.

A few of the members doubted the possibility of this in such cases.

The crimson man, who was a retired maltster of comfortable means,
ventru, and short in stature, cleared his throat, blew off his superfluous
breath, and proceeded to give the instance before alluded to of such
possibility, first apologizing for his heroine's lack of a title, it never
having been his good fortune to know many of the nobility. To his style
of narrative the following is only an approximation.

Dame the Sixth
Squire Petrick's Lady

By the Crimson Maltster

FOLK who are at all acquainted with the traditions of Stapleford Park will not need to be told that in the middle of the last century it was owned by that trump of mortgagees, Timothy Petrick, whose skill in gaining possession of fair estates by granting sums of money on their title-deeds has seldom if ever been equalled in our part of England. Timothy was a lawyer by profession, and agent to several noblemen, by which means his special line of business became opened to him by a sort of revelation. It is said that a relative of his, a very deep thinker, who afterwards had the misfortune to be transported for life for mistaken notions on the signing of a will, taught him considerable legal lore, which he creditably resolved never to throw away for the benefit of other people, but to reserve it entirely for his own.

However, I have nothing in particular to say about his early and active days, but rather of the time when, an old man, he had become the owner of vast estates by the means I have signified – among them the great manor of Stapleford, on which he lived, in the splendid old mansion now pulled down; likewise estates at Marlott, estates near Sherton Abbas, nearly all the borough of Millpool, and many properties near Ivell. Indeed, I can't call to mind half his landed possessions, and I don't know that it matters much at this time of day, seeing that he's been dead and gone many years. It is said that when he bought an estate he would not decide to pay the price till he had walked over every single acre with his own two feet, and prodded the soil at every point with his own spud, to test its quality, which, if we regard the extent of his properties, must have been a stiff business for him.

At the time I am speaking of he was a man over eighty, and his son was dead; but he had two grandsons, the elder of whom, his namesake, was married, and was shortly expecting issue. Just then the grandfather was taken ill, for death, as it seemed, considering his age. By his will the old man had created an entail (as I believe the lawyers call it), devising the whole of the estates to his elder grandson and his issue male, failing which, to his younger grandson and his issue male, failing which, to remoter relatives, who need not be mentioned now.

While old Timothy Petrick was lying ill, his elder grandson's wife, Annetta, gave birth to her expected child, who, as fortune would have it, was a son. Timothy, her husband, though sprung of a scheming family, was no great schemer himself; he was the single one of the Petricks then living whose heart had ever been greatly moved by sentiments which did not run in the groove of ambition; and on this account he had not married well, as the saying is; his wife having been the daughter of a family of no better beginnings than his own; that is to say, her father was a country townsman of the professional class. But she was a very pretty woman, by all accounts, and her husband had seen, courted, and married her in a high tide of infatuation, after a very short acquaintance, and with very little knowledge of her heart's history. He had never found reason to regret his choice as yet, and his anxiety for her recovery was great.

She was supposed to be out of danger, and herself and the child progressing well, when there was a change for the worse, and she sank so rapidly that she was soon given over. When she felt that she was about to leave him, Annetta sent for her husband, and, on his speedy entry and assurance that they were alone, she made him solemnly vow to give the child every care in any circumstances that might arise, if it should please Heaven to take her. This, of course, he readily promised. Then, after some hesitation, she told him that she could not die with a falsehood upon her soul, and dire deceit in her life; she must make a terrible confession to him before her lips were sealed for ever. She thereupon related an incident concerning the baby's parentage, which was not as he supposed.

Timothy Petrick, though a quick-feeling man, was not of a sort to show nerves outwardly; and he bore himself as heroically as he possibly could do in this trying moment of his life. That same night his wife died; and while she lay dead, and before her funeral, he hastened to the bed-side of his sick grandfather, and revealed to him all that had happened: the baby's birth, his wife's confession, and her death, beseeching the aged man, as he loved him, to bestir himself now, at the eleventh hour, and alter his will so as to dish the intruder. Old Timothy, seeing matters in the same light as his grandson, required no urging against allowing anything to stand in the way of legitimate inheritance; he executed another will, limiting the entail to Timothy his grandson, for life, and his male heirs thereafter to be born; after them to his other grandson Edward, and Edward's heirs. Thus the newly-born infant, who had been the centre of so many hopes, was cut off, and scorned as none of the elect.

The old mortgagee lived but a short time after this, the excitement of the discovery having told upon him considerably, and he was gathered to his fathers like the most charitable man in his neighbourhood. Both wife and grandparent being buried, Timothy settled down to his usual life as well as he was able, mentally satisfied that he had by prompt action defeated the consequences of such dire domestic treachery as had been shown towards him, and resolving to marry a second time as soon as he could satisfy himself in the choice of a wife.

But men do not always know themselves. The embittered state of Timothy Petrick's mind bred in him by degrees such a hatred and mistrust of womankind that, though several specimens of high attractiveness came under his eyes, he could not bring himself to the point of proposing marriage. He dreaded to take up the position of husband a second time, discerning a trap in every petticoat, and a Slough of Despond in possible heirs. 'What has happened once, when all seemed so fair, may happen again,' he said to himself. 'I'll risk my name no more.' So he abstained from marriage, and overcame his wish for a lineal descendant to follow him in the ownership of Stapleford.

Timothy had scarcely noticed the unfortunate child that his wife had borne, after arranging for a meagre fulfilment of his promise to her to take care of the boy, by having him brought up in his house. Occasionally, remembering this promise, he went and glanced at the child, saw that he was doing well, gave a few special directions, and again went his solitary way. Thus he and the child lived on in the Stapleford mansion-house till two or three years had passed by. One day he was walking in the garden, and by some accident left his snuff-box on a bench. When he came back to find it he saw the little boy standing there; he had excaped his nurse, and was making a plaything of the box, in spite of the convulsive sneezings which the game brought in its train. Then the man with the encrusted heart became interested in the little fellow's persistence in his play under such discomforts; he looked in the child's face, saw there his wife's countenance, though he did not see his own, and

fell into thought on the piteousness of childhood – particularly of despised and rejected childhood, like this before him.

From that hour, try as he would to counteract the feeling, the human
necessity to love something or other got the better of what he had called
his wisdom, and shaped itself in a tender anxiety for the youngster
Rupert. This name had been given him by his dying mother when, at
her request, the child was baptized in her chamber, lest he should not
survive for public baptism; and her husband had never thought of it as a
name of any significance till, about this time, he learnt by accident that
it was the name of the young Marquis of Christminster, son of the Duke
of Southwesterland, for whom Annetta had cherished warm feelings
before her marriage. Recollecting some wandering phrases in his wife's
last words, which he had not understood at the time, he perceived at last
that this was the person to whom she had alluded when affording him a
clue to little Rupert's history.

He would sit in silence for hours with the child, being no great
speaker at the best of times; but the boy, on his part, was too ready with
his tongue for any break in discourse to arise because Timothy Petrick
had nothing to say. After idling away his mornings in this manner,
Petrick would go to his own room and swear in long loud whispers, and
walk up and down, calling himself the most ridiculous dolt that ever
lived, and declaring that he would never go near the little fellow again;
to which resolve he would adhere for the space perhaps of a day. Such
cases are happily not new to human nature, but there never was a
case in which a man more completely befooled his former self than in
this.

As the child grew up, Timothy's attachment to him grew deeper, till
Rupert became almost the sole object for which he lived. There had been
enough of the family ambition latent in him for Timothy Petrick to feel
a little envy when, some time before this date, his brother Edward had
been accepted by the Honourable Harriet Mountclere, daughter of the
second Viscount of that name and title; but having discovered, as I have
before stated, the paternity of his boy Rupert to lurk in even a higher
stratum of society, those envious feelings speedily dispersed. Indeed,
the more he reflected thereon, after his brother's aristocratic marriage,
the more content did he become. His late wife took softer outline in his
memory, as he thought of the lofty taste she had displayed, though only
a plain burgher's daughter, and the justification for his weakness in
loving the child – the justification that he had longed for – was afforded

now in the knowledge that the boy was by nature, if not by name, a representative of one of the noblest houses in England.

'She was a woman of grand instincts, after all,' he said to himself proudly. 'To fix her choice upon the immediate successor in that ducal line – it was finely conceived! Had he been of low blood like myself or my relations she would scarce have deserved the harsh measure that I have dealt out to her and her offspring. How much less, then, when such grovelling tastes were furthest from her soul! The man Annetta loved was noble, and my boy is noble in spite of me.'

The afterclap was inevitable, and it soon came. 'So far,' he reasoned, 'from cutting off this child from inheritance of my estates, as I have done, I should have rejoiced in the possession of him! He is of blue stock on one side at least, whilst in the ordinary run of affairs he would have been a commoner to the bone.'

Being a man, whatever his faults, of good old beliefs in the divinity of kings and those about 'em, the more he overhauled the case in this light, the more strongly did his poor wife's conduct in improving the blood and breed of the Petrick family win his heart. He considered what ugly, idle, hard-drinking scamps many of his own relations had been; the miserable scriveners, usurers, and pawnbrokers that he had numbered among his forefathers, and the probability that some of their bad qualities would have come out in a merely corporeal child of his loins, to give him sorrow in his old age, turn his black hairs gray, his gray hairs white, cut down every stick of timber, and Heaven knows what all, had he not, or rather his good wife, like a skilful gardener, given attention to the art of grafting, and changed the sort; till at length this right-minded man fell down on his knees every night and morning and thanked God that he was not as other meanly descended fathers in such matters.

It was in the peculiar disposition of the Petrick family that the satisfaction which ultimately settled in Timothy's breast found nourishment. The Petricks had adored the nobility, and plucked them at the same time. That excellent man Izaak Walton's feelings about fish were much akin to those of old Timothy Petrick, and of his descendants in a lesser degree, concerning the landed aristocracy. To torture and to love simultaneously is a proceeding strange to reason, but possible to practice, as these instances show.

Hence, when Timothy's brother Edward said slightingly one day that Timothy's son was well enough, but that he had nothing but shops and offices in his backward historical perspective, while his own children, should he have any, would be far different, in possessing such a mother as the Honourable Harriet, Timothy felt a bound of triumph within him at the power he possessed of contradicting that statement if he chose.

So much was he interested in his boy in this new aspect that he now began to read up chronicles of the illustrious house ennobled as the Dukes of Southwesterland, from their very beginning in the glories of the Restoration of the blessed Charles till the year of his own time. He mentally noted their gifts from royalty, grants of lands, purchases, intermarriages, plantings and buildings; more particularly their political and military achievements, which had been great, and their performances in art and letters, which had been by no means contemptible. He studied prints of the portraits of that family, and then, like a chemist watching a crystallization, began to examine young Rupert's face for the unfolding of those historic curves and shades that the painters Vandyke and Lely had perpetuated on canvas.

When the boy reached the most fascinating age of childhood, and his shouts of laughter ran through Stapleford House from end to end, the remorse that oppressed Timothy Petrick knew no bounds. Of all people in the world this Rupert was the one on whom he could have wished the estates to devolve; yet Rupert, by Timothy's own desperate strategy at the time of his birth, had been ousted from all inheritance of them; and, since he did not mean to remarry, the manors would pass to his brother and his brother's children, who would be nothing to him, and whose boasted pedigree on one side would be nothing to his Rupert's after all.

Had he only left the first will of his grandfather alone!

His mind ran on the wills continually, both of which were in existence, and the first, the cancelled one, in his own possession. Night after night, when the servants were all abed, and the click of safety locks sounded as loud as a crash, he looked at that first will, and wished it had been the second and not the first.

The crisis came at last. One night, after having enjoyed the boy's company for hours, he could no longer bear that his beloved Rupert of the aristocratic blood should be dispossessed; and he committed the felonious deed of altering the date of the earlier will to a fortnight later, which made its execution appear subsequent to the date of the second will already proved. He then boldly propounded the first will as the second.

His brother Edward submitted to what appeared to be not only incontestable fact, but a far more likely disposition of old Timothy's property; for, like many others, he had been much surprised at the limitations defined in the other will, having no clue to their cause. He joined his brother Timothy in setting aside the hitherto accepted document, and matters went on in their usual course, there being no dispositions in the substituted will differing from those in the other, except such as related to a future which had not yet arrived.

The years moved on. Rupert had not yet revealed the anxiously expected historic lineaments which should foreshadow the political abilities of the ducal family aforesaid, when it happened on a certain day that Timothy Petrick made the acquaintance of a well-known physician of Budmouth, who had been the medical adviser and friend of the late Mrs Petrick's family for many years; though after Annetta's marriage, and consequent removal to Stapleford, he had seen no more of her, the neighbouring practitioner who attended the Petricks having then become her doctor as a matter of course. Timothy was impressed by the insight and knowledge disclosed in the conversation of the Budmouth physician, and the acquaintance ripening to intimacy, the physician alluded to a form of hallucination to which Annetta's mother and grandmother had been subject – that of believing in certain dreams as realities. He delicately inquired if Timothy had ever noticed anything of the sort in his wife during her lifetime; he, the physician, had fancied that he discerned germs of the same peculiarity in Annetta when he attended her in her girlhood. One explanation begat another, till the dumbfoundered Timothy Petrick was persuaded in his own mind that Annetta's confession to him had been based on a delusion.

'You look down in the mouth?' said the doctor, pausing.

'A bit unmanned. 'Tis unexpected-like,' sighed Timothy.

But he could hardly believe it possible; and, thinking it best to be frank with the doctor, told him the whole story which, till now, he had never related to living man, save his dying grandfather. To his surprise, the physician informed him that such a form of delusion was precisely what he would have expected from Annetta's antecedents at such a physical crisis in her life.

Petrick prosecuted his inquiries elsewhere; and the upshot of his labours was, briefly, that a comparison of dates and places showed irrefutably that his poor wife's assertion could not possibly have foundation in fact. The young Marquis of her tender passion – a highly moral and bright-minded nobleman – had gone abroad the year before

Annetta's marriage, and had not returned till after her death. The young girl's love for him had been a delicate ideal dream – no more.

Timothy went home, and the boy ran out to meet him; whereupon a strangely dismal feeling of discontent took possession of his soul. After all, then, there was nothing but plebeian blood in the veins of the heir to his name and estates; he was not to be succeeded by a noble-natured line. To be sure, Rupert was his son physically; but that glory and halo he believed him to have inherited from the ages, outshining that of his brother's children, had departed from Rupert's brow for ever; he could no longer read history in the boy's face, and centuries of domination in his eyes.

His manner towards his son grew colder and colder from that day forward; and it was with bitterness of heart that he discerned the characteristic features of the Petricks unfolding themselves by degrees. Instead of the elegant knife-edged nose, so typical of the Dukes of Southwesterland, there began to appear on his face the broad nostril and hollow bridge of his grandfather Timothy. No illustrious line of politicians was promised a continuator in that graying blue eye, for it was acquiring the expression of the orb of a particularly objectionable cousin of his own; and, instead of the mouth-curves which had thrilled Parliamentary audiences in speeches now bound in calf in every well-ordered library, there was the bull-lip of that very uncle of his who had had the misfortune with the signature of a gentleman's will, and had been transported for life in consequence.

To think how he himself, too, had sinned in this same matter of a will for this mere fleshly reproduction of a wretched old uncle whose very name he wished to forget! The boy's Christian name, even, was an imposture and an irony, for it implied hereditary force and brilliancy to which he plainly would never attain. The consolation of real sonship was always left him certainly; but he could not help groaning to himself, 'Why cannot a son be one's own and somebody else's likewise!'

The Marquis was shortly afterwards in the neighbourhood of Stapleford, and Timothy Petrick met him, and eyed his noble countenance admiringly. The next day, when Petrick was in his study, somebody knocked at the door.

'Who's there?'

'Rupert.'

'I'll Rupert thee, you young impostor! Say, only a poor commonplace Petrick!' his father grunted. 'Why didn't you have a voice like the

Marquis's I saw yesterday?' he continued, as the lad came in. 'Why haven't you his looks, and a way of commanding, as if you'd done it for centuries – hey?'

'Why? How can you expect it, father, when I'm not related to him?'

'Ugh! Then you ought to be!' growled his father.

As the narrator paused, the surgeon, the Colonel, the historian, the Spark, and others exclaimed that such subtle and instructive psychological studies as this (now that psychology was so much in demand) were precisely the tales they desired, as members of a scientific club, and begged the master-maltster to tell another curious mental delusion.

The maltster shook his head, and feared he was not genteel enough to tell another story with a sufficiently moral tone in it to suit the club; he would prefer to leave the next to a better man.

The Colonel had fallen into reflection. True it was, he observed, that the more dreamy and impulsive nature of woman engendered within her erratic fancies, which often started her on strange tracks, only to abandon them in sharp revulsion at the dictates of her common sense – sometimes with ludicrous effect. Events which had caused a lady's action to set in a particular direction might continue to enforce the same line of conduct, while she, like a mangle, would start on a sudden in a contrary course, and end where she began.

The Vice-President laughed, and applauded the Colonel, adding that there surely lurked a story somewhere behind that sentiment, if he were not much mistaken.

The Colonel fixed his face to a good narrative pose, and went on without further preamble.

Dame the Seventh
Anna, Lady Baxby

By the Colonel

IT was in the time of the great Civil War – if I should not rather, as a loyal subject, call it, with Clarendon, the Great Rebellion. It was, I say, at that unhappy period of our history that, towards the autumn of a particular year, the Parliament forces sat down before Sherton Castle with over seven thousand foot and four pieces of cannon. The Castle, as we all know, was in that century owned and occupied by one of the Earls of Severn, and garrisoned for his assistance by a certain noble Marquis who commanded the King's troops in these parts. The said Earl, as well as the young Lord Baxby, his eldest son, were away from home just now, raising forces for the King elsewhere. But there were present in the Castle, when the besiegers arrived before it, the son's fair wife Lady Baxby, and her servants, together with some friends and near relatives of her husband; and the defence was so good and well-considered that they anticipated no great danger.

The Parliamentary forces were also commanded by a noble lord – for the nobility were by no means, at this stage of the war, all on the King's side – and it had been observed during his approach in the night-time, and in the morning when the reconnoitring took place, that he appeared sad and much depressed. The truth was that, by a strange freak of destiny, it had come to pass that the stronghold he was set to reduce was the home of his own sister, whom he had tenderly loved during her maidenhood, and whom he loved now, in spite of the estrangement which had resulted from hostilities with her husband's family. He believed, too, that, notwithstanding this cruel division, she still was sincerely attached to him.

His hesitation to point his ordnance at the walls was inexplicable to those who were strangers to his family history. He remained in the field on the north side of the Castle (called by his name to this day because of his encampment there) till it occurred to him to send a messenger to his sister Anna with a letter, in which he earnestly requested her, as she valued her life, to steal out of the place by the little gate to the south, and make away in that direction to the residence of some friends.

Shortly after he saw, to his great surprise, coming from the front of the Castle walls a lady on horseback, with a single attendant. She rode straight forward into the field, and up the slope to where his army and tents were spread. It was not till she got quite near that he discerned her to be his sister Anna; and much was he alarmed that she should have run such risk as to sally out in the face of his forces without knowledge of their proceedings, when at any moment their first discharge might have burst forth, to her own destruction in such exposure. She dismounted before she was quite close to him, and he saw that her familiar face, though pale, was not at all tearful, as it would have been in their younger days. Indeed, if the particulars as handed down are to be believed, he was in a more tearful state than she, in his anxiety about her. He called her into his tent, out of the gaze of those around; for though many of the soldiers were honest and serious-minded men, he could not bear that she who had been his dear companion in childhood should be exposed to curious observation in this her great grief.

When they were alone in the tent he clasped her in his arms, for he had not seen her since those happier days when, at the commencement of the war, her husband and himself had been of the same mind about the arbitrary conduct of the King, and had little dreamt that they would not go to extremes together. She was the calmer of the two, it is said, and was the first to speak connectedly.

'William, I have come to you,' said she, 'but not to save myself as you suppose. Why, O, why do you persist in supporting this disloyal cause, and grieving us so?'

'Say not that,' he replied hastily. 'If truth hides at the bottom of a well, why should you suppose justice to be in high places? I am for the right at any price. Anna, leave the Castle; you are my sister; come away, my dear, and save thy life!'

'Never!' says she. 'Do you plan to carry out this attack, and level the Castle indeed?'

'Most certainly I do,' says he. 'What meaneth this army around us if not so?'

'Then you will find the bones of your sister buried in the ruins you cause!' said she. And without another word she turned and left him.

'Anna – abide with me!' he entreated. 'Blood is thicker than water, and what is there in common between you and your husband now?'

But she shook her head and would not hear him; and hastening out, mounted her horse, and returned towards the Castle as she had come. Ay, many's the time when I have been riding to hounds across that field that I have thought of that scene!

When she had quite gone down the field, and over the intervening ground, and round the bastion, so that he could no longer even see the tip of her mare's white tail, he was much more deeply moved by emotions concerning her and her welfare than he had been while she was before him. He wildly reproached himself that he had not detained her by force for her own good, so that, come what might, she would be under his protection and not under that of her husband, whose impulsive nature rendered him too open to instantaneous impressions and sudden changes of plan; he was now acting in this cause and now in that, and lacked the cool judgment necessary for the protection of a woman in these troubled times. Her brother thought of her words again and again, and sighed, and even considered if a sister were not of more value than a principle, and if he would not have acted more naturally in throwing in his lot with hers.

The delay of the besiegers in attacking the Castle was said to be entirely owing to this distraction on the part of their leader, who remained on the spot attempting some indecisive operations, and parleying with the Marquis then in command, with far inferior forces, within the Castle. It never occurred to him that in the meantime the young Lady Baxby, his sister, was in much the same mood as himself. Her brother's familiar voice and eyes, much worn and fatigued by keeping the field, and by family distractions on account of this unhappy feud, rose upon her vision all the afternoon, and as day waned she grew more and more Parliamentarian in her principles, though the only arguments which had addressed themselves to her were those of family ties.

Her husband, General Lord Baxby, had been expected to return all the day from his excursion into the east of the county, a message having been sent to him informing him of what had happened at home; and in the evening he arrived with reinforcements in unexpected numbers. Her brother retreated before these to a hill near Ivell, four or five miles off, to afford the men and himself some repose. Lord Baxby duly placed his forces, and there was no longer any immediate danger. By this time Lady Baxby's feelings were more Parliamentarian than ever, and in her fancy the fagged countenance of her brother, beaten back by her husband, seemed to reproach her for heartlessness. When her husband entered her apartment, ruddy and boisterous, and full of hope, she received him but sadly; and upon his casually uttering some slight-ing words about her brother's withdrawal, which seemed to convey an imputation upon his courage, she resented them, and retorted that he, Lord Baxby himself, had been against the Court-party at first, where it would be much more to his credit if he were at present, and showing her brother's consistency of opinion, instead of supporting the lying policy of the King (as she called it) for the sake of a barren principle of loyalty, which was but an empty expression when a King was not at one with his people. The dissension grew bitter between them, reaching to little less than a hot quarrel, both being quick-tempered souls.

Lord Baxby was weary with his long day's march and other ex-citements, and soon retired to bed. His lady followed some time after. Her husband slept profoundly, but not so she; she sat brooding by the window-slit, and lifting the curtain looked forth upon the hills without.

In the silence between the footfalls of the sentinels she could hear faint sounds of her brother's camp on the distant hills, where the soldiery had hardly settled as yet into their bivouac since their evening's retreat. The first frosts of autumn had touched the grass, and shrivelled the more delicate leaves of the creepers; and she thought of William sleeping on the chilly ground, under the strain of these hardships. Tears flooded her eyes as she returned to her husband's imputations upon his courage, as if there could be any doubt of Lord William's courage after what he had done in the past days.

Lord Baxby's long and reposeful breathings in his comfortable bed vexed her now, and she came to a determination on an impulse. Hastily lighting a taper, she wrote on a scrap of paper:

'*Blood is thicker than water, dear William – I will come*'; and with this in her hand, she went to the door of the room, and out upon the stairs; on second thoughts turning back for a moment, to put on her husband's hat and cloak – not the one he was daily wearing – that if seen in the twilight she might at a casual glance appear as some lad or hanger-on of one of the household women; thus accoutred she descended a flight of circular stairs, at the bottom of which was a door opening upon the terrace towards the west, in the direction of her brother's position. Her object was to slip out without the sentry seeing her, get to the stables, arouse one of the varlets, and send him ahead of her along the highway with the note to warn her brother of her approach to throw in her lot with his.

She was still in the shadow of the wall on the west terrace, waiting for the sentinel to be quite out of the way, when her ears were greeted by a voice, saying, from the adjoining shade –

'Here I be!'

The tones were the tones of a woman. Lady Baxby made no reply, and stood close to the wall.

'My Lord Baxby,' the voice continued; and she could recognize in it the local accent of some girl from the little town of Sherton, close at hand. 'I be tired of waiting, my dear Lord Baxby! I was afeared you would never come!'

Lady Baxby flushed hot to her toes.

'How the wench loves him!' she said to herself, reasoning from the tones of the voice, which were plaintive and sweet and tender as a bird's. She changed from the home-hating truant to the strategic wife in one moment.

'Hist!' she said.

'My lord, you told me ten o'clock, and 'tis near twelve now,' continues the other. 'How could ye keep me waiting so if you love me as you said? I should have stuck to my lover in the Parliament troops if it had not been for thee, my dear lord!'

There was not the least doubt that Lady Baxby had been mistaken for her husband by this intriguing damsel. Here was a pretty underhand business! Here were sly manœuvrings! Here was faithlessness! Here was a precious assignation surprised in the midst! Her wicked husband, whom till this very moment she had ever deemed the soul of good faith – how could he!

Lady Baxby precipitately retreated to the door in the turret, closed it, locked it, and ascended one round of the staircase, where there was a loophole. 'I am not coming! I, Lord Baxby, despise 'ee and all your wanton tribe!' she hissed through the opening; and then crept upstairs as firmly rooted in Royalist principles as any man in the Castle.

Her husband still slept the sleep of the weary, well-fed, and well-drunken, if not of the virtuous; and Lady Baxby quickly disrobed herself without assistance – being, indeed, supposed by her woman to have retired to rest long ago. Before lying down she noiselessly locked the door and placed the key under her pillow. More than that, she got a staylace, and, creeping up to her lord, in great stealth tied the lace in a tight knot to one of his long locks of hair, attaching the other end of the lace to the bedpost; for, being tired herself now, she feared she might sleep heavily; and, if her husband should wake, this would be a delicate hint that she had discovered all.

It is added that, to make assurance trebly sure, her gentle ladyship, when she had lain down to rest, held her lord's hand in her own during the whole of the night. But this is old-wives' gossip, and not corroborated. What Lord Baxby thought and said when he awoke the next morning, and found himself so strangely tethered, is likewise only matter of conjecture; though there is no reason to suppose that his rage was great. The extent of his culpability as regards the intrigue was this much: that, while halting at a cross-road near Sherton that day, he had flirted with a pretty young woman, who seemed nothing loth, and had invited her to the Castle terrace after dark – an invitation which he quite forgot on his arrival home.

The subsequent relations of Lord and Lady Baxby were not again greatly embittered by quarrels, so far as is known; though the husband's conduct in later life was occasionally eccentric, and the vicissitudes of his public career culminated in long exile. The siege of the Castle was not regularly undertaken till two or three years later than the time I have been describing, when Lady Baxby and all the women therein, except the wife of the then Governor, had been removed to safe distance. That memorable siege of fifteen days by Fairfax, and the surrender of the old place on an August evening, is matter of history, and need not be told by me.

The Man of Family spoke approvingly across to the Colonel when the Club had done smiling, declaring that the story was an absolutely faithful page of history, as he had good reason to know, his own people having been engaged in that well-known scrimmage. He asked if the Colonel had ever heard the equally well-authenticated, though less martial tale of a certain Lady Penelope, who lived in the same century, and not a score of miles from the same place?

The Colonel had not heard it, nor had anybody except the local historian; and the inquirer was induced to proceed forthwith.

Dame the Eighth
The Lady Penelope

By the Man of Family

IN going out of Casterbridge by the low-lying road which eventually
conducts to the town of Ivell, you see on the right hand an ivied manor-
house, flanked by battlemented towers, and more than usually distinguished by the size of its many mullioned windows. Though still of
good capacity, the building is somewhat reduced from its original grand
proportions; it has, moreover, been shorn of the fair estate which once
appertained to its lord, with the exception of a few acres of park-land
immediately around the mansion. This was formerly the seat of the
ancient and knightly family of the Drenghards, or Drenkhards, now
extinct in the male line, whose name, according to the local chronicles,
was interpreted to mean *Strenuus Miles, vel Potator*, though certain
members of the family were averse to the latter signification, and
a duel was fought by one of them on that account, as is well known. With
this, however, we are not now concerned.

In the early part of the reign of the first King James there was visiting
near this place of the Drenghards a lady of noble family and extraordinary beauty. She was of the purest descent; ah, there's seldom such
blood nowadays as hers! She possessed no great wealth, it was said, but
was sufficiently endowed. Her beauty was so perfect, and her manner so
entrancing, that suitors seemed to spring out of the ground wherever she
went, a sufficient cause of anxiety to the Countess her mother, her only
living parent. Of these there were three in particular, whom neither her
mother's complaints of prematurity, nor the ready raillery of the maiden
herself, could effectually put off. The said gallants were a certain Sir
John Gale, a Sir William Hervy, and the well-known Sir George
Drenghard, one of the Drenghard family before-mentioned. They had,
curiously enough, all been equally honoured with the distinction of

knighthood, and their schemes for seeing her were manifold, each fearing that one of the others would steal a march over himself. Not content with calling, on every imaginable excuse, at the house of the relative with whom she sojourned, they intercepted her in rides and in walks; and if any one of them chanced to surprise another in the act of paying her marked attentions, the encounter often ended in an altercation of great violence. So heated and impassioned, indeed, would they become, that the lady hardly felt herself safe in their company at such times, notwithstanding that she was a brave and buxom damsel, not easily put out, and with a daring spirit of humour in her composition, if not of coquetry.

At one of these altercations, which had place in her relative's grounds, and was unusually bitter, threatening to result in a duel, she found it necessary to assert herself. Turning haughtily upon the pair of disputants, she declared that whichever should be the first to break the peace between them, no matter what the provocation, that man should never be admitted to her presence again; and thus would she effectually stultify the aggressor by making the promotion of a quarrel a distinct bar to its object.

While the two knights were wearing rather a crestfallen appearance at her reprimand, the third, never far off, came upon the scene, and she repeated her caveat to him also. Seeing, then, how great was the concern of all at her peremptory mood, the lady's manner softened, and she said with a roguish smile –

'Have patience, have patience, you foolish men! Only bide your time quietly, and, in faith, I will marry you all in turn!'

They laughed heartily at this sally, all three together, as though they were the best of friends; at which she blushed, and showed some embarrassment, not having realized that her arch jest would have sounded so strange when uttered. The meeting which resulted thus, however, had its good effect in checking the bitterness of their rivalry; and they repeated her speech to their relatives and acquaintance with a hilarious frequency and publicity that the lady little divined, or she might have blushed and felt more embarrassment still.

In the course of time the position resolved itself, and the beauteous Lady Penelope (as she was called) made up her mind; her choice being the eldest of the three knights, Sir George Drenghard, owner of the mansion aforesaid, which thereupon became her home; and her husband being a pleasant man, and his family, though not so noble, of as good repute as her own, all things seemed to show that she had reckoned wisely in honouring him with her preference.

But what may lie behind the still and silent veil of the future none can foretell. In the course of a few months the husband of her choice died of his convivialities (as if, indeed, to bear out his name), and the Lady Penelope was left alone as mistress of his house. By this time she had apparently quite forgotten her careless declaration to her lovers collectively; but the lovers themselves had not forgotten it; and, as she would now be free to take a second one of them, Sir John Gale appeared at her door as early in her widowhood as it was proper and seemly to do so.

She gave him little encouragement; for, of the two remaining, her best beloved was Sir William, of whom, if the truth must be told, she had often thought during her short married life. But he had not yet reappeared. Her heart began to be so much with him now that she contrived to convey to him, by indirect hints through his friends, that she would not be displeased by a renewal of his former attentions. Sir William, however, misapprehended her gentle signalling, and from excellent, though mistaken motives of delicacy, delayed to intrude himself upon her for a long time. Meanwhile Sir John, now created a baronet, was unremitting, and she began to grow somewhat piqued at the backwardness of him she secretly desired to be forward.

'Never mind,' her friends said jestingly to her (knowing of her humorous remark, as everybody did, that she would marry them all three if they would have patience) – 'never mind; why hesitate upon the order of them? Take 'em as they come.'

This vexed her still more, and regretting deeply, as she had often done, that such a careless speech should ever have passed her lips, she fairly broke down under Sir John's importunity, and accepted his hand. They were married on a fine spring morning, about the very time at which the unfortunate Sir William discovered her preference for him, and was beginning to hasten home from a foreign court to declare his unaltered devotion to her. On his arrival in England he learnt the sad truth.

If Sir William suffered at her precipitancy under what she had deemed his neglect, the Lady Penelope herself suffered more. She had not long been the wife of Sir John Gale before he showed a disposition to retaliate upon her for the trouble and delay she had put him to in winning her. With increasing frequency he would tell her that, as far as he could perceive, she was an article not worth such labour as he had bestowed in obtaining it, and such snubbings as he had taken from his rivals on the same account. These and other cruel things he repeated till he made the lady weep sorely, and wellnigh broke her spirit, though she had formerly been such a mettlesome dame. By degrees it became perceptible to all her friends that her life was a very unhappy one; and the fate of the fair woman seemed yet the harder in that it was her own stately mansion, left to her sole use by her first husband, which her second had entered into and was enjoying, his being but a mean and meagre erection.

But such is the flippancy of friends that when she met them, and secretly confided her grief to their ears, they would say cheerily, 'Lord, never mind, my dear; there's a third to come yet!' – at which maladroit remark she would show much indignation, and tell them they should know better than to trifle on so solemn a theme. Yet that the poor lady would have been only too happy to be the wife of the third, instead of Sir John whom she had taken, was painfully obvious, and much she was blamed for her foolish choice by some people. Sir William, however, had returned to foreign cities on learning the news of her marriage, and had never been heard of since.

Two or three years of suffering were passed by Lady Penelope as the despised and chidden wife of this man Sir John, amid regrets that she had so greatly mistaken him, and sighs for one whom she thought never to see again, till it chanced that her husband fell sick of some slight ailment. One day after this, when she was sitting in his room, looking from the window upon the expanse in front, she beheld, approaching the house on foot, a form she seemed to know well. Lady Penelope withdrew silently from the sickroom, and descended to the hall, whence, through the doorway, she saw entering between the two round towers which at that time flanked the gateway, Sir William Hervy, as she had surmised, but looking thin and travel-worn. She advanced into the courtyard to meet him.

'I was passing through Casterbridge,' he said, with faltering deference, 'and I walked out to ask after your ladyship's health. I felt that I could do no less; and, of course, to pay my respects to your good husband, my heretofore acquaintance. . . . But O, Penelope, th'st look sick and sorry!'

'I am heartsick, that's all,' said she.

They could see in each other an emotion which neither wished to express, and they stood thus a long time with tears in their eyes.

'He does not treat 'ee well, I hear,' said Sir William in a low voice. 'May God in Heaven forgive him; but it is asking a great deal!'

'Hush, hush!' said she hastily.

'Nay, but I will speak what I may honestly say,' he answered. 'I am not under your roof, and my tongue is free. Why didst not wait for me, Penelope, or send to me a more overt letter? I would have travelled night and day to come!'

'Too late, William; you must not ask it,' said she, endeavouring to quiet him as in old times. 'My husband just now is unwell. He will grow better in a day or two, maybe. You must call again and see him before you leave Casterbridge.'

As she said this their eyes met. Each was thinking of her lightsome words about taking the three men in turn; each thought that two-thirds of that promise had been fulfilled. But as if it were unpleasant to her that this recollection should have arisen, she spoke again quickly: 'Come again in a day or two, when my husband will be well enough to see you.'

Sir William departed without entering the house, and she returned to Sir John's chamber. He, rising from his pillow, said, 'To whom hast been talking, wife, in th' courtyard? I heard voices there.'

She hesitated, and he repeated the question more impatiently.

'I do not wish to tell you now,' said she.

'But I will know!' said he.

Then she answered, 'Sir William Hervy.'

'By God, I thought as much!' cried Sir John, drops of perspiration standing on his white face. 'A skulking villain! A sick man's ears are keen, my lady. I heard that they were lover-like tones, and he called 'ee by your Christian name. These be your intrigues, my lady, when I am off my legs a while!'

'On my honour,' cried she, 'you do me a wrong. I swear I did not know of his coming!'

'Swear as you will,' said Sir John, 'I don't believe 'ee.' And with this he taunted her, and worked himself into a greater passion, which much increased his illness. His lady sat still, brooding. There was that upon her face which had seldom been there since her marriage; and she seemed to think anew of what she had so lightly said in the days of her freedom, when her three lovers were one and all coveting her hand. 'I began at the wrong end of them,' she murmured. 'My God – that did I!'

'What?' said he.

'A trifle,' said she. 'I spoke to myself only.'

It was somewhat strange that after this day, while she went about the house with even a sadder face than usual, her churlish husband grew worse; and what was more, to the surprise of all, though to the regret of few, he died a fortnight later. Sir William had not called upon him as he had promised, having received a private communication from Lady Penelope, frankly informing him that to do so would be inadvisable, by reason of her husband's temper.

Now when Sir John was gone, and his remains carried to his family burying-place in another part of England, the lady began in due time to wonder whither Sir William had betaken himself. But she had been cured of precipitancy (if ever woman were), and was prepared to wait her whole lifetime a widow if the said Sir William should not reappear. Her life was now passed mostly within the walls, or in promenading between the pleasaunce and the bowling-green; and she very seldom went even so far as the high road which then gave entrance from the north, though it has now, and for many years, been diverted to the south side. Her patience was rewarded (if love be in any case a reward); for one day, many months after her second husband's death, a messenger arrived at her gate with the intelligence that Sir William Hervy was again in Casterbridge, and would be glad to know if it were her pleasure that he should wait upon her.

It need hardly be said that permission was joyfully granted, and within two hours her lover stood before her, a more thoughtful man than formerly, but in all essential respects the same man, generous, modest to diffidence, and sincere. The reserve which womanly decorum threw over her manner was but too obviously artificial, and when he said, 'The ways of Providence are strange,' and added after a moment, 'and merciful likewise,' she could not conceal her agitation, and burst into tears upon his neck.

'But this is too soon,' she said, starting back.

'But no,' said he. 'You are eleven months gone in widowhood, and it is not as if Sir John had been a good husband to you.'

His visits grew pretty frequent now, as may well be guessed, and in a month or two he began to urge her to an early union. But she counselled a little longer delay.

'Why?' said he. 'Surely I have waited long! Life is short; we are getting older every day, and I am the last of the three.'

'Yes,' said the lady frankly. 'And that is why I would not have you hasten. Our marriage may seem so strange to everybody, after my

unlucky remark on that occasion we know so well, and which so many
others know likewise, thanks to talebearers.'

On this representation he conceded a little space, for the sake of her
good name. But the destined day of their marriage at last arrived, and it
was a gay time for the villagers and all concerned, and the bells in the
parish church rang from noon till night. Thus at last she was united to
the man who had loved her the most tenderly of them all, who but for
his reticence might perhaps have been the first to win her. Often did he
say to himself, 'How wondrous that her words should have been
fulfilled! Many a truth hath been spoken in jest, but never a more
remarkable one!' The noble lady herself preferred not to dwell on the
coincidence, a certain shyness, if not shame, crossing her fair face at any
allusion thereto.

But people will have their say, sensitive souls or none, and their sayings
on this third occasion took a singular shape. 'Surely,' they whispered,
'there is something more than chance in this. . . . The death of the first
was possibly natural; but what of the death of the second, who ill-used
her, and whom, loving the third so desperately, she must have wished
out of the way?'

Then they pieced together sundry trivial incidents of Sir John's
illness, and dwelt upon the indubitable truth that he had grown worse
after her lover's unexpected visit; till a very sinister theory was built up
as to the hand she may have had in Sir John's premature demise. But
nothing of this suspicion was said openly, for she was a lady of noble
birth – nobler, indeed, than either of her husbands – and what people
suspected they feared to express in formal accusation.

The mansion that she occupied had been left to her for so long a time
as she should choose to reside in it, and, having a regard for the spot, she
had coaxed Sir William to remain there. But in the end it was unfortunate; for one day, when in the full tide of his happiness, he was
walking among the willows near the gardens, where he overheard a
conversation between some basketmakers who were cutting the osiers for
their use. In this fatal dialogue the suspicions of the neighbouring
townsfolk were revealed to him for the first time.

'A cupboard close to his bed, and the key in her pocket. Ah!' said one.

'And a blue phial therein – h'm!' said another.

'And spurge-laurel leaves among the hearth-ashes. Oh-oh!' said a
third.

On his return home Sir William seemed to have aged years. But he said nothing; indeed, it was a thing impossible. And from that hour a ghastly estrangement began. She could not understand it, and simply waited. One day he said, however, 'I must go abroad.'

'Why?' said she. 'William, have I offended you?'

'No,' said he; 'but I must go.'

She could coax little more out of him, and in itself there was nothing unnatural in his departure, for he had been a wanderer from his youth. In a few days he started off, apparently quite another man than he who had rushed to her side so devotedly a few months before.

It is not known when, or how, the rumours, which were so thick in the atmosphere around her, actually reached the Lady Penelope's ears, but that they did reach her there is no doubt. It was impossible that they should not; the district teemed with them; they rustled in the air like night-birds of evil omen. Then a reason for her husband's departure occurred to her appalled mind, and a loss of health became quickly apparent. She dwindled thin in the face, and the veins in her temples could all be distinctly traced. An inner fire seemed to be withering her away. Her rings fell off her fingers, and her arms hung like the flails of the threshers, though they had till lately been so round and so elastic. She wrote to her husband repeatedly, begging him to return to her; but he, being in extreme and wretched doubt, moreover, knowing nothing of her ill-health, and never suspecting that the rumours had reached her also, deemed absence best, and postponed his return a while, giving various good reasons for his delay.

At length, however, when the Lady Penelope had given birth to a still-born child, her mother, the Countess, addressed a letter to Sir William, requesting him to come back to her if he wished to see her alive; since she was wasting away of some mysterious disease, which seemed to be rather mental than physical. It was evident that his mother-in-law knew nothing of the secret, for she lived at a distance; but Sir William promptly hastened home, and stood beside the bed of his now dying wife.

'Believe me, William,' she said when they were alone, 'I am innocent – innocent!'

'Of what?' said he. 'Heaven forbid that I should accuse you of anything!'

'But you do accuse me – silently!' she gasped. 'I could not write thereon – and ask you to hear me. It was too much, too degrading. But would that I had been less proud! They suspect me of poisoning him,

William! But, O my dear husband, I am innocent of that wicked crime! He died naturally. I loved you – too soon; but that was all!'

Nothing availed to save her. The worm had gnawed too far into her heart before Sir William's return for anything to be remedial now; and in a few weeks she breathed her last. After her death the people spoke louder, and her conduct became a subject of public discussion. A little later on, the physician who had attended the late Sir John heard the rumour, and came down from the place near London to which he latterly had retired, with the express purpose of calling upon Sir William Hervy, now staying in Casterbridge.

He stated that, at the request of a relative of Sir John's, who wished to be assured on the matter by reason of its suddenness, he had, with the assistance of a surgeon, made a private examination of Sir John's body immediately after his decease, and found that it had resulted from purely natural causes. Nobody at this time had breathed a suspicion of foul play, and therefore nothing was said which might afterwards have established her innocence.

It being thus placed beyond doubt that this beautiful and noble lady had been done to death by a vile scandal that was wholly unfounded, her husband was stung with a dreadful remorse at the share he had taken in her misfortunes, and left the country anew, this time never to return alive. He survived her but a few years, and his body was brought home and buried beside his wife's under the tomb which is still visible in the parish church. Until lately there was a good portrait of her, in weeds for her first husband, with a cross in her hand, at the ancestral seat of her family, where she was much pitied, as she deserved to be. Yet there were some severe enough to say – and these not unjust persons in other respects – that though unquestionably innocent of the crime imputed to her, she had shown an unseemly wantonness in contracting three marriages in such rapid succession; that the untrue suspicion might have been ordered by Providence (who often works indirectly) as a punishment for her self-indulgence. Upon that point I have no opinion to offer.

The reverend the Vice-President, however, the tale being ended, offered as his opinion that her fate ought to be quite clearly recognized as a chastisement. So thought the churchwarden, and also the quiet gentleman sitting near. The latter knew many other instances in point, one of which could be narrated in a few words.

Dame the Ninth
The Duchess of Hamptonshire

By the Quiet Gentleman

SOME fifty years ago the then Duke of Hamptonshire, fifth of that title, was incontestably the head man in his county, and particularly in the neighbourhood of Batton. He came of the ancient and loyal family of Saxelbye, which, before its ennoblement, had numbered many knightly and ecclesiastical celebrities in its male line. It would have occupied a painstaking county historian a whole afternoon to take rubbings of the numerous effigies and heraldic devices graven to their memory on the brasses, tablets, and altar-tombs in the aisle of the parish church. The Duke himself, however, was a man little attracted by ancient chronicles in stone and metal, even when they concerned his own beginnings. He allowed his mind to linger by preference on the many graceless and unedifying pleasures which his position placed at his command. He could on occasion close the mouths of his dependents by a good bomb-like oath, and he argued doggedly with the parson on the virtues of cock-fighting and baiting the bull.

This nobleman's personal appearance was somewhat impressive. His complexion was that of the copper-beech tree. His frame was stalwart, though slightly stooping. His mouth was large, and he carried an unpolished sapling as his walking-stick, except when he carried a spud for cutting up any thistle he encountered on his walks. His castle stood in the midst of a park, surrounded by dusky elms, except to the southward; and when the moon shone out, the gleaming stone façade, backed by heavy boughs, was visible from the distant high road as a white spot on the surface of darkness. Though called a castle, the building was little fortified, and had been erected with greater eye to internal convenience than those crannied places of defence to which the name strictly appertains. It was a castellated mansion as regular as a chessboard on its ground-plan, ornamented with make-believe bastions and machicolations, behind which were stacks of battlemented chimneys. On still mornings, at the fire-lighting hour, when ghostly housemaids stalk the corridors, and thin streaks of light through the shutter-chinks lend startling winks and smiles to ancestors on canvas, twelve or fifteen thin stems of blue smoke sprouted upwards from these chimney-tops, and spread into a flat canopy on high. Around the site stretched ten thousand acres of good, fat, unimpeachable soil, plentiful in glades and lawns wherever visible from the castle-windows, and merging in homely arable where screened from the too curious eye by ingeniously-contrived plantations.

Some way behind the owner of all this came the second man in the parish, the rector, the Honourable and Reverend Mr Oldbourne, a widower, over stiff and stern for a clergyman, whose severe white neck-cloth, well-kept gray hair, and right-lined face betokened none of those sympathetic traits whereon depends so much of a parson's power to do good among his fellow-creatures. The last, far-removed man of the series – altogether the Neptune of these local primaries – was the curate, Mr Alwyn Hill. He was a handsome young deacon with curly hair, dreamy eyes – so dreamy that to look long into them was like ascending and floating among summer clouds – a complexion as fresh as a flower, and a chin absolutely beardless. Though his age was about twenty-five, he looked not much over nineteen.

The rector had a daughter called Emmeline, of so sweet and simple a nature that her beauty was discovered, measured, and inventoried by almost everybody in that part of the country before it was suspected by herself to exist. She had been bred in comparative solitude; a rencounter with men troubled and confused her. Whenever a strange visitor came to her father's house she slipped into the orchard and remained till he was gone, ridiculing her weakness in apostrophes, but unable to overcome it. Her virtues lay in no resistant force of character, but in a natural inappetency for evil things, which to her were as unmeaning as joints of flesh to a herbivorous creature. Her charms of person, manner, and mind, had been clear for some time to the Antinous in orders, and no less so to the Duke, who, though scandalously ignorant of dainty phrases, ever showing a clumsy manner towards the gentler sex, and, in short, not at all a lady's man, took fire to a degree that was wellnigh terrible at sudden sight of Emmeline, a short time after she was turned seventeen.

It occurred one afternoon at the corner of a shrubbery between the castle and the rectory, where the Duke was standing to watch the heaving of a mole, when the fair girl brushed past at a distance of a few yards, in the full light of the sun, and without hat or bonnet. The Duke went home like a man who had seen a spirit. He ascended to the picture-gallery of his castle, and there passed some time in staring at the bygone beauties of his line as if he had never before considered what an important part those specimens of womankind had played in the evolution of the Saxelbye race. He dined alone, drank rather freely, and declared to himself that Emmeline Oldbourne must be his.

Meanwhile there had unfortunately arisen between the curate and this girl some sweet and secret understanding. Particulars of the attachment remained unknown then and always, but it was plainly not approved of by her father. His procedure was cold, hard, and inexorable. Soon the curate disappeared from the parish, almost suddenly, after bitter and hard words had been heard to pass between him and the rector one evening in the garden, intermingled with which, like the cries of the dying in the din of battle, were the beseeching sobs of a woman. Not long after this it was announced that a marriage between the Duke and Miss Oldbourne was to be solemnized at a surprisingly early date.

The wedding-day came and passed; and she was a Duchess. Nobody seemed to think of the ousted man during the day, or else those who thought of him concealed their meditations. Some of the less subservient ones were disposed to speak in a jocular manner of the august husband and wife, others to make correct and pretty speeches about them, according as their sex and nature dictated. But in the evening, the ringers in the belfry, with whom Alwyn had been a favourite, eased their minds a little concerning the gentle young man, and the possible regrets of the woman he had loved.

'Don't you see something wrong in it all?' said the third bell as he wiped his face. 'I know well enough where she would have liked to stable her horses to-night, when they have done their journey.'

'That is, you would know if you could tell where young Mr Hill is living, which is known to none in the parish.'

'Except to the lady that this ring o' grandsire triples is in honour of.'

Yet these friendly cottagers were at this time far from suspecting the real dimensions of Emmeline's misery, nor was it clear even to those who came into much closer communion with her than they, so well had she concealed her heart-sickness. But bride and bridegroom had not long been home at the castle when the young wife's unhappiness became plainly enough perceptible. Her maids and men said that she was in the habit of turning to the wainscot and shedding stupid scalding tears at a time when a right-minded lady would have been overhauling her wardrobe. She prayed earnestly in the great church-pew, where she sat lonely and insignificant as a mouse in a cell, instead of counting her rings, falling asleep, or amusing herself in silent laughter at the queer old people in the congregation, as previous beauties of the family had done in their time. She seemed to care no more for eating and drinking out of crystal and silver than from a service of earthen vessels. Her head was, in truth, full of something else; and that such was the case was only too obvious to the Duke, her husband. At first he would only taunt her for her folly in thinking of that milk-and-water parson; but as time went on his charges took a more positive shape. He would not believe her assurance that she had in no way communicated with her former lover, nor he with her, since their parting in the presence of her father. This led to some strange scenes between them which need not be detailed; their result was soon to take a catastrophic shape.

One dark quiet evening, about two months after the marriage, a man entered the gate admitting from the highway to the park and avenue which ran up to the house. He arrived within two hundred yards of the walls, when he left the gravelled drive and drew near to the castle by a roundabout path leading into a shrubbery. Here he stood still. In a few minutes the strokes of the castle-clock resounded, and then a female figure entered the same secluded nook from an opposite direction. There the two indistinct persons leapt together like a pair of dewdrops on a leaf; and then they stood apart, facing each other, the woman looking down.

'Emmeline, you begged me to come, and here I am, Heaven forgive me!' said the man hoarsely.

'You are going to emigrate, Alwyn,' she said in broken accents. 'I have heard of it; you sail from Plymouth in three days in the *Western Glory*?'

'Yes. I can live in England no longer. Life is as death to me here,' says he.

'My life is even worse – worse than death. Death would not have driven me to this extremity. Listen, Alwyn – I have sent for you to beg to go with you, or at least to be near you – to do anything so that it be not to stay here.'

'To go away with me?' he said in a startled tone.

'Yes, yes – or under your direction, or by your help in some way! Don't be horrified at me – you must bear with me whilst I implore it. Nothing short of cruelty would have driven me to this. I could have borne my doom in silence had I been left unmolested; but he tortures me, and I shall soon be in the grave if I cannot escape.'

To his shocked inquiry how her husband tortured her, the Duchess said that it was by jealousy. 'He tries to wring admissions from me concerning you,' she said, 'and will not believe that I have not communicated with you since my engagement to him was settled by my father, and I was forced to agree to it.'

The poor curate said that this was the heaviest news of all. 'He has not personally ill-used you?' he asked.

'Yes,' she whispered.

'What has he done?'

She looked fearfully around, and said, sobbing: 'In trying to make me confess to what I have never done, he adopts plans I dare not describe for terrifying me into a weak state, so that I may own to anything! I resolved to write to you, as I had no other friend.' She added, with dreary irony, 'I thought I would give him some ground for his suspicion, so as not to disgrace his judgment.'

'Do you really mean, Emmeline,' he tremblingly inquired, 'that you – that you want to fly with me?'

'Can you think that I would act otherwise than in earnest at such a time as this?'

He was silent for a minute or more. 'You must not go with me,' he said.

'Why?'

'It would be sin.'

'It *cannot* be sin, for I have never wanted to commit sin in my life; and it isn't likely I would begin now, when I pray every day to die and be sent to Heaven out of my misery!'

'But it is wrong, Emmeline, all the same.'

'Is it wrong to run away from the fire that scorches you?'

'It would look wrong, at any rate, in this case.'

'Alwyn, Alwyn, take me, I beseech you!' she burst out. 'It is not right in general, I know, but it is such an exceptional instance, this. Why has such a severe strain been put upon me? I was doing no harm, injuring no one, helping many people, and expecting happiness; yet trouble came. Can it be that God holds me in derision? I had no supporter – I gave way; and now my life is a burden and a shame to me. . . . O, if you only knew how much to me this request to you is – how my life is wrapped up in it, you could not deny me!'

'This is almost beyond endurance – Heaven support us,' he groaned. 'Emmy, you are the Duchess of Hamptonshire, the Duke of Hamptonshire's wife; you must not go with me!'

'And am I then refused? – O, am I refused?' she cried frantically. 'Alwyn, Alwyn, do you say it indeed to me?'

'Yes, I do, dear, tender heart! I do most sadly say it. You must not go. Forgive me, for there is no alternative but refusal. Though I die, though you die, we must not fly together. It is forbidden in God's law. Goodbye, for always and ever!'

He tore himself away, hastened from the shrubbery, and vanished among the trees.

Three days after this meeting and farewell, Alwyn, his soft, handsome features stamped with a haggard hardness that ten years of ordinary wear and tear in the world could scarcely have produced, sailed from Plymouth on a drizzling morning, in the passenger-ship *Western Glory*. When the land had faded behind him he mechanically endeavoured to school himself into a stoical frame of mind. His attempt, backed up by the strong moral staying power that had enabled him to resist the passionate temptation to which Emmeline, in her reckless trustfulness, had exposed him, was rewarded by a certain kind of success, though the murmuring stretch of waters whereon he gazed day after day too often seemed to be articulating to him in tones of her well-remembered voice.

He framed on his journey rules of conduct for reducing to mild proportions the feverish regrets which would occasionally arise and agitate him, when he indulged in visions of what might have been had he not hearkened to the whispers of conscience. He fixed his thoughts for so many hours a day on philosophical passages in the volumes he had brought with him, allowing himself now and then a few minutes' thought of Emmeline, with the strict yet reluctant niggardliness of an ailing epicure proportioning the rank drinks that cause his malady. The voyage was marked by the usual incidents of a sailing-passage in those days – a storm, a calm, a man overboard, a birth, and a funeral – the latter sad event being one in which he, as the only clergyman on board, officiated, reading the service ordained for the purpose. The ship duly arrived at Boston early in the month following, and thence he proceeded to Providence to seek out a distant relative.

After a short stay at Providence he returned again to Boston, and by applying himself to a serious occupation made good progress in shaking off the dreary melancholy which enveloped him even now. Distracted and weakened in his beliefs by his recent experiences, he decided that he could not for a time worthily fill the office of a minister of religion, and applied for the mastership of a school. Some introductions, given him before starting, were useful now, and he soon became known as a respectable scholar and gentleman to the trustees of one of the colleges. This ultimately led to his retirement from the school and installation in the college as Professor of rhetoric and oratory.

Here and thus he lived on, exerting himself solely because of a conscientious determination to do his duty. He passed his winter evenings in turning sonnets and elegies, often giving his thoughts voice in 'Lines to an Unfortunate Lady', while his summer leisure at the same hour would be spent in watching the lengthening shadows from his window, and fancifully comparing them with the shades of his own life. If he walked, he mentally inquired which was the eastern quarter of the landscape, and thought of two thousand miles of water that way, and of what was beyond it. In a word he was at all spare times dreaming of her who was only a memory to him, and would probably never be more.

Nine years passed by, and under their wear and tear Alwyn Hill's face lost a great many of the attractive characteristics which had formerly distinguished it. He was kind to his pupils and affable to all who came in contact with him; but the kernel of his life, his secret, was kept as snugly shut up as though he had been dumb. In talking to his acquaintances of England and his life there, he omitted the episode of Batton Castle and Emmeline as if it had no existence in his calendar at all. Though of towering importance to himself, it had filled but a short and small fragment of time, an ephemeral season which would have been wellnigh imperceptible, even to him, at this distance, but for the incident it enshrined.

One day, at this date, when cursorily glancing over an old English newspaper, he observed a paragraph which, short as it was, contained for him whole tomes of thrilling information - rung with more passion-stirring rhythm than the collected cantos of all the poets. It was an

announcement of the death of the Duke of Hamptonshire, leaving
behind him a widow, but no children.

The current of Alwyn's thoughts now completely changed. On
looking again at the newspaper he found it to be one that was sent him
long ago, and had been carelessly thrown aside. But for an accidental
overhauling of the waste journals in his study he might not have known
of the event for years. At this moment of reading the Duke had already
been dead seven months. Alwyn could now no longer bind himself
down to machine-made synecdoche, antithesis, and climax, being full of
spontaneous specimens of all these rhetorical forms, which he dared not
utter. Who shall wonder that his mind luxuriated in dreams of a sweet
possibility just laid open for the first time these many years? for
Emmeline was to him now as ever the one dear thing in all the world.
The issue of his silent romancing was that he resolved to return to her at
the very earliest moment.

But he could not abandon his professional work on the instant. He did
not get really quite free from engagements till four months later; but,
though suffering throes of impatience continually, he said to himself
every day: 'If she has continued to love me nine years she will love me
ten; she will think the more tenderly of me when her present hours of
solitude shall have done their proper work; old times will revive with
the cessation of her recent experience, and every day will favour my
return.'

The enforced interval soon passed, and he duly arrived in England,
reaching the village of Batton on a certain winter day between twelve and
thirteen months subsequent to the time of the Duke's death.

It was evening; yet such was Alwyn's impatience that he could not
forbear taking, this very night, one look at the castle which Emmeline
had entered as unhappy mistress ten years before. He threaded the park
trees, gazed in passing at well-known outlines which rose against the
dim sky, and was soon interested in observing that lively country-people,
in parties of two and three, were walking before and behind him up the
interlaced avenue to the castle gateway. Knowing himself to be safe
from recognition, Alwyn inquired of one of these pedestrians what was
going on.

'Her Grace gives her tenantry a ball to-night, to keep up the old
custom of the Duke and his father before him, which she does not wish
to change.'

'Indeed. Has she lived here entirely alone since the Duke's death?'

'Quite alone. But though she doesn't receive company herself, she likes the village people to enjoy themselves, and often has 'em here.'

'Kind-hearted, as always!' thought Alwyn.

On reaching the castle he found that the great gates at the tradesmen's entrance were thrown back against the wall as if they were never to be closed again; that the passages and rooms in that wing were brilliantly lighted up, some of the numerous candles guttering down over the green leaves which decorated them, and upon the silk dresses of the happy farmers' wives as they passed beneath, each on her husband's arm. Alwyn found no difficulty in marching in along with the rest, the castle being Liberty Hall to-night. He stood unobserved in a corner of the large apartment where dancing was about to begin.

'Her Grace, though hardly out of mourning, will be sure to come down and lead off the dance with neighbour Bates,' said one.

'Who is neighbour Bates?' asked Alwyn.

'An old man she respects much – the oldest of her tenant-farmers. He was seventy-eight his last birthday.'

'Ah, to be sure!' said Alwyn, at his ease. 'I remember.'

The dancers formed in line, and waited. A door opened at the further end of the hall, and a lady in black silk came forth. She bowed, smiled, and proceeded to the top of the dance.

'Who is that lady?' said Alwyn, in a puzzled tone. 'I thought you told me that the Duchess of Hamptonshire—'

'That is the Duchess,' said his informant.

'But there is another?'

'No; there is no other.'

'But she is not the Duchess of Hamptonshire – who used to—' Alwyn's tongue stuck to his mouth, he could get no farther.

'What's the matter?' said his acquaintance. Alwyn had retired, and was supporting himself against the wall.

The wretched Alwyn murmured something about a stitch in his side from walking. Then the music struck up, the dance went on, and his neighbour became so interested in watching the movements of this strange Duchess through its mazes as to forget Alwyn for a while.

It gave him an opportunity to brace himself up. He was a man who had suffered, and he could suffer again. 'How came that person to be your Duchess?' he asked in a firm, distinct voice, when he had attained complete self-command. 'Where is her other Grace of Hamptonshire? There certainly was another. I know it.'

'Oh, the previous one! Yes, yes. She ran away years and years ago with the young curate. Mr Hill was the young man's name, if I recollect.'

'No! She never did. What do you mean by that?' he said.

'Yes, she certainly ran away. She met the curate in the shrubbery about a couple of months after her marriage with the Duke. There were folks who saw the meeting and heard some words of their talk. They arranged to go, and she sailed from Plymouth with him a day or two afterward.'

'That's not true.'

'Then 'tis the queerest lie ever told by man. Her father believed and knew to his dying day that she went with him; and so did the Duke, and everybody about here. Ay, there was a fine upset about it at the time. The Duke traced her to Plymouth.'

'Traced her to Plymouth?'

'He traced her to Plymouth, and set on his spies; and they found that she went to the shipping-office, and inquired if Mr Alwyn Hill had entered his name as passenger by the *Western Glory*; and when she found that he had, she booked herself for the same ship, but not in her real name. When the vessel had sailed a letter reached the Duke from her, telling him what she had done. She never came back here again. His Grace lived by himself a number of years, and married this lady only twelve months before he died.'

Alwyn was in a state of indescribable bewilderment. But, unmanned as he was, he called the next day on the, to him, spurious Duchess of Hamptonshire. At first she was alarmed at his statement, then cold, then she was won over by his condition to give confidence for confidence. She showed him a letter which had been found among the papers of the late Duke, corroborating what Alwyn's informant had detailed. It was from Emmeline, bearing the postmarked date at which the *Western Glory* sailed, and briefly stated that she had emigrated by that ship to America.

Alwyn applied himself body and mind to unravel the remainder of the mystery. The story repeated to him was always the same: 'She ran away with the curate.' A strangely circumstantial piece of intelligence was added to this when he had pushed his inquiries a little further. There was given him the name of a waterman at Plymouth, who had come forward at the time that she was missed and sought for by her husband, and had stated that he put her on board the *Western Glory* at dusk one evening before that vessel sailed.

After several days of search about the alleys and quays of Plymouth Barbican, during which these impossible words, 'She ran off with the curate,' became branded on his brain, Alwyn found this important waterman. He was positive as to the truth of his story, still remembering the incident well, and he described in detail the lady's dress, as he had long ago described it to her husband, which description corresponded in every particular with the dress worn by Emmeline on the evening of their parting.

Before proceeding to the other side of the Atlantic to continue his inquiries there, the puzzled and distracted Alwyn set himself to ascertain the address of Captain Wheeler, who had commanded the *Western Glory* in the year of Alwyn's voyage out, and immediately wrote a letter to him on the subject.

The only circumstances which the sailor could recollect or discover from his papers in connection with such a story were, that a woman bearing the name which Alwyn had mentioned as fictitious certainly did come aboard for a voyage he made about that time; that she took a common berth among the poorest emigrants; that she died on the voyage out, at about five days' sail from Plymouth; that she seemed a lady in manners and education. Why she had not applied for a first-class passage, why she had no trunks, they could not guess, for though she had little money in her pocket she had that about her which would have fetched it. 'We buried her at sea,' continued the captain. 'A young parson, one of the cabin-passengers, read the burial-service over her, I remember well.'

The whole scene and proceedings darted upon Alwyn's recollection in a moment. It was a fine breezy morning on that long-past voyage out, and he had been told that they were running at the rate of a hundred and odd miles a day. The news went round that one of the poor young women in the other part of the vessel was ill of fever, and delirious. The tidings caused no little alarm among all the passengers, for the sanitary conditions of the ship were anything but satisfactory. Shortly after this the doctor announced that she had died. Then Alwyn had learnt that she was laid out for burial in great haste, because of the danger that would have been incurred by delay. And next the funeral scene rose before him, and the prominent part that he had taken in that solemn ceremony. The captain had come to him, requesting him to officiate, as there was no chaplain on board. This he had agreed to do; and as the sun went down with a blaze in his face he read amidst them all assembled: 'We therefore commit her body to the deep, to be turned into corruption, looking for the resurrection of the body when the sea shall give up her dead.'

The captain also forwarded the addresses of the ship's matron and of other persons who had been engaged on board at the date. To these Alwyn went in the course of time. A categorical description of the clothes of the dead truant, the colour of her hair, and other things, extinguished for ever all hope of a mistake in identity.

At last, then, the course of events had become clear. On that unhappy evening when he left Emmeline in the shrubbery, forbidding her to follow him because it would be a sin, she must have disobeyed. She must have followed at his heels silently through the darkness, like a poor pet animal that will not be driven back. She could have accumulated nothing for the journey more than she might have carried in her hand; and thus poorly provided she must have embarked. Her intention had doubtless been to make her presence on board known to him as soon as she could muster courage to do so.

Thus the ten years' chapter of Alwyn Hill's romance wound itself up under his eyes. That the poor young woman in the steerage had been the young Duchess of Hamptonshire was never publicly disclosed. Hill had no longer any reason for remaining in England, and soon after left its shores with no intention to return. Previous to his departure he confided his story to an old friend from his native town – grandfather of the person who now relates it to you.

A few members, including the Bookworm, seemed to be impressed by the quiet gentleman's tale; but the member we have called the Spark – who, by the way, was getting somewhat tinged with the light of other days, and owned to eight-and-thirty – walked daintily about the room instead of sitting down by the fire with the majority, and said that for his part he preferred something more lively than the last story – something in which such long-separated lovers were ultimately united. He also liked stories that were more modern in their date of action than those he had heard to-day.

Members immediately requested him to give them a specimen, to which the Spark replied that he didn't mind, as far as that went. And though the Vice-President, the Man of Family, the Colonel, and others, looked at their watches, and said they must soon retire to their respective quarters in the hotel adjoining, they all decided to sit out the Spark's story.

Dame the Tenth
The Honourable Laura

By the Spark

IT was a cold and gloomy Christmas Eve. The mass of cloud overhead
was almost impervious to such daylight as still lingered; the snow lay
several inches deep upon the ground, and the slanting downfall which
still went on threatened to considerably increase its thickness before the
morning. The Prospect Hotel, a building standing near the wild north
coast of Lower Wessex, looked so lonely and so useless at such a time as
this that a passing wayfarer would have been led to forget summer
possibilities, and to wonder at the commercial courage which could
invest capital, on the basis of the popular taste for the picturesque, in a
country subject to such dreary phases. That the district was alive with
visitors in August seemed but a dim tradition in weather so totally
opposed to all that tempts mankind from home. However, there the
hotel stood immovable; and the cliffs, creeks, and headlands which
were the primary attractions of the spot, rising in full view on the
opposite side of the valley, were now but stern angular outlines, while
the townlet in front was tinged over with a grimy dirtiness rather than
the pearly gray that in summer lent such beauty to its appearance.

Within the hotel commanding this outlook the landlord walked idly
about with his hands in his pockets, not in the least expectant of a visitor,
and yet unable to settle down to any occupation which should compen-
sate in some degree for the losses that winter idleness entailed on his
regular profession. So little, indeed, was anybody expected, that the
coffee-room waiter – a genteel boy, whose plated buttons in summer
were as close together upon the front of his short jacket as peas in a pod
– now appeared in the back yard, metamorphosed into the unrecogniz-
able shape of a rough country lad in corduroys and hobnailed boots,
sweeping the snow away, and talking the local dialect in all its purity,

quite oblivious of the new polite accent he had learned in the hot
weather from the well-behaved visitors. The front door was closed, and,
as if to express still more fully the sealed and chrysalis state of the
establishment, a sand-bag was placed at the bottom to keep out the
insidious snowdrift, the wind setting in directly from that quarter.

The landlord, entering his own parlour, walked to the large fire which
it was absolutely necessary to keep up for his comfort, no such blaze
burning in the coffee-room or elsewhere, and after giving it a stir
returned to a table in the lobby, whereon lay the visitors' book – now
closed and pushed back against the wall. He carelessly opened it; not a
name had been entered there since the 19th of the previous November,
and that was only the name of a man who had arrived on a tricycle, who,
indeed, had not been asked to enter at all.

While he was engaged thus the evening grew darker; but before it was
as yet too dark to distinguish objects upon the road winding round the
back of the cliffs, the landlord perceived a black spot on the distant
white, which speedily enlarged itself and drew near. The probabilities
were that this vehicle – for a vehicle of some sort it seemed to be –
would pass by and pursue its way to the nearest railway-town as others
had done. But, contrary to the landlord's expectation, as he stood
conning it through the yet unshuttered windows, the solitary object, on
reaching the corner, turned into the hotel-front, and drove up to the
door.

It was a conveyance particularly unsuited to such a season and
weather, being nothing more substantial than an open basket-carriage
drawn by a single horse. Within sat two persons, of different sexes, as
could soon be discerned, in spite of their muffled attire. The man held
the reins, and the lady had got some shelter from the storm by clinging
close to his side. The landlord rang the hostler's bell to attract the
attention of the stable-man, for the approach of the visitors had been
deadened to noiselessness by the snow, and when the hostler had come
to the horse's head the gentleman and lady alighted, the landlord
meeting them in the hall.

The male stranger was a foreign-looking individual of about eight-
and-twenty. He was close-shaven, excepting a moustache, his features
being good, and even handsome. The lady, who stood timidly behind him,
seemed to be much younger – possibly not more than eighteen, though
it was difficult to judge either of her age or appearance in her present
wrappings.

The gentleman expressed his wish to stay till the morning, explaining somewhat unnecessarily, considering that the house was an inn, that they had been unexpectedly benighted on their drive. Such a welcome being given them as landlords can give in dull times, the latter ordered fires in the drawing- and coffee-rooms, and went to the boy in the yard, who soon scrubbed himself up, dragged his disused jacket from its box, polished the buttons with his sleeve, and appeared civilized in the hall. The lady was shown into a room where she could take off her snow-damped garments, which she sent down to be dried, her companion, meanwhile, putting a couple of sovereigns on the table, as if anxious to make everything smooth and comfortable at starting, and requesting that a private sitting-room might be got ready. The landlord assured him that the best upstairs parlour – usually public – should be kept private this evening, and sent the maid to light the candles. Dinner was prepared for them, and, at the gentleman's desire, served in the same apartment; where, the young lady having joined him, they were left to the rest and refreshment they seemed to need.

That something was peculiar in the relations of the pair had more than once struck the landlord, though wherein that peculiarity lay it was hard to decide. But that his guest was one who paid his way readily had been proved by his conduct, and dismissing conjectures he turned to practical affairs.

About nine o'clock he re-entered the hall, and, everything being done for the day, again walked up and down, occasionally gazing through the glass door at the prospect without, to ascertain how the weather was progressing. Contrary to prognostication, snow had ceased falling, and, with the rising of the moon, the sky had partially cleared, light fleeces of cloud drifting across the silvery disk. There was every sign that a frost was going to set in later on. For these reasons the distant rising road was even more distinct now between its high banks than it had been in the declining daylight. Not a track or rut broke the virgin surface of the white mantle that lay along it, all marks left by the lately arrived travellers having been speedily obliterated by the flakes falling at the time.

And now the landlord beheld by the light of the moon a sight very similar to that he had seen by the light of day. Again a black spot was advancing down the road that margined the coast. He was in a moment or two enabled to perceive that the present vehicle moved onward at a more headlong pace than the little carriage which had preceded it; next, that it was a brougham drawn by two powerful horses; next, that this carriage, like the former one, was bound for the hotel-door. This desirable feature of resemblance caused the landlord once more to withdraw the sand-bag and advance into the porch.

An old gentleman was the first to alight. He was followed by a young one, and both unhesitatingly came forward.

'Has a young lady, less than nineteen years of age, recently arrived here in the company of a man some years her senior?' asked the old gentleman, in haste. 'A man cleanly shaven for the most part, having the appearance of an opera-singer, and calling himself Signor Smittozzi?'

'We have had arrivals lately,' said the landlord, in the tone of having had twenty at least – not caring to acknowledge the attenuated state of business that afflicted Prospect Hotel in winter.

'And among them can your memory recall two persons such as those I describe? – the man a sort of baritone?'

'There certainly is or was a young couple staying in the hotel; but I could not pronounce on the compass of the gentleman's voice.'

'No, no; of course not. I am quite bewildered. They arrived in a basket-carriage, altogether badly provided?'

'They came in a carriage, I believe, as most of our visitors do.'

'Yes, yes. I must see them at once. Pardon my want of ceremony, and show us in to where they are.'

'But, sir, you forget. Suppose the lady and gentleman I mean are not the lady and gentleman you mean? It would be awkward to allow you to rush in upon them just now while they are at dinner, and might cause me to lose their future patronage.'

'True, true. They may not be the same persons. My anxiety, I perceive, makes me rash in my assumptions!'

'Upon the whole, I think they must be the same, Uncle Quantock,' said the young man, who had not till now spoken. And turning to the landlord: 'You possibly have not such a large assemblage of visitors here, on this somewhat forbidding evening, that you quite forget how this couple arrived, and what the lady wore?' His tone of addressing the landlord had in it a quiet frigidity that was not without irony.

'Ah! what she wore; that's it, James. What did she wear?'

'I don't usually take stock of my guests' clothing,' replied the landlord drily, for the ready money of the first arrival had decidedly biassed him in favour of that gentleman's cause. 'You can certainly see some of it if you want to,' he added carelessly, 'for it is drying by the kitchen fire.'

Before the words were half out of his mouth the old gentleman had exclaimed, 'Ah!' and precipitated himself along what seemed to be the passage to the kitchen; but as this turned out to be only the entrance to a dark china-closet he hastily emerged again, after a collision with the inn-crockery had told him of his mistake.

'I beg your pardon, I'm sure; but if you only knew my feelings (which I cannot at present explain), you would make allowances. Anything I have broken I will willingly pay for.'

'Don't mention it, sir,' said the landlord. And showing the way, they adjourned to the kitchen without further parley. The eldest of the party instantly seized the lady's cloak, that hung upon a clothes-horse, exclaiming: 'Ah! yes, James, it is hers. I knew we were on their track.'

'Yes, it is hers,' answered the nephew quietly, for he was much less excited than his companion.

'Show us their room at once,' said the uncle.

'William, have the lady and gentleman in the front sitting-room finished dining?'

'Yes, sir, long ago,' said the hundred plated buttons.

'Then show up these gentlemen to them at once. You stay here to-night, gentlemen, I presume? Shall the horses be taken out?'

'Feed the horses and wash their mouths. Whether we stay or not depends upon circumstances,' said the placid younger man, as he followed his uncle and the waiter to the staircase.

'I think, Nephew James,' said the former, as he paused with his foot on the first step – 'I think we had better not be announced, but take them by surprise. She may go throwing herself out of the window, or do some equally desperate thing!'

'Yes, certainly, we'll enter unannounced.' And he called back the lad who preceded them.

'I cannot sufficiently thank you, James, for so effectually aiding me in this pursuit!' exclaimed the old gentleman, taking the other by the hand. 'My increasing infirmities would have hindered my overtaking her to-night, had it not been for your timely aid.'

'I am only too happy, uncle, to have been of service to you in this or any other matter. I only wish I could have accompanied you on a pleasanter journey. However, it is advisable to go up to them at once, or they may hear us.' And they softly ascended the stairs.

On the door being opened a room too large to be comfortable was disclosed, lit by the best branch-candlesticks of the hotel, before the fire of which apartment the truant couple were sitting, very innocently looking over the hotel scrap-book and the album containing views of the neighbourhood. No sooner had the old man entered than the young lady – who now showed herself to be quite as young as described, and remarkably prepossessing as to features – perceptibly turned pale. When the nephew entered she turned still paler, as if she were going to faint. The young man described as an opera-singer rose with grim civility, and placed chairs for his visitors.

'Caught you, thank God!' said the old gentleman breathlessly.

'Yes, worse luck, my lord!' murmured Signor Smittozzi, in native London-English, that distinguished Italian having, in fact, first seen the light as the baby of Mr and Mrs Smith in the vicinity of the City Road. 'She would have been mine to-morrow. And I think that under the peculiar circumstances it would be wiser – considering how soon the breath of scandal will tarnish a lady's fame – to let her be mine to-morrow, just the same.'

'Never!' said the old man. 'Here is a lady under age, without experience – child-like in her maiden innocence and virtue – whom you have plied by your vile arts, till this morning at dawn—'

'Lord Quantock, were I not bound to respect your gray hairs—'

'Till this morning at dawn you tempted her away from her father's roof. What blame can attach to her conduct that will not, on a full explanation of the matter, be readily passed over in her and thrown entirely on you? Laura, you return at once with me. I should not have arrived, after all, early enough to deliver you, if it had not been for the disinterestedness of your cousin, Captain Northbrook, who, on my discovering your flight this morning, offered with a promptitude for which I can never sufficiently thank him, to accompany me on my journey, as the only male relative I have near me. Come, do you hear? Put on your things; we are off at once.'

'I don't want to go!' pouted the young lady.

'I daresay you don't,' replied her father drily. 'But children never know what's best for them. So come along, and trust to my opinion.'

Laura was silent, and did not move, the opera gentleman looking helplessly into the fire, and the lady's cousin sitting meditatively calm, as the single one of the four whose position enabled him to survey the whole escapade with the cool criticism of a comparative outsider.

'I say to you, Laura, as the father of a daughter under age, that you instantly come with me. What? Would you compel me to use physical force to reclaim you?'

'I don't want to return!' again declared Laura.

'It is your duty to return nevertheless, and at once, I inform you.'

'I don't want to!'

'Now, dear Laura, this is what I say: return with me and your Cousin James quietly, like a good and repentant girl, and nothing will be said. Nobody knows what has happened as yet, and if we start at once, we shall be home before it is light to-morrow morning. Come.'

'I am not obliged to come at your bidding, father, and I would rather not!'

Now James, the cousin, during this dialogue might have been observed to grow somewhat restless, and even impatient. More than once he had parted his lips to speak, but second thoughts each time held him back. The moment had come, however, when he could keep silence no longer.

'Come, madam!' he spoke out, 'this farce with your father has, in my opinion, gone on long enough. Just make no more ado, and step downstairs with us.'

She gave herself an intractable little twist, and did not reply.

'By the Lord Harry, Laura, I won't stand this!' he said angrily. 'Come, get on your things before I come and compel you. There is a kind of compulsion to which this talk is child's play. Come, madam – instantly, I say!'

The old nobleman turned to his nephew and said mildly: 'Leave me to insist, James. It doesn't become you. I can speak to her sharply enough, if I choose.'

James, however, did not heed his uncle, and went on to the troublesome young woman: 'You say you don't want to come, indeed! A pretty story to tell me, that! Come, march out of the room at once, and leave that hulking fellow for me to deal with afterward. Get on quickly – come!' and he advanced toward her as if to pull her by the hand.

'Nay, nay,' expostulated Laura's father, much surprised at his nephew's sudden demeanour. 'You take too much upon yourself. Leave her to me.'

'I won't leave her to you any longer!'

'You have no right, James, to address either me or her in this way; so just hold your tongue. Come, my dear.'

'I have every right!' insisted James.

'How do you make that out?'

'I have the right of a husband.'

'Whose husband?'

'Hers.'

'What?'

'She's my wife.'

'James!'

'Well, to cut a long story short, I may say that she secretly married me, in spite of your lordship's prohibition, about three months ago. And I must add that, though she cooled down rather quickly, everything went on smoothly enough between us for some time; in spite of the awkwardness of meeting only by stealth. We were only waiting for a convenient moment to break the news to you when this idle Adonis turned up, and after poisoning her mind against me, brought her into this disgrace.'

Here the operatic luminary, who had sat in rather an abstracted and nerveless attitude till the cousin made his declaration, fired up and cried: 'I declare before Heaven that till this moment I never knew she was a wife! I found her in her father's house an unhappy girl – unhappy, as I believe, because of the loneliness and dreariness of that establishment, and the want of society, and for nothing else whatever. What this statement about her being your wife means I am quite at a loss to understand. Are you indeed married to him, Laura?'

Laura nodded from within her tearful handkerchief. 'It was because of my anomalous position in being privately married to him,' she sobbed, 'that I was unhappy at home – and – and I didn't like him so well as I did at first – and I wished I could get out of the mess I was in! And then I saw you a few times, and when you said, "We'll run off," I thought I saw a way out of it all, and then I agreed to come with you-oo-oo!'

'Well! well! well! And is this true?' murmured the bewildered old nobleman, staring from James to Laura, and from Laura to James, as if he fancied they might be figments of the imagination. 'Is this, then, James, the secret of your kindness to your old uncle in helping him to find his daughter? Good Heavens! What further depths of duplicity are there left for a man to learn!'

'I have married her, Uncle Quantock, as I said,' answered James coolly. 'The deed is done, and can't be undone by talking here.'

'Where were you married?'

'At St Mary's, Toneborough.'

'When?'

'On the 29th of September, during the time she was visiting there.'

'Who married you?'

'I don't know. One of the curates – we were quite strangers to the place. So, instead of my assisting you to recover her, you may as well assist me.'

'Never! never!' said Lord Quantock. 'Madam, and sir, I beg to tell you that I wash my hands of the whole affair. If you are man and wife, as it seems you are, get reconciled as best you may. I have no more to say or do with either of you. I leave you, Laura, in the hands of your husband, and much joy may you bring him; though the situation, I own, is not encouraging.'

Saying this, the indignant speaker pushed back his chair against the table with such force that the candlesticks rocked on their bases, and left the room.

Laura's wet eyes roved from one of the young men to the other, who now stood glaring face to face, and, being much frightened at their aspect, slipped out of the room after her father. Him, however, she could hear going out of the front door, and, not knowing where to take shelter, she crept into the darkness of an adjoining bedroom, and there awaited events with a palpitating heart.

Meanwhile the two men remaining in the sitting-room drew nearer to each other, and the opera-singer broke the silence by saying, 'How could you insult me in the way you did, calling me a fellow, and accusing me of poisoning her mind toward you, when you knew very well I was as ignorant of your relation to her as an unborn babe?'

'O yes, you were quite ignorant; I can believe that readily,' sneered Laura's husband.

'I here call Heaven to witness that I never knew!'

'Recitativo – the rhythm excellent, and the tone well sustained. Is it likely that any man could win the confidence of a young fool her age, and not get that out of her? Preposterous! Tell it to the most improved new pit-stalls.'

'Captain Northbrook, your insinuations are as despicable as your wretched person!' cried the baritone, losing all patience. And springing forward he slapped the captain in the face with the palm of his hand.

Northbrook flinched but slightly, and calmly using his handkerchief to learn if his nose was bleeding, said, 'I quite expected this insult, so I came prepared.' And he drew forth from a black valise which he carried in his hand a small case of pistols.

The baritone started at the unexpected sight, but recovering from his surprise said, 'Very well, as you will,' though perhaps his tone showed a slight want of confidence.

'Now,' continued the husband, quite confidingly, 'we want no parade, no nonsense, you know. Therefore we'll dispense with seconds ?'

The Signor slightly nodded.

'Do you know this part of the country well ?' Cousin James went on, in the same cool and still manner. 'If you don't, I do. Quite at the bottom of the rocks out there, just beyond the stream which falls over them to the shore, is a smooth sandy space, not so much shut in as to be out of the moonlight; and the way down to it from this side is over steps cut in the cliff; and we can find our way down without trouble. We – we two – will find our way down; but only one of us will find his way up, you understand ?'

'Quite.'

'Then suppose we start; the sooner it is over the better. We can order supper before we go out – supper for two; for though we are three at present—'

'Three ?'

'Yes; you and I and she—'

'O yes.'

' – we shall be only two by-and-by; so that, as I say, we will order supper for two; for the lady and *a* gentleman. Whichever comes back alive will tap at her door, and call her in to share the repast with him – she's not off the premises. But we must not alarm her now; and above all things we must not let the inn-people see us go out; it would look so odd for two to go out, and only one come in. Ha! ha!'

'Ha! ha! exactly.'

'Are you ready ?'

'Oh – quite.'

'Then I'll lead the way.'

He went softly to the door and downstairs, ordering supper to be ready in an hour, as he had said; then making a feint of returning to the room again, he beckoned to the singer, and together they slipped out of the house by a side door.

The sky was now quite clear, and the wheelmarks of the brougham which had borne away Laura's father, Lord Quantock, remained distinctly visible. Soon the verge of the down was reached, the captain leading the way, and the baritone following silently, casting furtive glances at his companion, and beyond him at the scene ahead. In due course they arrived at the chasm in the cliff which formed the waterfall. The outlook here was wild and picturesque in the extreme, and fully justified the many praises, paintings, and photographic views to which the spot had given birth. What in summer was charmingly green and gray, was now rendered weird and fantastic by the snow.

From their feet the cascade plunged downward almost vertically to a depth of eighty or a hundred feet before finally losing itself in the sand, and though the stream was but small, its impact upon jutting rocks in its descent divided it into a hundred spirts and splashes that sent up a mist into the upper air. A few marginal drippings had been frozen into icicles, but the centre flowed on unimpeded.

The operatic artist looked down as he halted, but his thoughts were plainly not of the beauty of the scene. His companion with the pistols was immediately in front of him, and there was no handrail on the side of the path toward the chasm. Obeying a quick impulse, he stretched out his arm, and with a superhuman thrust sent Laura's husband reeling over. A whirling human shape, diminishing downward in the moon's rays further and further toward invisibility, a smack-smack upon the projecting ledges of rock – at first louder and heavier than that of the brook, and then scarcely to be distinguished from it – then a cessation, then the splashing of the stream as before, and the accompanying murmur of the sea, were all the incidents that disturbed the customary flow of the lofty waterfall.

The singer waited in a fixed attitude for a few minutes, then turning, he rapidly retraced his steps over the intervening upland toward the road, and in less than a quarter of an hour was at the door of the hotel. Slipping quietly in as the clock struck ten, he said to the landlord, over the bar hatchway –

'The bill as soon as you can let me have it, including charges for the supper that was ordered, though we cannot stay to eat it, I am sorry to say.' He added with forced gaiety, 'The lady's father and cousin have thought better of intercepting the marriage, and after quarrelling with each other have gone home independently.'

'Well done, sir!' said the landlord, who still sided with this customer in preference to those who had given trouble and barely paid for baiting the horses. ' "Love will find out the way!" as the saying is. Wish you joy, sir!'

Signor Smittozzi went upstairs, and on entering the sitting-room found that Laura had crept out from the dark adjoining chamber in his absence. She looked up at him with eyes red from weeping, and with symptoms of alarm.

'What is it? – where is he?' she said apprehensively.

'Captain Northbrook has gone back. He says he will have no more to do with you.'

'And I am quite abandoned by them! – and they'll forget me, and nobody care about me any more!' She began to cry afresh.

'But it is the luckiest thing that could have happened. All is just as it was before they came disturbing us. But, Laura, you ought to have told me about that private marriage, though it is all the same now; it will be dissolved, of course. You are a wid— virtually a widow.'

'It is no use to reproach me for what is past. What am I to do now?'

'We go at once to Cliff-Martin. The horse has rested thoroughly these last three hours, and he will have no difficulty in doing an additional half-dozen miles. We shall be there before twelve, and there are late taverns in the place, no doubt. There we'll sell both horse and carriage to-morrow morning; and go by the coach to Downstaple. Once in the train we are safe.'

'I agree to anything,' she said listlessly.

In about ten minutes the horse was put in, the bill paid, the lady's dried wraps put round her, and the journey resumed.

When about a mile on their way they saw a glimmering light in advance of them. 'I wonder what that is?' said the baritone, whose manner had latterly become nervous, every sound and sight causing him to turn his head.

'It is only a turnpike,' said she. 'That light is the lamp kept burning over the door.'

'Of course, of course, dearest. How stupid I am!'

On reaching the gate, they perceived that a man on foot had approached it, apparently by some more direct path than the roadway they pursued, and was, at the moment they drew up, standing in conversation with the gatekeeper.

'It is quite impossible that he could fall over the cliff by accident or the will of God on such a light night as this,' the pedestrian was saying. 'These two children I tell you of saw two men go along the path toward the waterfall, and ten minutes later only one of 'em came back, walking fast, like a man who wanted to get out of the way because he had done something queer. There is no manner of doubt that he pushed the other man over, and, mark me, it will soon cause a hue and cry for that man.'

The candle shone in the face of the Signor and showed that there had arisen upon it a film of ghastliness. Laura, glancing toward him for a few moments, observed it, till, the gatekeeper having mechanically swung open the gate, her companion drove through, and they were soon again enveloped in the white silence.

Her conductor had said to Laura, just before, that he meant to inquire the way at this turnpike; but he had certainly not done so.

As soon as they had gone a little further the omission, intentional or not, began to cause them some trouble. Beyond the secluded district which they now traversed ran the more frequented road, where progress would be easy, the snow being probably already beaten there to some extent by traffic; but they had not yet reached it, and having no one to guide them their journey began to appear less feasible than it had done before starting. When the little lane which they had entered ascended another hill, and seemed to wind round in a direction contrary to the expected route to Cliff-Martin, the question grew serious. Ever since overhearing the conversation at the turnpike, Laura had maintained a perfect silence, and had even shrunk somewhat away from the side of her lover.

'Why don't you talk, Laura,' he said with forced buoyancy, 'and suggest the way we should go?'

'O yes, I will,' she responded, a curious fearfulness being audible in her voice.

After this she uttered a few occasional sentences which seemed to persuade him that she suspected nothing. At last he drew rein, and the weary horse stood still.

'We are in a fix,' he said.

She answered eagerly: 'I'll hold the reins while you run forward to the top of the ridge, and see if the road takes a favourable turn beyond. It would give the horse a few minutes' rest, and if you find out no change in the direction, we will retrace this lane, and take the other turning.'

The expedient seemed a good one in the circumstances, especially when recommended by the singular eagerness of her voice; and placing the reins in her hands – a quite unnecessary precaution, considering the state of their hack – he stepped out and went forward through the snow till she could see no more of him.

No sooner was he gone than Laura, with a rapidity which contrasted strangely with her previous stillness, made fast the reins to the corner of the phaeton, and slipping out on the opposite side, ran back with all her might down the hill, till, coming to an opening in the fence, she scrambled through it, and plunged into the copse which bordered this portion of the lane. Here she stood in hiding under one of the large bushes, clinging so closely to its umbrage as to seem but a portion of its mass, and listening intently for the faintest sound of pursuit. But nothing disturbed the stillness save the occasional slipping of gathered snow from the boughs, or the rustle of some wild animal over the crisp flake-bespattered herbage. At length, apparently convinced that her former companion was either unable to find her, or not anxious to do so in the present strange state of affairs, she crept out from the bushes, and in less than an hour found herself again approaching the door of the Prospect Hotel.

As she drew near, Laura could see that, far from being wrapped in darkness, as she might have expected, there were ample signs that all the tenants were on the alert, lights moving about the open space in front. Satisfaction was expressed in her face when she discerned that no reappearance of her baritone and his pony-carriage was causing this sensation; but it speedily gave way to grief and dismay when she saw by the lights the form of a man borne on a stretcher by two others into the porch of the hotel.

'I have caused all this,' she murmured between her quivering lips. 'He has murdered him!' Running forward to the door, she hastily asked of the first person she met if the man on the stretcher was dead.

'No, miss,' said the labourer addressed, eyeing her up and down as an unexpected apparition. 'He is still alive, they say, but not sensible. He either fell or was pushed over the waterfall; 'tis thoughted he was pushed. He is the gentleman who came here just now with the old lord, and went out afterward (as is thoughted) with a stranger who had come a little earlier. Anyhow, that's as I had it.'

Laura entered the house, and acknowledging without the least reserve that she was the injured man's wife, had soon installed herself as head nurse by the bed on which he lay. When the two surgeons who had been sent for arrived, she learnt from them that his wounds were so severe as to leave but a slender hope of recovery, it being little short of miraculous that he was not killed on the spot, which his enemy had evidently reckoned to be the case. She knew who that enemy was, and shuddered.

Laura watched all night, but her husband knew nothing of her presence. During the next day he slightly recognized her, and in the evening was able to speak. He informed the surgeons that, as was surmised, he had been pushed over the cascade by Signor Smittozzi; but he communicated nothing to her who nursed him, not even replying to her remarks; he nodded courteously at any act of attention she rendered, and that was all.

In a day or two it was declared that everything favoured his recovery, notwithstanding the severity of his injuries. Full search was made for Smittozzi, but as yet there was no intelligence of his whereabouts, though the repentant Laura communicated all she knew. As far as could be judged, he had come back to the carriage after searching out the way, and finding the young lady missing, had looked about for her till he was tired; then had driven on to Cliff-Martin, sold the horse and carriage next morning, and disappeared, probably by one of the departing coaches which ran thence to the nearest station, the only difference from his original programme being that he had gone alone.

During the days and weeks of that long and tedious recovery Laura watched by her husband's bedside with a zeal and assiduity which would have considerably extenuated any fault save one of such magnitude as hers. That her husband did not forgive her was soon obvious. Nothing that she could do in the way of smoothing pillows, easing his position, shifting bandages, or administering draughts, could win from him more than a few measured words of thankfulness, such as he would probably have uttered to any other woman on earth who had performed these particular services for him.

'Dear, dear James,' she said one day, bending her face upon the bed in an excess of emotion. 'How you have suffered! It has been too cruel. I am more glad you are getting better than I can say. I have prayed for it – and I am sorry for what I have done; I am innocent of the worst, and – I hope you will not think me so very bad, James!'

'O no. On the contrary, I shall think you very good – as a nurse,' he answered, the caustic severity of his tone being apparent through its weakness.

Laura let fall two or three silent tears, and said no more that day.

Somehow or other Signor Smittozzi seemed to be making good his
escape. It transpired that he had not taken a passage in either of the
suspected coaches, though he had certainly got out of the county;
altogether, the chance of finding him was problematical.

Not only did Captain Northbrook survive his injuries, but it soon
appeared that in the course of a few weeks he would find himself little
if any the worse for the catastrophe. It could also be seen that Laura,
while secretly hoping for her husband's forgiveness for a piece of folly
of which she saw the enormity more clearly every day, was in great
doubt as to what her future relations with him would be. Moreover, to
add to the complication, whilst she, as a runaway wife, was unforgiven
by her husband, she and her husband, as a runaway couple, were
unforgiven by her father, who had never once communicated with
either of them since his departure from the inn. But her immediate
anxiety was to win the pardon of her husband, who possibly might be
bearing in mind, as he lay upon his couch, the familiar words of Brabantio,
'She has deceived her father, and may thee.'

Matters went on thus till Captain Northbrook was able to walk about.
He then removed with his wife to quiet apartments on the south coast,
and here his recovery was rapid. Walking up the cliffs one day, supporting him by her arm as usual, she said to him, simply, 'James, if I go on
as I am going now, and always attend to your smallest want, and never
think of anything but devotion to you, will you – try to like me a little ?'

'It is a thing I must carefully consider,' he said, with the same
gloomy dryness which characterized all his words to her now. 'When I
have considered, I will tell you.'

He did not tell her that evening, though she lingered long at her
routine work of making his bedroom comfortable, putting the light so
that it would not shine into his eyes, seeing him fall asleep, and then
retiring noiselessly to her own chamber. When they met in the morning
at breakfast, and she had asked him as usual how he had passed the
night, she added timidly, in the silence which followed his reply, 'Have
you considered ?'

'No, I have not considered sufficiently to give you an answer.'

Laura sighed, but to no purpose; and the day wore on with intense
heaviness to her, and the customary modicum of strength gained to
him.

The next morning she put the same question, and looked up despairingly in his face, as though her whole life hung upon his reply.

'Yes, I have considered,' he said.

'Ah!'

'We must part.'

'O James!'

'I cannot forgive you; no man would. Enough is settled upon you to keep you in comfort, whatever your father may do. I shall sell out, and disappear from this hemisphere.'

'You have absolutely decided?' she asked miserably. 'I have nobody now to c-c-care for—'

'I have absolutely decided,' he shortly returned. 'We had better part here. You will go back to your father. There is no reason why I should accompany you, since my presence would only stand in the way of the forgiveness he will probably grant you if you appear before him alone. We will say farewell to each other in three days from this time. I have calculated on being ready to go on that day.'

Bowed down with trouble she withdrew to her room, and the three days were passed by her husband in writing letters and attending to other business-matters, saying hardly a word to her the while. The morning of departure came; but before the horses had been put in to take the severed twain in different directions, out of sight of each other, possibly for ever, the postman arrived with the morning letters.

There was one for the captain; none for her – there were never any for her. However, on this occasion something was enclosed for her in his, which he handed her. She read it and looked up helpless.

'My dear father – is dead!' she said. In a few moments she added, in a whisper, 'I must go to the Manor to bury him. . . . Will you go with me, James?'

He musingly looked out of the window. 'I suppose it is an awkward and melancholy undertaking for a woman alone,' he said coldly. 'Well, well – my poor uncle! – Yes, I'll go with you, and see you through the business.'

So they went off together instead of asunder, as planned. It is unnecessary to record the details of the journey, or of the sad week which followed it at her father's house. Lord Quantock's seat was a fine old mansion standing in its own park, and there were plenty of opportunities for husband and wife either to avoid each other, or to get reconciled if they were so minded, which one of them was at least. Captain Northbrook was not present at the reading of the will. She came to him afterward, and found him packing up his papers, intending to start next morning, now that he had seen her through the turmoil occasioned by her father's death.

'He has left me everything that he could!' she said to her husband. 'James, will you forgive me now, and stay?'

'I cannot stay.'

'Why not?'

'I cannot stay,' he repeated.

'But why?'

'I don't like you.'

He acted up to his word. When she came downstairs the next morning she was told that he had gone.

Laura bore her double bereavement as best she could. The vast mansion in which she had hitherto lived, with all its historic contents, had gone to her father's successor in the title; but her own was no unhandsome one. Around lay the undulating park, studded with trees a dozen times her own age; beyond it, the wood; beyond the wood, the farms. All this fair and quiet scene was hers. She nevertheless remained a lonely, repentant, depressed being, who would have given the greater part of everything she possessed to ensure the presence and affection of that husband whose very austerity and phlegm – qualities that had formerly led to the alienation between them – seemed now to be adorable features in his character.

She hoped and hoped again, but all to no purpose. Captain Northbrook did not alter his mind and return. He was quite a different sort of man from one who altered his mind; that she was at last despairingly forced to admit. And then she left off hoping, and settled down to a mechanical routine of existence which in some measure dulled her grief, but at the expense of all her natural animation and the sprightly wilfulness which had once charmed those who knew her, though it was perhaps all the while a factor in the production of her unhappiness.

To say that her beauty quite departed as the years rolled on would be to overstate the truth. Time is not a merciful master, as we all know, and he was not likely to act exceptionally in the case of a woman who had mental troubles to bear in addition to the ordinary weight of years. Be this as it may, eleven other winters came and went, and Laura Northbrook remained the lonely mistress of house and lands without once hearing of her husband. Every probability seemed to favour the assumption that he had died in some foreign land; and offers for her hand were not few as the probability verged on certainty with the long lapse of time. But the idea of remarriage seemed never to have entered her head for a moment. Whether she continued to hope even now for his return could not be distinctly ascertained; at all events she lived a life unmodified in the slightest degree from that of the first six months of his absence.

This twelfth year of Laura's loneliness, and the thirtieth of her life drew on apace, and the season approached that had seen the unhappy adventure for which she so long had suffered. Christmas promised to be rather wet than cold, and the trees on the outskirts of Laura's estate dripped monotonously from day to day upon the turnpike-road which bordered them. On an afternoon in this week between three and four o'clock a hired fly might have been seen driving along the highway at this point, and on reaching the top of the hill it stopped. A gentleman of middle age alighted from the vehicle.

'You need drive no further,' he said to the coachman. 'The rain seems to have nearly ceased. I'll stroll a little way, and return on foot to the inn by dinner-time.'

The flyman touched his hat, turned the horse, and drove back as directed. When he was out of sight the gentleman walked on, but he had not gone far before the rain again came down pitilessly, though of this the pedestrian took little heed, going leisurely onward till he reached Laura's park gate, which he passed through. The clouds were thick and the days were short, so that by the time he stood in front of the mansion it was dark. In addition to this his appearance, which on alighting from the carriage had been untarnished, partook now of the character of a drenched wayfarer not too well blessed with this world's goods. He halted for no more than a moment at the front entrance, and going round to the servants' quarter, as if he had a preconceived purpose in so doing, there rang the bell. When a page came to him he inquired if they would kindly allow him to dry himself by the kitchen fire.

The page retired, and after a murmured colloquy returned with the cook, who informed the wet and muddy man that though it was not her custom to admit strangers, she should have no particular objection to his drying himself, the night being so damp and gloomy. Therefore the wayfarer entered and sat down by the fire.

'The owner of this house is a very rich gentleman, no doubt?' he asked, as he watched the meat turning on the spit.

' 'Tis not a gentleman, but a lady,' said the cook.

'A widow, I presume?'

'A sort of widow. Poor soul, her husband is gone abroad, and has never been heard of for many years.'

'She sees plenty of company, no doubt, to make up for his absence?'

'No, indeed – hardly a soul. Service here is as bad as being in a nunnery.'

In short, the wayfarer, who had at first been so coldly received, contrived by his frank and engaging manner to draw the ladies of the kitchen into a most confidential conversation, in which Laura's history was minutely detailed, from the day of her husband's departure to the present. The salient feature in all their discourse was her unflagging devotion to his memory.

Having apparently learned all that he wanted to know – among other things that she was at this moment, as always, alone – the traveller said he was quite dry; and thanking the servants for their kindness, departed as he had come. On emerging into the darkness he did not, however, go down the avenue by which he had arrived. He simply walked round to the front door. There he rang, and the door was opened to him by a manservant whom he had not seen during his sojourn at the other end of the house.

In answer to the servant's inquiry for his name, he said ceremoniously, 'Will you tell the Honourable Mrs Northbrook that the man she nursed many years ago, after a frightful accident, has called to thank her?'

The footman retreated, and it was rather a long time before any further signs of attention were apparent. Then he was shown into the drawing-room, and the door closed behind him.

On the couch was Laura, trembling and pale. She parted her lips and held out her hands to him, but could not speak. But he did not require speech, and in a moment they were in each other's arms.

Strange news circulated through that mansion and the neighbouring town on the next and following days. But the world has a way of getting used to things, and the intelligence of the return of the Honourable Mrs Northbrook's long-absent husband was soon received with comparative calm.

A few days more brought Christmas, and the forlorn home of Laura Northbrook blazed from basement to attic with light and cheerfulness. Not that the house was overcrowded with visitors, but many were present, and the apathy of a dozen years came at length to an end. The animation which set in thus at the close of the old year did not diminish on the arrival of the new; and by the time its twelve months had like-wise run the course of its predecessors, a son had been added to the dwindled line of the Northbrook family.

At the conclusion of this narrative the Spark was thanked, with a manner of some surprise, for nobody had credited him with a taste for tale-telling. Though it had been resolved that this story should be the last, a few of the weather-bound listeners were for sitting on into the small hours over their pipes and glasses, and raking up yet more episodes of family history. But the majority murmured reasons for soon getting to their lodgings.

It was quite dark without, except in the immediate neighbourhood of the feeble street-lamps, and before a few shop-windows which had been hardily kept open in spite of the obvious unlikelihood of any chance customer traversing the muddy thoroughfares at that hour.

By one, by two, and by three the benighted members of the Field-Club rose from their seats, shook hands, made appointments, and dropped away to their respective quarters, free or hired, hoping for a fair morrow. It would probably be not until the next summer meeting, months away in the future, that the easy intercourse which now existed between them all would repeat itself. The crimson maltster, for in-stance, knew that on the following market-day his friends the President, the Rural Dean, and the Bookworm would pass him in the street, if they met him, with the barest nod of civility, the President and the Colonel for social reasons, the Bookworm for intellectual reasons, and the Rural Dean for moral ones, the latter being a staunch teetotaller, dead against John Barleycorn. The sentimental member knew that when, on his rambles, he met his friend the Bookworm with a pocket-copy of something or other under his nose, the latter would not love his com-panionship as he had done to-day; and the President, the aristocrat, and the farmer knew that affairs political, sporting, domestic, or agricultural would exclude for a long time all rumination on the characters of dames gone to dust for scores of years, however beautiful and noble they may have been in their day.

The last member at length departed, the attendant at the museum lowered the fire, the curator locked up the rooms, and soon there was only a single pirouetting flame on the top of a single coal to make the bones of the ichthyosaurus seem to leap, the stuffed birds to wink, and to draw a smile from the varnished skulls of Vespasian's soldiery.

Notes

Wessex Tales

The Three Strangers. The situation which develops in this story has endowed it with a lasting appeal. At the suggestion of J. M. Barrie, Hardy produced a dramatised version, *The Three Wayfarers*, which was first performed in London with other short plays in June 1893, and judged by the *Times* critic to be the 'best piece of the evening'. The manuscript gives 'Higher Polenhill' for 'Higher Crowstairs'. The change introduced by Hardy in the 1912 edition, giving its distance from the 'county-town' as 'not three' instead of 'not five', probably reflects its location more accurately. To judge from the direction likely to be taken by the prisoner and his brother, it lies roughly north-north-east of Dorchester. The constable belongs to the same order as the 'rusty executors of the law' in *The Mayor of Casterbridge*, and all three owe something to Shakespeare.

A Tradition of Eighteen Hundred and Four. This brief but memorable story illustrates Hardy's mastery of the vernacular. Like the next, it is in some ways a by-product of his research for *The Trumpet-Major*. The main setting is above Lulworth Cove when a French invasion was expected at various points along the Dorset coast. King George's watering-place is Weymouth. Though Hardy's 'tradition' was wholly fictional, he discovered years later that his story had actually been established it (see F. E. Hardy, *The Life of Thomas Hardy, 1840–1928* (1962), pp. 391–2).

The Melancholy Hussar of the German Legion. The evidence for the shooting of the deserters from the York Hussars was found by Hardy in the *Morning Chronicle*, 4 July 1801, in the British Museum, and entered among the records he kept in preparation for *The Trumpet-Major*. A note in the *Life* for 27 July 1877 shows that he was familiar with the story long before he began to write the novel:

> James Bushrod of Broadmayne saw the two German soldiers shot on Bincombe Down in 1801. It was in the path across the Down, or near it. James Selby of the same village thinks there is a mark.

(This suggests that Hardy not only interviewed James Selby, but also used

his surname reminiscentially for the narrator of the previous story.) The
bodies of the deserters were buried by the church at Bincombe, immediately below the downs north of Weymouth. In his first preface to *Life's
Little Ironies* (1894), Hardy related how the woman who 'at the age of
ninety' pointed out their graves to him lingered 'pathetically' in his
memory. The story gives the actual names of the deserters, and everything relating to their attempt to escape is based on the facts Hardy
recorded in his notebook.

The Withered Arm. Hardy believed that a story must be unusual to be
worth the telling. This is undoubtedly one of his most striking, and its
powerful climax is effectively sprung on the reader. 'Davies' was the actual
name of the hangman. He had been a friend of the Hardy family, and it
may therefore have been from him indirectly that the author heard of the
superstition around which the climax was constructed. Leslie Stephen
thought that the reader should have been given a clue to this irrational
element, but Hardy's view was that this would weaken the narrative effect
in the unfortunate manner of Mrs Radcliffe.

The change for the date of the hanging from 'near twenty years' after
1813 (end of section VI) to 'near twelve years' was made in the 1912
edition. There were many outbreaks of rioting and incendiarism among
agricultural labourers after the Napoleonic Wars. Penalties were harsh,
and a youth was hanged because he was 'present by chance' when a rick
was fired. It was a story which drove 'the tragedy of life' more deeply into
Hardy's mind than any other he heard from his father.

Originally Farmer Lodge lived in 'Stickleford', and the dairy farm at
which Rhoda Brook worked was in the 'Swenn' valley. No changes were
subsequently made in the descriptive background. Rushy-Pond (half a
mile from Hardy's boyhood home) was unnamed. The ending of the
story was changed before it appeared in *Blackwood's Magazine*: Farmer
Lodge died 'a chastened man, rather than by his own hand'.

Fellow-Townsmen. This novelette illustrates the main element in Hardy's
tragic vision of life: man is a victim of chance or 'the whimsical god . . .
known as Circumstance'. The story appealed to the author, no doubt for
this reason (reflections on his own marriage may also have enlisted his
sympathy for Mr Barnet), and he thought his novelist friend Mrs Henniker
right in preferring it to 'The Three Strangers'. It may, nonetheless,
appear over-contrived and too unrelievedly sombre.

The original opening was revised considerably. It emphasised the
contrast between the two homes, and presented sufficient detail to make
Bridport easily recognisable as the setting, although there was no reference to Port-Bredy.

Interlopers at the Knap. The Knap was a house in Melbury Osmond, the
village where Hardy's mother was born; it probably belonged to her
collateral ancestors the Childses or Swetmans (see *Life*, p. 6). Its peculiar

features show that it is identical with the house in his poem 'One Who Married Above Him'. Except for place-names, the story was altered little. The most interesting topographical detail in the first version shows that the travellers at the opening followed the north-west road from Caster-bridge along Holloway (Holway) Lane; 'north' and 'Long-Ash Lane' were substituted when the story was revised for *Wessex Tales*. The first route shows more clearly where the wrong road was taken and how The Knap was subsequently three miles off to the left. The climbing of the guide-post and the late arrival are based on the adventures of Hardy's father when walking late at night to Melbury Osmond for his marriage the next day. From Puddletown he was accompanied across country by the brother-in-law of the bride (Hardy's mother).

The stress on Darton's wealth is related to *The Mayor of Casterbridge*, the subject of which Hardy had in mind when he wrote this story. The great economic gap between the wealth of farmers and the plight of labourers is an important feature of its background.

The Distracted Preacher. Hardy's humour and interest in smuggling history combine to make this an attractive romance. It was written just before *The Trumpet-Major*, and Hardy's notes for the latter include a number on coastal smuggling. He knew that his grandfather had allowed his house on the edge of the heath at Higher Bockhampton to be used as a station where cross-country carriers could conceal their tubs of spirits. For further notes relating to this aspect of the story, see Hardy's preface to *Wessex Tales*, p. 11.

BIBLIOGRAPHICAL NOTE

The *Wessex Tales* published in May 1888 when Hardy's fame as a novelist had almost reached its peak consisted of five stories only. 'An Imaginative Woman' was added to the 1896 edition, to be replaced in 1912 by 'A Tradition of Eighteen Hundred and Four' and 'The Melancholy Hussar of the German Legion'. This arrangement was dictated by background, all the stories in the final collection being set in districts central to Wessex (within twenty miles of Dorchester) and at various periods dating back to French invasion threats at the beginning of the nineteenth century.

As all were written for magazines or weekly newspapers after Hardy's success with *Far from the Madding Crowd* and *The Return of the Native*, it is reasonable to assume that little time elapsed between their completion and first publication. Their chronological order and probable dates of composition are as follows:

The Distracted Preacher	1878–9
Fellow-Townsmen	1880
A Tradition of Eighteen Hundred and Four	1882
The Three Strangers	1883

Interlopers at the Knap   1884
The Withered Arm   1887
The Melancholy Hussar of the German
    Legion   1889

With the exception of the last, the dates provided by Hardy at the end of
the stories indicate when they were first published. 'The Melancholy
Hussar' was sold in October 1889 to Tillotson & Son for distribution to
provincial newspapers, and made its first appearance in January 1890.

Only two of the tales are known to survive in manuscript: 'The Three
Strangers' in the Berg Collection in the New York Public Library, and
'The Melancholy Hussar' in the Huntington Library, California.

A Group of Noble Dames

Whatever Hardy says in his preface, the veracity of the accounts of
private lives in some at least of these stories must remain very suspect.
To varying extents, history enters most, if not all, of them. The relevant
genealogies and historical background for half of them (1, 2, 6, 7, 8) were
traced by Hardy in his copy of John Hutchins, *The History and Antiqui-
ties of the County of Dorset*, 3rd ed. (1861–73); and these are the only
ones for which the settings are in no way conjectural. He informed his
friend Edward Clodd that most of the tales were founded on fact. When
one considers the provenance of the non-historical portions, it is hardly
surprising that no significant evidence for substantiating them has come to
light. After a discussion with Hardy, Miss Rebekah Owen noted that all
were true, though Mrs Hardy excepted 'Barbara of the House of Grebe';
he had 'got traditions from old people who got them from old family
servants of the great families'.[1] It seems a fair inference that when they
returned home or retired they indulged in gossip and scandal in those parts
of Dorset, near Dorchester and at Melbury Osmond in particular, where
the Hardys were well known. The collection may be regarded therefore
as a curious amalgam of history, tradition, scandal, and fiction.

The six stories (2–7) which were published in the Christmas number of
The Graphic, 1890, were set in a slight narrative framework. For the larger
collection of the first edition, this was revised and extended, though in
general it remained almost minimal and perfunctory. It has obvious
parallels to that of Boccaccio's *Decameron*. The character and interest of
the stories may be appropriate to the narrators, but only occasionally does
the manner of telling reflect their personalities. Originally their meeting-
place was the old museum in Trinity Street, Dorchester, but there can be
little doubt that Hardy in revising the text had in mind its successor, the
present County Museum, which was opened in 1884. Here the Dorset

---

[1] Carl J. Weber, *Hardy and the Lady from Madison Square* (1952), p. 238.

Natural History and Antiquarian Field Club, of which he was a member, held important meetings.

Two significant overtones result from fitting the tales to this particular setting: the pervasive irony of stories which associate deceit, hypocrisy, and cruelty with noble bearing in 'dear, delightful Wessex', where 'the honest squires, tradesmen, parsons, clerks, and people still praise the Lord with one voice for His best of all possible worlds'; and the relative insignificance of noble dames and lords as they take their place in geological and archaeological time with the ichthyosaurus and varnished skulls of Vespasian's soldiery.

I. *The First Countess of Wessex*. The illustrations accompanying the story in *Harper's New Monthly Magazine* showed that it related to the Ilchesters of Melbury House near the village of Melbury Osmond where Hardy's mother was born. 'Squire Dornell' is Thomas Horner of Mells Park, near Frome, Somerset; he died in 1741. In 1736 his daughter Elizabeth (born in 1723) married Stephen Fox, who became the first Earl of Ilchester (Hutchins, vol. II, pp. 663, 667, 669).

In the original story Phelipson died as a result of a fall when descending from Betty's window by the ladder which Tupcombe, thinking that Reynard was with her, had placed in an insecure position. The story of her infection did not appear; neither did the amusing confession of the secret meetings which made Betty's public marriage urgent in the eyes of her mother.

From the outset Hardy stressed that 'Little Hintock' (see the end of the story) is 'several miles eastward' of 'King's-Hintock village'. The latter is Melbury Osmond, the 'Great Hintock' of *The Woodlanders* in its first edition (1885). Hardy had realised how indiscreet he had been – with the possibility of annoying the Ilchesters (as he did at first) by the publication of this story – to expose himself to the charge that the seductive Mrs Charmond of the novel could be associated with their home. With very slight descriptive alterations, he therefore took the first opportunity of ensuring that 'the Hintocks' in *The Woodlanders* were sited further east, in the region of High Stoy. He anticipated this move in 'The First Countess of Wessex'.

II. *Barbara of the House of Grebe*. This story incurred the inquisitorial condemnation of T. S. Eliot in *After Strange Gods* (1934). His criticism was unjustified; he knew very little about Hardy's works, as he admitted then and confirmed in *To Criticize the Critic* (1965), when, attempting to extenuate himself, he instanced 'the lack of a sense of humour' as a 'failing' in Hardy. Eliot found a 'world of pure Evil' in the story, and thought it was written 'solely to provide a satisfaction for some morbid emotion' in Hardy. (Would one give such a diagnosis for the blinding of Gloucester on the stage in *King Lear*?) Hardy was moved by man's inhumanity, and knew that its clear, clinical presentation would kindle the right sympathies as well as horror. It is his pity which makes him face the harsher realities unflinchingly.

The story is based on the life of Barbara Webb, wife of the fifth Earl of Shaftesbury (Hutchins, vol. III, pp. 298, 594). 'Knollingwood Hall' is St Giles's House, Wimborne St Giles, near Cranborne; 'Chene Manor' is Canford Manor, near Wimborne.

III. *The Marchioness of Stonehenge.* The manuscript shows that the first title was 'The Lady Caroline'; to this was added 'afterwards Marchioness of Stonehenge'. Originally she had married the Marquis of Athelney (Somerset), a fact which makes one wonder how reliable are some of the geographical hints for settings in *A Group of Noble Dames*. 'Stonehenge' and 'the Earl of Avon' have suggested Wilton House west of Salisbury as the 'classical mansion . . . standing not a hundred miles from the city of Melchester'. The Avon flows south a few miles to the east of Stonehenge and Wilton.

The final tragedy is aptly expressed through an allusion to King Lear's

> How sharper than a serpent's tooth it is
> To have a thankless child!

IV. *Lady Mottisfont.* The name 'Ashley Mottisfont' probably came from a map showing Ashley Down and Mottisfont Priory to the north of Romsey, Hampshire. Reference to Hardy's map of Wessex shows that 'Deansleigh Park' is Broadlands (home of Lord Palmerston), one mile south of Romsey. 'Fernell Hall' is thought to be Embley (home of Florence Nightingale), two miles to the west, though Hardy places it further north by the river. The Contessa resembled the Contessa M——, 'a great beauty' to whom Hardy was introduced in Venice (see *Life*, pp. 194–5).

V. *The Lady Icenway.* Hardy's map suggests that Icenway House is Herriard House (now demolished), south of Basingstoke and ten miles from the *Via Iceniana*, the old Roman road running south-west from Silchester. The first wife of George Purefoy Jervoise of Herriard House (1770–1847) was the daughter and heiress of Thomas Hall, Preston Candover, Hampshire; his second, the eldest daughter of Wadham Locke of Rowdeford House, Bromham, near Devizes, Wiltshire. He died without issue.

From 1895 to 1911 Hardy had accepted a map of Wessex (in the uniform edition of his fiction) which showed Heymere House where the story leads one to expect it. It seems to have coincided with Churchill Court, ten miles south-west of Bristol. Hardy's interest may have arisen through trying to trace a link between the Churchills here and the Churchills of Colliton House, Dorchester. No relationship, however, has been found between Herriard House and Churchill Court, and the question arises whether Hardy combined 'facts' from two places which had no historical association whatever. The reference to Leyland may be no more than a feint (at the expense of a member of the Antiquarian Club). Leyland uses 'maner place' for a country residence or mansion, and 'a faire maner place' with reference to Newton St Loe, near Bath.

VI. *Squire Petrick's Lady*. The manuscript of *A Group of Noble Dames* includes only 'The Lady Penelope' and the six stories which were published in *The Graphic*. This is the only one where the bowdlerised passages are blue-pencilled (with a note stating that they were 'deleted [from *The Graphic*] against author's wish, by compulsion of Mrs Grundy'). It is difficult to see why they were considered offensive, until it is realised that magazine editors were afraid of offending upper-class readers in any way.

'Squire Petrick' was Peter Walker of Stalbridge House, north Dorset. He was the grandson of Peter Walker who acquired vast estates and died in 1745 at the age of eighty-three (Hutchins, vol. III, p. 671). One change in the text is of interest: in 1891 'the Marquis of Trantridge, son of the Duke of Hamptonshire' became 'the Marquis of Christminster, son of the Duke of Southwesterland'. This shows that Hardy (as the preface to the novel confirms) had already made plans for *Jude the Obscure*, in which 'Christminster' is Oxford.

VII. *Anna, Lady Baxby*. Mainly historical, this relates to Anne, Lady Digby of Sherborne Castle. Her brother was the Earl of Bedford (Hutchins, vol. IV, pp. 269, 473).

VIII. *The Lady Penelope*. Lady Penelope Darcy married Sir George Trenchard of Wolfeton House, a mile north of Dorchester. On his death, she inherited his estate. Her second husband was Sir John Gage; her third, Sir William Hervey. She was buried in the church at Charminster (Hutchins, vol. III, pp. 326, 329).

The magazine version shows that the most imaginative description in this moving story (on the rumours which 'rustled in the air like nightbirds of evil omen') was an afterthought.

IX. *The Duchess of Hamptonshire*. This was the first short story by Hardy to be published in England, and it is impressive in the pathos of its romance and the hauntingly effective way in which the tragic climax turns upon the irony of an extraordinary chance. It first appeared in 1878 as 'The Impulsive Lady', its heroine being Lady Saxelbye of Croome Castle. When it was published in New York in 1884 as 'Emmeline, or Passion vs. Principle', she was Lady Emmeline of Stroome Castle. These two versions do not differ in any important respect from 'The Duchess of Hamptonshire'.

Though 'Hamptonshire' is the old name for Hampshire, it does not follow that the Duke lived in the county after which he took his title. 'Batton Castle' appeared on Wessex maps before 1912 (and it is still shown on the smaller map) at a point which suggests Tottenham House, southeast of Marlborough. The fictional name resembles that of the historic neighbouring borough of Bedwyn. Recently Denys Kay-Robinson has suggested that 'Croome', 'Stroome' and 'Batton' might indicate Badminton near Castle Combe, ten miles north-east of Bath. No clue to the story has been discovered, though a slight parallel may be found in one of the reminiscences of Mrs Hardy's brother-in-law (*Life*, p. 155).

x. *The Honourable Laura*. Though probably not written long before its publication in December 1881 under the title of 'Benighted Travellers', this is one of Hardy's earliest short stories. Whether he knew the part of Devon he romantically describes is not known; it forms a suitable setting to his story. The most interesting revision before its appearance in *A Group of Noble Dames* was in the name of the heroine. It had been 'Lucetta'; but, after choosing that name for a tragic lady in *The Mayor of Casterbridge*, Hardy preferred another.

BIBLIOGRAPHICAL NOTE

A Group of Noble Dames was first published at the end of May 1891. It consisted of a group of six stories (which Hardy agreed in April 1889 to write for *The Graphic*) and four others: 'The First Countess of Wessex', 'The Lady Penelope', 'The Duchess of Hamptonshire' and 'The Honourable Laura'. All except the last two were written when Hardy disengaged himself from the problems which arose from the serialisation of *Tess of the d'Urbervilles*. 'The First Countess of Wessex' appeared in *Harper's New Monthly Magazine* in December 1889, and 'The Lady Penelope' in *Longman's Magazine* in January 1890. 'The Duchess of Hamptonshire' was first published in 1878; 'The Honourable Laura' in 1881.

The six stories undertaken for *The Graphic* were completed in just over a year after they had been commissioned, but Hardy had to bowdlerise and modify them before they were accepted for the special Christmas number of *The Graphic* in 1890. The original text was published in America, where they appeared about this time as instalments in four numbers of *Harper's Weekly*. It was preserved when the ten stories first appeared in book form in 1891.

The manuscript of the six stories for *The Graphic* and that of 'The Lady Penelope' were presented to the Library of Congress, Washington, in 1911. The manuscript of 'The First Countess of Wessex' was sold in New York in 1906 but its whereabouts remains unknown; that of the 1884 version of 'The Duchess of Hamptonshire' belongs to the Pierpont Morgan Library, New York (see R. L. Purdy, *Thomas Hardy: A Bibliographical Study* (1954) pp. 64–5).

Glossary of Dialect Words

a-scram withered
athwart across
barton farmyard
bleachy saltish
chimmer bedroom, chamber
climm climb
clitch crook
coddle self-indulgent person
coomb small valley on the flank of a
    hill
crope crept
culpet culprit
cunning-man wizard, 'knowing'
    man
dazed damned
en him
ewe-leases downs or meadows for
    sheep
glum gloom
hackle cone-shaped straw roof of a
    beehive
hang-fair a hanging the public
    were allowed to watch
het hot
home-along going home

innerds stomach
jack-o'-lent numskull
laved baled, drew
mid may
'nation damnation
no'thern stupid
Ooser grotesque mask
out-step out of the way
overlooked looked upon with an
    evil eye
pink in draw in
pinner pinafore
rathe soon, early
skimmer-cake cake baked on a
    metal skimming-ladle
slack-twisted spineless
small light, weak (drink)
strake section of an iron wheel-rim
stoor to-do, commotion
tisty-tosty round, buxom
tole draw, lure
vamp sole
yaller yellow
zeed saw
zull plough

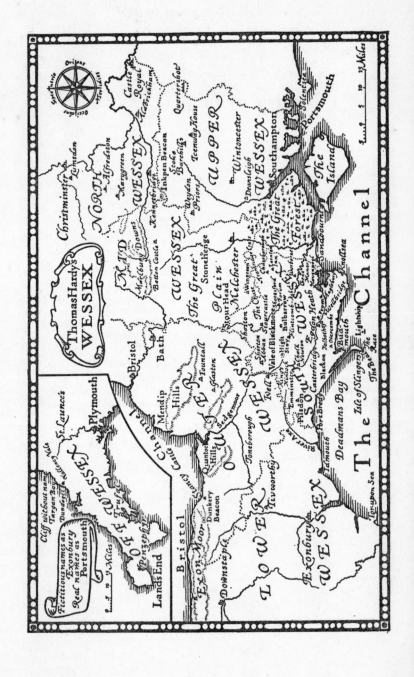

Glossary of Place-Names

N.B. (1) Identifications which are provided in the Notes are not included below. (2) Locations of smaller places are given in mileage and direction with reference to well-known places in Dorset.

ABBOT'S-CERNEL. Cerne Abbas, 7N Dorchester.
ANGLEBURY. Wareham.
BUDMOUTH (REGIS). Weymouth.
CASTERBRIDGE. Dorchester.
CHALK-NEWTON. Maiden Newton, 7½NW Dorchester.
CHRISTMINSTER. Oxford.
CLIFF-MARTIN. Combe Martin, N. Devon.
DAGGER'S GRAVE. Dagger's Gate, 1NW Lulworth Cove.
DOWNSTAPLE. Barnstaple, N. Devon.
EGDON (HEATH). Puddletown Heath and eastward, north of the Frome valley.
EVERSHEAD. Evershot, 6WNW Cerne Abbas ('Abbot's-Cernel').
EXONBURY. Exeter.
HAVENPOOL. Poole.
HOLMSTOKE. In the region of West Holme, Stokeford, and East Stoke, 2–4W Wareham.
IVELL. Yeovil.
KING'S-HINTOCK. Melbury Osmond, 7NW Cerne Abbas ('Abbot's-Cernel').
KINGSBERE. Bere Regis, 10ENE Dorchester.
KNOLLSEA. Swanage.
LORNTON. Horton, 5NNE Wimborne.
LULWIND. Lulworth Cove.
MARLOTT. Marnhull, 6WSW Shaftesbury.
MELCHESTER. Salisbury.
MILLPOOL. Milborne Port, 3NE Sherborne.
NETHER-MOYNTON. Owermoigne, 6SE Dorchester.
PORT-BREDY. Bridport.
RINGSWORTH. Ringstead Bay, 5½ENE Weymouth.
SHERTON (ABBAS). Sherborne.
SHOTTSFORD-FORUM. Blandford Forum.
STICKLEFORD. Tincleton, 5E Dorchester.

TONEBOROUGH. Taunton.
WARBORNE. Wimborne.
WINTONCESTER. Winchester.
YEWSHOLT LODGE. Farrs House, $1\frac{1}{2}$W Wimborne.

Warm'ell Cross is the crossroads near Warmwell; here the road to Weymouth turns off from the Wareham–Dorchester road.